THE
DANCE
OF
DESTINY

"Tell me again what it's like to die."

C.D. MCKENNA

The Dance of Destiny
The Vorelian Saga
Copyright © 2024 C.D. McKenna
Published by C.D. McKenna

First Edition: May 2024
Printed in the United States of America

eISBN: 979-8-9902901-0-5
979-8-9902901-1-2 (paperback)
979-8-9902901-2-9 (hardcover)

Library of Congress Control Number: 2024904886

www.thevoreliansaga.com

Cover Design by Cherie Foxley
Map Illustrations by Eve's Worldbuilding
Interior Design and Formatting by Dragan Bilic
Morei Geral Illustration by George Patsouras

To my Ghost Writer.
None of this would have been possible without your
four paws and insatiable love for coffee.

Diyra
Volkeri Island
The Shade
Assane
Junok's Port
Junok
Merrél Sea
Mowvale Mountains
N
City of Liral
The Delfic Forest
Raveer
Whale Village
The Gulf of Beritisian
Crown Port
Jasper Village
Nighthunter Federation
Ronin's Port

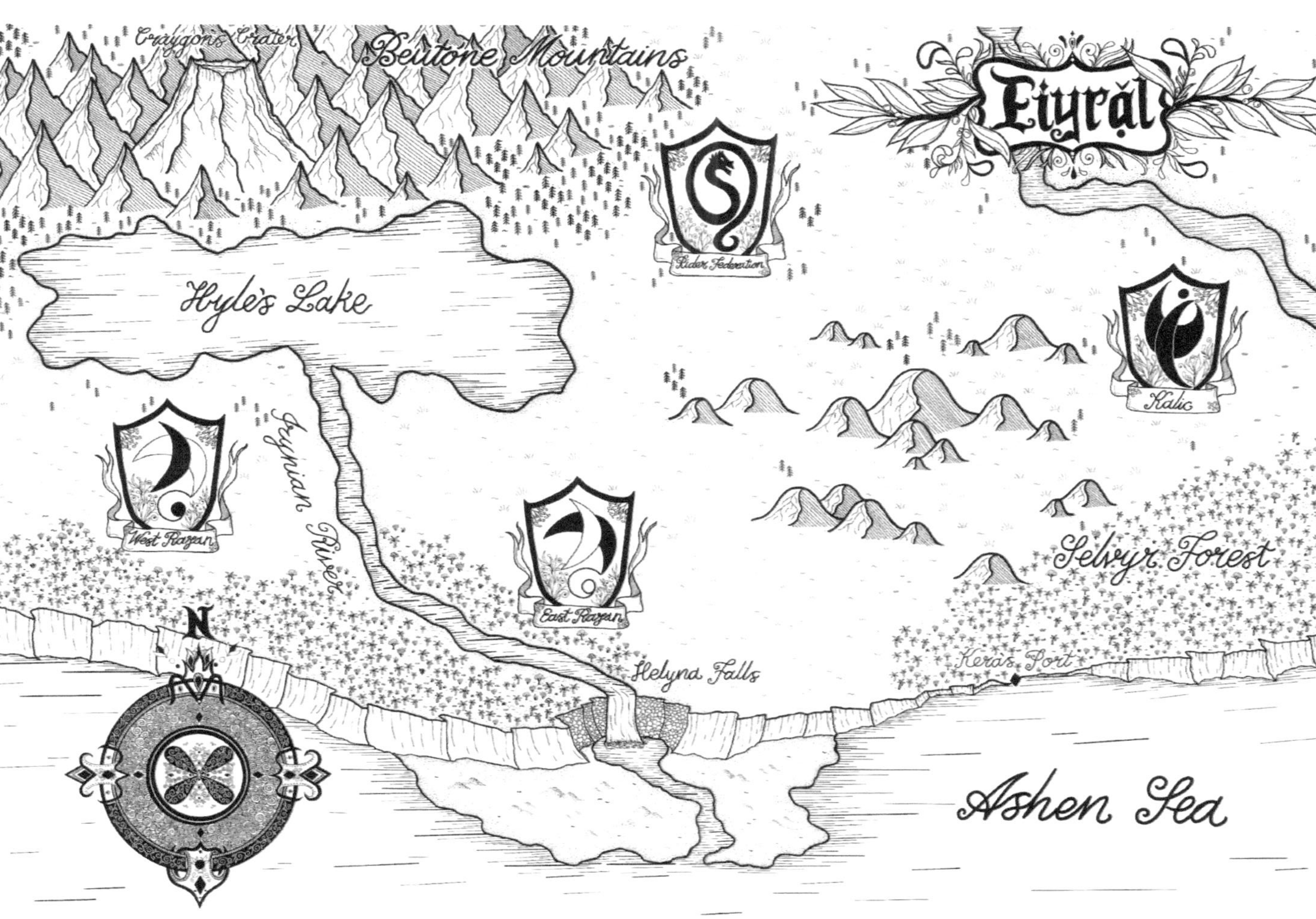

Craygon's Crater
Beltoire Mountains
Eiyral
Rider Federation
Hyle's Lake
Kalic
Fynian River
West Razan
East Razan
Selvyr Forest
N
Helyna Falls
Kera's Port
Ashen Sea

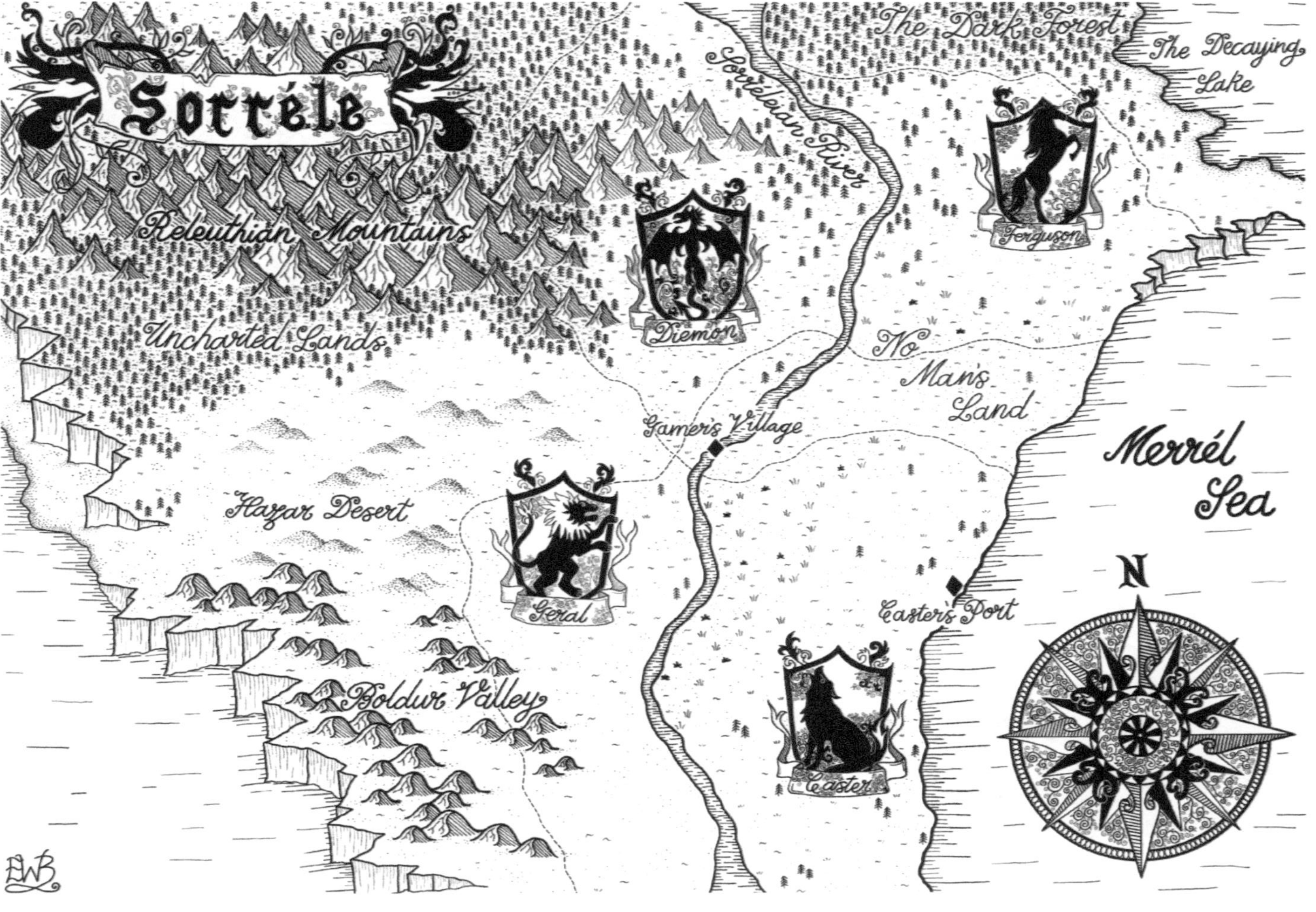

Sorréle
The Dark Forest
The Decaying Lake
Sorrélean River
Releuthian Mountains
Ferguson
Diemon
Uncharted Lands
No Man's Land
Gamer's Village
Merrél Sea
Hazar Desert
Geral
Caster's Port
Boldur Valley
Caster
N

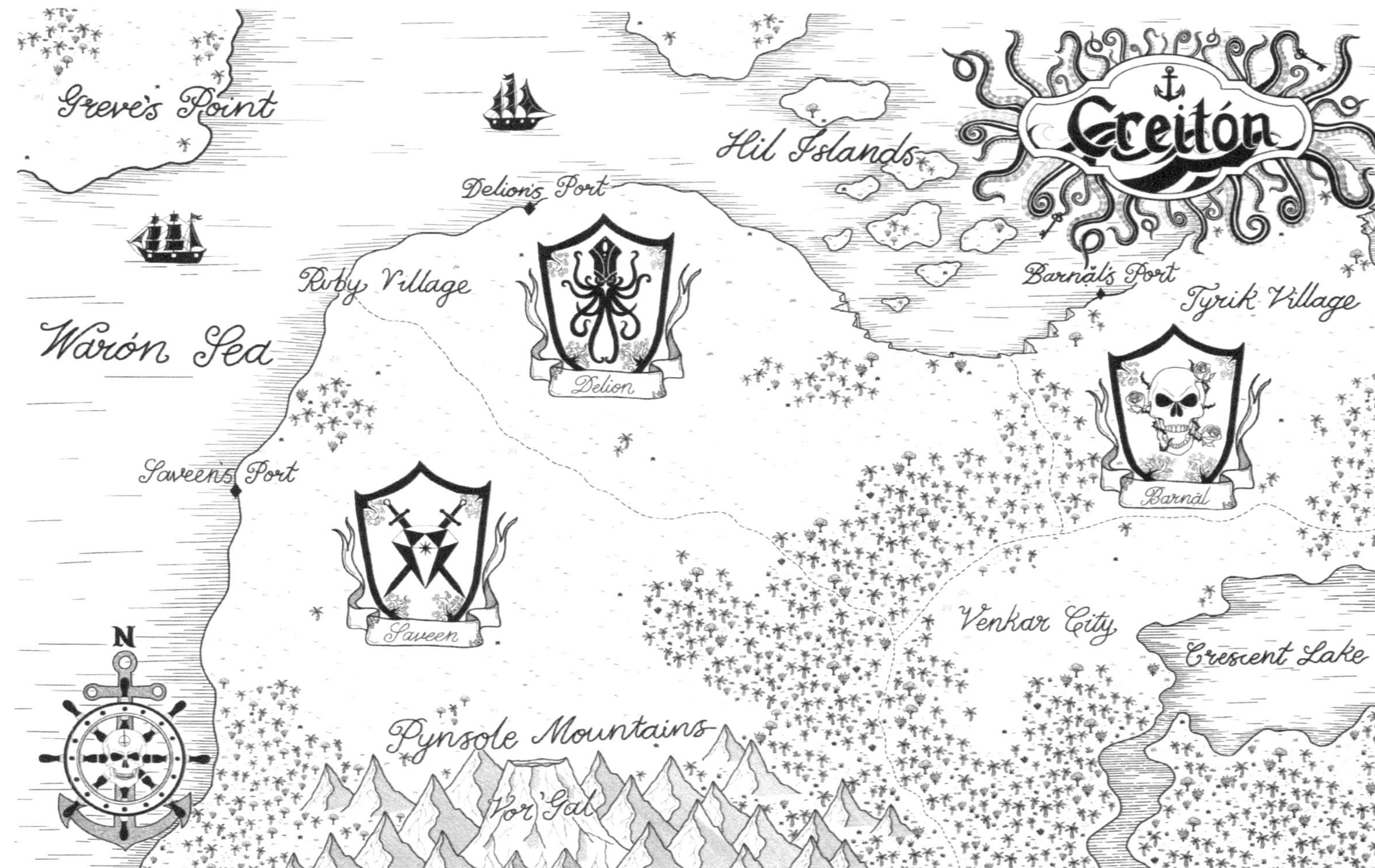
Greve's Point
Hil Islands
Creitón
Delion's Port
Ruby Village
Warón Sea
Delion
Barnál's Port
Tyrik Village
Saveen's Port
Barnál
Saveen
Venkar City
Crescent Lake
N
Pynsole Mountains
Vor'Gal

CONTENTS

PART 1

"Throw a man to the sun and he'll make fire.
Throw a God to the sun and he'll conquer the world."
~ Vorelian Scrolls

CAPTAIN OF THE WRETCHED

The sea was no place for the restless. Nerius had learned of such things when he came aboard *Mercy* last season. These men were different, even compared to the rest of the crews he'd ever worked with. It had been a few summers now that he had been aboard ships, working the deck, but this was the first where the men turned on each other.

It was a funny thing, being stuck in the middle of the sea with men he wasn't certain wouldn't stab him while he slept. Couldn't necessarily blame them, though—Captain Jones was not the nicest he'd worked with. The old man was cruel, rude, and crass. Not a thing went under the captain's nose without someone hearing about it. Just last night, Jones had blown up with a drink in hand over how the knots were done. Nerius rolled his eyes just thinking about it, and he knew the other men felt the same. They were tired of Jones and his games.

A few days ago, a man had gone overboard. Accidents happened out on these waters. That was what the men called them. *Accidents.* Murder was considered one too. Chip was the fellow's name—Nerius couldn't say he liked it. A bit childish. Though Chip wasn't a day over sixteen, either. He'd picked a fight with one of the older seaman, one they called Parrot because he always had a feather tucked behind the ear, even when the wind was wild. The men on *Mercy* knew that having words with Parrot, who stood a head taller than them all and was missing teeth, was dumb. The man had seen more seasons on a boat than land, and when they asked why he hadn't become a captain, he always flashed them a toothless grin and told them a title like that didn't warrant loyalty.

So Chip got drunk and said some things. It had been his first season on a boat, and of all ships, he'd chosen *Mercy.* Foolish or just bad luck, Nerius couldn't decide. This ship could crack the will of any man. He dared believe a God wouldn't last a moon cycle onboard.

Chip certainly hadn't.

Nerius had spent time on quite a few different ships, and he could smell out a rotten one. The crew here didn't trust each other. They knew everyone was in it for a job, but the trust ended there. Nerius's first night had almost ended fatally when he'd accidentally assumed he was entitled to *two* biscuits instead of one. They were sea biscuits—hard, flavorless, and used to soak up the bile in a man's stomach after a long day of no food. Men had been in his face, cursing, and he'd even earned himself a black eye before Jones had shown up and threatened to throw Nerius overboard himself for being a fool.

He certainly hadn't started off on the right foot, but he'd made a promise to prove himself. After that, he'd always been the first to offer his services. Nerius wasn't a moron. It didn't take a seasoned expert to know that there was a fine line between being helpful and pissing off a crew of highly volatile and prideful men. But he'd managed to earn their respect for his skills aboard *Mercy*—nobody else could man the wheel like he could when the captain wasn't around.

Shouts from the main deck drew his attention outward. He had been off duty and napping some, listening to the constant slosh of waves against the wall to his left. The sea had been quite calm up until a bit ago, but by the harshness of the ship's tilt, he knew a storm was coming. The tiny windowpane that peeked out of the room was mostly submerged as the waves grew taller and bolder.

He stood from his cot, putting a hand out to steady himself when the ship rocked sharply to the right. Holding himself up, he heard something fall in the other room—a moron who had likely not strapped anything down. Dan, no doubt. That one-eyed fellow was on everyone's nerves.

Movement caught his attention, and he turned back to the window, narrowing his eyes. Strange, but not surprising. It was probably seaweed, although he always wondered what else lurked in the depths. Stories were one thing, but seeing something was different.

More shouts. Nerius rolled his eyes and made his way to the hall. The wood groaned under the increasing force of the waves, a sound he had grown to adore with time. Stepping out, he moved his foot just in time for a metal cup to roll sideways. He watched it go—the last person who had been responsible for the galley was Dan. Always Dan.

Nerius looked to his left and saw more items from the galley roll out and into the hall. Raising an eyebrow, he knew that was a task for later. All he could hope was that the food wasn't rolling all over the place as well. That would really ruin his night. There was nothing more annoying than fishing for one's own food aboard a ship this size. It made catching fish, especially when they didn't have a proper net, that much more challenging. He'd done it once, and he had pledged never again to work a ship that made the crew fight for their own food after dealing with the sea all day.

Turning right, he walked to the steep stairs—perhaps it was better to call them a ladder, given it was nearly a vertical climb to the door. He made his way up, sniffing the stench of algae and seawater, and pushed the door open. The handle was flimsy, and it was only a matter of time before that broke too. Felt like this whole damn ship was falling apart.

Curse of the Grave. That was what everyone said, anyway. They were too close to the Grave of the Sea, and the waters grew fierce and wild out here, but Jones had insisted on sailing through it to avoid the storm that was now upon them.

"Tie that down!" the captain barked from above. Nerius turned in time to see the wheel spinning dangerously fast. Everything else, he took in as quickly as he could.

It was chaos. The entire ship was groaning, the winds whipping the masts left and right, and the ominous black clouds had a green tinge that foretold a nasty storm. The waters were restless, creating waves nearly as tall as the ship, and everywhere men ran about in a frenzy. They were trying to tie things into place, to keep the ship from being controlled by the sea. It was futile. Nerius had come to learn that one never controlled these waters; the men were at the service of the waves. They either learned to let the sea do as she wished or get out of the way.

Kye slammed into him. The fellow had a rope wrapped around his forearm and was soaked to the bone. His red hair was plastered to his face. "You help the captain get that wheel under control!" He was already running to the other side of the deck toward Dan, who was struggling with some loose barrels that were toppling about.

Nerius should have panicked, should have been running, but he wasn't. There was something about the madness of it all that brought him immense peace. He took his time walking up those slick stairs, keeping one hand on the rail, as the waves struck him over and over. He was dripping by the time he made it to the top, and it was there that he could see the Grave.

The waters were no longer vibrant blue but a wicked gray. Lifeless. An island too far to reach jutted from the horizon. He'd heard stories about that place before, grand tales, because nobody had ever actually made it there and lived to come back. But he'd heard about monsters and flying creatures, things with leather-like skin and the faces of men. By the grace of Greve, he'd heard it all.

"What're you starin' at, son?" The voice came from his left, and he turned to see Jones's ugly face glaring at him. Another deckhand was trying to control the wheel, but his strength was failing miserably by the looks of it. "Get over there and help Scales out!"

Scales. Right. He knew the deckhand. They'd started calling him that after the sun had turned his skin to a crisp. Nerius approached, his body tipping with the sway of the ship, and he grabbed onto the wheel with Scales on the other side.

"You're doing good," Nerius gritted out. The wood was stressed and making all sorts of noises, but he could feel the ship steady herself under the hold. The sky lit up with a bolt of lightning—but it was green.

Nerius was dumbstruck. Green lightning was not normal, and neither was the gray-colored sea. This was the doing of magic.

Energy, his mother corrected him from the depths of his mind. Even after all these summers of her being dead, she still spoke to him. She was like a song that could not be forgotten, a tune he hummed constantly, despite not having heard the lyrics in so long. Everything had changed when his mother died.

The crack of thunder shook him out of his thoughts, but he was not staring at the sky anymore. He was staring at the woman who was now aboard. She had beautiful green and blue hair, the color of the sea, and her big eyes were inhumanly perfect, with slits for pupils and irises a vivid green as well. She smiled at him, revealing dagger teeth, but they looked stunning on her.

She stood some bit away, and nobody else seemed to take note of her. She did not sway like the others did with the motion of the ship—she just stood perfectly still. And when she spoke, her voice carried right to him with the utmost clarity.

"The Grave requires a soul," she told him, the words like honey. "Give a soul and I will spare your ship, Prince."

Prince. Nerius's muscles shook from the weight of the wheel, yet he felt his mind completely elsewhere. Crowns, jewels, and grand halls . . . Memories of a life he'd run from flitted by, stealing his senses for just a moment. The sounds of this world muted, replaced by a ringing in his ear before her voice broke through again.

"Nobody ever escapes these parts, Prince," she continued. "My kind make sure of it."

A single soul . . .

"Yes," she answered again. The woman could hear his thoughts. "Choose wisely, though. We do not like weak-boned men." She flashed a grin. "Their bones are too easy to eat."

Nerius stared. Scales was yelling at him for something, but his words went unheard. The only thing he could hear was her, even as the sky lit up once more with the strange lightning.

"There must be another way," he muttered, and shook his head. "I can't—I can't do this."

A hand ran over his arm, slithering up to his shoulder and squeezing in encouragement. "Your heart is so pure, Junok." The woman stood next to him now, her body radiating a frigid air that made the hairs on his arm stand on end. "But you mustn't deny the Grave. Do you wish to end the lives of all these men?"

Mute, he shook his head, eyes ahead. He'd never killed a man before. Nerius put on a brave front, even had punched and stabbed people, but he'd never taken a life. He was not a killer, never had wanted to be. Such crimes were reserved for monsters.

"Your captain would do," she told him—no, begged him, he was certain of it. "His spirit is cruel, and his heart beats with violence. We would be satisfied with him."

To kill his captain . . . Nerius was uncertain. Jones was ruthless, but he did not know if that was just cause. Yet if he did not satisfy this woman's needs, all the men aboard this ship would perish.

"This would satisfy my kind—and your crew," she added with a hint of amusement. "Do not deny your disdain for him. I can feel it."

Was he a coward? The grip on the wheel tightened as the ship groaned under the strain of the hungry waters. But as her hand slipped away from his shoulder and she disappeared, a burning desire filled his core. Nerius was not a coward. He was a prince, a rightful heir to a throne that had not been granted to him, and he would prove to these men that he was willing to do anything to protect them.

Still, there were risks. The ship's politics were shaky at best, but they existed.

If anyone found out, they'd throw him overboard, wouldn't they? The whole crew hated him, felt like he was nothing but a nasty authoritarian who got off on being cruel. The crew might celebrate him, but more importantly, they wouldn't ask questions.

Even as he came to that conclusion, he saw the woman smile knowingly, her eyes gleaming with delight. Nerius let go of the wheel and didn't wait to see how Scales would do—it didn't matter. He turned to face his captain, watching as the man did nothing while his crew fought to keep this ship afloat. Unsheathing his dagger from his side, Nerius lunged for Jones.

The captain never expected it, and the ease with which the blade cut through the fragile skin of Jones's neck was almost as surprising to Nerius as it was to the captain. The man's eyes went wide, his mouth opening in a stunned O, but no words came out. It wasn't like Nerius gave him the chance. He pushed him overboard, watching as the captain's body struck the water belly-first.

But it was the dozen tentacles that kept his eyes glued to the water. The creature wrapped around Jones, even as he thrashed, and yanked him under.

The woman was beside him again. "You're a strong man, Prince. We like you."

At once, the waters calmed. The storm was still upon them, but the rain and winds were bearable as the sea relented. He turned to see Scales staring, wide-eyed, hands still latched on to the wheel. The dagger in Nerius's hand was soaked in blood that dripped to the boards below. He tossed it over the edge, no longer wanting anything to do with that weapon. It felt right to get rid of it—the woman would be proud.

Men clambered up from the main deck, shouting questions and asking what to do. They were anticipating seeing their captain standing there with that never-ending smug expression, but instead they found Nerius and Scales. They halted, surprised.

When Nerius looked around, the woman was gone.

"Where's the captain?" Kye asked.

"Dead," Nerius answered with far too much ease. It was the summers in royalty that had taught him how to lie without remorse. "Fell overboard when the waters got bad."

The real test was Scales. Nerius turned his gaze on the young seaman, who hadn't moved from his spot. His eyes hardened with resolve. "He's right," Scales agreed. "Watched the whole thing."

Good. Nerius knew then that he had his loyalty. No seaman turned on his fellow when the goings got tough. And he knew without a shadow of a doubt that if anyone was going to confess what had happened, it was here and now. Out at sea, the crew was the judge. If Scales had hated Nerius, well, he'd already be dead.

Dan piped up, breaking the stunned silence. Even as the rain pelted them now, nobody seemed to care. "Well, who's going to be captain?"

"A vote," Scales offered. "Does anyone disagree?"

When Nerius looked over at him then, he saw something flash in the young man's eye. Recognition. Scales had seen the woman, at least in the end, and he had seen the waters return to normal after Jones had been killed. This sea was a strange place, and only the wildest dared to sail it.

Scales lifted his hand. "All in favor of Nerius taking charge, say aye."

The majority of the men immediately agreed. Nerius was surprised. He had not anticipated so many to trust him with their lives. Tense silence filled the air, noted only by the ship's lazy rocking. Men eyed each other. Nobody spoke, and there was only one elected official to guide this ship.

Nerius swallowed, feeling an immense weight on his shoulders. Somehow, he would have to get this ship out of the Grave—a task nobody else wanted to take responsibility for— and while the woman had told him she would help, he didn't trust her entirely.

"Then it's official," Scales said, voice firm. "Nerius is our captain." He turned his eyes upon him once more. "Captain, what is your first order?"

Deep down, he knew they would be safe. There was no question about it. He knew they had to deal with the storm, and they'd surely manage, but he was confident that they would see the sun rise tomorrow, too. His heart beat with a steady rhythm that gave him peace, while his limbs shook with nerves and uncertainty. He was a murderer, but the crew was safe.

"Get something to eat," he said. "And get the galley tidied up. It's a disaster down there."

The men obeyed without question. They scampered off, yet as Scales let go of the wheel, Nerius stopped him. "Stay here, Scales. Keep your hands on the wheel." He approached the young seaman as everyone disappeared.

"You saw her, didn't you?" he asked.

Scales nodded.

That confirmed his theory. He turned his eyes toward the distant island, which was now engulfed in a wall of rain.

"Tsu'ran," the man said out of nowhere. Nerius turned back and raised a brow. "She was a Tsu'ran."

The legend danced across his mind. The shape-shifters of the sea. Dangerous, devious, taking on the form of what their victims desired most. "What are you saying?"

Scales swallowed and turned to him, his brown eyes full of worry. His next words were heavy, final. "You just made a deal with a monster. She will seek something in return."

Nerius fell quiet and looked away. His first order of business was to have his men eat, but he could not shake what Scales had said.

He knew the man was right.

A MIST OF DEATH

Present

orei's boots crunched under the branches. The air was wet on his tongue and coated his skin with a fine cool layer. The dense trees with their thin, needlelike leaves surrounded him wherever he turned. A mist had turned the world dreary, blue and gray, and it kept Morei from seeing any farther than what lay immediately ahead of him. When he looked up, he saw nothing but the thick fog. The trail he was walking on, at least in the narrow circle of ground he could see, appeared well-loved despite the littering of branches.

He continued down the path, trusting his instinct, but his eyes wandered. Morei had spent his entire life in the Hazar Desert—the only trees he'd ever seen were in paintings. He'd become so accustomed to the hot sand that he'd believed he'd never see a tree in person. Yet here he was, in the middle of some unnamed forest and unsure where he was going. Glancing down again, he found he bore no weapon of any sorts, only a simple tunic and pants, but the black veins of his ailment still glared back at him, a tragic reminder of his past and future.

His ears strained for any strange noises, but as he'd never spent time in a forest, everything felt strange. In the abnormal quiet, his steps were too loud. A twig snapped under the weight of his boot, and the sound echoed for what felt like leagues. Perhaps this forest never ended. Maybe this was what death felt like—an endless path that took him nowhere and never changed.

But as he let his thoughts wander down that avenue, he heard distinct steps next to him. Morei looked over to see a woman with fiery red hair that trailed halfway down her back in long waves. She was dressed in travel clothing and had porcelain skin with faint freckles along her nose and cheekbones. The woman stood a head shorter than him, but she walked with the certainty of someone who knew exactly where they were going. And he couldn't say he was surprised. The gait fit her as well as the red hair.

Syra Castello.

"Have you been here the whole time?" Morei asked. His words echoed, deafening, and he wondered if anything else was lurking in these woods.

Syra turned her eyes up at him. Green, but unlike anything he had ever seen before—perhaps what some might have called true emerald. They complemented her skin so well. "Will you tell me a story, Morei?" Her voice rolled through the trees.

He looked at her, curious that she wouldn't answer his question but too caught up in the moment to care. Her gaze was haunting. A thousand stories locked in those orbs, desperate to have a voice. When he found his tongue, the words came out barely above a whisper. "What do you want to hear?"

A handful of heartbeats slipped by, and Morei thought the mist had grown denser. He was preparing to repeat his question, believing she hadn't heard the first time, when she finally spoke. *"Tell me again what it's like to die."*

What a tragic request. Perhaps they were both dead. He found solace in the passing time, in the crunch of the twigs and soil. Despite the boots he wore, he could not shake the frigid sensation that managed to seep right through the leather and into his feet before slowly crawling up his legs.

"Cold," he blurted out, breaking the long silence. "Death is cold, but it doesn't start that way. The moments leading up to her embrace"—he shook his head—"are warm. The memories are sweet, and there's this intense euphoric sensation that washes over you. One could say you were drunk off life." That statement made him smile. "And perhaps you are, in those final moments."

He slowed his pace, no longer certain about the path he was taking them on. "But then the warmth fades just as your heart slows, and the blood that has kept you alive ceases movement, no longer filled with purpose. You can hear it, you know, the moment your heart stops. That silence that follows, the hollowness in your chest, cannot be replicated." Morei bit his tongue, finding himself lost in thought. "For me, there was no white light or family waiting for me. I was alone, in the trees—I have never been among so many trees before. It was beautiful and so quiet. I was walking, but I don't know where."

Morei fell quiet and submitted himself to the silence of the forest. This time, though, he could have sworn he heard a bird caw, its call muffled by the dense mist.

"I was standing on a port," Syra responded. "And I was watching the sun rise before I felt pulled and woke up." She stretched her hand out and looked up at him. "Let me take your hand, Morei."

He stared, unsure of such a request. "Why?"

"To see if this is real," she whispered.

Morei reached out, their steps slowing to a near stop. Warmth, soft skin, life flooded his senses, and he inhaled sharply as she wrapped her delicate but strong fingers around his hand—

He jolted awake, blinking at the stars above him.

Morei patted himself down, checking to make sure he was real, that this moment was real, that what he had just experienced was a dream. Nothing felt out of the ordinary—it was night, and he was just outside Gamer's Village, in the heart of the Sorréle country.

Next to him, Sunny snorted in his sleep, lying flat on his side. The Shire was the last thing he owned from Geral besides the clothes on his back and the sword at his hip. He was a traitor, a killer, and a monster.

He had to find her.

That revelation hung so heavily in his thoughts that for once, he was forgiven for the monstrous images that flashed behind his eyes—the crimes he'd committed against the very citizens he once swore to protect. They deserved it, he told himself; they were going to kill him if he didn't first.

He folded his hands behind his head and took a deep breath. The air was still warm, and he had shushed the fire hours ago. He noted the placement of the wide moon in the sky. It was close to dawn, but still that odd hour in the night where sleep was expected regardless of the oncoming light.

Syra Castello. The woman he swore had something to do with all that had happened to him. Why and how, he did not know, but he hoped to find out sooner rather than later. She'd been showing up more and more in his dreams, but always fleeting. Tonight was different. Tonight, he could not deny the strange realness of the dream. He could still feel her hand around his, the way the cold mist had settled on his skin.

There were things happening that he did not understand, but he intended to.

Morei lay there for a long while, lost in the memory of the dream, reliving the details and listening to the forest's rustle.

No matter how many times he played that moment over and over again, he could not shake one thing. He found himself repeating the phrase over and over again.

"Tell me again what it's like to die."

Then he felt the ground shake underneath him.

Sunny popped up, blinking with wide eyes as Morei rolled over to stand. The darkness of his surroundings did not rest well with him—he couldn't see anything beyond his outstretched hand. Soldiers always used to say that a man without a fire was as good as dead. He had wanted to avoid attention, but it seemed the attention had already found him.

Morei strained his ears, and in one quick flick of his wrist, he summoned Dark Energy in the palm of his hand. The flames burst to life, the touch ice cold despite the obvious heat that radiated off the dancing fire. The voices bombarded him at once, shouting to be heard in the mess of his scrambled thoughts, but he hushed them with a single command. As he cast his hand forward, lighting his surroundings with an orange glow, he was met with not a physical presence, but something else entirely.

The blades of grass disappeared as his vision turned inward. The cold night air was muted by the intense heat that seared his body and mind, the fire that burned in his hand extinguished by a force well beyond his own. The Dark Energy, so readily available to him, was yanked from his grasp as a much more intense and otherworldly power slithered across his mind.

Morei shuddered and collapsed, feeling the ground shake beneath his hands as the presence *moved* below him. Deep underground, among soil, root, and rock, something large shifted. He could feel it, as certain as he was that the sun would rise. A voice he could not recognize or hear well passed through his thoughts in one gust of wind.

And then it was gone.

Morei blinked, feeling now the cold grass on his hands and knees. He should have moved, but he didn't. He stared into the ground, expecting the presence to come back at any time. To his right, Sunny snorted, oblivious to the otherworldly energy that had just made itself known to Morei.

He should have done anything else—gotten up, screamed, called out, anything. Instead, he continued to stare and wait, unsure if the ground would open up right there and swallow him whole.

There was something down there. Something ancient.

PIRATE COUNTRY

Cyrus had grown tired of the sea. The vast blue waters had become the only scenery for nearly a full moon cycle, only broken up by the occasional islands from Eiyrȧl to Creitón. He had grown quite fond of island hopping, enjoying the discovery of each and using the ground to center himself—he loved flying, but he had grown restless. Time was constantly on his mind.

They were flying for a purpose. The night he left Razan behind, Cyrus had felt a massive weight released from his shoulders. He'd gotten too close there—Zorya, the princess and daughter of the king, proved that—and the farther he flew, the freer he felt. Behind, memories grew duller with distance, and ahead a new purpose. He would find his mother, break the curse that kept him from harvesting energy, and fulfill his duty as a Dragon Rider by returning to Leonzo to raise the two female dragons.

Sozar's growth had caused strain on the leather. It was the same he'd fled Razan with. The dragon's belly had widened, his shoulders bulking out and his neck thickening. While Sozar still had more development ahead, he had struck a growth spurt on their travels, and it had forced them to become creative with the leathers. About halfway through the flight, they had landed on an island with large leaves, so Cyrus had stripped several branches and turned the leaves into a girth, cutting the leather to stop the strain on it. It worked, but it was not tough, and Cyrus had spent many a day eying for islands to replace the leaves—even the dragon's soft scales were too rough for the plant.

The Rider's Sword had become imperative, cutting fish, leather, leaves, clearing paths, all of it. His arm was defined from constant use, his skin kissed by the sun, his hair brighter than ever before. The salt in the air had dried his skin and lips, cracking the sensitive areas between his knuckles until the scabs were thick enough to protect and his body adjusted to the harsher conditions. Unbelievably, though, the metal of his sword had remained intact, with no sign of erosion. For once, Cyrus could do nothing but thank Eazon for sparing the one thing keeping him alive.

Sozar's midnight scales had become encrusted in buildup, thanks to the sea's brutal presence, and Cyrus had found himself picking crud out from underneath where salt particles had accumulated during their flights. The area around his neck managed to constantly harvest sea crystals—what he had come to call them after the fourth round of this.

Cyrus tried not to complain much during the flight, but one thing he had concluded far too soon was his absolute disdain for fish. They had become his only meal, and while it kept him alive, he nearly gagged at the sight now. Sozar had managed to stay fed by hunting the islands for larger prey and had found some wild beasts roaming about, oblivious to predators. Cyrus had managed to start several fires during their travel to cook some of the meat, but he hadn't been born a cook and had generally turned the meat into charred leather. Not the finest meals, but it had still been better than fish.

Regardless of the adventurous flight, Cyrus could not suffocate the guilt that turned his tongue sour every time he let his thoughts wander too long in the past. There were people, like

Zorya, who did not deserve anything cruel to happen to them. Even his disdain for the king did not warrant a merciless hand.

More than anything, though, he could not shake the feeling that Dameon and Ashtir had done something terrible.

What's done is done. Sozar had told him that relentlessly, and he had to accept it. Cyrus could not change his actions in the past, but he could change the future.

The thrill that bubbled just under the surface of his skin was for what lay ahead. Creitón, the land of pirates, or so the stories told. The land was ancient; some believed the first true settlements of the Vore people originated here. Cyrus didn't know the accuracy of that versus Eiyrăl, and frankly, he didn't care.

Because he wasn't here for that—he had flown all this way to find his mother in the city of Delion. Leonzo had promised it. The man would be waiting for Cyrus upon his return, where he'd been told to fly to the outskirts of Jasper Village and continue north until he found the large boulder that was shaped like a ship's anchor. Leonzo would wait there on the third full moon from his departure. That was two cycles from now, which gave Cyrus time to recuperate, find his mother, and get answers.

Once that was finished, Leonzo would teach him how to harvest energy, and he would have say over the two female dragon eggs that remained now in the man's care. The thought of raising the young generation of dragons made him antsy, even after all this time. This was it—the key to the future, a new generation of Dragon Riders at his fingertips.

Nothing could be more fulfilling than that.

And so, despite the way his bones ached and his legs cramped as Sozar settled on the coast of the city and he descended from the dragon's back, Cyrus felt purpose boil his blood. The sun had slipped under the horizon, the light fading at a rapid pace, but that was to his favor. Cyrus's silver eyes would no doubt give him away before he spoke a word, and he had no hood to protect himself from prying gazes. The dragon would remain hidden behind the jagged rocks of the coast until Cyrus had more answers. Until then, he was to wander the streets of Delion, near the coast, and find the small cottage that Leonzo had told him about.

That was all he knew, truthfully—where her home would be, and that a Krakí statue would mark it. Leonzo had said it had been many, many summers since he himself had last seen Cyrus's mother, and he couldn't say what she looked like now. He would have to go off trust and intuition once he arrived at the cottage. Something told Cyrus that he would simply know once he laid eyes on her.

He gave the dragon a solid pat on the neck, the scales slick with moisture but warm. "Rest your wings, my friend," he mumbled. Sozar turned his beefy head toward him and met his eyes with his a single fiery one. The pupil dilated, then contracted again. Sozar let a hot huff of air wash over Cyrus's body.

Be safe, the dragon grumbled. The exhaustion was audible, and Cyrus sympathized. To be so close, to finally have reached the country—it made him want to curl up on the sand beneath his feet and sleep. His head was heavy, and his shoulders were tight from the constant tensing of his muscles in flight, but his mind was alive.

This was it.

He stretched, relishing in this moment of silence, of preparation. Despite the days of solitude, his heart still thudded with nerves. He tried to swallow the building anticipation, but it was lodged in his throat.

Sozar nudged his shoulder. *Go.*

And he did. With one warn boot in front of the other, Cyrus made his way through the sand of the coast. The crashing waves were left behind, the waters no longer charming, and he trudged forward. The beach soon gave way to pebbles, and it took little time before he found a small and narrow path, made from countless summers of use by the looks of it. He kept his eyes peeled for anyone, but no one was out around here. He was alone.

Buildings sprouted in the distance, their shingled roofs gray in the failing light. He noted the exteriors all looked the same—rough stone, no wood. A few people mingled about, but they kept to themselves and were obviously in no mood to chat, which was fine by him. Cyrus slowed, not wishing to enter the outer edge of the city without first knowing he would not be followed or tracked. He looked around—no soldiers that he could tell. Either that, or the soldiers here dressed in mundane civilian clothes.

Swords were common on the hips of many, at least, which made his own sheathed weapon less of an anomaly. Someone was roasting meat, and the succulent scent made his mouth water—it had been too long since he had had a proper meal, and the idea of digging into real food nearly turned him savage.

Stomach grumbling, he avoided eye contact with anyone. No one would know who he was if he didn't make it obvious. To them, he'd just look like another citizen. A rough, dirty, and perhaps smelly one, but a citizen nonetheless.

As he wove his way along the simple paths, he took in the houses. Leonzo had told him his mother had settled in a nice cottage by the sea, where she could overlook the water and sit on the slabs of stone near the shore. "Her home will be obvious—your mother was always eccentric in nature," the man had told him. "Look for the large Krakí. Her father gave it to her before he passed many summers ago."

So many questions, and yet he could not remember half of what he wished to ask her—the anxiety was making him uncomfortable in his own skin. Exhaustion fell away, replaced by adrenaline he hadn't known he possessed. If he laid his head down now, he had no doubt he would sleep soundly for the next six days—what he would give for a bath!

He kept his eyes locked to his right, where he anticipated her home to be. The pace of his steps increased as the night grew bolder. Time felt like it was slipping between his fingers, and if he did not find her now, he might never.

Cyrus sidestepped to avoid bumping into a woman carrying a basket of goods. From his peripheral vision, he saw her smile at him, but he did not risk looking at her directly to return it.

Her steps faded behind him as he continued onward. The homes to his left grew denser, while those on the right grew sparse, broken up by countless paths beaten into the ground. Patches of thin grass broke out between sections of pebbles and large rock. Salt corrosion had damaged the sea-facing homes. Some looked to have been scrubbed, while others had given up, choosing to consider it a part of the build. However, it had dug itself deep in some spots, and many people clearly hadn't even attempted to reverse the damage.

It was reflective of the city, really, what the homes looked like, and it was apparent to Cyrus that people simply got by here, nothing more.

That did not reflect highly on their king.

A king, he realized, he wanted nothing to do with. He had learned a valuable lesson in Razan—trust was nonexistent. Anybody could be an enemy, even his own mother. And while he hoped beyond hope and truly believed that this wasn't the case, there was still a small part of him that doubted.

Cyrus grunted to himself, agitated at his own thoughts. Again and again, he spiraled, and again and again, he scolded himself. This was no way to live, and he certainly couldn't go the rest of his life second-guessing every act. That would drive him mad.

Through their mental link, he could hear Sozar snort with amusement. He knew what the dragon thought, because it was the exact same as he did—that he was being ridiculous.

Ahead, Cyrus saw it, and his steps faltered on the path. The Krakí statue. Bold, bright blue, and on the porch of a small home. Grass grew tall around the stone walls, the shingles looked like their best days were well behind, and a light burned inside. A single window faced his direction, and he saw a woman walk by, basket in hand.

That was her.

Or so he wanted to believe. The thought drifted away, leaving behind the reality of what was before him: a home. A light did burn, but he couldn't actually see anyone inside, not right now. The statue, though. His body remained motionless, as if carved in stone itself while he stared. He knew he needed to approach, but the only thing he wanted to do was turn around and run.

Sozar urged him forward. This was his destiny.

The air was cool on his tongue as he scrambled up the steps. From the front door, a stunning image caught his attention—a freshly painted scene from out at sea, with a ship crashing through waves, a flag held high. The flag carried an unknown crest, perhaps some sort of pirate's, and tiny figures had been painted on the main deck, swords raised. In the background, a sunset turned the blues into oranges before fading back into the wood grain of the door. For a moment, Cyrus stared, stunned at the beauty of it all. This was done by the hand of someone talented. Could his own mother do such a thing?

The sea creature to his right had a chunk of stone missing from the back of its head, and here, he could see that the blue was a cover-up for an original tan color. He wasn't sure what kind of paint had been used that would hold up against the sea's intensity, although he was certain that berries had been used as the foundation for the color—

Focus, Sozar interjected.

The dragon was right—Cyrus was scattered, his mind no longer fully his own. Nerves made his palms sweat and his fingers restless. This was it. He was here. So much had gone into this moment. So many summers spent alone in the mines of Diemon, dreaming of the day they'd be reunited. Was it normal to be so . . . anxious?

One foot in front of the other, he ascended the two steps onto the beaten porch, where the wood gave away his position immediately. It groaned under his weight, and he wondered if it might give out completely, but it held as he closed in on the door and raised his shaking hand.

Cyrus took a large, deep breath and knocked. For a fleeting moment, as the steps inside began to track their way toward him, he wanted to turn and run, run from it all before it ever happened, but something held him there. A force, perhaps, that he didn't entirely understand.

As the door drew open and he beheld her fully for the first time, a wave of a hundred different emotions crashed over him.

Disbelief. Rage. Exasperation.

It was not his mother. He knew because she had to be no older than him. The woman stood there, mouth agape. Her dark hair was braided atop her head, her ebony skin covered in ink that depicted ships and unnamed monsters. Small gold hoops covered both ears, and she smiled, although somewhat guarded based on the troubled gleam in her honey-brown eyes.

"Can I help you?"

Cyrus's lung failed to work. Everything he had been told was poured into this moment, and yet before him stood a stranger. There were hardly any words to describe the frustra-tion that boiled over in his chest. All he knew how to do was back up.

The wood groaned again as he stumbled down the steps. "My apologies. I've got the wrong house."

Yet she continued to stare—no doubt stunned by the color of his eyes. With a quick turn, he ran.

DREAMER

The air was frigid, and Syra pulled the giant fur blanket tighter, her cheeks bitten by the cold breeze. The cave entrance was high above the forest, and one small move would plummet her to her death, but she found solace here. The stone around her was decorated with icicles from the oncoming winter. In the distance, snow clung to the mountaintops. Clouds hung low, thick with moisture, but she didn't move. This was her sanctuary in the disaster that had become her life.

For life hadn't been easy. In the moon cycle that had passed, Syra had been herded to the depths of the Mourale Mountains by the Infernol—a secret organization of over five thousand misfits and rebels. It was they who had ambushed the group that day in the rolling hills. She could still remember the fear that had gripped her as the boots approached.

Feverish, Syra had relied heavily on Zarek over the days they traveled east and past Raveer. The Infernol had said little, only that they had been sent to "retrieve" her and her comrades. When questions were asked about her illness, Zarek brushed it off, and with a Guardian speaking for her, no one challenged it. Or so she told herself—they had surely stared though.

Zarek had been frustrated, to say the least. He had demanded that Syra somehow summon Sekar so that he could confront the God once and for all, but Syra had pleaded that it did not work that way. Though when he asked how she could be so certain, she couldn't answer him. When no one was looking, the Guardian would glare at her, having an entire conversation through looks alone that she wished she didn't comprehend. He was angry, upset, and most importantly, concerned that she was in over her head. Not that she had a choice, did she? Zarek didn't think she was prepared to take on such a monumental selection, but Syra had already told him how it all happened— how Sekar had torn her free from this realm—and it was quite clear that none of this had ever been her choice.

It wasn't that the Guardian didn't think she was capable, it was that he believed all of this to be happening too soon. Zarek was a planner, methodical about his approach. What occurred had derailed everything. When she tried to tell him that it would be okay, he dismissed her and told her to let him think.

Zane, the ex-commander of Raveer, knew almost everything, but certain things remained kept from him for his safety. It had not changed his humor or actions, but it had altered how much he spoke. He was cautious, and everything he said sounded well thought out. The man was wary, and rightfully so. He had accompanied them for a chance at a new life but had unwillingly been tossed into the fire of Destiny's jaws. Understandably, he was a bit stunned. But Zane was still Zane— loveable, caring, and passionate about doing the right thing. When he could, he offered to help, like when the Infernol were struggling with lighting a fire one night on their travels, and he stepped in. Or when one of the Infernol men came back with fresh kills for food, Zane helped skin and prepare the meat to cook. By now, he had embedded himself into the military ranks of the organization and was often so busy teaching, advising, and planning that Syra hardly saw him on the main floors of the Infernol.

Now that Syra thought about it, it had actually been three whole days since she had run into Zane, but she was happy for him. He needed a purpose like this, something to help him stay busy, so that he didn't ask too many questions. Sure, he knew of Syra's situation, but he didn't know that she was destined by the Guardians to restore the Soul Realm. Or that the bond she had with Sekar, the Zyulë Bond, was fatal if either party got stabbed, burned alive, drowned . . . the list went on. But Zane did know that she and Sekar were connected now, something he was not entirely comfortable with. It wasn't like the God of Dreams had left a positive impression on him.

But while Sekar could undoubtedly find her, he hadn't tried. The God had just disappeared. During her travels and now her stay, Syra had anticipated his arrival, but he had yet to show himself. The Infernol had been proud to announce that their extraordinary Energy Harvesters—a set of twins who had an abnormal way about them—had the place well protected and that they would sense any fluctuation in the energy fields around them, but Syra questioned it. She didn't doubt their abilities, but she did doubt that they extended to one like Sekar. The God of Dreams was a master of illusions and Chaos; he had spent lifetimes perfecting his craft to hide even from his own siblings. If he wanted to see her, he would.

Try as Syra might, she could not sense Sekar. She tried to call upon the bond the same way she had with Light Energy, but it failed repeatedly. Her hope was that if she could summon the power that connected them, she could feel out the God's location and call on him. He had abandoned her, and she wasn't sure how to even begin navigating her new abilities.

Zarek didn't know how either. As proud as the Guardian was, he outright admitted that a God's power was well beyond his comprehension and that he wouldn't know where to begin. Harvesting Chaos was an entirely separate league of energy harvesting. Only a God could teach such power, for it was only a God who understood it in its fullest.

One thing Syra had learned was that she was dreaming more vividly than ever before. She had spent many nights wandering coastal seas of cities she'd never heard of, shared wine with women and men she'd never meant, had even relived memories of her own childhood. Syra relished it. Most of her dreams had been nothing but a great adventure, a welcome escape from her current reality, but after last night . . . Syra shuddered. Her dreams were growing more vivid. Unpredictable.

The touch of the Geral king was still warm on her hands, even though a day had passed. He had looked so stoic, certain, but he had not fooled her. Morei Geral was lost and had forgotten his purpose. His hands, decorated with the ailment of his curse, had not scared her but filled her with sorrow. She didn't know why she'd seen him or what to make of it. All she knew was that the dream now haunted her.

"I thought I'd find you here." The voice startled her, and she whirled around. Approaching was the man of the hour, Zarek, dressed in a simple white tunic and pants. Death's Sword was always on his hip, and he had taught her to wear hers the same way. The Infernol leader, Keryn, had insisted that no violence was tolerated and there had not been any crimes in many, many cycles. The Guardian had waved him off and said that nothing would convince them otherwise.

And the truth was, the Infernol had not been as warm as they'd wanted. People stared, and rumors that their arrival marked the end of times, that they were conduits for something far more evil, had spread like wildfire. They had tried to address them, but the more they fought back, the grander the tales became. When they brought this to Keryn's attention, he'd challenged their integrity. The leader didn't trust them, and it would seem they were walking on thin ice.

The real question was why they'd been intercepted in the first place—Keryn had told them he'd received a tip about their whereabouts from a stranger. When Zarek pressed him about who, he said he didn't know the name and had never gotten the chance to learn because the man had disappeared.

Then there was Vic Resanson, the man Dryl had tasked her to find. He was an agent for the Infernol and, as the Guardian had said, the answer. She had held on to that note all the way here, and when she'd originally presented it to Keryn, he had told her that Vic was not here and he wasn't sure when—or even if—he'd be back. The campaign he was on was by his own accord, not the Infernol's. Syra hadn't believed him, but she'd been in no place to challenge his authority. Not yet.

Syra patted the ground next to her and shifted the fur blanket. She had recently found a little cave that overlooked the forest of the Mourale Mountains. Never in her life had she seen so many trees clustered at once. Caster had trees, but nothing like this—there had to be thousands of pine trees in just her view alone. The evening air was crisp, the clouds fat with moisture, which was why she had taken a fur blanket with her. The cave was far up; the drop alone would kill her, so she kept a little distance between herself and the steep rocky edge.

The Guardian's pale blue skin looked dark in the fading of the light, but his piercing red gaze twinkled with amusement as he sat down next to her. A wave of warmth washed over Syra at his presence. "How long have you been here?"

She shrugged. "The clouds weren't this thick a bit ago." Syra pulled the fur blanket up to her chin. "I like it here. It's quiet."

"I don't blame you," the Guardian replied softly. "It's not like the people have been the most welcoming."

"Even for you?" She raised an eyebrow. Guardians of Death were supposed to be revered by the Infernol, and she'd suspected a little more respect would be shown to him after he'd been requested to join the last meeting. They had only been here for a little over fifteen days. The travel had taken longer than anticipated after a reroute to avoid the disarray of Raveer, which had alerted the northern city, Assane, who sent troops. In fact, the commotion at Raveer had been so large that they'd been able to see smoke for leagues after. Yalana, as Sekar had called the massive Firóle, had truly done what she had set out to do: get revenge.

While they had spoken routinely, Syra and Zarek had not recently discussed their feelings about the secret organization. They'd promised to give it a little bit of time and see if the rumors and glares settled. The only person who blended right in was Zane, but it was easy to see why—he was a soldier, another resource for the undeniable approaching war.

Zarek took a deep breath, the sound cutting the silence that sat between them. He looked down at her—even sitting, he towered over her. "It isn't what they say, it's how they act. Their council—if that's what you can call them—does not trust me. It's not their fault. They've been bred into an era of impending doom. But still." Zarek shrugged. "I didn't come here for them. I came here for you."

She nodded, although slowly. "Do you think this is what Dryl would have wanted, though?" The ring he'd given her always sat in her pouch. It served as a reminder of her constant promise to him and to the brother of the Guardian who now sat next to her. Syra motioned to the trees beneath them. "Dryl wanted me to come here, and I have, but I don't think he anticipated any of the hostility."

"Maybe that's why he gave you the ring," the Guardian countered. "Perhaps he knew the Infernol would not be so welcoming."

The reply surprised her, and she looked at him fully. "You think so?"

"Dryl was strategic. He knew there were risks in everything he decided to do. When he left the Soul Realm and turned his back on the order, he knew what he was doing. When he found you and chose to stay, he also knew what he was doing, and when he gave you the sword and ring, he had planned that. Dryl was no fool. Every decision was carefully calculated. That ring you have was given as protection." Zarek smiled, but it looked strained. "Did you see the way Keryn looked at you when you showed it to him?"

She had. Syra recalled the annoyance, even though it was fleeting, that had crossed his blue eyes. The leader of the Infernol had been drilling her about who she was, how she came to be, and Syra had quickly revealed the ring and spoken of Dryl. At that, Keryn had ceased all interrogation. But the tension between them all hadn't gone ignored by her. Even now, more than two weeks later, she could still feel it whenever she was near Keryn. He wasn't fond of her. She wanted to believe that it was because he saw her as a liability to his control, but it felt like more than that.

"It's an obligation," she mumbled. Dryl had been heavily involved with the Infernol—the ring symbolized such things— but that didn't mean the Infernol was happy to uphold that promise.

While it all seemed rather obvious, admitting it out loud left a sour taste on her tongue.

"This place has to work, though—it's too dangerous out in the open," Zarek continued. "It provides us some form of security, even if it's short term, so that we can plan our next steps." He didn't sound too convinced.

"I don't trust anyone," she confessed.

"And nor should you." The Guardian raised his brow. "If you trusted anyone here, I'd have doubts about everything."

She restrained a playful smile. "There you go again—"

"With what?" he pressed.

Syra dropped her voice to try to mimic Zarek's, although it was a far cry. "Your first lesson: Everyone has an incentive."

The Guardian eyed her, his expression unchanged. "Are you proud of yourself?"

Syra waved him off. Such a short time together, but she could already tell he was putting on a tough face on purpose. "Don't deny it, you were impressed."

He nodded, and she caught his shoulders relax. "Will you stay out here much longer?"

The subject change forced her back into the current reality—that she was hiding out in a cave above the forest to avoid interacting with the Infernol altogether. "Seems to be the only spot I can be without starting a war," she replied, and looked back at the trees. The clouds had broken on a distant mountain, and she could see the flurries chasing one another. Snow.

The season was officially on them, and already, she missed the warmth and humid touch of the sea.

"Have you tried training more?" Again, a subject change. Zarek was prodding for information.

Her potential to harvest Chaos was the last thing she wanted to discuss. He knew the answer to that—had known it for days now. "You know as well as I do what I will say."

Zarek shrugged, unperturbed by the change in her tone. "And would I be upholding my oath if I didn't ask?"

Syra glared at him. "Am I just a task then?"

Now, the Guardian looked miffed. "Syra, you know that's not what I meant."

She bit her tongue, trying to keep herself from saying something she might regret. Truthfully, she was angry at the world. It all felt rather bleak when she stared too long; nothing was exactly going to plan. Sekar had abandoned her to traverse this new world of energy harvesting on her own, the Infernol wanted nothing to do with her, and she was no longer sure what her purpose was. Sure, she had a bloodline in the Soul Realm, but accepting and acting on that were two entirely separate things. And she knew she was in no shape to confront Shevana.

So, essentially, she was just sitting here, and that did little for her self-esteem.

"Syra," Zarek spoke up. His agitation was gone. "Don't think so little of me after everything we've been through."

And he was right, that she knew. She avoided his demanding gaze and tried to wiggle herself deeper into the blanket, hoping to suffocate her fears, but she was already engulfed in them. Her remark had been callous and unfair. Of all people, Zarek deserved accolades—Zane too—especially after all the madness her very existence had put everyone through. But that did not mean she didn't sometimes feel like a task to the Guardian. He was direct, abrasive at times, and without remorse for things that he said. And while she had grown accustomed to his way of speaking, it did not lessen the occasional frustrations she felt with his behavior.

"I know," she finally admitted, barely above a whisper.

For a long time, neither spoke. They just sat and watched the oncoming storm. The wind shifted several times, bitterly cold, making her appreciate the fur blanket even more. Although, when she glanced over, Zarek looked rather comfortable, and it occurred to her that she had no idea if Guardians got cold. It was a strange thought that surged itself to the forefront of her mind.

One day, she might ask about it, but not now. Right now, she felt oppressed by the noise of the realms and what was expected of her. As if Destiny had snatched her tongue right from her.

The sound the wind made as it traversed through the trees was a melody she'd never heard until entering these mountains. It whistled, low and long, and filled the air with nature's tune. Syra listened, entranced that the rustling of pines against a breeze could make such a noise. It grew louder and louder as it traveled closer to their nook in the mountain, and only when the wind struck her exposed face and disturbed her hair did she blink.

"You asked if this was what Dryl wanted," Zarek said out of nowhere, without looking her way. "What he wanted was peace, to salvage what was left of the Soul Realm and start again. He always believed in the power of the Guardians, even as our numbers dwindled. He knew our very existence was part of the balance so carefully crafted by what many call destiny. Naïve, I used to call him, but now, I wonder if it's the right thing to do at all."

That alarmed her. "You think it's better to let the Soul Realm perish?"

He let out a cold laugh. "Why not? What good would it do if we charged in there and declared a resurrection of the old ways?" Before she could interject, he waved her off, as if sensing her words. "Let's play this out, Syra. You embrace your new abilities and title—Goddess and heir to the Soul Realm—and reclaim the throne. You banish the demons, get control of the wretched monsters that now call the realm of the dead their home, and declare that a new order of Guardians will begin. Congratulations, you have officially staked your claim. What now?"

Syra turned to face him better. His expression was innocent, but his eyes and the way they squinted told her he wasn't happy with the outcome he foresaw. She could not see her way out of one very big problem, though. "If we fail to restore the Soul Realm to what it once was, then the balance of all things is lost. The dead cannot pass successfully to the Afterlife, demons overrun the realm and then this one will be next. Needless we forget the beasts you mentioned on our travels. Already, we know that there is a spike of possessions—Jared said so himself." At the mention of the healer from the Nighthunter Federation, she internally cringed. Another death she was responsible for.

Zarek motioned as he spoke, using his fingers to count off. "Your first problem is dealing with the original Guardians who have grown accustomed to the ways of Shevana. Once that is dealt with, you must also face the demons who will not see you as ruler, but as an opportunity to take the Soul Realm for themselves—"

"Honuyál," she blurted out.

"The Honuyál demons are the least of your problems, Syra. There are things that live within the Soul Realm that take no form and feed on souls—without proper protection, they will slip through the covers and embed themselves right into your body without you ever knowing."

Zarek lifted his third finger. Syra flinched at the motion, momentarily speechless. He'd never shared that with her before, and she wasn't sure what to make of such an enemy. "Who's to say the Gods want the Soul Realm restored at all?" he asked. "If they were so keen on keeping it going, then why have they not intervened? Now, you have them to consider. Do I need to keep going?"

Syra swallowed. There was a lot to unpack in all of this, and while she hadn't considered the implications of each issue, she was more surprised by Zarek's sudden tone. "What's gotten into you? You've proclaimed nothing but wanting to make sure the prophecy is fulfilled, upholding duties, all of that. Why this?"

Zarek turned his gaze upward, as if the answers lay somewhere in the stone above them, before redirecting his crimson eyes back to her with a fierceness that could have lit a fire. "I want nothing more than to continue the oath I took centuries ago, Syra. But I will not do so with blood on my hands. Do you understand me?"

"No," she spat, "I don't. Your biggest concern is a little blood on your hands? If those deaths meant restoring balance and keeping the realms going, isn't that worth it?"

Zarek's jaw ticked. "And what if that blood was yours, Syra? Would you still feel the same?"

His answer struck her hard, tearing the air from her lungs. For a long moment, she just stared, unsure of what to say or how to say anything at all. Frankly, she wasn't even sure she comprehended his meaning.

It seemed he knew that. "I don't see this ending the way you want it to, Syra. If I did, I would tell you, but I don't. This—" Zarek reached forward and snatched her wrist up. The ugly gray scar revealed itself to them. "This will be your downfall. You are bound to a God who thrives in madness, a God who has spent lifetimes living in illusions. You don't think he will tailor you to meet his needs?" He dropped his voice to a low hiss. "Do you really believe there's an ending with both of you in it?"

The breath caught in her throat. "The Zyulë Bond—"

"You're in denial." His grip tightened. "How many times do I have to tell you a bond like that won't stop him from doing whatever he wants to do with you?"

He was right. This was not the first time they'd had this conversation, and it might not be the last. The God of Dreams was unpredictable, and he had her right where he wanted her. That brought her no comfort, not after everything he had done to her and her friends. This was a man who had brought a city to its knees to prove a point. The bond was not to protect her, as Sekar had once promised, but to control her. Zarek had told her that over and over, but it was sinking in now. The reality of her situation was bleak—she was bound to a God who would stab her in the back if it meant he could save his own neck.

Syra pulled her wrist free, and he obliged. Free from him, she shook her head. Everything was happening too fast and not adding up. Sekar had spoken with her, told her he would be there for her, and he had even taken her back to them on her request. If this was all about control, then why hadn't he held her against her will? Why let her lose and not speak for a moon cycle?

Zarek believed that Sekar was using her, utilizing the strength of the bond to keep them connected, but she wanted to—*needed to*—believe otherwise. No more could she take of being toyed with. No more could she handle being tricked and manipulated. If one more person tried to take advantage of her, she would . . . she would . . .

Bring this world to its knees.

The thought was so loud in her head that it startled her. Syra gulped in air and looked around. It felt like she had just screamed; even her throat was dry. All of a sudden, she felt like a foreigner in her own body.

Syra was ashamed of her thoughts. In the last half cycle, she had been experiencing changes to her mind that she didn't quite understand. Never in her life had she felt so . . . *violent* with the world around her. It had felt like she was constantly the running joke in Destiny's games, and she was growing quite tired of it all. These feelings were unlike her, though, and she knew that. She was the girl who rescued the insect from the dock of Caster, not the one who stepped on it and kept walking. Now, she was quick to think the worst—to *want* the worst.

"Are you all right?" Zarek asked. She blinked and looked at him. He was watching her intensely.

Syra cleared her throat and made to stand. The blanket was gripped in her hands, acting as some sort of pacifier for all the emotions washing over her at once. "I'm fine, but I think this discussion is done."

"You can't just storm off when the truth is too hard to he—" Zarek started.

"In case you forgot," she cut in. "I didn't ask for any of this, and if you try to push me around one more time, I will shame-lessly punch you in the face."

Death's Sword bounced on her hip as she strode down the cavern. There were no lanterns hung—it was not a main hall for the Infernol, more like a forgotten section of the mountain—but she knew her way quite well. This was not the first time she'd walked this stone path.

She needed to leave. Get away from everyone and be alone. Her heart raced too forcefully, her hands shook with an unrecognizable compulsion to hit something, and her head swam with visions of what she wanted to say to the people who failed to understand her. Most of all Zarek. But Syra knew this wasn't her, and she didn't want to say or do anything she would regret. Enough had been done already. The last thing she needed was to hurt the one person who had defended her on more than one occasion already.

It seemed all she ever needed was protecting, and that made her feel defenseless.

Zarek didn't come after her, and she was relieved. The Guardian had enough awareness to sense her turmoil, but she knew she'd have to face him again, probably sooner than she wanted to admit. Until then, she kept walking.

Chaos's new child, heir to a throne she couldn't figure out if she wanted or not, and all she could think about was why she had dreamt of Morei Geral last night. If it was just a dream, it had been the most vivid of her life, but if it was real . . .

Well, then, Syra wanted to find out.

SEEK THE HUNTER

amer's Village was not big, perhaps what one would call a slightly larger town, but it was perfect. It was not advertised by any means, but this village was home to the misfits, and that meant it was safe for Morei. His boots crunched the gravel, the breeze tousled his cloak, and Sunny walked beside him, snorting. The steed would need a place to rest while he stayed, so he steered toward the barn, which was hard to miss. The large structure stood taller than any of the homes and inns here, the smell of livestock wafting through the streets nearby.

People glanced once or twice as they walked, but none stopped or asked questions. The temperature was cooler with the oncoming season change, but not cold enough for gloves, as he wore now. Morei could not risk being recognized—misfits or not, he was being hunted and had a hefty bounty on his head.

He still recalled the dream and the trembling ground. As he listened to the people passing by, none spoke of any strange happenings like the ground shaking. He was still uneasy from last night—the vivid vision of Syra clung to his thoughts like mold. If it was a dream, then he could not explain why it felt so real. In such a short time, the world had grown unrecognizable. Morei missed the simplicity of ruling Geral. It'd had its ups and downs, but it was still something he understood. He didn't understand the strange presence he'd felt last night or the dream, and it all made him homesick.

For once, he gave himself the right to reminisce about the people of Geral, including Ezra. The young Energy Harvester had managed to wiggle his way into Morei's inner circle of friendship without even trying. He cared about Ezra, and a part of him sympathized with how the Energy Harvester would be navigating politics and rule with zero experience. Peter would be there, and Morei had no doubt the chancellor was making it seamless, but that still didn't give him peace.

Deep down, the only regret he had was leaving Ezra with an immense mess to clean up. Between Cu'cel, Morei's actions, and the political divide, the new king of Geral had no doubt entered a disastrous phase of cleanup. Morei didn't need proof to know that—he could make that assumption simply because he knew how running a city went.

Ezra was tough, though. There were characteristics of the young Energy Harvester that reminded Morei of himself, and that included resilience. He wanted to believe that Ezra was thriving, if only to squash the guilt over his own actions.

"Afternoon, sir," the barn hand greeted and cut into his thoughts. The man's voice was hoarse, his skin leathery and dark, the color of soil. "You lookin' for a place for this fella?"

Morei looked about, drawn back to the current reality. Horses whinnied from their stables, and he heard another man yell back as if talking to them. "So long as you've got room for him," he replied, "and a big stable. I don't want him cramped."

The barn hand waved him off. "Nonsense. We got space. Let me show you, yeah? You tell me if it'll make the boy happy. He's a big one, too. What is he, seventeen hands?"

"Eighteen," Morei corrected.

He was led to the barn, passing a pen of cattle as they went. There was a young boy milking one, and he waved at Morei as they passed, his blue eyes innocent and bright. Morei strained a smile, wanting to look pleasant, and it seemed to please the young lad. When they got to the stables, Morei tossed the reins over Sunny's bulky head and raised a hand to the steed. "Just you wait a moment, my friend."

In response, the horse snorted and turned his head to focus one large dark eye on him.

"I don't want to hear it," he mumbled, and turned around. The barn hand was staring, clearly amused.

"You two travel a lot together, eh?" he asked as he motioned to the empty stalls to the left. "Got a man who comes through here quite often, and he's got somethin' similar with his horse. She ain't big like this fella, though, only about fourteen hands. Small thing, but good for endurance."

Morei nodded but didn't reply. He eyed the stalls, noting the width and height. The ground looked well cared for, the shade abundant under this sun and any weather, and there was even a bucket of water. "You take them out, you said?"

"Twice a day for a good long walk. More'n happy to do more, if you need."

"Hm." He looked back at Sunny, who still stood where he had been left, and then back at the stall again. The last thing he wanted to do was leave Sunny here, but it was for the best. There was no space in the inns for horses, and he certainly didn't want to attract any attention by doing anything out of the ordinary. Normal travelers boarded their horses, so he would have to play by those rules.

Still, it was a smaller space than what Sunny was used to back at the palace barn.

"Get him out three times a day," Morei said, and reached for a coin pouch underneath the cloak.

"No problem. Just so you know, that'll be extra—"

"Price is not the concern," he cut in. "He's a spoiled boy, and if you want your stall to be in the same condition as it is now, he'll need lots of time out. We got a deal?"

The barn hand looked stunned. Morei had now made it clear he was rich, and maybe they didn't see many of his kind around. Finally, the older man cleared his throat and nodded. "You got it. How long are you wanting to keep him?"

"Jasper is his name," Morei added. The lie would help protect him if anyone came asking questions. "Keep the gear out of the sun, too. I don't want that accidentally getting moved anywhere where it could be damaged. It's expensive stuff and was custom fitted to him. Three times out, and make sure his water is freshened every day, although I'm sure you and your men do that already. And he is a grazer, so don't expect him to eat his hay all at once—" He stopped and looked about. It was all dirt in the barn with some wood. "Or do you let them eat grass?"

"A little of both."

"Ah, good." Morei eyed the steed. "He'll appreciate that. He does like water, so if you got a good spot near the river where he can get his hooves wet and dip his nose in, he'll be your best friend. No need for whips or stern words with him, either. He'll follow you, if you let him. If you need him to stay, just do as I did with my hand and he'll listen."

"Um." The barn hand licked his lips and cocked his head to the side. "H—How long is he . . . staying?"

A punch to his gut. "At least a moon cycle. I have business to take care of." Before the man could say more, he tossed the coin bag in his direction and the man caught it.

He remained silent as the guy counted, watching his eyes go wide and his mouth open and close several times before he finally blurted out, "This's enough for a cycle."

Morei nodded. "If anything occurs and I need him to stay a bit longer, I'll make sure you are taken care of."

"If you don't mind me asking," the man began as he tucked the coin pouch into a pant pocket, "what're you doin'?"

He swallowed. "Business," he repeated, slower this time. "Business that I cannot speak about. Am I to trust that you do not speak of your clients to anyone?"

"You mean privacy? Yeah." The barn hand sounded more and more uncertain, though.

"I would hope there is confidentiality," Morei said, and forced a smile. "Now, are we all set?"

The man cleared his throat. "We're good to go. I just need a name to tell the boys, if you come back and I ain't here?"

"Ah." Morei licked his lips. "Garrison is the name."

The man reached out to shake, and Morei took it. "Pleasure doin' business with yah, Garrison. Name's Beckett. You come back and I ain't here, it's either James or Kraig here. Them boys are good fellas. They'll take good care of Jasper, I promise that."

Morei pulled his hand away. "Good to hear. I'll say goodbye and be out of your way, then." What he couldn't voice was the sheer stress he felt at this next part. He'd known it was coming, known that Sunny would be left here for a prolonged period, but he could not shake the feeling that if something went wrong with him, he would never see his steed again.

Facing Sunny, he closed the gap between them and rested his head against the bridge of his head. Morei rubbed his thumbs through the short fur, which was silky smooth and hot from travel. The skin underneath was soft where the fur gave way toward the mouth, and he savored the touch, for it would be a long time before he would see this friend again.

"You behave yourself," he whispered to Sunny. "You don't stir up any trouble, and when I'm ready, I'll come back for you." Emotions stormed his senses, and he closed his eyes. His limbs felt like dead weight, his heart beat with an agonizing thump, and his mind was engulfed in all the things that could go wrong.

But this next leg of the journey was far too risky for Sunny, and he could not stomach the idea that something could happen to the horse because of him. This was the safest place for the steed, and deep down, between all the aches and doubts, he knew that. Sunny had been a rock, where his life had been a river of misfortunes.

"All right," he breathed, and looked up. Morei ran his hand along the entire bridge of Sunny's face, soaking in the touch one last time. *Only for now, though*, he reminded himself. This was temporary. "Until next time."

And with that, he bid farewell to Beckett and the barn. The weight that bore down on his shoulders as he left nearly brought him to his knees, but he kept one foot in front of the other, and soon, there was relief.

He had made it this far, and now, there was nothing anchoring him. Morei had no one but himself to worry about, and there was something incredibly freeing about that.

As he wound his way through the streets, he found an inn close to the river, the raging waters audible at the end of the small road. Morei had never seen the Sorréleian River in person, but he'd heard stories about its sheer size and power. The river cut right through the heart of Sorréle and fed this town, but it also supplied Geral when the water supplies of the desert kingdom fell low, which happened on occasion.

River's Inn, where he would stay, was crowded as he entered. The lights were warm, offering just enough to make the place feel open, and he wove his way through a handful of bulky men who looked to belong to the sea rather than here. Their dreads were interlaced with gold rings, one wearing a silver medallion around his neck, while the other spoke in a choppy tongue. There was no doubt that they weren't from around here, but he didn't care to stick around and ask where they hailed from.

He approached the front, a small counter in the corner of the lobby where a man stood. His stomach fought against the pull of the white fabric, the buttons groaning as he leaned up against the wood at Morei's approach. He was a bald man, his skin covered in scars from a past life, and his eyes were hard, despite their soft brown color.

Voices rose from behind as someone started to sing a song that Morei was unfamiliar with. "Welcome to River's Inn, lad. You checking in?" Despite his harsh exterior, his voice was warm and soft.

"Room for one," he answered, "and perhaps a room farther away from the singing, although I won't complain if you don't have one." He reached for the other pouch of coins on his belt and opened it. "Three nights."

The innkeeper nodded and fished under the counter for a moment. A metal clanging echoed, and he shoved a drawer closed before laying a bronze key down on the rough wood. "Got one down the hall, not too far, but it isn't close either. You okay with that?"

"That'll do. How much?"

"You checking out morning of or evening?"

Morei thought for a moment. "Morning, and if anything changes, I'll let you know."

The innkeeper laid out his hand. "Call it eight then, meals included."

"Thanks." Morei counted out eight Krye and dropped them in the man's beefy hand. The key was right there, so he grabbed it. The metal was cold to the touch, a wonderful relief after the sun. "Meals are served all day?"

The innkeeper grunted. "Supposed to be. If someone tells you no, it's because they're cooking it."

That made him smile. "Got it."

"Enjoy the stay, lad. Washbasin's in the room, but for a more proper wash, there's a bathing room behind the lobby. Can't miss it."

Perfect. Morei nodded, satisfied, and made his way back through the crowd. It was growing denser as the afternoon gave way to early evening. He would wait this out and come back to eat when the majority of these people shuffled out of the way. Shoulders bumped into one another, hands touched places he would've very much rather they not have, and people's faces practically kissed his own as he shoved his way through the dining room. The bar was packed to his right, the bartender covered in ink with long, dark hair braided down one side. His hands were covered in rings, and he shouted to different patrons, placing tall mugs of mead and ale in their faces before telling them to get out of the way.

The scent of body odor followed him even as he broke free from the crowd and made his way down the hall. It was darker, but still cozy, and he saw two doors close to the end. He took a gamble and reached for the door on the left, relieved to find that the key worked. With creaky hinges, the door swung open to reveal a small room with a cot, some shelves, and a washbasin to the right. A mirror was positioned next to the basin, and he cringed, remembering the lady he had seen in the mirror when he'd visited the city. The thought brought back a cold chill that sent goosebumps across his body.

He would cover that with one of the blankets.

Morei locked the door with a metal clasp and let a long sigh escape his lips as he set the key down on one of the shelves. The hood came off and he rubbed his face hard, hoping to wipe away some of the tiredness. His bones ached, his skin was dry from travel, and his cheeks, once so smooth from constant shaving, were now coarse with a short beard. He hated it.

It represented just how disheveled he felt.

The washbasin had a bucket of water next to it and—

Morei nearly lunged for the blade that sat next to the basin. He had missed that the first time. Finally, after all this time, he could properly shave.

Later, once he knew the bathing room was not occupied, he would slip in for a deep clean. For now, Morei reached over, ripped the top blanket off the cot and dumped it over the mirror, covering it and removing the sight of him—he was unrecognizable, save for what lay beneath these gloves. That was familiar to his eyes, and so too was the sword at his hip, but nothing else. Everything else about him felt foreign.

All he needed was a moment to settle, so he sat down. The act alone made him stifle a groan. Maybe a nap would do—perhaps that was what he needed most. He could get a nap and then freshen up before a meal.

By the Gods, that sounded good.

Morei leaned over and kicked his legs up, boots and all, onto the cot. After the hard ground, this less-than-quality cot felt like a little slice of paradise, and his bones and muscles ate it up. There was nothing like this.

The sword, belt, and cloak stayed on as he lay there. In a little pouch, though, along with some Krye, sat the Lirallian Ring. Morei was not done with it. He intended on using it when the time was right, but not now. Now, what was important was knowing that he had it and nobody else. One thing he struggled to admit to was that he was terrified of putting it back on. He feared that the woman would return and this time, he would not be so lucky.

But the urge was there, always, just nibbling away at his control, begging him to slip the metal back on because only then would he be able to witness the future.

His thoughts swam with possibilities as he lay there, and eventually, after slumber teased him for a while, she finally pulled him under.

BRIBES DON'T MAKE FRIENDS

Cyrus was still reeling from the failure of his encounter the night before. He had sat at the edge of a cliff on a fjord for the entire night, watching the city. The air had grown chilly with the darkness, but also humid. With the sky clear, Cyrus watched the speckled light show. Stars—hundreds of them—stared down at him in awe. Such a clear view.

When he was younger, stories about the stars being the souls of old kings and queens would fill pubs late into the evenings. Cyrus had heard it all, and he had once believed it, but as time shifted, he heard other theories, like how the lights in the sky were portals to the Soul Realm. Or how they were balls of pure energy—Chaos.

He didn't know what to believe. He was content simply calling them stars.

Cyrus had felt angry at Leonzo for leading him onto a dead trail, but that frustration had been short-lived. There was nothing he could do but shout at the sky or kick the ground until all that emotion was out of his system. Then he'd sat with his back against Sozar's shoulder until the first signs of dawn. When he saw the horizon decorated with oranges and pinks, he stood and stretched with newfound purpose.

His mother was here. Somewhere.

Now, as he strolled the dusty streets of the out village of Delion, he listened and observed. Cyrus was desperate—he could feel it thick like sludge in his bones—and to keep himself from spiraling too far into his own head, he decided the best thing he could do was move forward. It didn't help ease his concerns—that perhaps she wasn't here at all—but it at least made him feel productive. For now.

Sozar rested on the fjord where they had spent the night, waiting for his updates. The dragon was far from the public eye, which meant Cyrus's only concern was the same he'd had when he had entered Razan: his eyes.

Avoid direct eye contact, and he should be able to meander the streets without issue. Still, that made him uneasy. He wished he had a cloak to help conceal his features, but unless he found one lying about, he had nothing to help shield his silver gaze.

He was careful with his steps—too quick and he'd draw attention for his abrupt pace, too slow and people would wonder what he was up to. So he kept a hand constantly on his hip, as if he were someone lost in thought, and he watched as the village came to life. Market stands had been erected and people shouted in greeting to one another, as the smells of fresh goods started to waft through the air. Pastries, jams, even roasted fish.

He wrinkled his nose at the last. There were a variety of kinds being prepped for sale, and the constant thud of striking knives rang through the air, carrying the pungent smell of the raw sea.

He had been hungry before. Now, he wasn't.

The Rider's Sword on his hip was thankfully not the only beautiful weapon carried about. Cyrus saw some prestigious designs on both men and women alike, some with scarves tied on the hilt, while others had jewels embedded. The people here clearly took their weaponry seriously. It was a stark contrast to the culture he had been exposed to in Razan, where carrying even a dagger was frowned upon.

As the village outside of Delion came to life more, sellers of crafts and supplies came about. Birds started calling as the late morning warmed the air. The dock that hugged the village—no doubt Delion's Port—was full of ships and crews unloading and loading goods. Some seamen were accompanied by guards dressed in green and silver, and Cyrus wondered what they could possibly be unloading that would require armed forces. Gold? Ancient smuggled relics?

He turned, heading down a street that he had traveled already five times this morning. He wasn't sure how to find his mother. She had to be here, but he wasn't sure exactly what he was looking for. There were women everywhere, of all ages, all appearances. He had no idea what she looked like, beyond the expectation that she would likely share some of his features.

Leonzo hadn't even told him her name. He'd told her that in her line of work, she went by many different names to keep herself out of the king or queen's eye. In fact, Leonzo had never known her real birth name, only that she had been Everly—over two decades ago. She was a trader of particularly rare goods, and sometimes that meant working with people who were banned from the Delion territory. Samantha, Rose, Gaella, Jasmine—Leonzo had given him a variety of names that she had gone by when he was around.

Essentially, he was looking for a ghost.

Sozar urged him to put those thoughts aside, and he obliged and turned his attention back to the market stands he was passing. People went by, laughing, pushing each other in play, some even holding hands. Children bolted through the crowds, and one even had a bundle of red fruit he'd never seen before, likely a variety unique to Creitón.

"... hear about the ship that went down off the coast of Greve's Point?"

"King thinks it was an attack by the Red Queens. Tell you what, it was the Krakí."

The voices came and went. Cyrus listened, enjoying the changes of topic he overheard as he passed by a dense group of people. He'd never seen a Krakí before, not even on his flight, so he considered himself lucky. He didn't want to see a beast like that.

"Barnǎl's king is sick—"

"Lies."

"—been missing for a moon cycle—"

"Can I have both necklaces?"

A woman snorted, loud. "Your prices have gone up!"

Cyrus shook his head, amused. The people were so engrossed in their daily affairs that they hardly noticed a man like him squeezing through the moving crowd. Although as he cut close to one stand, he spied the silver beads that he had grown so accustomed to seeing in Diemon.

Hyle's Beads. Cyrus slowed just enough to eye the dozens that hung in all different sizes. They could be worn as bracelets or necklaces, or used as décor for a home. Drügalism had never been Cyrus's strong suit. Many Sorréleians considered themselves avid followers of the polytheistic religion, but Cyrus had never thought himself a strong one. That didn't mean he didn't know the stories, though, or what the people did to show their faith.

The God of Courage, Hyle, was an anomaly amongst the believers. He was the only God with silver eyes, and because of this, many believed he'd once been a Dragon Rider before he'd been chosen to serve as a deity. Many dismissed this—there were no records remaining of the fallen Rider Federation that would be evidence that there was ever a Hyle to serve the federation. But Cyrus thought that theory outrageous—the Rider Federation was in ruins. There were no records of anything anymore. When he was a boy, Cyrus had always wanted to believe the God of Courage was once a Dragon Rider—perhaps was even *still* a Dragon Rider. He would daydream about how the Vore God flew across the world on the back of some giant dragon.

He had been so young when he dreamed up those stories, though. As the summers passed by, he had come to believe that Hyle was just like the rest of the deities. A mystery. A bundle of stories that evolved with each generation of Vorelians. By the time he was fifty, he was certain there would be a new version of the origin stories of each Vore God. The heart of the stories all remained, like how Greve was a king who'd been stabbed in the back by his own chancellor, but the details around that shifted depending on who told the story.

Cyrus continued on his way, eyeing the different pieces used to appreciate each Vore God. The familiar wooden stakes and cloth were not what surprised him but rather the bone necklaces and sharpened teeth painted with Old Tongue sigils in a variety of colors.

"Bless your sea travels with these gifts!" a man declared. "Come now, Eazon himself has touched these!"

No amount of Krye could get him to wear any of that.

Cyrus continued to wander. The day had long since passed high noon, and the heat of the sun was at its most intense. Perspiration dotted his brow and back, and he was starving now, damn the reek of fish. He had some Krye in the pouch on his belt, but he was not so keen on the idea of having any direct interactions with these people. The way that woman had stared the night before unsettled him. The last thing he needed was to be cornered by the people before he could find his mother.

Sozar stirred. *Take a break. Clear your head.*

Cyrus raised his brow, despite not being anywhere near the dragon. *And for what? So that I can waste time?* It felt like the later the day got, the more he failed, and that emotion bled over into his response. Patience was not his gift, and he was growing more and more irritated as each passing face became familiar. There went the man again with the front gold tooth, the woman with the purple scarf who carried baked breads to sell on the spot, which now looked delicious, and the grouchy old man who stood no taller than Cyrus's chest who grumbled constantly about pirates.

At this point, he was certain people would start to recognize him, and that made him nervous. The original plan of searching for his mother had been built on finding a lead early in the day. His muscles ached, and his feet started to grow sore as he walked the same routes over and over. The excitement of landing had long worn off, and he wanted to lay his head down and sleep for a long while.

Yet, he continued on. It felt like if he didn't find her today, he never would. Sure, he could make his way into the heart of the city and search there, but he dreaded that thought. Too risky. Here, he was protected by the thrill of markets, the sea, and the bustle of simple life. Closer to the center of the city, there was a greater risk of soldiers who would be looking for anyone who stood out—such as a man who was walking in circles.

Time crawled on like an incessant rodent. Cyrus knew Sozar could sense his irritation, but the dragon did not try to ease his nerves. Certain things, like flying across the Vore World to find his mother who could be the key to his future, just couldn't be talked away with a couple of words. He knew Sozar adored him—their bond made that feeling palpable, despite the annoyance of the day—but he was growing sick and tired of the sand and the smell of the sea.

And he turned down a street nestled up next to the port and saw the tents. Those were new. He'd been down this street six times already, but they were new. And while the thick leather structures were a strange sight to behold, the pirates were what caused him to slow his steps.

Cyrus had never met or seen a pirate directly, but he didn't have to question that these men were from the sea. Their grimy attire, tall leather boots, shaggy hair that was either braided or windblown, all gave it away. Some were covered in black or colored ink, with others choosing to wear jewels on every finger and ear. Swords were strapped to belts that looked to have been eaten by the harsh sea weather, and some of the men wore wide-brim hats to keep the sun out of their faces. Their skin was leathered from long travel under relentless heat, but their eyes, even from his distance, were undeniably *alive*. They were right where they wanted to be.

Cyrus watched as the four shuffled into the first tent, removing their hats and ducking low. He approached, too curious to turn around, pulled by a deep need to see what or who was inside. He picked up the pace, hoping to not miss anything said, then slowed to a stop, just outside the entrance, as he heard voices.

"… find no other like it." It was a woman, and she sounded rather pleased with herself.

"Come now, Ruth, you've worked with us before. Cut the price—you know we'll send interest your way. We're reliable to your … *business.*" The man who was speaking had a thick accent from an unknown origin, and Cyrus had to strain to hear better. He kept his arms crossed and his head lowered, hoping to look more like someone waiting their turn than an eavesdropper.

Sozar stretched, the image coming across clear in his mind. *Found something of interest?* the dragon asked through a yawn.

Cyrus answered with a mental nod.

"And you and I both know that certain trades are far more valuable than others. You won't find this anywhere else," Ruth countered. "You've been given priority because I trust what we have, but we all know the Red Queens are due to land any time this evening, and they always pay for what they want."

"Don't play that game with me," another pirate shot back. "Those fools steal their gold. We work for ours."

"It's all the same once it reaches my hand. Do we have a deal or not?"

Cyrus would have paid a lot of coin to see whatever it was they were buying. Based on the grumbles he heard, he was certain they would pay. After another moment, he heard heavy coin pouches being set down. One, two, three … *four*. Cyrus couldn't even contain his shock. Nothing he knew cost that much, and as far as he was aware, only royalty paid in such sums at once. He'd always been taught that the pirates were scavengers, poor even, but this suggested something else entirely.

"Pleasure doing business with you, Til. You always know I love our deals," Ruth told him as the sound of something heavy was adjusted. "Just be careful with that compass, okay? The story given to me was that if you treated the item poorly, it brought bad luck. Take good care of it, and it will bring you riches. You know that though, or you wouldn't have sought it out. Until next time."

Cyrus stepped away from the entrance, just around the tent, as the men emerged, one carrying a small chest under his arm. They exchanged glances with each other and didn't even bother looking behind them to see Cyrus. They were too caught up in the purchase, thrilled to have possession of something so rare. He couldn't blame them. A compass like that?

"Destiny does not tolerate people like you," the woman said, peeking her head around the corner. "And I don't either."

Cyrus jumped. His eyes met hers almost immediately, and he wanted to say something snarky in return to her comment, but the words died on his tongue. The honey-blond hair, tan skin, and brown eyes felt undeniably familiar. She was the right age, and her choice of work hinted to what Leonzo had told him. The small details didn't bog him down; rather, it was the strange sensation that he'd seen her before. The entire day melted away in an instant—all the aches and pains and hunger disappeared with the newfound revelation before him.

This was her. Cyrus knew it as well as he knew the tiny scar on the base of his thumb that he'd earned with Sozar's hatching. This was his mother.

They stood there for what felt like a season but had to be only seconds before she whispered, "Do I know you?"

Slowly, scared that she might disappear in the blink of an eye, he nodded.

Ruth—though that was likely not her real name—put a hand over her mouth, not taking her eyes off him. He could hardly move, despite his inner voice telling him that if they stood there long enough like this, people would notice. A thousand different stories crossed her gaze at once, and when she spoke, it was not the crass seller's voice, but something softer.

"I thought I'd never see you again."

VOLKERI ISLAND

eep in the Mourale Mountains, where stone and wood met and the Infernol made their home, Syra was gathered with a dozen other close members of the secret organization. Many were the inner circle, showcasing rings similar to Dryl's, and then there were the twins, whom she'd learned were named Eva and Arik, as well as Zarek, Zane, Keryn, and the Infernol commander, Bane. They were standing around a large round table that was carved out of thick stone, polished to showcase the blue gemstone. Laid out was a map of the Vore World—something Syra had never seen before. She had heard stories about where everything was, seen bits and pieces of maps, but never one that encompassed the whole world.

She had never felt more out of place. When she tried to capture the leader's eye, he avoided her.

Many were still dressed in sleeping attire, and Syra was too, but she'd put her cloak around her to keep warm. The floors were cold, and she was barefoot, and the air had a thick chill to it that clung to the halls and chambers. The gathering had been hasty, and nobody appeared dressed for the occasion. The only person who looked the part was Keryn, with an embellished cloak that spoke as if he'd just gotten out of another important meeting.

Syra didn't know what could be so important—this certainly wasn't one of the Infernol's scavenger campaigns—but she could see that the Infernol leader was visibly alarmed. He held a scroll, which looked to have been damaged in transit, and next to him, a hawk stood on a perch. The bird was fluffed up, relaxed, and it occasionally blinked with an air of sluggishness. Syra felt they were disturbing the hawk's slumber after its long flight home.

Keryn cleared his throat, and the room fell silent at once. "Ladies and gentlemen, thank you for your quick arrival. It's not ideal to be called at this hour, but I could not wait until morning." He gestured at the hawk behind him. "Lue has arrived from Volkeri Island with information that I believe must be shared now." Keryn laid the scroll down but did not open it. The twine was untied, and it was obvious he had already read through the parchment.

Instead, he laid his hands flat on the table, showcasing a number of rings with massive jewels embedded. Green, blue, and even gold glittered in the lanterns that lit the chamber.

"My resource tells me that during his travels on Volkeri Island, he has stumbled on a massive fracture of realms." Murmurs spread throughout the room. "I'm not entirely sure how to describe that. Allow me to give the floor to Eva and Arik."

Eva's chest rose and fell, as if she had suddenly come to life, while her brother looked borderline dead—his skin sick and pale, his eyes abnormally gray. "A fracture occurs when balance is disrupted. It is believed, although not proven, that the only thing that could cause a literal crack separating realms is a huge fluctuation of Chaos." Eva spoke in a monotone voice, unnaturally so. Syra shrank in her cloak—she did not like the twins. There was something odd about them. "Cracks can be seen by anyone."

Bane cleared his throat. "So … there's a crack just sitting—*hanging?*—in the air?"

Arik still did not speak, so Eva answered. "Realms mirror one another in some way or another. Imagine a crack in the mirror you look at every day—that crack is obvious. Now, imagine some other light spilling forth from that fracture. Sometimes, if the crack is large enough, you can see the other realm." Still, her tone did not change.

"Greve give us strength," someone mumbled.

Eva continued, unperturbed. "Cracks like this have only happened once before. At the time it is believed Chaos converged with the living, well before our existence—"

"Can this be stopped?" That was one of the inner circle's members. Syra wasn't sure of her name and didn't bother to ask, but she recognized the Infernol ring on her finger. The older woman's wild hair was held together by a clip that was failing miserably at its task. She clutched an oversized cloak around her chest and leaned forward over the table, face stretched wide in terror. "Can this be stopped?" she repeated, quieter.

Another wave of murmurs. Eva and Arik did not immediately reply. Their eyes locked, sharing a silent conversation. While the rest were too caught up in the turmoil to study the exchange, Syra did. A thousand things said all at once—while their expressions did not change, their gray eyes did.

"We don't know," Arik finally answered. His response deafened the room, and as everyone gaped, he added, "There are no records, although we can assume only a God could do such a thing."

Syra took a quick peek at her cloak's sleeve—it covered the scar and concealed the knowledge she possessed. Better that way. These people would devour her whole if they knew what she was.

Zarek pressed up behind her. She looked up. His crimson gaze was stern, calculative. The earlier conversation felt leagues away, and the devastating reality of what this crack meant was quite clear: The living realm was in danger. This went above and beyond everything she was worried about.

"So"—Keryn spoke now—"we need a God to resolve this?" He looked like he was grappling for the right word to say, and he motioned at the scroll instead. "My resource tells me the answers lie here ..."

Bane slammed his hand against the table. "Here? Am I expected to send my soldiers into an unknown situation and expect them to be okay with any of this?" A vein bulged along his forehead as he hissed, "This is not swords or combat, Keryn—this is outside my army's scope, and I refuse to send men with weapons into a situation where metal against metal is not how we win."

The leader gave a slow nod. "Understood. Although I did not assume you." His eyes looked over at the twins. "You two are powerful—perhaps combined you could create some solution?"

"It's risky." Arik rolled his shoulders as he spoke—the biggest movement Syra had seen from either of them. "There are patterns we must look for when dealing with this kind of power. The disruption of balance may disrupt how we harvest."

"What are you saying?"

"Exactly that . . . *Gonsín.*" The Old Tongue for leader. Syra recognized it from old tales she used to read when she was small in Caster, but it was obvious to her that Arik was not using it with a tone of respect. "The energies we harvest are not by accident. Energy Harvesters spend meticulous time learning and understanding the type of energy they manipulate, not just because we think it's fun, but because it will save our lives. If we harvest the wrong energy, say Dark Energy, when we are not capable of withstanding its strength, we will be killed in the process." Arik's mouth hardly moved as he spoke. "If the very essence of the energy we harvest is tampered with, as it will likely become with the disruption of balance, we put ourselves at risk."

Silence filled the room. The tension was rising, and as it thickened, it became harder to breathe. Syra licked her lips, wanting to ask the question that was weighing heavily on her. But just as she sucked in the courage, Zarek laid a hand on her shoulder and squeezed. He did not want her to speak, for reasons she did not understand.

She obeyed. Despite everything, she trusted him.

Zane cleared his throat. "Is this resource a member of the Infernol?"

"Why don't we know who this person is?" another asked.

And then the dreaded question. "Why is *she* here?"

Keryn raised his hand to silence more oncoming questions. "For his protection, he remains anonymous to you all, but I assure you that he is trustworthy and reliable. There is no one else I would have requested this of." Finally, his eyes landed on her, blue and frigid. "She's here because I assumed she knew of this."

A blade twisted itself in her back. They were all mad with desperation. When Zarek's grip didn't persuade her either way, she said, "If I knew about any of this, why would I waste my time here subjecting myself to your poor attitude?"

If there was ever a time when Syra knew she'd made an enemy, this was it. There were concerns about this Infernol leader, Zarek had said so, but standing here now, she knew he had other motives. Keryn glared at her as if he wanted to stab her right here and now. The room remained quiet, horrifyingly so, but she did not tear her eyes away.

"What now?" the woman asked, clutching her cloak even tighter. Syra could see that her knuckles had turned white, but she'd never been so appreciative of an interruption. "Do we wait for this . . . *resource* to tell us more?"

"No," Keryn said, "we plan. We have other matters to deal with, like the resurrection of the Lirallian Empire."

"Excuse me?" Bane asked, and did a double take at the room. "I am your commander, Gonsín—why am I just hearing about this?"

"Because this is information I knew of only moments prior to this letter arriving," Keryn replied without hesitation. If he was still fuming, as she assumed, he did not show it. "It's been a very eventful evening, one might say."

Syra looked up at Zarek. This time, he returned her gaze. The Lirallian Empire was centuries old and supposed to be dead, a piece of history. The empire had massacred millions, led by Henry Junok. If an empire like that was to return, and attempt to stake its claim on this world, then the living realm had much bigger problems to deal with. But Henry was dead, his execution public. This was not adding up.

"I'm sorry," someone whispered, and raised a hand in sub-mission. It was another woman, a handful of summers younger than the other. Her hair was cut short, accentuating her jaw-line. "The Lirallian Empire is . . . I mean, wasn't the Infernol supposed to make sure this didn't happen?"

Keryn nodded, just barely. "It appears they have worked in secret over the past decade or longer. Their forces have tripled in just the past season, and with great dissatisfaction I must tell you that Junok is presumed to be under their control now."

An uproar. Curses, yells, shouts, and a hundred questions were lost in the commotion that overtook the room. Syra was stunned, all words vacant from her tongue. Junok was the larg-est territory in Diyră. If the City of Liral had that, then they had immense resources to call upon, including their very own port. There was supposed to be a queen there, a council—her mind was racing now.

Zarek stepped forward, and his movement shattered her spiraling thoughts. His impressive stature took over the room as he cut in front of everyone to stand before the map and face Keryn directly. The Infernol leader was dwarfed by the Guardian, both in spirit and in size. The room's noise ceased.

"Movement such as overthrowing Junok should have been reported well in advance," Zarek said. "The Infernol's duty was to observe the City of Liral, and yet, an entire city was ambushed and seized right under your noses? Tell me, Keryn, Gonsín, whatever it is you would like to be called, why?"

Syra swallowed, hoping to remain a fly on the wall in this exchange. The Guardian was infuriated. She recognized that tone all too well. From across the room, Zane locked eyes with her, and she adjusted her cloak.

Zarek cleared his throat and swallowed, the sound audible in the surrounding silence. Keryn was prey in this moment. He licked his lips. "To be honest, I don't have an answer," he confessed.

Nobody moved. That was not enough.

"If I had an answer, a reason, you all would be the first to hear it," Keryn continued. "I know that's not what you want to hear. It's not what I want to hear either. Centuries ago, this place—the Infernol—started with the sole purpose of protecting the Vorelians. We wanted to ensure that a monster empire like Liral never came to see the light again. All of us have spent summers and many long nights strategizing about what to do if any of our what-ifs came to fruition. Some of us"—he motioned at Bane—"have generations of family attached to the Infernol. It's all we've ever known."

Now, Keryn met Zarek's gaze once more and lifted his chin. "Your people entrusted us with this, and we failed. Whatever Liral has done to circumvent us is still under heavy consideration, but nothing we learn will change the problems we now have to address."

As Keryn spoke, he regained his confidence; his shoulders straightened, his eyes burned brighter, and his voice grew more certain. Syra knew the look well, the feeling. The Infernol leader was going to use this to his advantage—admit his fault and leverage it as an opportunity to strengthen his control over these people. It was strategic, and she couldn't blame him.

She still didn't have the courage to make any noise from her position, and Zarek was still not satisfied. His expression remained stoic, his eyes devoid of any emotion—it was the Guardian's way of saying he was unconvinced without ever saying a word. She'd received that look herself at least twice since they'd met.

"Junok," Zane muttered. "If Liral has Junok, they'll go for the next closest city, and that's Raveer. It's a stone's throw away from the City of Liral."

"Assane, if you consider all the tribesmen and outer towns," Bane retorted, but without insult. "If they combine their forces, they would be nigh indestructible."

"Then they'd actually have to agree on something," the older woman observed, and shook her head.

"Yana," Keryn said, and looked her way. "Bane and Zane"—he shared looks with each—"your concerns are what my next point is. We must get ahead of Liral. They will go for the entire country, that is without a doubt."

The twins exchanged a glance. Syra watched them—it was hard not to.

"Raveer was nearly brought to its knees after the Firóle attack," Keryn said. "In some reports, it was, while others have declared that the city is doing just fine now. Regardless, it is my belief that Liral will go for Raveer next because of this."

The Guardian inhaled, and all eyes turned to him, though he paid them no mind. "Your theory is that Liral is not going to stop at Diyră."

Keryn pursed his lips. "No."

"You believe without intervention, Liral will take this across the Merrél Sea and to Sorréle," Zarek added. "But if that happens, why stop there? Liral has the opportunity and now the armed forces to overthrow another country. Less risk of backlash if there are more loyal followers. More control, less chances of the Lirallian Empire ever falling again. So"—Zarek raised a hand to halt Keryn from talking—"let's play this out by Liral's standards. We've overthrown Diyră and Sorréle after a few summers of wars and plenty dead. We're feeling powerful, our numbers are growing, but we've lost a few—that's to be expected with such aggressive movements—and so we want to take on either Eiyrăl or Creitón. Both ancient and well-developed countries with families older than even Liral. That makes them incredibly dangerous."

The Guardian gestured at the world map between them. "Eiyrăl is home to two families, but the Razan historically have remained rather peaceful, despite their bloody past. Although Kalic is rumored to be one of the most barbaric families to date, so they would put up quite a fight, but Liral isn't interested in that. They're interested in allies. Kalic would be perfect—give them one damn good reason to draw their sword and they'll do it. So now, you have armed forces from Sorréle, Diyră, and Kalic all pointed at Razan. That family will bend the knee, and I'm sure Liral is quite aware of this. They may act tough, but they hide behind wealth and ancient practices."

Zarek drew his finger down to the pirate country. "This is, logistically, one of the best options available to Liral. Creitón is not a country that shies away from war. Historically, they are the ones starting it. Their open system provides pirates from all over the world an ability to call this place"—he tapped a pale blue finger on the parchment—"home. Barnăl, Saveen, and Delion are ruthless in their own rights. Many still practice ancient torture rituals, and the political system there is built off who's stabbing who in the back. But give them a common threat and they could destroy half of the Vore World, if they so pleased."

Syra was impressed, though she couldn't say she was surprised. Zarek was older than anyone in this room, so of course he would know more than anyone here about the geopolitics involved. Zarek had watched these cities over the last four centuries—his knowledge would be better than even what could be gleaned from ancient texts.

Now, the Guardian straightened and met Keryn's gaze. "You wish to seize Raveer before Liral does and utilize the weapons and soldiers to your purpose."

The leader flared his nostrils as the crowd muttered among themselves. "And what do you suppose we do, Death Seeker?"

"You'll never win," Zarek replied. "You will be chasing the tail of Liral for many summers to come if you think you'll ever be ahead of them. Men are replaceable, and we both know the only incident in history with reports of undead soldiers was from the Lirallian Empire during the Diyrąllian Massacre. You are a fool if you believe they will not repeat that now."

Keryn crossed his arms. "Only one person was capable of pulling a ritual like that off to obtain immortality."

Syra tried to keep her nerves subdued but couldn't, and she couldn't tell who to stare at. There was a hidden conversation passing between the two of them that was lost to the rest of the room.

"You already know the answer," the leader prodded. "So why don't you get it over with."

Syra stared, waiting. There was only one piece of information that she knew could be big enough to cause this much tension. They had discussed it once, in passing, but with the pressure of staying alive, Syra hadn't given the subject much more thought. Perhaps that made her a fool. She looked around, watching shoulders tense and the eyes narrow around the room. She wondered if Roman's words had been true, or if they had been exaggerated.

Zarek's shoulders tensed as well, but only a fraction. "Liral has not acted alone and could not successfully have infiltrated Junok without the aid of a powerful Energy Harvester. With Junok's vast history in energy and extensive lineage in energy harvesting, they would be the least likely of targets for a small city like Liral. But if you have someone like Henry Junok driving the charge, then Liral would be unstoppable."

A man cleared his throat. "This is all a bit much." It was Zane, eyes wide. "You downplayed this all when we were at Roman's. You didn't even confirm if—"

"Would you have come?" Zarek countered. "Careful with what you say now, Commander. I am in no mood for this. And for the record, I never denied anything either." He stared down Keryn. "We know Henry Junok is alive and driving the charge. And there are certain . . . scopes of my work that provide me the ability to learn information that is not shared. Like how it was knowledge to the Infernol that the Lirallians were already amassing in numbers even last summer, and how Junok had reported well in advance their concerns of sabotage and ambush, but you did nothing."

Keryn huffed. "You're blowing—"

"Or how the Lirallians have already infiltrated different countries to gather information to return to Henry with. Do you take me as a fool, Keryn? Have you forgotten what I do? I know you wish to believe the best, but do you *really* believe every member in the Infernol is pure of heart? Do you truly believe you've only just learned of Junok because it just happened, or because someone was baiting you?"

Zarek turned to leave, but as he did so, he gestured at the room. His next words came out with a scoff. "Be careful who you speak to, *Gonsín*. There are traitors everywhere, and one of them just might be a Lirallian."

An uproar followed as Keryn tried to yell at the Guardian. There was a mass surge, and Syra felt herself forced forward by the bodies behind her. Her mind was racing—a Lirallian, here? If that was the case, they weren't safe anywhere they went, and if so, Henry already knew their whereabouts—or was going to. But why not tell her this in private? The way these people acted, like savage animals, she knew they hadn't been aware of this either. She could hardly contain her frustrations, and she nearly screamed when a hand latched itself on to her arm.

Zarek's voice radiated over her ear in hot breaths. "Follow me."

She didn't have a say. The Guardian yanked her with him through the crowd by one arm, and she used her other hand to keep the cloak from falling off.

With all the commotion unfolding, nobody dared to stop the two as they slipped out and Zarek slammed the door. It echoed down the quiet hall. Not a soul walked by—it was well into the early hours of the morning, and everyone else was still sleeping.

Syra didn't have time to consider the implications of it all. The Guardian was in her face almost immediately. "You avoid Keryn. I don't trust him one bit. Do you understand?"

She blinked. Distrusting Keryn felt leagues from where her mind was. Zarek was still holding on to her. That was apparently becoming a natural thing for him. "Why are you telling me all this now? We've been here for fifteen days. *Fifteen*! If there's a Lirallian here, they already have everything they want."

"The only information a Lirallian will have is knowledge that me, a Guardian, and you are here. That is all." He narrowed his gaze. He was implying that nobody knew who she was, which gave some relief. Nobody needed to know they had a new Vore God running about their halls. Not yet. "Unless you've done something else that I'm not aware of."

The threat was blatant, and she shrank back from him. "Do you think I'm a moron? I've done everything you've told me to." She couldn't stop there—she wouldn't dare. This was too close to home now, and the cold touch of familiar emotions made the hairs on her neck stand on end. "Why didn't you tell me any of that before? Why were you hiding that from me?" It wasn't the information about Henry that she was angry about, it was everything else. She'd thought he would share these concerns with her, but he hadn't.

The Guardian let go and took a step back. "I didn't tell you because there was no reason—no proof. While you've been wallowing in self-pity, I've been busy exploring and learning as much as I can."

That was a low strike. She might as well have been stabbed. For a long moment, she could do nothing but stare. Zarek's hostility was borderline aggressive, and she couldn't be sure he wasn't going to punch the wall behind her or storm off. Never had she seen him so frazzled. In the room behind them, something shattered. People were clearly upset in there too, but the sounds of their voices were muffled by the thick stone and door.

Syra tore her sleeve up and brandished the Zyulë Bond. "Remember this? Remember what we talked about? Have you forgotten what happened to me? Or are you too busy trying to right all your wrongs after you spent the last, what, three centuries ignoring everything so you could fuck Shevana?"

That was it. Zarek snatched her collar and yanked her forward. Syra nearly lost her footing, but it didn't matter, because the Guardian lifted her until her toes could barely brush against the cold surface. She grabbed his arm to steady herself. Never in their time together had they outright discussed his relationship with the queen of the Soul Realm, but they didn't have to. Syra had her suspicions.

"Have you spent so long believing you were alone that you would do everything in your power to tarnish the only friendship you have?" Zarek's voice was low, and she wanted to shrink but couldn't. "You have spent a lifetime sheltered from the cruelty that life offers, while I have spent lifetimes sleeping with the dead. If you think your words offend me, you are wrong, but they tell me everything I need to know about you."

He let her go, and her knees wobbled as her feet tried to find ground. Syra stumbled and put a hand out to the wall to steady herself, but she could barely straighten her shoulders from the immense guilt that crushed her. Here she was, being rude. Zarek hadn't deserved that. When had she become so careless in her words?

"Zarek—"

"Don't," he snapped, not stopping his pace. His boots echoed, but they were already fading. "Goodnight, Syra."

His words, harsh and quick, paralyzed her. She could not recall ever hearing such anger in the Guardian's voice. Anger caused by her. Her cheeks flushed with shame, and her entire chest felt like it would cave in from anxiety. They were dealing with so much, and with such little time—they couldn't afford to argue like this, yet she had done it.

But why? She couldn't answer that. Syra didn't know what had come over her, and she wanted to tell Zarek she was foolish, but she remained in place. Now was not the time to go begging for forgiveness. It wasn't that she wanted the Guardian, not after what had just happened, but that she wanted to ensure that their dynamic—their friendship, as he had called it—was still the same. If not for her own self-preservation, then for her security.

The realms were in danger, and she was picking fights. Was this how she'd been raised to be?

Syra huffed and stared after Zarek, who disappeared around the corner. Not once did he look back, nor did his steps falter. He was certain, confident, without remorse. This was not someone who would ever feel guilty for driving a blade through the heart of a lover if it meant proving the point he so desperately needed to prove. No. Zarek had spent lifetimes learning to smile when the agony was too much to bear.

Syra felt small. No longer brave or proud or even angry that he had withheld information she deserved to know—she felt like a fool.

As the muffled shouts on the other side of the door grew, she turned and walked away. It was the long way back to her chamber, but she did not want to risk seeing him again, not now. Right now, they needed to cool down. That much was clear.

As she walked, she let her mind drift over everything that had happened.

Zarek had accused Keryn of wanting to seize Raveer, and the Infernol leader had not denied it. That bothered her. Liral was supposed to be the enemy, not the reason to be violent. To take an entire city was grounds for war, and the Infernol seemed rather okay with that idea. At this rate, Syra was no longer sure who was more justified—a dead empire driven by revenge or an organization finding any excuse to seize a city and potentially take innocent lives to prove their ruthlessness. If she'd been a woman made to bet, she would have staked her claim on that Raveer would not go easy, no matter the political persuasion.

This also did not address the biggest two problems: There was likely a Lirallian here, and there was a fracture in the realm at Volkeri Island. There was no guidance on how to handle any of this. Back at Roman's in Jasper Village, there had been a discussion that Henry was alive. At the time, it had seemed like just a rumor. Life had turned into a maddening dance of staying alive, and she had gotten so caught up in the tune of running that she hadn't stopped to consider there might be another song far more devastating.

That there might not be a world to run from.

She tossed this thought around in her head, suffocating in it. Her steps faltered as she approached her room. When she laid everything out, it felt like Henry was one step ahead, and they might never catch up. It felt like she'd fallen right into the claws of a beast she couldn't defeat. Zarek's cruel nature didn't help either.

For a fleeting moment, she felt utterly alone.

Then she opened her door, and froze.

TEA AND BISCUITS

The bread was flaky, the salt just right, and Cyrus must have used an entire serving of butter for one bite because his mother had already refilled the dish three times since he'd started eating. It had been his first proper meal since leaving Razan, and while he should have been used to the pattern of it all by now—long flights and little food—he wasn't. Which made it undeniably the best biscuit he'd ever had.

Tea came and went, flavored with honey and milk. It was more dessert than anything, and he'd downed four cups by the time he'd gotten to his second biscuit. His mother, who he'd come to learn was named Meredith, sipped her tea and apologized profusely that she did not have anything else prepared.

It did not escape him that perhaps this was another fake name, but he didn't challenge it. Down the road perhaps he would speak more on the matter, but right now, he was simply grateful for this opportunity. When she'd realized that Cyrus was her son, she had embraced him right there by the tent with the biggest hug he'd ever received.

With little more said, they'd grabbed all of her belongings and walked the short distance to her current home. It was still by the sea, but it was plainer than he'd anticipated. The door was a soft red, the wood and stone in need of replacement from the harsh conditions, but the porch was newly fixed, based on the fresh, polished look. There was no statue as Leonzo had promised. Perhaps she had moved.

The interior was quite the opposite. So many different things drew his eyes, but most notably was the table that held all the food between them. It was painted with a massive depiction of a ship battling waves, chased by a sea creature that Cyrus could not identify. The one-eyed beast reached out with a dozen different hooks, eager to drown the people and ship. He'd found himself staring at it on more than one occasion as the silence rested between them.

Cyrus was nervous and used the food in front of him as an excuse for the awkward quiet. Meredith kept busy, constantly moving her hands; she had hardly sat still since they came in. There were so many thoughts passing through him. Did his mother love him, was he what she expected, did she even want him here? And the nastiest one: If she'd given him up, then maybe she'd hoped to never see him again. Cyrus found his thoughts spiraling before he knew what to do. He'd spent his life dreaming of this moment, but now, he felt like a fraud of a child, forcing his way into her life. All those insecurities presented themselves in their hideous glory, suffocating out the initial excitement he'd felt.

You're overthinking again, Sozar observed gently between their link.

He gripped the cup tighter in his hand, staring at the back of his mother's head as she fretted with the fire. *Can you blame me?*

No matter how he tried to justify it, he'd been abandoned. Despite Leonzo telling him that she was the key to breaking the curse that had been bestowed on him, he regretted sitting here. The nerves made it impossible to see clearly.

"I'm going to the market tomorrow morning," she told him, and plopped another log on the fire. It raged with delight, which he found soothing. "I was planning on making a big stew tomorrow night, if that suits you?"

He swallowed and reached for more bread, hoping to look calmer than he felt. "I don't wish to be a burden," he confessed. "I can find my own place."

Meredith scrunched up her face. "Nonsense. There's a spare room I always keep done up. Sailors come and go. They don't have places to stay sometimes, so I keep a room ready, in case they need a night or two here to rest before they set off again."

He nodded and took a big gulp of tea. If she had wished him to leave, she wouldn't have offered a room, of course.

The living area was small, with the galley only five paces away. It would take no more than ten steps to reach the back of the home. A wonder how she managed to keep the place organized, despite her quirky collection of feathers, beads, and tiny skulls. When he'd inquired about them, she'd told him they were gifts from the sea that she'd found washed up on shore on her morning walks.

Even though he was in the presence of the one person he'd dreamed of seeing all his life, he found himself more frayed than when he'd met the king of Razan. Sozar kept some of that away with his massive presence—always calm, always collected.

His mother set her tea down and clasped her hands together. The movement startled Cyrus, and he nearly choked on the bite he'd been chewing. This was it—the moment he'd been too terrified to broach for fear of upsetting her.

"I know you must have a lot of questions," she began. "I want to do my best to answer them. You said . . . I mean, you—" Meredith paused, her eyes searching for an answer.

"Dragon Rider," he offered after he swallowed. He couldn't say he was surprised about her inquiry—mother or not, she had recognized his eyes. "I'm a Dragon Rider."

She exhaled, and he watched her hands tighten. "And your dragon . . . where is he? She?"

"He's safe," Cyrus answered. "As much as I'd love to bring him around, the people would panic." He shrugged. "It's not like we've had the best of luck."

"I see."

He took the opportunity to ask the question that was burning on his tongue. "Why did you do it?"

Leonzo had told him already, but that was not enough. He needed to hear it from her directly. Abandoning a child a country away to the service of a queen was not something any parent did lightly, nor was it one he accepted.

Meredith stared at him. It lasted so long that he started to regret the question. It seemed as if it had triggered a montage of events in her mind, things he would never wish to see—or maybe he did. Perhaps in the long seconds that followed, she was reliving every single act that had led up to his abandonment.

He hoped it hurt.

Because he'd spent a lifetime in agony, wondering what he'd ever done to deserve such a thing. All he wanted was to be accepted—being abandoned by his parents had haunted him for too many summers to count.

"I, um—" Meredith blinked and looked away, her gaze locked on the window to the sea. Cyrus couldn't see the waters—it was too dark for that now—but she would know exactly where they lay. "I have spent many summers dreaming about you, where you've gone, who you've become, who you'd marry . . ." She smiled at the window. "I haven't got much of an excuse for why I did what I did, except that I was afraid. Afraid to fail you, afraid I'd fail at being a mother—"

A tear rolled down her cheek as the words stopped. Cyrus watched, stunned and confused. He wanted to go over to her and hug her, tell her it was all right and that he didn't wish to make her cry, but he didn't. The initial impulse dissolved just as quickly as it had arrived. He was determined to prove a point, so he stayed where he was, appetite gone, and waited. The old version of him would have wanted to apologize for making her uncomfortable. The new him, forged by betrayal and callused by the brutal hand of fate, knew better.

Meredith wiped the tear away and looked at him. "You were born for great things, Cyrus, but I was not the mother I should have been. Not a day goes by that I don't regret what I did, but I believe it was for your good. You were destined for great things, and look at you now"—she gestured his way—"a Dragon Rider!"

It was not the answer he wanted. "Even someone like me needs a mother's love."

Sozar stirred in their link, sensing his growing frustration. *People cope in different ways—*

Don't, Cyrus warned.

"Do you want an apology from me?" she asked, and wiped her eyes again. "Do you want me to get on my knees and beg for your forgiveness?"

For a long while, only the crack of the fire filled the room.

When Cyrus replied, he kept his voice as steady as possible, devoid of the anger that filled him. "No mother would abandon their son like you did without a valid reason. Were you afraid of me?"

"I already told you," she said. "I was afraid to fail you."

"So you sent me away to a different country?" Cyrus pressed. "Why? Here you sit, asking if I want an apology for the actions that left me, your son, alone for the better part of his life? Why must I beg for your forgiveness?"

The air had turned sour, the tension thick. This was not how he had anticipated this to go. Frankly, he wasn't sure how it was supposed to go. Cyrus had always imagined that he'd been sent away because of a war or because . . . because his parents were dead. To have one sit before him now did not satisfy his soul. It enraged him. She'd lived her life without ever trying to find him, while he'd spent his life dreaming of this very day.

"I think you're missing the point," Meredith said. "I was afraid to fail you because you were well beyond my control. You displayed abilities that no boy should have; you were in danger staying here. You displayed abilities that, if the wrong person found out . . . you might not be sitting here with me."

Despite himself, he heard the words escape his mouth. "But I was safe a country away from you?" Agitation flooded his voice. Sozar tried to reach him, but Cyrus would not hear any of it.

His mother raised her hand. "I will not defend my choices. It's been two and a half decades since I did what I did, and I cannot hash up the past for the sake of your peace. It destroyed me for many, many summers. What's done is done, and we're here now."

Cyrus stared at the floor. The light reflected the grains of wood that had been worn from use—long, dark stretches accented the almost grayish surface. He had overstepped, and he knew it, but he did not regret it.

She had made a choice and learned to live with it. Meredith had gone about her life in the end, comfortable that she'd done the right thing. Cyrus had never had a choice. He'd been thrust into a life he'd never asked for—all because of her.

He had poured so much emotion into this moment, and he was not satisfied. Meredith seemed almost fine with what she'd done to him. His stomach twisted, and he tightened his grip on the chair. What *had* he expected?

To be honest, he'd expected her to embrace him, to tell him she was forced to abandon him and that she'd gone her whole life looking for him. Not this. He felt like he'd traveled all this way for nothing. Leonzo had sent him, sure, but what Cyrus had hoped more than anything was to find what it meant to be loved—to be accepted.

Again, he felt like a fraud, forcing his way into her life when she'd have gladly gone the rest of her life without him. His chest hollowed out as he turned his eyes to the fire. What had once brought him reassurance now reminded him that he was, essentially, in a stranger's home.

"How long do you intend to stay?" she asked suddenly. If she felt the tension, her tone did not imply it.

He shrugged. "I would like to spend a little time here. I—" Cyrus took a deep breath. It was time to broach the next big topic. "I wanted to talk to you about what you did to me when I was an infant. Leonzo said—"

"Ah," Meredith interrupted. "The Don'sul."

"Is that . . . Is that what this is?"

She nodded. "I asked Leonzo for a way to protect you from yourself. From the moment you were conceived, things started to change. As you developed, objects would move when you kicked in the womb, and I would have the strangest dreams. Vivid, otherworldly, and starry. Then, when you were born, you would laugh and send things flying around the house." Meredith chuckled. "There was one time when you tipped over an entire basket of cherries and started giggling like a madman. No one knew how, and I quickly left with you in my arms. But you see . . . despite how much I loved it, I was scared. Leonzo was in and out of my life, busy with obligations that sometimes took him far away for several moon cycles at a time, and I didn't know anything about harvesting energy. I didn't trust strangers with you, and your abilities were growing more volatile. You would act out, cry, and something would shatter—and then you would sleep for an entire afternoon."

His mother was twisting her hands, staring at him hard. "I was a single mother with one purpose: to protect you. It didn't matter how or what it did to me, it was always about you. Leonzo warned me about the dangers of what would happen if you did not receive proper training at such a young age. You could have died, and there were several times that you should have, but by the grace of the Gods, you didn't."

Cyrus swallowed the lump in the back of his throat. "Then why didn't he step in? He's a powerful Energy Harvester—he could have done it."

"There was discussion about that," Meredith replied, and sipped her tea. "There were plenty of late nights we stayed awake talking about your future, but in the end, I was the one who asked for the Don'sul. Not him—he wanted to train you, you know. He saw the potential, and when he could be here, he did everything in his power to help you, but you were too young still. You could hardly speak, let alone understand what you were doing, so how could he tell you what to do?"

Her voice dropped as she continued. "And Delion was not the same city it is. There are terrible people out there who would do anything to enslave a child like yourself into a violent cause. The king has done incredible things to rid the city of that, but back then, I knew that if they got their hands on you, you would live a life of servitude. And that is no life to live, regardless of what your potential could be."

Cyrus nodded, but the question remained. "How could I be safe in another country then? Alone?" He added the last part intentionally—he needed her to understand how this sounded to him.

Meredith scoffed. "I'm not a good person," she said, and ran a hand over the skirt of her dress. "I have done terrible things. What you see you now"—she motioned at the home—"is me trying to be normal. When you were born, I was involved with illegal things—it's the only life I've ever known. I . . . was a thief of high-value items. I mingled with very dangerous people. I'm *still* in that business. My reputation keeps me in it." Her fingers fidgeted, clearly anxious. "The Don'sul was to protect you from yourself, but I sent you away to protect you from me."

He leaned forward. "But you still abandoned me. If I knew how to control this, you wouldn't have had to do any of this."

"I worked for people who would have slit my throat to get to you if they knew of your abilities. One can never fully leave a business like that. I made decisions based on what I knew then, and my priority was to keep you out of harm's way." Her eyes darted down at the cup on the table. "I gave you to a woman who promised she would take care of you. Someone who Leonzo knew, and so I trusted her."

These were the answers he'd wanted for so long, but now that he was hearing them, he wished he'd never asked. "I was raised in an orphanage in Diemon. The children there were raised to work for the queen, to harvest gems, that sort of stuff. That is the life I knew. Is that what you wanted for me?"

Meredith's answer came out soft. "No."

Somewhere inside him, that was all he'd wanted to hear. Affirmation that the life he'd been forced to live was not the one she had intended for him.

In the broad silence that followed, he felt the icy fingers of awkwardness creeping back up his spine. He rubbed his hands against his thighs and felt his back tense from the stress. He wanted to change the topic. "Then how do we reverse it? This Don'sul?"

She sighed, and he noted the way her shoulders slumped with relief at the shift. "There's a way we can do it, but it's an exhausting process for both parties. It may not be successful either. Do you understand?"

Cyrus nodded. There was no other choice.

"Then we'll do it tomorrow, okay?" Meredith stood and grabbed the plate of biscuits from the table. "You must be tired after your travels. I assume you're done with these?"

Cyrus stood and grabbed his tea, along with the butter. "Let me help."

He followed her into the galley and set everything next to the sink, where water had already been poured for cleaning. Fibers of wood were braided together in a round ball for scrubbing.

She waved him away. "I'll take care of all this in the morning. Why don't you go and get some sleep? Tomorrow will be a big day, and I'd like to know you got some rest. I'm sure you'll sleep well." Meredith laid a hand on his forearm and gave it a squeeze. Her palm was warm. "How rude of me to presume. What of your dragon? Will you return to him?"

Unless you wish to sleep on cold rock, the dragon mused, *I suggest you take her offer.*

Cyrus noted the humor in Sozar's voice. He could sense the dragon's satisfaction with the situation, and that gave him some reassurance. "A bed will be just fine. Thank you." The idea of a warm blanket and soft pillow brought a smile to his face.

His mother raised her brow. "Can he hear us?"

Cyrus nodded. "Aye. Our minds are linked—he can hear my thoughts, and I can hear his too."

"Incredible." She grinned. "What an amazing gift you have been given." Meredith motioned toward the hall. "Rest, Cyrus. I know you must be tired, as am I."

"Will I see you in the morning?"

"I will leave early for the market, but I'll have fresh biscuits out for you—and don't fret, they are easy to make, so it's no trouble at all. When I'm back, you can help me prepare the stew, and then we'll address your harvesting."

Cyrus's steps were already carrying him onward to the room on the left, where he would be sleeping for the night. "Thank you," he called. It felt important to say that, given how tense things still were. He wanted her to at least understand that he appreciated the hospitality, even if they had a lot to work on—even if he wasn't sure he wanted to work on it at all.

"Goodnight."

The room was small, private, decorated with a simple cot and some shelves. There was a cabinet with a round mirror, where he could see how rough he looked. His beard made him look summers older, and he could not wait to shave it. Another task for tomorrow—he had spent many nights with this itchy thing on his face, and he could spend one more. He was sure that if his mother hosted sailors, there must be a short blade around here somewhere to shave with, though it was probably dull.

He closed the door behind him, wanting a little more seclusion, and peeled his clothes off. There was no way in Greve's name that he would sleep in his clothes tonight. Once he was stripped, he slipped under the sheets and let out a large exhale as his body embraced the comforts of a bed.

It had been too long since he'd been this comfortable.

Sozar's presence snuggled up to his own, and he could practically hear the waves crashing against whatever cliff the dragon had chosen for the night. It felt strange to be so far away from him, but he reminded himself that it was only for a short time. And more importantly, they could communicate with emotions and thoughts, as they did now. Sometimes, words weren't necessary.

He let himself be engulfed in the dragon's warmth, and he returned it as he closed his eyes from the world.

This would surely be the best sleep he'd had in ages.

STEW WITH STRANGERS

orei was starving. His mouth watered at the smells wafting through the hall as he made his way to the dining room. It was quieter at this hour, well after dark, and he was relieved to finally consider himself clean. His beard was gone, his body washed, and even though he was still in the same attire, he felt cleaner just from the simple bath.

His boots made the floorboards creak as he meandered into the room and found a table in the corner. A woman was standing at the end of the bar, talking to the man from earlier, and at the sight of him, she waved. "Hi there, handsome. Something to drink and eat for you?" she called from across the room. Her dress was tight, her bust spilling out, and her red hair was clipped high atop her head.

Morei nodded. "That'd be great."

The chair squeaked as he repositioned himself and got comfortable. He had napped, barely making it out of bed to fulfill his promise of washing and eating. Exhaustion still hung heavy on him as he sat there, and he was determined to eat as quickly as possible and then return to bed. He had no idea how quickly the next part would happen, but a good night's sleep was well overdue.

For he intended on bringing King Drexis of Caster to his knees. The mere thought of his plans consumed him with immense purpose.

"Here you go," the lady said, and set a large bowl down before him. "Ox okay for you, hun?"

"That's wonderful," he replied. It had been a long while since he'd had ox meat. "Do you have any fresh bread? I smell it."

She nodded. "Just pulled it. You want some?"

He nodded and reached for the mug. The liquid was dark. "Thanks."

"Enjoy. I'll be back in a moment."

As she walked off, Morei took a large gulp of the ale, relishing it. It was smooth to the tongue and had an aftertaste of cinnamon. It would go perfectly with the stew.

He dug into the meat without hesitation, only stopping when the lady returned with some fresh bread, which he then used as another means to soak up the stew's broth. His stomach warmed with the meal, and the headache that had been teasing the edges of his thoughts was shushed once and for all. He would sleep well tonight—if he could, he'd sleep for the next five days straight. It would cleanse him of the crimes, the travel, everything he had done so willingly.

"Seat taken?"

Torn from his isolation, Morei looked up to see a man standing there, with eyes an unnaturally bright amber and dark hair that was tied up in a loose bun. Gold bands decorated the man's wrists, which peeked out from beneath a gray tunic, and his expression settled into a pleasant smile as he sat across from Morei without receiving an answer.

"Uh—" Morei swallowed and pointed at the room. "Plenty of tables. And I'd much prefer you find another spot."

The man exhaled and clasped his hands together over the table, meeting his gaze directly. "I'd prefer to stay."

"Welcome." It was the waitress, and she was standing there. Morei looked between her and the man across from him, trying to figure out if he was going to be an asshole or not. All he wanted was some privacy and peace. Was that so hard these days?

"Something to drink or eat for you?" she asked.

"Just to drink. I'll have whatever my friend's got here," the man replied with far too much warmth. It made the hairs on the back of Morei's neck stand on end.

As she turned and walked away, he snapped, "Friend? What game are you playing?"

"The only game you know how to play, Morei."

A cold blade shoved itself into his heart, and he froze. He'd known he was taking a risk, but he hadn't anticipated anything this quickly. And he had not factored this into his plan.

"I think it's best you move on," Morei whispered. "I wouldn't want to ruin that nice shirt of yours."

The man seemed unperturbed. "That's awfully nice of you, but I think I'll take my chances."

He fumed. "This is my last warn—"

"Shh." The man raised his hand. "Let's not say anything quite yet. I'd like to get my drink."

Morei would have stabbed him with his fork right there, but he refrained. A part of him was curious to hear what the stranger had to say before he did anything violent. Although another, much more gratifying part, wished to burn him alive from the inside out and skip the discussion altogether. In the end though, he kept his mouth shut until the waitress returned.

"Here's that ale," she said, and set the mug down in front of the stranger. "Let me know if you two need anything else. I'll be cleaning."

"Thank you," he said with a nod. As she walked away, he picked up the mug and took a drink. He swallowed, then inhaled sharply. "That's a good one." He set the mug down and tilted his head at Morei. "Relax. I'm not here for any of that bounty stuff, all right? I just want to talk."

Morei eyed him, not believing a word. What kind of trap was this?

"Keep eating, or you're going to make this awkward for both of us."

He tightened his grip on his spoon. "You already made it awkward the moment you sat down uninvited."

"To the rest, we look like friends catching up. But we won't if you look like you want to put a blade through my eye."

"Well, maybe I do."

The man laughed. "Good sense of humor."

Morei reached for his own drink, trying to look natural despite his growing ire. "So, what do you want?" He took a drink, but this time, he could hardly taste it.

He shrugged. "I told you, to chat."

Morei wanted to reach over and punch him. "I get it. What do you want to talk about? My bloody record?"

"You."

That nearly made him laugh. "Humor me, stranger. What do you want to know?"

"I want to know why the king of Geral is running."

That made his blood turn hot. "I'm not running—"

"Then tell me this," he interrupted, leaning forward. "What do you intend to gain by removing yourself from Geral all together?"

Morei sat back, not having it. "Who are you?"

"I asked a question."

"Don't bullshit me. Tell me who you are and then maybe I'll entertain you."

"Your voice is rising," the stranger warned. Morei looked about and saw the waitress avert her eyes. "Friends, remember?" He picked up his mug again. "Some call me Reyd."

"Some?" Morei clarified.

Reyd took a drink and shrugged. "I like it, so you can call me that."

Morei waved that comment off, not having the tolerance for this man. "Then tell me this, Reyd—why are you asking me that question? Are you waiting for the rest of your army? Is Drexis behind this?"

He shook his head, an amusing twinkle in those amber eyes, as if he found Morei funny. "How's that curse treating you?"

This man knew too much. Sure, the citizens of Geral had known something was wrong with him—they'd started rumors over it—but Morei didn't need to ask Reyd to know that this man knew *exactly* what he was talking about. He was only showing half the cards in his hand.

Morei couldn't help it. He flinched.

"Guilt is a dangerous enemy," Reyd muttered, then tilted his head. "How bad?"

"It grows stronger every day," Morei confessed. Why he would tell this stranger, he did not know, but it suddenly didn't seem to matter much to him. Reyd already knew a lot, and he didn't have the desire to banter.

Reyd motioned at his hands. "The gloves?"

"My hands are marked."

"Ah." Reyd nodded slowly. "Your symptoms?"

"Why do you care so much?"

The man didn't acknowledge the question. "Your symptoms?" he repeated.

"If you know everything, then you know that answer."

Reyd raised an eyebrow. "Am I upsetting you because I care?"

"You're upsetting me because you're overstepping. Big difference."

The man wagged his finger. "That temper of yours will get you in trouble, but it already has, hasn't it?"

That was it. His appetite was ruined, his stomach knotted, and his muscles tensed with rage. Morei stood and shoved his chair back. "We're done here."

As he turned, a hand latched on to his wrist with an iron grip. His entire body lurched as Reyd yanked him close and hissed, "The ring in your pocket will destroy you. Do not seek that power out."

Morei tore his arm free and stumbled back. There was not a single soul who knew of that relic. Impossible. Fear snaked her way up his back and made him shudder. This was unnatural. Everything about it was. He needed to leave.

"We're done here," he whispered, and shook his head. "Do not follow me."

Reyd sat back and grinned wide. "You would never know if I did, my friend."

Morei found nothing to say to that, and so he left. His steps had an extra skip to them as he made his way back to his room as fast as possible, almost at a run.

This was not normal—that much, he knew. A sensation engulfed his entire body, one he had not felt in many, many cycles, one that made sweat sprout along his brow and down his back, soaking his clothes.

Terror.

As he shut the door behind him and locked it, he sank to the floor. The panic evolved into rage. This was not him, this was not the man he was raised to be. Terror was not an emotion he was familiar with feeling. And yet, he could not face that door, could not face the conversation he had left. He could not even stand.

Instead, he dug into his pouch on his belt and pulled out the ring. There it was, cold against his fingers but familiar despite the time apart. The Lirallian Ring revealed itself to him; the large emerald in the center wrapped in silver was undeniably hideous. But knowing it was there, at his fingertips, provided him with comfort. This was a power that he could call upon at any time, when he was ready, and no stranger or city could take that from him.

WICKED AS THE DEAL

The meeting with the Infernol leader slipped between Syra's fingers in an instant. The words she and Zarek had shared, no matter how cruel, were meaningless given what now stood before her. The door handle in her hand was cold, and she could hardly feel the floor beneath her own feet as she stared ahead.

There he was. The man who had turned her life into a game of survival; the God who had plunged the Demon Killer right into her heart and resurrected her into something that she didn't even understand. A moon cycle had slipped by, and no matter how many times she had demanded he return, face her, and answer her questions, she went ignored. Frankly, she had no idea if he had heard any of her pleas.

Sekar was dressed simply, all in black and with no weapon that she could see, but he didn't need one. The God of Dreams could snap his fingers and bend reality itself into his own personal playground. Illusions were his gift. That awful smirk was permanently in place, and his dark eyes held a twinkle in them that could have passed for devious joy. It was always there, Syra realized that now, but she had never seen the look in such clarity until this moment.

"Hello, Syra," he greeted, voice smooth as always. There was never a concern in the world with Sekar.

She opened her mouth to say something but closed it just as quickly when she realized that she actually had no idea what. She'd been so caught up with her thoughts and current situation with Zarek that she hadn't even considered what she would say if Sekar actually showed up. At this point, she had assumed he would leave her to fend for herself—it seemed to be a pastime for him.

Instead of speaking, she closed the door, but still she did not approach the God right away. Suddenly, the nerves were there, scrambling everything she thought she knew. Her mind argued against what she wanted to believe and what the Guardian had told her. If the God of Dreams was trustworthy, wouldn't she have figured that out by now? It wasn't like he had made it easy—he'd spent the majority of their friendship pretending to be a Guardian when he wasn't. And then he had taken the relic right from her hands and left while Dryl had been surrounded by Nighthunters. Then there was the question about Henry Junok . . . Maybe he was reporting back to the false god for the Lirallian Empire, and perhaps this was all a façade to trick her. There were so many possibilities flashing through her mind that she couldn't think straight.

But she still saw the man who had spent countless evenings with her next to the fire, who had shared stories, listened to her own, and constantly told her she could be anything she wanted. The man she had come to know before all the secrets had unfolded had been playful, compassionate, and so full of life. Those parts couldn't be faked.

"Don't look so pleased to see me," Sekar commented, looking about. Syra pulled her cloak tighter, feeling exposed. "They haven't changed, have they? All the same."

Was he referring to the Infernol? "I didn't expect you," she said.

"Why would you?" he countered. "Where were you?"

Syra swallowed. "There was a meeting. I'm sure you're aware of everything that was discussed. If not, you will be." She knew he had Onyes that wandered for him like a second pair of eyes, but she was sure he had other means of learning information. Sekar seemed to know far too much for his own good. She was sure he knew everything about the Infernol, even its agents who were placed in cities across the world—like Saveen and Delion, and even Geral.

The God eyed her, his expression unchanged. "Have you experienced anything that feels out of the ordinary?"

She returned his skeptical look with her own. "Why?" Ordinary was a broad description. At this point, Syra wasn't sure what was supposed to be normal. Life hadn't been *ordinary* since she fled Caster.

"A fracture like the one on Volkeri Island will cause disruptions in the energies, including lifeforces. You may have more vivid dreams, be quicker to react, be more sensitive to different things, like Dark Energy, or you may just want to sleep and have a drink." The last part had a sarcastic edge, but Syra hardly heard it. She *had* been having more vivid dreams—Morei was that example—and she felt like she couldn't keep her emotions in check at times. Although maybe that was because of everything that was happening.

She shrugged. "Dreams," she confessed. "I've been having those a lot."

That seemed to satisfy him. "I am too."

Her bones were tired, her eyelids heavy, and she wanted to sleep off this day and start anew tomorrow. "Why are you here at this hour? Why not during the day?"

Sekar took a half step toward her. "Because there's no guarantee you'll be here during the day. But at night, I know it—"

"Can't you find another time?"

He flashed her a smile. "The night is my favorite time, Syra. I don't think I need to explain myself."

She crossed her arms and raised an eyebrow. "I'm really not in the mood."

"That's too bad," he replied, "because this is the only time I have available."

"Busy, hm? Working on those obligations you have? Like Henry Junok?" It was a long shot, but she had nothing to lose, and Sekar could handle himself. It was time to get everything out in the open. If he was determined to come here now, then he would have to deal with fessing up to where his loyalties really lay.

The muscle in his jaw ticked, and she felt a sliver of triumph pass through her. "Certain things are better left unsaid, Syra." A warning.

"I would have settled for that before you stabbed me," she retorted. "I want answers."

"Mm, so bold. Chaos suits you well, my little flower." Sekar approached, but his steps were still slow, calculated, as if he anticipated her to strike at any moment. Or maybe he was feeling her out, seeing how close he could get before she told him to stop. She should have spoken up, but her tongue wouldn't cooperate. "You're right. My obligations are to Ku'sar, but that does not sway my loyalty to you."

The weight of his words smashed into her, and she tried to inhale but couldn't. Yes, there were theories, and people could spend a lifetime saying what they thought was true or what could happen, but hearing it from him was different. More than anything, she had wanted to believe otherwise. Wanted to be wrong.

Deep down, a part of her had always known, even if she had refused to acknowledge it.

"You can't be loyal to both of us," she whispered. "He's a monster—"

"And you think the Infernol is so much better?" Sekar challenged, his voice still steady. He was only a few paces away. "You don't think the Infernol is desperately trying to become the ultimate source of power and authority?"

Syra shook her head. "You can't compare the two. Liral, Henry, they killed millions. There is nothing good that will come out of this. Junok is already in their hands, although I'm sure you helped with that too, so that's not a surprise. Sekar, this is a war we're talking about."

"And you continue to ask the wrong questions. Have you learned anything at all?"

He always had a way of getting under her skin. She nearly let it show, but she forced her expression to remain the same. "What should I be asking, Sekar? Whether you'll be so kind as to spare me when this is all over?"

Now, he tilted his head. "The Zyulë Bond—"

"Don't," she interjected. "You'll find some way to outsmart even it so that you can save yourself. That's what it's always about with you, isn't it? Staying alive?"

Those dark eyes did not leave her, and she forced herself to hold their wicked gaze. "You remind me a lot of Dryl, you know. Never quite pleased by anything you hear, always questioning, and never smart enough to listen—even when your instincts are begging you to shut it."

At that, he snapped his fingers, and the world dissolved around her. The stone floor gave way to dirt that her toes sank into, and the rich scent of pine filled her nose. Birds chirped loud and a doe bolted at their arrival. Syra turned, but she didn't have to look long before she saw it: the purple lake he had once told her about. It shimmered with an aura, the color so rich and deep that she felt like she had found herself in a world well beyond her own. The surface of the water didn't move, even as a wind rushed through the trees and their branches swayed.

They were in the Delfic Forest, still in the Mourale Mountains. The visions Sekar created were so vivid, it was no wonder he was deemed mad. Anyone would go mad with this kind of power. He could create entire worlds with a flick of the wrist. Even if they were just illusions, what she saw now felt so real.

"I know about the realm fracture," Sekar whispered from behind. "I've known for a long time."

Syra couldn't tear her gaze away from the enchanting waters, no matter how much she wanted to. "Why didn't you say anything?"

"What good would it do to burden you with something you couldn't change?"

Syra shook her head. "We could stop it."

"Do you know why I brought you here?" he asked.

She didn't, but she recognized this place from the story he'd once told her, at Jared's. She had known he could create illusions, but she'd had no idea he could build an entire scene from a single memory.

"Watch."

And so she did.

Before her, from out of the brushes, a stallion appeared, but it was no ordinary one. Its fur was blacker than midnight, large feathering decorated its wide hooves, and its piercing black gaze was ever-knowing. It walked with caution but confidence and moved its head all about to take in its surroundings. From its forehead jutted a horn that was sharpened to a point, black, the same color as its fur.

The unicorn approached the purple lake and slowed to a stop, where it dipped its head toward the surface. An exhalation of air rippled the water, but only slightly, before it drank. So beautiful was the stallion that she barely noticed the flash of light that engulfed the lake. And just like that, silence consumed the forest. Birds ceased, the wind stopped, but the unicorn continued to drink without a care. It occurred to her then that this stallion knew exactly what it had done.

There were so many stories out there that spoke of the creature now before her. Stories that promised these unicorns were only a myth, a tall tale to keep the imaginations of listeners running wild.

"What I never mentioned was that this was what I saw when I arrived here," Sekar said from behind. "This memory is one I relive many times, and no matter how often I revisit this place, I still have not seen the same thing." The unicorn lifted its head then and looked back toward them. "This is when he saw me," Sekar explained before the creature dissolved into dust. Syra felt her jaw go slack. *Gone.* In the same instant, the chatter of birds began once more.

"Created by pure Dark Energy," he continued. "Old texts refer to the unicorn as Mo'lüre, which literally translates to Walker of Realms. The unicorn earned that name because of what you just saw. It does not remain in any realm permanently. No other creature can do what the Mo'lüre can do, not even a dragon." Sekar stepped forward, his arm brushing against her shoulder. "So pure is the energy that forms the unicorn that you cannot physically touch the creature without permission. If you do, the Mo'lüre will consume your lifeforce."

"I thought they were a myth," she mumbled.

"As does most of the Vore World," Sekar said. "These creatures don't show themselves by accident. If you see one, it's because they wanted to show themselves."

She looked up at his dark gaze. "Why?"

He shrugged. "If we knew that answer, we'd likely find a way to abuse it for our own gain." Sekar smiled. This time, it looked genuine, handsome even. The illusion faded, dissipating just like the unicorn had, and they were back in her chamber. The cold touch of the stone against Syra's bare feet sent a chill up her spine.

The God was still standing close to her—too close. The heat of his body radiated over her in waves. "I came here to offer you help, Syra. I know what I did to you was unfair and that you were unprepared. But I also don't regret it. The Gods have all grown restless and greedy, so twisted by the coercion of Chaos and her ways. Someone like you—a soul so pure—is needed. Without intervention, I fear the others will end the realms for one reason or another."

Syra swallowed, understanding. "You think I can stop it all?"

"I *know* you can." Sekar reached out and brushed a strand behind her ear. "You are the prophecy among the Guardians. Your blood is royal, strong, and Chaos needs the balance. The actions of the Gods directly influence Chaos. The fracture between realms, the instability of energies, the failing Soul Realm—this is all consequences of centuries of imbalance."

Syra folded her arms over her chest. "I've been trying to harness Chaos, but I can't."

"That's because you aren't looking in the right places." He pressed a finger just where her heart would be. "Chaos comes from here. It always has. It does not suck the lifeforce from you like Light or Dark Energy does, it literally becomes you. Master yourself and you master Chaos." Sekar removed his hand and gestured all around. "Light and Dark Energy are derived from Chaos. They are what we pull from all around—they make up everything we know—and this is why you have learned to harvest as you have. It is why you tire when you harvest Light and Dark Energy. But Chaos, once she chooses you, lives in the very blood that moves through you."

"How do I know what . . . what I can do? You can use illusions, manipulate dreams. Someone like Helyna"—he grimaced at her name—"is apparently some master of love. How do I know what I can do?" she repeated.

"Practice." Sekar inhaled deeply. "When you begin to harvest Chaos, you will learn what your gift will be. The more you harness these abilities, the easier it will become. But—" The

God hesitated and looked away. "There will be consequences. There always are."

That made her uncomfortable. "What kind?"

Again, he shrugged. "It varies. No God is the same—if they were, I'd tell you. But no power such as Chaos comes freely. You are enslaved to her now, and she is a part of you." Sekar turned his haunting eyes back at her. "What do you want, Syra?"

The question brought her back. She blinked several times before she could force the words out of her mouth. "I want to help in any way I can. I don't want to run anymore, but I don't know where to begin."

The God nodded. "Then you start by learning how to harness Chaos. From there, you have the choice to go and do whatever you want. I cannot stop you."

Syra raised her brow. "Even if it's to bring an end to Liral and Henry?"

Sekar's expression did not change as he whispered, "I have spent lifetimes watching empires rise and fall. If you bring Liral to its knees once and for all, there will be another one in its place."

"Then why are you obligated to help Henry?" Sekar was complicated, perhaps not entirely sane, and she was beginning to wonder if he knew it.

"It was never a problem to see this all play out until you came along," the God replied. "Ku'sar"—he looked at her pointedly—"what the Lirallians call Henry Junok, he knew of your existence well in advance because I shared it with him—a bonus living among the Guardians for so long. The goal was to take you to him, so that he could mold you into his own personal puppet, but . . . things have changed."

"Changed?" she blurted out, a tinge of annoyance coating her words. "You have the Demon Killer, you come and go as you please, as if you can't pick a side, and now you tell me you spared me from him because, what? You had a change of heart? None of this adds up. You can't expect me to believe Henry, Ku'sar—whatever he wishes to be called—doesn't know you're here."

"He doesn't," Sekar said, but she was on a roll.

"What kind of obligations would tie you, a *God*, to a man like him?"

He regarded her, those eyes twisting into something unrecognizable. "If I told you, you'd sympathize with me, and I do not wish for you to carry that burden."

That answer bewildered her. He did not wish for her to feel bad for him because he thought it a weight she didn't wish or need to carry. Syra hated him. Hated his self-righteousness and contorted moral compass. He had ruined her life, torn it down to the bone, and now he stood here believing that after all this time together, he could tell her how she was supposed to feel. Like he was doing her a favor by withholding information that could make her see him in a different way.

Sekar continued before she could find the right words to reply with. "You have until tomorrow night to decide if you want my help. I will train you in every aspect that I can, but you must be aware that there will be consequences to tapping into this force. You just have to be prepared for it."

Syra's mind was racing. This was what she had wanted all along—to be trained properly—so why was she hesitating? Nothing was ever straightforward with Sekar, and while she wanted to take his words and pocket them, she couldn't. There would be a catch, as there always was. But he was also the only God in the Vore World willing to train her in Chaos. If she didn't hone her abilities, she was borderline useless to both the living and dead.

She licked her lips. People spent their entire lives wondering if the Gods were real, and she was over here making a deal with one. "What will you gain in doing this?"

"What do you mean?"

Syra gestured at him. "I am not a fool, Sekar. Everything you've ever done for me has come at a cost. What will this cost me?"

That earned her a grin, so wicked that she immediately regretted asking. "Your time."

She shook her head. "That is not an ans—"

"I don't seek material and I don't seek coin—I have everything I will ever need and more. I seek companionship. Is that too high a price for the daughter of Nala?"

The request was simple—he would train her, and she would return it by giving him friendship—but it did not add up. They'd spent time together, and she had, at once, thought they were friends, but it was Sekar who had destroyed that. She didn't trust him or his intentions—everything felt like a game with him, and she couldn't decide if this was just another one.

It pissed her off. In a matter of no time, he'd twisted this all back on her. Her thoughts were scattered. It felt incomprehensible that this would be it. "I don't understand."

"Spend centuries alone, and then tell me if you understand." His voice was low. "I will be back tomorrow evening. You decide."

And just like that, he was gone. The solidity of his body dissipated into black mist before disappearing altogether. Without his presence, she felt awfully isolated, and the chamber seemed too large. She hated how he made her feel. Sekar was a force to be reckoned with—he was loud, bold, and confident, and the way her soul reacted to his presence as if she had known him for lifetimes already was unfair. There was a comfort about him though, despite all his wrongdoing, that she could not describe. Perhaps he intentionally had made it this way, so that it would be that much harder to turn her back on the one God she'd come to despise.

If Sekar was being honest and that was all he wanted from her, the answer would be easy. But it never was, and she was terrified about the "what ifs." There would come a day when he would want something in return—something far more than just her time. The God of Dreams was a walking anomaly, a volcano ready to erupt at any point. Give him a good reason why he should destroy an entire city, and he would do it without a sliver of remorse.

Raveer was just him having fun—that much was clear to her now.

Syra swallowed, trying to regain her composure. She felt alone, and she wanted to confess her confusion to someone. The walls were closing in around her—she needed a way out. Harvesting Chaos was that way. If she embraced who she was, learned to control her abilities—damn the consequences—then she could make a change. The Soul Realm was dying. The living realm would be consumed by Chaos or demons, whichever came first, and that meant that no matter how much she wanted to run, she couldn't anymore.

She accepted that.

But the cost to fulfill whatever Destiny wanted of her? To let Sekar into her life willingly, knowing he might turn on her at any point? He'd already hurt her once, plunged a blade into her, and she was supposed to ignore all that for the sake of the realms. It was a savage blow to her morals.

Syra didn't make it to bed. She couldn't. She sank down to the floor and leaned against the wall. There were no tears—those would do no good—but the same emotions stormed her senses as if she were sobbing. Syra didn't want to feel helpless, didn't want to turn her back on the realms anymore. But she also wanted guidance and answers. For the first time in her life, nobody was telling her what to do, because they couldn't. The next part would be entirely decided by her, and that was terrifying.

Her thoughts wandered to Morei again. He was raised to make decisions, raised to look at the world as a threat, or so she thought. Rulers weren't ignorant or naïve—if they were, their reign would be nonexistent. Kings and queens didn't have time to second-guess or show vulnerability—the citizens they led would devour them whole.

It was so much more than kings and queens, though, no matter how much Syra wanted to compartmentalize this. If she failed to become what she was destined to be, then she would fail the lives of people all across the Vore World, born and unborn. Not to mention the souls of those who still wandered in the realm of the dead, seeking guidance. Her destiny had been carved centuries before she'd ever been born.

She either accepted that or damned everyone.

FORGED BY BETRAYAL

Cyrus awoke to rays of sun breaking through his window. Overlooking the coast, he could see the waves splashing lazily up against the shore, the sky bright. Clouds scattered by, likely the remaining few from the storm that had blown in overnight. Several times, he'd awoken to hear thunder but had quickly succumbed back to sleep. It would be a good day, he realized, one that gave him a deep thrill.

For a long moment, he stared at the coast. So long he had dreamed of such a thing! And now, here he was, in his mother's home, finally getting all the answers he could ever need to move on. A part of him was satisfied—he could finally close this chapter and embrace the future.

Whatever that may be.

He nudged his mind toward Sozar. *Sleep well?*

The dragon was sunning himself on the cliff, wings stretched wide. *Peaceful.*

Cyrus smiled as he threw on the clothes he'd grown accustomed to. The material was stiff from long exposure to the sea, and the colors had faded. Sozar still had the pouch that carried the *Book of Liral*, but Cyrus had the sword and belt next to him. He reached for it now and strapped it around his hips—a habit he would die without breaking.

With a good stretch, he made his way out of the room. The floor creaked at his weight, and he paused for a moment to listen. No other sounds followed, which meant his mother had already left. That was not a surprise—he'd anticipated it, but it still felt weird to even think that she, this woman who'd accepted him into her home, was his mother. Still, Meredith had responsibilities to attend to, and he did not wish to get in her way. He'd help wherever he could, if only to prove that he was willing to make this relationship work.

Cyrus looked around the neat living space. He pursed his lips—he was hoping to do something productive around here to show his appreciation. As he approached the galley, he saw a plate of biscuits and a piece of parchment with a note scrawled on it: *Enjoy—be back soon.*

Butter had been set out for him, along with a glass of water. Cyrus took a large gulp of it, finding it cool, and set it down before eyeing the galley. There were no dishes to put away, the cleaning water had already been tossed, and everything looked nearly spotless. She cleaned in the mornings, it seemed, before the day got ahead of her, which he appreciated. Sometimes mornings were the most peaceful part of the day.

Cyrus grabbed a biscuit and took a big bite. Despite having had them the night before, he still found them succulent. After days and days of fish and the sea, he was more than eager to indulge in bread and anything sweet. His next stop would be a pastry—what he would give for a butter cake.

The first went down quickly, and he dove into a second. As he ate, he roamed the home, eyeing the eccentric nature of the decorations and hoping to learn more about this woman. Meredith loved to use these skulls she found as holders, placing feathers and jewelry in the eye sockets. He found a human skull in her bedroom, placed right in the center of a dresser. It was staring at him when he peeked in, and it made his skin crawl, so he darted back out before he could study the purple drapes and mural painted across the wall in more detail.

Where he was from, people didn't use skulls as decorations. In Cyrus's opinion, the dead stayed dead, and nobody should use the remains of anyone as placeholders. The idea that he could wake up in the middle of the night and be faced with a skull that belonged to someone who'd died was creepy. What if a soul was still attached to that? Nobody knew. Nobody but a Soul Speaker, and he didn't know any offhand that he could summon. Frankly, he'd never even met one before.

He stepped toward the living room and stumbled, dropping the second biscuit to the ground. Cyrus shook his head, suddenly disoriented. He tried to stand but felt all his strength draining in one quick sweep. Stomach cramping, Cyrus gagged and crawled forward on all fours.

Panic crashed over him as he heard the door slam open. Men shouted just as Sozar roared from his place on the cliff. The dragon launched himself in the air and started toward him at a dangerous speed. The terror that streaked his mind black from Sozar tore the air right from his lungs.

Drugged.

Cyrus had been drugged. He looked up to see a hand reach for him. He swatted at it and tried to jerk away but was too slow and weak to do so. Words failed to come out properly; he wanted to curse the soldiers coming for him, but all that came out was a beastlike groan. Vision fading, he reached for Sozar, not wanting the dragon to come his way—this was dangerous. This was like Geral. They simply could not afford the both of them here, but he couldn't reach Sozar anymore. His thoughts were closing in on him, so quickly that his head spun.

Breaths uneven, he shoved himself away from all the prying hands, but then his face slammed into something hard. He blinked—the wood was glaring back at him. He forced his hands underneath him to continue to try and get away, but a force yanked him backward.

"Come on, son, don't make this difficult," a man said. "Tie him up, let's get out of here."

The last thing he saw was his mother's ugly scowl, staring down at him.

SLEEP DOES NOT WELCOME THE WICKED

It was the cracking of the child's neck that echoed; the limp body that dropped to his feet spared no weight on his soul, for she was only one of dozens. Morei stepped around the child, a resounding crunch filling the space as he walked. He looked down and found that his boots didn't press against sand or dirt, but bones. Hundreds, possibly thousands, of bones.

From afar, he saw a murder of crows in the sky. The black splotches grew as they came closer, and their shouts filled the gap between his steps. He felt a vibration in his bones and smiled—there was nothing quite like Dark Energy. Her presence was a constant, a way to keep him steady, a surety in all this mess.

She was satisfied, that he knew, for the carnage that lay around him would feed her. Her, he mused. When had that become natural for him?

"You make me proud," a voice called from behind.

Morei spun on his feet and saw a man there. Red markings covered his sickly skin and piercing blue eyes glared. In his arms, a woman. Syra. She was gagged and bound, and her muffled screams only reached so far.

"Who—" He stopped himself and stepped forward. "What are you doing?"

A black blade glinted under the sun, a feverish grin stretched across the man's face. "Power comes with consequences, boy. Surely you must know that by now."

And before anyone could say more, that sinister blade swept itself cleanly across the woman's neck, as if her skin had been begging for it. Syra's struggle ceased as the man dropped her to the ground, blood dripping freely from the Demon Killer. Her body convulsed once, twice, and then no more.

A guttural roar sounded, and Morei realized it was coming from his own throat—

He jolted awake. Skin slick with sweat, he practically threw himself out of the bed. Breaths rasped, and he fell on all fours, crawling away from the cot. The sheet dragged behind him, tangled in his feet until it finally relented halfway across the room. Once Morei was far enough away, he leaned up against the adjacent wall, still fighting for air. It felt like he was being choked to death right here; a grip around his throat tightened, squeezed, until he scrambled away from the wall, falling before the mirror. The bottom half remained visible, and he coughed and sputtered a scream when he saw fingers around his throat.

Morei threw his hands up and pulled hard against the hands, but they wouldn't budge. His skin was turning red, his eyes bloodshot as he suffocated, and then he saw it—the glint of metal.

"No—"

Morei gasped and shot up from his spot in the cot. He reached for his neck, felt for any signs of hands. His lungs burned, and he kicked the sheets off and pulled himself up against the wall.

A dream. Nothing more.

But he could not shake himself free from the panic that still bound his senses in disarray. The dark felt oppressive, and for once, he wished to not be alone. The dreams were growing more violent, more vivid. They had started when he fled Geral, but now they were coming almost nightly.

Time was not on his side, and he wasn't sure when it had started working against him.

Morei looked down at his hands. Despite the dark, he could still see the black veins that were crawling up his arms and over his chest. The ailment was worsening, growing stronger, and he was losing his grip. One day, he might not know the difference between dream and reality.

But that was not today, and until then . . . he closed his hands into fists.

He would kill King Drexis for what the man had taken.

For a long while, he sat there listening to the creaks and groans of the wood around him. Someone walked down the hall, their steps fading. In the next room over, he could hear something drop something, and a loud curse followed by silence. He wondered if Reyd was in any of these rooms, waiting to surprise him once more.

The stranger did not sit well with him. In different circumstances, Morei may have just killed the man to resolve the issue, but he was trying to be strategic. He knew someone from the city of Caster would come for him, and that was his primary goal—someone was bound to recognize him from the poor sketches that hung in the village center.

With a man like Reyd around, Morei didn't feel entirely in control of the situation. Reyd was . . . different. Morei recognized power when he saw it. He recognized danger, too.

He'd seen the same look in his own eyes before.

CARESSED BY THE BLADE OF FATE

rying to find Zarek had turned into a task that had consumed the entire first part of Syra's day. Every time she found someone who knew of his whereabouts, she would arrive to find he was already somewhere else, and it had turned into a game of cat and mouse. The Infernol's structure was massive. The entire mountain range had been carved away to conceal the housing, resources, and so many chambers that Syra had literally no idea what all happened here. It would take a lifetime to learn all of this organization's secrets. The Infernol was its own self-sustaining city, completely removed from the rest of the world. Bakers, blacksmiths, soldiers, clothing, even farming—if she named it, she knew she could find it.

There were three levels to this world the Infernol had built, with spiral staircases connecting each one in various places. On the north side, closer to Assane's territory, she had learned that livestock was kept, because they'd have more access to natural grass while still being concealed. Horses were held there too. To the west lay the chambers she had grown accustomed to, with many meeting rooms and sleeping rooms. To the south were training grounds and where soldiers of the Infernol were found. It was here that Zane was often reported to be. And finally, to the east, a large portion of the markets, farming, and supplies—many people would take day trips over to the East Markets to shop for anything they might need because the travel alone between regions took half a day.

Syra kept to the west and had barely explored the rest of the Infernol, but she hoped to do that soon. There was so much to see still. Staying on the west side had grown a bit monotonous, and she was feeling antsy, bold even. Perhaps she would head there in the next couple of days when she could leave early.

Or maybe she was desperately holding on to the idea of normalcy.

Back on the west side, she wrapped around another hall. She wasn't sure if she had been down this one already or not—they all looked the same around here. The Infernol had not built for style but for practicality, so the walls were all smooth gray, the ceilings rounded, with metal hooks hammered in to hold lanterns throughout. Doors were scattered about, leading to various chambers that were identified by Old Tongue sigils. By now, Syra had learned that the sigil with the circle and six jagged lines was for sleeping chambers, although she still didn't know how anyone knew which room was theirs. Though, she supposed, if someone spent their entire life here, it wouldn't be difficult navigating these countless halls.

Coming up to a door, she checked the sigil. It had three sharp lines interlaced with another three, and a half circle cut right through it. Zarek had told her it meant unity, which made sense, given the purpose of the chamber. She tried the handle and found that it gave, so she opened the door.

"Hello?" she called—she didn't want to be rude.

"Is someone looking for me?" It was a woman's voice. She was crouched behind some furniture. Her dark hair was peppered with white strands, the pants and shirt she wore were tattered and covered in some kind of oil, and her eyes were vivid purple, which struck Syra as the woman met her gaze "Oh! You're the one everyone keeps talking about."

Syra didn't have to ask to know what that meant. She was the redhead who had been brought back with the Guardian. For the first few days, their arrival had been all that anyone could talk about, much to her dislike. She had spent so much time trying to avoid the world, and now here she was, the center of attention. Syra had heard that some thought she was a bad omen, because no mortal should be escorted by what many called Death Seekers. On the other hand, with the rising geopolitical tensions, some believed she was a bringer of hope. Nobody knew that she was the new Vore God, or that she was bonded with the Sekar. Still, her heart fluttered at the idea that these people might know who she really was.

With all the rumors, it was unclear who accepted or despised her. "That's me," she replied with a forced laugh. "Have you seen the Guardian? Zarek?"

The woman sighed and adjusted the cloth from one hand to the other—it was soaked in dark oil. She was clearly polishing the furniture in here, which looked to be a strange assortment of various wood pieces. "I saw him quite a while ago, but I don't think that helps you, does it?"

She shook her head. "No, but I appreciate your help."

Syra was turning to leave when the lady spoke up. "Do you know what they say about you?"

"Who?" But she knew that answer already. Instinctively, she dropped a hand to the hilt of her sword. For all she knew, this woman was preparing to ambush her and call her the bringer of evil. It wasn't like she'd heard a lot of good things about her arrival here.

The woman looked at her cloth and offered the faintest of smiles before meeting her gaze. "They say you're it, the Fräurune—that you will end all wars."

Syra stared. There were so many things people called her, and she still didn't know if any of it was true or not.

"You have not heard of it then, have you? No matter. All I'm saying is the people talk about you and it's because they believe in you."

"Ah." The word came out of her mouth before she could stop herself. "Thank you." Slowly, not wanting to be too sure or rude, she lowered her hand from her weapon.

"You're quieter than we predicted," the woman continued, unperturbed. "We don't think it's in a bad way, nothing like that, but"—she shrugged—"many of us have spent many a summer telling tall tales about who the Light Bringer might be."

"How . . ." Syra furrowed her brow. "How do you know that term?" That was a Soul Realm term, a part of their legend and something she could've sworn only the Guardians knew of. It had been Dryl who had shared that with her. Dryl and Kar— well before he revealed his true identity.

"Old records shared long ago by Guardians," the woman answered nonchalantly. "Some of us still read those; others have long since forgotten or choose to focus their attention on other things." She gestured at her rag. "I should get back to it. I was hoping to finish these pieces up by the end of the day."

Syra hesitated to move. There was an acute sense of realization that this was all so much bigger than her. She felt like a bystander in her own body, staring at a woman who knew nothing but grand tales of who she was supposed to become. These people truly believed she was to bring change and good fortune—that she would end all wars. Syra had known the Soul Realm spoke of her, but she had not been prepared to think that the living thought so highly of her. Well, some of them. She had spent the last season on the run with a bounty. Now, in this instant, she was revered by a stranger.

Oh, how the times had changed.

"Your name?" Syra asked. There was an obligation now to know. Perhaps she would remember the name, perhaps not, but regardless, she wanted the woman to feel acknowledged.

The cloth in her hand rested on a furniture piece. "Irsilla," she answered, and smiled. "It's an old name."

"It's beautiful," Syra commented, smiling back. "I'm Syra. It was a pleasure to meet you today. I'll see you around."

"Farewell, Fräurune."

As the door shut behind her, Syra let a large exhale out through her lips. So many questions, but she felt overcome with the need to find Zarek.

She had made a mental note of the term. Someone would have to tell her what "Fräurune" translated too. Was it just another word for Light Bringer? Possibly. Not that it mattered—everyone had a name for her these days—but it was still nice to know.

"Syra?"

She spun on her heels to see Zarek approaching, looking surprised to see her. He was dressed in a dark gray button-down, with Death's Sword sheathed at his hip.

Tension from their confrontation the night before immediately made itself known in her shoulders, back, and head. They'd left things unpleasantly before Sekar's surprise visit. While she had managed to catch a little more sleep, it hadn't been restful, and Syra had no doubt that by the end of the day, she would require a hot bath and a bit of solitude to relax and rest.

"I've been looking everywhere for you," she told him as he came to a stop before her. There was no one else in the hall with them, but she wasn't necessarily comfortable talking here. "Can we find somewhere private?"

"Sure." Zarek motioned for her to follow, so she did, quickly falling into step next to him. There was an obvious tension between them—his simple response was clipped—but she did not press. Now was not the time, although she hoped he understood she wasn't here to dig up faults. Mistakes had been made, and while she needed to apologize, she wanted to address the larger problem that had forced her on this adventure to begin with.

The Guardian tried a door with the unity sigil engraved on it, and it opened freely. They entered, and he shut the door behind them, giving them total privacy. The chamber was smaller than the one she'd just been in, and as she scanned the shelves and small desk with its few plush chairs, she realized this had to be someone's office. "Is this okay?" she asked.

"It doesn't matter," Zarek replied, his tone brisk. It was clear that their fight was still there, festering like an infected wound. "There are a dozen of these chambers on this level alone." Crossing his arms, he leaned against the wall. "You wanted to talk?" She nodded, but it felt weak. Countless reasons popped into her head why this was a bad idea and why she should have just asked for forgiveness later. "I'm not quite sure where to start . . . but—" Syra licked her lips and shoved her doubts aside. "Sekar visited last night—"

"Here?"

"Yes. In my chamber."

Zarek raised a hand. "Excuse me?" "Not like that." Syra glared at him. "What are you thinking? Never mind, I really don't want to know. But he offered to train me—"

"No." The answer was firm.

She fumbled on her words for a moment. "What?"

"The answer is no," he stated. "Have you lost your fucking mind?"

She crossed her arms. "I didn't come here to ask for permission."

The Guardian huffed. "So you came here to tell me what would happen. You've already made up your mind without consulting anyone?"

"No." She wanted to shake some sense into him. "You've got this all wrong, Zarek. I came here to talk to you because if he helps me harness Chaos, I can help restore the Soul Realm. I can be who I need to be."

"And you've got this all wrong, Syra," he countered. "You really think Sekar is the safest option?"

They were only a step apart, but it felt like he was screaming in her face with how much his words dripped with loathing. "I need a God to train me. You and I both agreed on that."

"I agreed on *a* God, not Sekar. He is dangerous, unstable, and unpredictable. Not to mention his potential and likely affiliation with Liral. Is that really who you want to spend your time with?"

Syra threw her hands up, frustrated. "Shall I summon another then?"

"You seem determined to involve yourself with that monster every moment you get, so go right ahead," the Guardian replied coolly.

She needed him to understand where she was coming from. This was not exactly the ideal scenario, but she could not turn down an offer like this. She and Sekar had history, and while he wasn't the most reliable person she'd come to know, he was there, and it would be absurd to turn this offer down.

The truth was, she was terrified that she'd never see an opportunity like this again, or at least not in time to save the realms. Even if Sekar's attitude rubbed her wrong. "Listen, he's all I have. He's all we have, Zarek. We can't risk passing this up when there's so much at stake. What good will I be to any of you if I can't do anything? If there was another God to train me, I'd take it, but he's all we've got."

Zarek raised his brow. "*Would* you?"

The challenge was clear. Syra took a step back, appalled. The Guardian was in quite a mood, and frankly, she didn't have time for it. "I know you might not like him, and that's fine. I'm not an idiot—he's not been the greatest, and I'd be lying if I said I was totally comfortable with this, but he told me he wanted to help. That he believed in me." Zarek was making this impossible—his animosity was putting her in a corner that she was not entirely comfortable with. Here she was *defending* Sekar.

"And he'll be the last person you see when he drives that dagger through your heart," Zarek said with a sneer. "Your choice."

She put a hand up in defeat. Flustered, annoyed, and overwhelmed, Syra was trying to do the right thing. This seemed like the lesser of two evils. "You're not thinking clearly, Zarek. He might not be exactly what we want—"

"He's only working for Henry Junok," the Guardian pointed out. "Seems like a rather safe option."

"Sekar told me things have changed," she continued, ignoring his comment. "I don't know what that means, but I intend to find out."

Zarek's nostrils flared as he glared down at her. This was her decision and hers alone—she knew it was risky, knew there were likely obstacles ahead that she would not be able to face alone, but she also hoped that the Guardian would understand that this was all they had. No matter how he felt, he could not deny that to be anything of value, she *needed* to master her abilities. Syra was going on faith here that Sekar would not betray her. The history they had—no matter what Zarek had to say on the matter—and the Zyulë Bond were things she was putting her trust heavily in. Even if she was scared to death, she had to make a decision or risk being a bystander in her own life. Sekar was complicated, mad. She loathed his smugness, how it was like he already *knew* what she'd do, but he was the only option she had. Last night, she'd learned that there was a fracture between the realms. A moon cycle ago, Sekar had told her the Gods wanted her dead and she'd learned she was the daughter of Nala. If she failed to embrace her purpose, she feared that it would cost countless lives. Sekar was the quickest option she had to resolve all of this once and for all.

Zarek stepped away and back toward the door they had entered through. "Where are you going?" she asked.

He laid a hand on the handle. "I'm leaving. There's nothing more to say on the matter. Your decision was made prior to you ever finding me, and nothing I say will change what you want to do. Just know that my loyalty lays in the Soul Realm, Syra. Whatever happens today will impact the future of that realm, so if he harms that in any way, I'll kill him with my bare hands." His eyes dipped. "And that means you too."

He opened the door and walked out, leaving it wide open behind him.

Syra felt no celebration, no pride. She wasn't jumping up and down because she had made a decision and was running with it, damn what anyone would say. Instead, she felt devoid of any emotions. Numb, to be precise. Syra had spent her entire life catering to the needs of others, always ensuring everyone got along, and now that she was entrusted with such a responsibility, she was farther from everyone than ever before.

The cost of embracing her destiny was steeper than she liked to admit. Hopefully, this would be temporary. Internally, she begged that Zarek would understand once she successfully harvested Chaos with Sekar's help. She no longer had time to go searching for everyone's approval. She knew now that that was what this had been.

Syra shook herself free from her thoughts and lifted her chin high. Tonight couldn't come fast enough.

A COLD REALITY

is wrists were weighed down, his feet numb. Cyrus could smell the wretched scent of defecation and decay, and he gagged as it all struck him. Rolling over, he spit and coughed until bile came up, burning his throat and tongue. The yellow goop painted the stone floor beneath him and reeked instantly. Turning back over on his ass, he inhaled deeply in an attempt to calm his racing heart. It was pounding painfully hard against his chest as he looked about.

The dungeon was in terrible shape, the stone coated in a layer of moisture, and dark. So dark. There was no window, nothing to tell the time, and his body could still feel the effects of the drug. Metal clasps were locked around his wrists, and chains dragged every time he moved—a sound that he loathed. A primitive fear gripped his bones and turned his blood cold, being at the mercy of men and rulers who dared for things far grander than themselves. Nothing would keep them from getting what they wanted. It was never a matter of sympathy—it was about outsmarting them.

Cyrus had been trying to outsmart these rulers since the day Sozar had hatched. He hadn't run because he was a coward but because he knew no deals could ever be made that would benefit him, the Dragon Rider. He could not lean on gaining sympathy, not in a time of impending war. His life had become a game of cat and mouse. After Razan and even Dameon, Cyrus had considered himself skilled in this chase. But he was wrong. These chains were proof that he'd never outsmarted anyone, he'd just gotten good at running. Sooner or later, though, Destiny was bound to catch up to him.

"Sozar?"

His voice was rugged, hoarse, barely audible to his own ears. Nothing.

Taking a deep breath, he searched within his mind for their mental link—any sign of the dragon's presence.

Nothing.

Terror filled him in an instant. "Sozar!" he screamed. This was not happening, *couldn't be*. The void in his mind was large, unused—it left him feeling empty. It was a feeling he'd only experienced once before, in the dungeons of Geral, but this . . . this was something else entirely. It was as if the dragon didn't even exist.

Alone. Cyrus was utterly alone.

It was him and his thoughts—whatever they were, because he couldn't quite think straight yet. He knew he was in a dungeon, could remember that he'd only just arrived in Delion, but the conclusions were coming too slow.

One thing stuck clear, though: he had been betrayed by his mother, locked up by kings, and stabbed in the back. All in a matter of a few seasons now. How he was still trying to see the good in people was beyond his comprehension. No, he was well past being furious.

He clenched his shaking hands into fists and gritted his teeth. Fiery tears rolled down his cheeks. This was no one else's fault but his own. Cyrus had walked right into danger, so distracted by old dreams and bitter wishes that he'd willingly strolled into unknown territory. Who was he to blame the others when he so willingly put himself in this danger? When he, a Dragon Rider, was so fucking gullible?

Cyrus had spent most of his life dreaming of finding his mother, and while he had known there was tension, he had never imagined she would abandon him again. She had sounded so convincing, like she had wanted this to work as much as him. She'd lied, though. He had spent so long trying to be loved, and now his own mother turned him over like scum. He felt like a fool. Worthless.

A loud bang broke the spell, and he shoved himself further into the back of the cell, until his back met cold stone. Muffled voices, then the deafening screech of metal sliding against metal as a door opened before him. A man stepped in, holding a lantern. It was the first time Cyrus was able to see his own hands, dirty from the dungeon's grime.

The man stood no taller than Cyrus's shoulder. His deep olive complexion and black hair contrasted boldly with those pale hazelnut eyes. It was an eye color Cyrus had not seen before, and he was momentarily caught off guard.

"Comfortable?" the man asked, voice thick with the Southern accent of Creitón. It was a mixture between Sorréle's tongue and something else entirely.

"No."

"Good." The man stepped forward, and Cyrus caught sight of two soldiers behind him. As his eyes fell back on the man holding the lantern, realization dawned on him. Despite the plain clothing, the man who stood before him was not just some guard—he was the king.

"Is it customary for kings to be assholes?" Cyrus asked. The last word had barely left his lips before the blunt sting of a slap burned his cheek. The king had struck him so hard that his neck swiveled and strained.

"It is when people like you are disrespectful."

"Where's my dragon?"

"Why are you here?" the king countered.

"Maybe I'll answer your questions if you answer mine."

That earned a cruel smile. "You are not in a position to make deals, Rider, and you know that. Let me tell you something." He leaned over and placed the lantern on a hook that was well beyond Cyrus's reach, then knelt to his level. "Your mother came to the palace in the middle of the night to turn you in. Told us you didn't mean anything to her, and that she wanted to prove her loyalty to the crown. She'd rather have a lifetime supply of coin than be your mother. That's got to hurt."

Cyrus gritted his teeth once more, not wanting to show a single emotion. The whole evening they'd shared, she'd been planning to report him to this king, all so she could pocket more coin. It was hideous. Yet more than anger, he felt that deep sense of abandonment.

Nobody wanted him. Not unless he could become exactly what they needed him to be: a weapon.

"Let me ask again," the king hissed. "Why are you here?"

A part of him knew he should comply—that same part that was begging him to play by the rules, so that he had a better chance at staying alive—but the other part of him was furious. Furious at the world, at the king, at his mother, at himself. Cyrus watched and waited, letting the moment settle between them in a stew of tension.

"No," he whispered. The word came out slow, low, and bold.

"Hm." The king cocked his head to the side. "Is that your final answer?"

Cyrus glared into the depths of those hideous eyes. As the seconds slipped between them, he reached out over and over to Sozar, trying to make contact but failing every time. That barrier that kept them apart was made of iron, thick and impenetrable. It made him reel with rage. After everything they'd been through, he should have been more equipped and prepared to protect the dragon.

Suddenly, the man's hands wrapped around his throat—hot—and squeezed. Cyrus jerked backward, but it was too late.

The claws had him. He grabbed at the hands, trying to yank them away, but his muscles were sluggish and weak. Fire lit his neck, a deep agony seeping all the way to his spine. The king's expression contorted into savagery, teeth bared. He pushed Cyrus back, and his head slammed against the stone with a burst of pain as he gasped for air. Already, his lungs were screaming.

"Father!"

The call shattered the moment, and the king lessened his grip. Another man appeared, with those same haunting eyes and black hair but far younger. He stood in the doorway, the guards pressed up behind him, as if terrified by their own ruler. "Are you done playing with your new toy?"

As the king retracted his grip, Cyrus inhaled sharply. His throat burned, but his lungs savored the air and his body tingled. Blinking, he reached for his neck and rubbed it—the skin was already tender. The newcomer was eying him.

"Do not interrupt my proceedings," the king retorted, and stood. "What is it that you want?"

His son smiled, eyes devoid of affection. "I've come to introduce the great King Raj and his son, but it seems you've already started." His words dripped with cold sarcasm.

Cyrus bit his tongue, no longer trusting himself to speak. What he wanted to ask was where Sozar was kept, or if they had him at all, but he refrained.

"You were late, Alaric," the king snapped. "A habit your mother taught you."

"But I have my father's ruthlessness," the prince countered, "don't forget that."

"Mm." The king turned his attention back to Cyrus. "You should consider your answers before I come back, Rider. Alaric may not interrupt me next time."

The words burst from his mouth before he could catch himself. "Why am I here?"

"Wouldn't you like to—"

Alaric stepped up to the king and hissed, "Careful, Father."

The dynamic between the two was tense, devoid of love, that much was clear. Cyrus watched a muscle in the king's jaw twitch as he ground his teeth and his shoulders rose and fell. There was an unspoken conversation that was happening between the two—Alaric posturing over his father, the king, who looked more apt to kill than a starved beast. It turned the humid air cold and made Cyrus want to crawl underneath the stone.

Finally, the king rolled his shoulders. "There cannot be a Dragon Rider in this country," he stated firmly. "Imagine what that would do to my authority. You're better off here than out there." He turned to leave but stopped just outside the door. When he glanced back, his eyes flashed with humor, as if he found this all entertaining. Perhaps he did. "It's amazing what a dragon is willing to do to keep his Rider alive."

And then he was gone.

The guards stood there, waiting for Alaric, who hovered just at the door. Cyrus lurched forward, engulfed by panic. "What have you done to him?" His voice shook, his body overcome by an impulse to run. "Tell me!"

Alaric regarded him for what felt like an eternity before he lifted his chin. "Your mother turned you in, Rider. How does that make you feel?"

Cyrus blinked. Was it their only goal, father and son, to remind him that he had no one to turn to? He should have returned to Sozar and not accepted the offer to stay. The tension that had been unresolved when he'd gone to sleep should have been proof enough that she was not to be trusted yet. But he had blindly accepted the offer in the belief that his mother would not be so cruel, even if they had issues they were working through.

He swallowed and met the prince's pale gaze. No response was needed. There was nothing he could say to this stranger. This prince didn't know his life, only what he wanted to believe, and Cyrus was comfortable letting him believe it for the time being.

Alaric smiled. "It hurts, doesn't it?"

He left, and the guards slammed the door behind him. The only light now was from that lantern hanging beyond his chained reach, and he wasn't sure how long that would last. He didn't even want the light. The darkness would at least hide his own hands from sight, the very hands that had gotten him here. A tear rolled down his cheek, fat and cold, until it splashed into the palm of his hand.

All he could do was wait. His head swam, his body weak still from the drug. He just hoped that it would all wear off soon enough, so that he could reach Sozar to make sure he was all right. Only then could he plan a way out.

THE BOY IN BLUE

here was very little that Morei let get to him, but last night had wiggled its way through his barriers and embedded itself into his chest. He routinely checked to make sure the ring was in its pouch rather than on his finger. While he was terrified of the relic, he couldn't justify *not* putting it on. There were answers in wearing it—answers that could guide him to some sort of redemption, control.

Yet Reyd's words nagged him, and no matter how often he shoved them aside, they still managed to crawl their way back to the forefront of his mind, like some pesky fly that wouldn't leave one alone. Better yet, it felt like he'd shoved his hand into a mound of ants and now couldn't shake them off.

It didn't sway his opinion, though. It only angered him.

Morei would not be scared, and he certainly wouldn't let the unknown change his opinion. Enough had already been taken away from him—he would not have his choices taken as well.

The sun's rays were cooler today, but with the gloves and cloak, the heat was unbearable. Thankfully, they wouldn't be necessary much longer.

He had waited to show himself, so that King Drexis would have time to receive word of the massacre at Geral, gather troops, and send them out to hunt for him. Drexis had forced his hand. The king had threatened to withhold valuable resources, made him a monster to his council if he did not obey Caster demands, and now he would have his revenge.

Everything had to be done strategically, though. First, he needed to find the right person, a person who would talk.

Morei made his way to the main street, finding it filled with people bustling about and market stands selling all sorts of goodies, from weapons, leather, and clothing, to art, to fruits, fish, and pastries. A community board stood at the center of the small village, covered in announcements and bounties. A poor sketch of him had been hung up, warning readers that he was a murderer and a traitor. Morei's bounty was considered a royal matter—the bounty didn't ask for commoners to confront him, but to report to the nearest soldier, trusting that word would reach Geral. They would be rewarded handsomely for their tip.

Next to his sketch was one of Syra Castello, the same he'd seen back in Geral. There were several other common thieves, but they were nowhere near as exciting.

When Morei had studied the board long enough, half-way hoping for someone to recognize him then and there, he strolled away. He bought himself a small batch of berries, which were sold in wrapped parchment and sealed with twine. When the lady had taken his Krye, he took the bundle and undid it as he walked through the crowd, enjoying the berries and people-watching.

A little girl tugged at her father's pants, pointing at a nearby pastry stand. The father, hands full with a basket of purchases that appeared to be tools for blacksmith work, motioned for her to grab some currency out his pocket, and she did so, running over to the stand and asking for one of the large twisted fried breads. He stood there, patient, until his daughter had what she needed, and then they were off.

To Morei's right, just behind the stands, several people were trading goods, although based on their scowls and callused hands, he assumed the items were illegal. A pouch slipped here and there between the two and then a quick nod before they were off on their respective ways.

Looking ahead as he brushed through the crowd, Morei found a dark-eyed gentleman walking toward him. His gait was certain, his eyes older than his skin, and his belt was engraved with gold. Around his throat, a necklace hung with a gold-shaped pendant that peeked out from between the folds of the tunic.

Nighthunter.

The necklace was a dead giveaway. Becoming a king came with an immense amount of education that the public was not given, and one thing that all rulers were beaten to know was the recognizable traits of the deadly Nighthunters. Necklaces were one—specifically, necklaces with the Old Tongue sigil, for courage. While anyone could wear sigils like that, the Nighthunter's was always custom-made to have *Brotherhood* inscribed along the bottom. Morei was too far to read such small scripture, but he was confident in his judgment. Especially with the wicked black ink of a tattoo just visible from underneath the man's collar. Tribal stuff that the Nighthunters did to emulate the Death Seekers, who bore what many simply knew as Marking.

Whoever he was here for, or where he was going, Morei wished the target luck. Nighthunters could fool most of the public, but not him. He had made sure to learn as much as he could about the assassins in hopes that he'd never have to come face-to-face with one.

Morei popped a few more berries into his mouth and chewed slowly. All about, the noises meshed into a raging storm. Yells, shouts, laughter, and beckoning—so much sound that he could allow himself to get lost, the voices in his head silenced. Dark Energy was always close by, her whispers constantly begging him to listen, but one did not listen to the song of the dead. To do so was a sure way to go mad.

The urge was getting stronger, though, and one day he might give in.

A caw caught his attention, and he turned his attention to a barrel on his left. It was just outside the river of people, and he saw a raven perched there. A single white tail feather contrasted vividly against its midnight coat and eyes. Something he had never seen before. Morei had heard of white ravens in the past, which some believed to be messengers from the Soul Realm, but he'd never seen one.

The raven bounced on the barrel and flapped its wings. Morei broke from the crowd and approached cautiously. A couple of berries wouldn't hurt the thing, and he was intrigued by it.

"Hey there," he greeted, voice low. The bird couldn't understand him, of course, but that didn't stop him from talking to the creature. Getting within four paces, he stopped as the bird took a step back. "Fair enough," he mumbled. It was closer than he'd thought he would manage.

He glanced into his hand. Five berries left—that would do. Stretching out his arm, he slowly opened his hand to the raven, showing it the food. When the bird cocked its head and took a half step forward, he did too.

The tuff of fur on the raven's beak bounced as it opened its mouth and cawed again, then bounced where it stood before another hop forward. Morei felt more confident now and closed the gap between them. He lay his hand beneath the bird's head.

A smile tugged at his lips; he felt like a boy again, completely oblivious to the world around him as the raven plucked a berry out of his hand and ate it. This bird was clearly used to being fed by people. "Smart one," he complimented, more to himself. "If I was a bird, I'd hang out here too."

And if he were a bird, he'd fly far from here and disappear entirely from the world. But it seemed Destiny had other plans, plans that he no longer wished to ignore. If Destiny chose him to do her bidding, he would abide and court the monsters in his head.

Morei had already turned his back on his own people, burned innocent lives, and slaughtered in hatred, so what would be the difference if he made the entire city of Caster his own personal playground?

An empire, a voice whispered to him. His own. He would build an empire and make Geral pay for what it had taken from him.

The raven took the last berry and swallowed it, then turned its head slightly to stare at Morei. As he met its gaze, he felt a chill encompass his body. There was such intelligence in this little creature's look, it felt like he was meeting the eyes of another man rather than a bird.

With a few flaps, the bird took off, disappearing above him and over a building. Morei retracted his hand and stood there for a long moment, absorbing the little silence he had been bestowed. The world was a loud place, and he realized then how much he wished to be back in the desert, amid the leagues of untouched land.

"Sir?"

Morei tore his gaze from the empty barrel to find a small boy standing next to him. He was dressed in blue, and an ugly scar stretched across his lip and over his left cheek, making his upper lip abnormally shaped and his front teeth more exposed. A mop of black hair sat on his head over big brown eyes. He looked tiny for his age, and Morei knelt to meet him at eye level.

There was a force coming from this boy, a sensitivity to the world of energy harvesting. Morei could feel it brush up against his own consciousness. The first thing he thought of was Ezra. He had never encountered another Energy Harvester with Ezra's potential—save for the boy who now stood before him. He swallowed and shoved that thought aside.

He would be perfect. With a nod, Morei asked, "Can I help you?"

The boy stared at him. He opened his mouth to speak but then closed it again. Morei tilted his head. "Are you lost?" Doubtful, but he still wanted to ask.

With a shake of his head, the boy glanced around. His eyes looked leagues away, as if he could see beyond the living realm. Warmth spread over Morei's entire body—this boy was not lost, but curious.

"You feel it," he observed, and leaned over to pick up a handful of dirt with his gloved hand. "Have you done anything yet with this ability of yours?"

A big grin stretched across the boy's face. "I made a flower for Mother!"

That made him laugh. Innocence was precious. "Did she like it?"

"Yeah."

"Good," he replied. "Then bring her this." Morei pulled upon the Light Energy around him—lifeforces from the grass, bugs, people passing by who would never know the slight draw from the power they could never reach, and even his own from within—to evolve the dirt into a simple pink rose. Only once before had he been so intentional: when he'd carved a blue stone out from the heart of a flower to show Ezra what power was. He wondered if the new King Geral still held that stone.

The stem was short, but the flower itself was big, plump, and alive. He carefully unfolded his hand to meet the growth and revealed it to the little boy. "Do you think she'll like this?"

His brown eyes were wide, his grin permanent. "Yes!"

Morei rested the flower in the boy's hands. "Careful with it, then. If she asks, you tell her a king made it." The boy wouldn't understand, but he had no doubt his mother would, and that was all he needed. Word would travel quickly after that.

The boy nodded.

"Your ability to harvest will strengthen as you grow older," Morei continued, "but don't ever do something you do not know for sure you can succeed in. Your energy harvesting is only as strong as you, do you understand?" There was no certainty that this boy had a mentor to look up to in his life, and he suddenly felt responsible to shove as much education into this moment as he could without overwhelming the child.

"You may think yourself greater than the rest, even your parents, but don't let this gift define your actions. You are responsible for this gift as much as for the horse you are gifted. Take care of it and it will bring you good things."

"Okay," the boy mumbled.

"Dark Energy." Morei motioned to the fire pit that danced with life across the street. The boy's eyes drew toward it, already entranced by those flames. "Such power takes great mastery. You mustn't seek that until you have mastered Light Energy. It may call to you—perhaps it already does—but do not listen. It will eat you alive if you allow it."

Morei watched the boy, noting how he crinkled his brow in concern but his eyes remained unwavering. He was scared, as he should be.

"Fire will harm those it does not control," he warned. "Any element of Dark Energy will, for that matter." That was something he did not need to experiment with to know. He was a servant to Dark Energy, and for that, he'd been saved from the torturous end of being burned alive. To some, maybe that would've been a benefit. To Morei, it was a reminder that the option of ending his life had been taken from him.

"Run along," Morei blurted out, no longer wishing to entertain the boy. His heart was beating slower, his limbs felt cold, and his thoughts had turned sour. The boy disappeared among the hordes of people.

With a final glance at the barrel, still finding it empty, Morei made his slow way back to River's Inn. The afternoon was growing older, the shadows taller, and it would not be long before dusk had her time. When that happened, he intended to be nestled away with a full stomach in his room, waiting.

Waiting for Caster.

BAD OMEN

Syra wandered the halls. She didn't feel any rush to get back, but she also didn't feel like exploring. She let her feet carry her to wherever they desired. In time, she would work her way back to her chamber, have a bath, eat, and rest before the coming night. For now, her emotions were still in shambles from the earlier confrontation with Zarek.

Life was complicated, and it was becoming more so with each passing day. No longer were her concerns focused on Caster's Port and the fishermen who arrived each day to deliver their catch, shop, and then set sail once more. It was about the future of realms, Chaos, and her heritage with the Soul Realm. There was simply no way to digest who she had become.

Syra slowed next to a door with a sigil she did not recognize. It was a crescent moon with arching lines above it. She stared, but she could not place the Old Tongue meaning, although if it was in this west region, it had to be related to some sort of meeting chamber? Still, she didn't open it—that felt intrusive.

All about, people wandered by. Most kept to themselves, but a few stared hard at her, or so she felt, as if they were trying to tell her something without ever opening their mouths. Maybe they *did* have something to say, but she didn't wait long enough to see.

Syra averted her gaze. It felt like everyone here wanted to devour her whole. The tension was palpable, the steps of those around her slowed, as if they were ready to pounce.

Footsteps echoed loud behind her, and Syra turned just in time to see a man spit at her. The wad of saliva landed just next to her boot as he latched on to her arm and yanked her close. "You are a disgrace," he hissed. Onlookers glanced but kept moving along. Nobody stopped or demanded he let go of her, and she couldn't tell what shocked her more: the man's hatred for her or the lack of intervention.

He released her just as quickly, and she dropped a hand to the hilt of her sword. The sheath always remained unlatched for this very reason. Syra held her tongue and waited. There was no point in wasting her energy on verbal insults—if this was going to turn into a clash, she needed to be prepared.

His eyes dropped to the weapon and then rose back to her face. His lip curled up in a snarl. "I wouldn't waste my strength on you."

Coward.

"The world will eat you up," he told her. "Better that way."

A force slammed into her back, and Syra stumbled to catch her footing. Behind her, two more men now stood, cornering her. One was missing his front tooth and looked like he hadn't bathed in at least a cycle.

"Pretty sword you got there." He jutted his chin in her direction. "Pay a lot of coin just to have that one around—"

"I'll stab you with it," she snapped, heat rising to her cheeks. The three were taller than her, but she wasn't going to let it get to her. She let her eyes meet each of theirs, annoyed that they had interrupted her day. "If you intend to intimidate me, you can't."

The first one tried to grab her arm, but she yanked it free before he could tighten his grip. "Touch me or hurt me in any way, and I'll be the least of your problems," she told them.

When they paused, she added, "Piss off a Guardian and he might damn your souls himself."

Zarek would be an issue. No matter what was transpiring between them, he would have her back if she were hurt, but she withheld the threat of Sekar. Better for no one to know about him. If they thought a vengeful Guardian was scary . . .

She smiled.

"What're you smilin' about?" the guy on the left asked—the toothless one. "He ain't even said anything back."

The answer slipped before she could even stop herself. "Your deaths."

Now they took a step back. Bad omen or not, she wondered what they believed to have warranted such a reaction. Did they think she would burst into flames right here? Regardless, she would use it to her advantage.

The first one still scowled, while the middle one curled his upper lip. The one on her right hissed, "We're going to wipe that smile right off your face."

He turned and slipped back into the passing crowd, and the others followed immediately. A few onlookers watched, keeping their tongues to themselves, and Syra returned their stares—hard. She wanted them to know she was watching them. Always.

But she was still shaken up underneath the hard exterior. She knew there were people who didn't like her—that much had become clear—but this was the first time they had become physical with her. She felt flush from the sudden encounter, and if she could have submerged herself in some sort of ice bath, she would have. She forced deep breaths in. That man could have done more to her, and she wasn't sure she'd have been able to act quick enough to protect herself. Bound to Chaos or not, she still didn't know yet how to harvest it.

The twins, Eva and Arik, had told Keryn that she possessed powerful energy harvesting skills and that she should be further questioned. The leader's questions had not been as intense as Syra anticipated, but clearly the twins knew something was different about her. Hopefully not the truth. If they knew, then they'd also know she was something more, something . . . otherworldly. A Goddess. A term she loathed—merely thinking about it made her cringe.

There was no longer a reason for her to be wandering these halls. Her mood had soured, and her muscles were tired. She did not take her hand off the hilt of the sword as she made her way back to her chamber. Several times, she got lost and found herself more irritated than she would've been before. There was simply no way to navigate these halls consistently.

She didn't ask for help, of course. After today, she was just grateful she hadn't stabbed someone. Her patience was running thin with them all. The old Syra would have shed a tear. The person she was becoming was angrier, quicker to snap, and had less tolerance for the world. In a summer, she might be unrecognizable even to herself.

Though her stomach grumbled, she refused to stop or look for the galley. Syra would eat later, once the tension in her shoulders eased.

When she finally found her chamber, she nearly yelled in celebration. It had been quite some time, and she knew the afternoon was well upon her. She recognized the door, which had a gold-plated sun—representative of an honorary guest, thanks to Keryn—and she knew it was hers from the tall plant outside with its wide leaves and orange flowers.

She entered and closed the door behind her. Probably too quickly, given how relieved she was to be alone, away from the rest of this place. There were far too many people with their own motives, and that made her uncomfortable. Syra locked the door—a simple bolt that slid over and hooked into a loop.

It was time for a bath.

SHATTER THE BOLD

The cold sting of the slap radiated down his jaw. Cyrus coughed and kicked out, his foot landing true on the soldier's groin. The guard moaned and stumbled backward just as the other one yanked Cyrus forward by his chains. His jaw struck the floor hard, his shoulder following, and he tasted copper. There was no time to react before a kick lit up his side with fiery pain.

"Ready to eat, Rider?" the first guard asked. "Or do you want to continue?"

He didn't move. They were drugging the food to keep his senses dull, and he was refusing to eat. It had only taken one skipped meal for them to figure it out, and now he was suffering the consequences. But Cyrus was desperate to reach Sozar, and he knew he was close—all he needed was *time*.

His stomach clenched as two strong hands hoisted him up and shoved him back against the wall. Blinking, he stared at the men as one held his hands down with enough force for the metal to dig into the skin. It was only a matter of time before the skin broke or he'd rub them raw—already, the area was bruised and tender.

Cyrus tried to kick out again, but a punch to the jaw stilled him. His head spun as the other guard approached him with a mug, undoubtedly to drug him. He knew Sozar was near, that much had become obvious, but he could not yet reach the dragon. It was like a dense fog that wouldn't clear.

It had all happened so fast. One day, Cyrus was flying over the endless blue waters and filled with purpose, the next he was in a dark stone dungeon surrounded by men who thought he was the literal reason everything was wrong with the world. In the haze that had become his normalcy, Cyrus couldn't fathom how he'd ended up here. It felt like he had finally gotten life under control, despite all the obstacles, only to have Destiny wrap her callused fingers around his throat. Fate's joke had never been so cruel as it was now.

"Open up."

Cyrus jerked himself away and kicked again. This time, he struck the leg of the soldier who held the liquid, and he relished the moment as the man almost dropped the mug. Liquid sloshed and splashed to the ground, and then Cyrus received a kick directly into the ribs. Agony filled his chest—hot, unrelenting—and he hissed, but he refused to show the pain.

They would not win there.

"You're scum," said the man to his left. He took the chains and wrapped them around Cyrus's wrists and hands, over the cuffs, and tightened them as far as he could. Bruising pain radiated up his arms as he tried to move his hands, but he was pinned now, and the same soldier grinned. "You like that?"

"Kick him," the other guard ordered. "We got orders to give this, but we weren't told how. Guess that means we can do whatever we want with you."

And then, in one flash, the world caved in on him. Both men started kicking and punching relentlessly. Cyrus tried to move, to jerk away, anything to avoid the assault, but he couldn't. Boots made contact with every part of his body, punches targeted his head and chest, and he started wheezing. The pain all evolved into one continuous wave—he could not pinpoint what was hurt, if anything was broken, or if he was going to die, and it didn't matter.

Cyrus's strength was sapped. He slouched against the stone, hardly able to move or adjust himself. He was certain, given the sharp stab he felt every time he breathed, that a rib or two was broken, but still he did not cry out. He wouldn't. A tear rimmed his eye and rolled down his cheek without his permission.

Hands clawed at his mouth and pried his lips apart. Cyrus's mind raced. He wanted—no, needed—to do something, but he could hardly move. His body rejected his orders, and his vision swayed in and out of focus. This was how he would die.

"Give me space," one of them said, and he felt his mouth stretched as wide as it would go, cheek muscles straining. He was now acutely aware that the warmth on his tongue was blood. His blood.

Ice-cold liquid splashed over his face and then into his mouth. Cyrus tried to refuse it, but the soldier squeezed his nose shut. With his head shoved up against stone and his neck strained, he could no longer breathe, and he couldn't turn to spit it out. There was a pungent taste to the liquid that made him want to gag—was it water? With no saying how much of the drug they'd put in, he couldn't tell if swallowing this was going to severely impair him to a point of no return, or even kill him.

His lungs screamed, his heart pounded frantically, and his mind twisted into a desperate need to live by getting air. Cyrus choked the liquid down, burning all the way to his stomach.

It was already happening. The poison, drug, toxin—it was changing him.

The soldier pinching his nose released, and Cyrus gulped in air. The chains around his hands and wrist loosened, and he slumped over to his side without fight, gasping.

"Sleep well," one of them said, and laughed. They retreated from the room and slammed the door shut.

Cyrus just lay there, staring at the base of the door. The light from a new lantern hung to his left, but the oil was low. It was already fading, and he was sure it would die in a matter of minutes and plunge him into darkness. With the drug coursing through him, his senses impaired, he was no longer entirely sure how much time was passing.

All he knew was that he was starving, and that he needed to somehow reach Sozar. He had no idea what they had done to the dragon, and as he couldn't feel anything from their bond, he worried about all the possible tortures. The king himself had hinted as much on their meeting, yet he'd not seen the man since. Cyrus was supposed to be the one protecting Sozar, chosen because the dragon had trusted his soul. Yet here they were, separated and unable to connect. He'd tried hard to listen for noises, hopeful that he might hear something—anything—that could indicate Sozar was closer than he realized. All hopeless.

If he was this drugged and blocked from communication, from feeling the dragon, would he even know if Sozar was seriously harmed? The possibility that they had done something terrible made it hard to focus on anything. There was no way Cyrus could ever live with himself if they had.

Fueled by this thought, he pulled himself up onto his knees. His mind was sluggish, his entire body engulfed in a fire, and his left eye pulsing with a life of its own—he was sure it was swollen based on the way the skin tugged every time he blinked.

Perhaps he would be a blind Dragon Rider by the end of it all. The Rider who lost his vision from being imprisoned and beaten. The thought crossed his mind, and he tried to laugh, but nothing came out. Nothing but a wheeze.

As his stomach twisted in discomfort from what lay within, he raised his right hand and placed two fingers on his tongue. Desperation was so heavy on his mind that he would do anything to rid himself of what they'd fed him. Cyrus shoved his fingers into the back of his throat and started to cough. He lurched forward but kept his fingers in place, holding himself up with his left hand. He started to gag, and his stomach heaved its contents.

The liquid came up in one foul swoop and splashed all over the floor in front of him. His throat burned, and his stomach convulsed. He stayed there, weak, unable to move as he beheld the liquid. Drool dripped from his lips and joined its companion below until he collapsed to his side.

The cold stone had never felt as welcoming as it did then, and he submitted himself to the slumber that awaited.

CROOKED AS THE WOLF

Patience was not a trait Morei had ever prided himself on. He was impatient at times, intolerable at others; he was a man who wanted to get things done. But sometimes there were things well beyond his control, and waiting was the name of the game.

Sitting on the cot in his rented room, Morei waited. The commotion from outside was loud—the bar full, the patrons cheering and singing—and he listened. Men and women yelled, mugs were slammed into the tables, creating a ruckus of noise that made him want to stab the nearest person. Peace, that was what he desired. It had become more and more a requirement for his soul as the days had worn on. Noise meant chaos; noise kept his senses frayed and his ears alert. Silence gave him a chance to prepare.

Tonight, however, as the entertainment went on, it was a harsh quietness that he searched for. And it would happen soon, he had no doubt.

He sat there as patient as one could be when they knew their time of freedom was almost up. And amid that, he felt not anxiety but excitement for the future. What happened next would be *his* decision and no one else's. There was nothing more liberating than that.

The blanket still hung over the mirror, and his thoughts returned to the night before. Answers evaded him; he could not determine whether what he'd experienced had been a dream or real. If it was real, that gave him pause. It unsettled him to think this dark woman, whoever she may be, was haunting him, even if the ring was not on. Yet he could not ignore such power. To control this kind of relic was to control the world.

Suddenly, the music halted, and a chair squealed.

It was time.

Shouts, followed by a muffled conversation. Morei glanced down at his gloved hands, which rested on his thighs, and double checked that the Lirallian Ring rested in the palm of his hand between the leather and skin. They would pat him down, strip him of his weapon and belt, and try to demoralize him, but they wouldn't succeed.

After all, this was his decision, not theirs.

Heavy boots neared, and his grip tightened on his legs. Breaths escaped quicker, and the hot embrace of excitement engulfed him.

The steps stopped before his door, hesitation filling the space. Then, a weak knock.

"Uh—" It was the innkeeper's voice. "Sir?"

Pathetic.

Morei cleared his throat, eyes locked on the little bit of the mirror that wasn't covered. He could see his boots and the edges of his cloak. "Can I help you?"

"Could you—" His voice was swept away from pounding on the door. That was more like it.

"Open the fucking door," a man growled. "We know you're in there."

Morei almost laughed. "And who might I be?"

"I ain't playin'," the man said, and slapped the door hard. "I'll bust the door down—"

With a flick of his wrist, Morei turned the lock from where he sat. It didn't take much, just a slight draw of lifeforce to manipulate the energy that made up the bolt. As he felt the final tug of metal slide against metal, he announced, "It's open."

The door swung open, yet still no noise came from the room where the patrons sat—all presumably awaiting the grand piece of entertainment. A crowd of men in blue and gold uniform surrounded the fat innkeeper. Morei gestured at them and asked, "What took you so long?"

Then, as if a fire had burst to life, Caster soldiers stormed into the room and grabbed him in every spot imaginable. Hands held his arms and legs, a punch met his jaw, and the shrieking cry of metal shackles echoed as they were clasped around his wrists with bruising force. Another man ripped his belt off, taking away the familiar weight that he had once found so reassuring, another searched his cloak and clothes, patting him down with unnecessary force to ensure he had no other weapons. Hands slipped inside his boots to pull out the dagger he so often forgot about and handed the weapon to another who had his belt. Never once did they stumble on the ring, because it lay comfortably inside his glove.

When they had exhausted their assault and yanked him off his cot to stand, two men took up either side, holding his arms with an iron grip. "Let's move," a soldier ordered from near the door. His scruffy beard made him look dirty, his piercing blue eyes twinkling with a sense of triumph. *What it must feel like to capture and detain the Demon King*, he mused to himself as they started to walk.

As he approached the innkeeper, Morei met his eyes and nodded. "Thanks for the room."

The man opened his mouth and then closed it again before another soldier snapped, "Shut it, murderer."

Boots creaked along the floor, offering a break from the foreboding silence as Morei was escorted out of the room and down the hall. His hands rested in front of him, the chains wrapped around his waist to keep so they wouldn't drag on the floor. He did not speak, did not argue or fight, just obeyed their commands.

As they exited the hall, he became the entertainment of all the feasting eyes of the dining room. Morei leveled his gaze with everyone. There was not a single person who could hold his eyes, and that made him smile.

The dark humor in all this did not escape him, even as he was shoved out of the inn and into the street where horses awaited. The sky was dark, the stars muffled by town lights, and the crisp cool air forced goosebumps along his arms, despite the cloak. He was used to the desert heat, not the chill of oncoming winter.

They stopped him in front of a white horse dressed simply in reins and a saddle, not like the other steeds, which were garnished with Caster attire and the wolf imprint. Morei did not wait for orders. He lifted his hands as far as they would go before the chains ceased movement. Three men encircled him and, without comment, hoisted him up. He swung his leg around, latched on to the front of the saddle, and adjusted himself until he was comfortable in the seat.

The reins were longer and tied to the left side of a soldier's saddle, keeping the horses incredibly close. In a final call, the soldiers all jumped on as a crowd of onlookers watched from afar. Nobody cheered or groaned; nobody even spoke. It was as if the entire scene unfolding was taboo, yet no one dared to look away.

Maybe they couldn't. Maybe the sheer idea of the Demon King in the small town of Gamer's Village was too unbelievable and they all had to see it for themselves. He had been missing for nearly a moon cycle, and many had likely believed him dead among the desert storms.

As they all started outward, toward the bridge that made the village so famous, the soldier who had his horse twisted in his seat and asked, "How's it feel to be the prisoner, eh?" His tone was dismissive and challenging at the same time. He was looking for a response.

Morei flashed him a cold smile, certain that he would make the man squirm. "It's exactly where I wanted to be, soldier."

The smug expression contorted, and the man grumbled, turning away again.

They rode in silence, but Morei never stopped smiling. This was the start of the end—this was how he would bring the city of Caster to its knees and under his control.

This was how he would build an empire.

THE GRAY REALM

yra paced, then sat down on her bed. Then she paced again and sat once more. It was a vicious cycle that had consumed her time since she had finished eating. Once she had cleaned up and dressed herself in a blue wool sweater and pants, she'd made quick use of the galley down the hall and grabbed a plate of fresh bread, fruit, and a few cured slices of lamb. The staff was refreshingly friendly and had even offered to bring her food as needed, but she had declined. It would do little good to have staff bringing her food when she had no idea her whereabouts or even when Sekar would show. More importantly, it was too risky. Just because three staff members were nice didn't mean the rest would be just as welcoming.

The empty plate sat on a dresser—she would take care of it once she was done, but she had been too anxious to return it to the galley. He could show at any time, and she wanted to be here for it.

Her heart pounded like she had gone for a run, but it was only from nerves. It had been a long time since she had felt this way—where her fingers tingled and her lungs felt like they were being strangled. At this point, she was sure her cheeks had flushed from the building anxiety, but she hoped otherwise. When she was younger, she had been teased constantly for her red cheeks, and while she had grown accustomed to it and even learned to ignore the naysayers when she was older, it occasionally still bothered her.

Syra shook out her hands. Why was she so worried about that? This was Sekar she was talking about—they had ridden on horseback and traveled together for over two moon cycles. If anyone knew her best, it was him. He hadn't cared about the grungy attire or the days they would go without bathing. They had made it work and been forced to make friends quick, but that had been easy—

A noise caught her attention, and she straightened in the bed. When she turned her head, there he was, dressed in gray and black with a hilt and sword and a satisfied smile. *Knowing.* Her suspicion had been right—he had expected her to say yes. For a fleeting instant, she wished she'd said no, just to see his reaction.

"Blue looks good on you," he complimented. "And I see you're dressed. Am I to assume we have a deal?"

"You're late," she announced, standing. It was well past when she had expected to see him, and she made sure to show her annoyance. He wanted the world to revolve around him, but she wouldn't be a part of that.

Sekar did a dramatic bow. "Obligations made me late, my princess."

She rolled her eyes. "All right, don't call me that."

"Accept who you are," he responded, and approached. "Princess of the Soul Realm, daughter of Nala, and heir to the throne. Or do you want to ignore that all?"

Syra held up a hand. "I'm not here to start an argument. I just don't want to be called princess. It's . . ." *Odd.* The word never left her tongue. Between his proximity and her impulsive urge to tell him to leave—a desperate need to keep the peace between her mind and soul—the words failed her.

"Very well." Sekar stood before her now, smelling rich with cinnamon and other spices. For all she knew, he had come from a bakery. But he didn't press her for an explanation, which relieved her. He reached out with a gloved hand and cupped her jaw. Gentle and warm. She hated how the touch made her feel, how his gaze consumed her. She was angry at him, rightfully so after what he'd done to her, yet without thought, she'd let his hand wander too close. "Have we a deal, Syra?"

Zarek's warning rang through her head. "How do I know I can trust you?"

The question did not alarm him like she'd expected. His expression remained the same. "If I did not care for you or the Soul Realm, you would have never made it to the Infernol."

His eyes held the same storm she had come to know so well, before she knew him to be the God of Dreams. They always had a way of picking apart every piece of her without ever trying. Slowly, she muttered, "Then we have a deal."

Sekar grinned like a boy who had received his first sword. "A good choice."

"Where will we train?"

He slipped his hand from her jaw to around her waist in one quick motion. The act made her want to disappear in to the floor as he pressed himself against her. "The Gray Realm. Hold on."

Syra knew better than to ask questions. She grabbed him in return and squeezed as the world around her turned to mist. The familiar sensation of being tugged engulfed her, so she held him tighter, afraid to be torn away into a void between realms. That, she assumed, would be an eternal prison, and she wanted nothing to do with that.

The darkness was fleeting before oranges and grays filled her vision. As her feet felt the ground beneath her, the air was ripped from her lungs.

It was hot, but not in a sense that made her sweat. The air was charged—*alive*—and she felt like one wrong breath might turn the ground into a burning pit of metal and consume them both. Even the air tasted different, metallic. All around, an endless desert landscape that stretched for leagues, and the mountains in the far distance didn't look ordinary. They appeared as giant horns jutting from the world, sharpened to points and the color of blackened charcoal. Even the sand had an orange tint to it that made it look unnatural, and when Syra knelt to run her fingers through it, it dissolved like dust and was swept away in an unseen wind.

Above her, the sky was a pale grayish orange. Not a cloud occupied the endless sky, only the red sun that hung low over the horizon ahead.

As she straightened, Sekar said, "Welcome to the Gray Realm."

"Is . . . Are we the only living things here?" she asked, unable to take her eyes off the horn-like mountains. Here, the world of her emotions felt out of reach.

"There are things here," he began, and gestured about them, "that will not harm us. They are beyond the natural creations of prey and predator. They exist as a result of pure concentration of Chaos. You may see them during your time here, but they do not come about easily."

"This place," Syra said, "what is it?"

"Home to Chaos," Sekar said. "Here, all forms of energy exist at once. Any form of energy harvesting will not harm you, and if anything is destroyed here, it will regenerate. If you tried training in the living realm, you would risk significant consequences."

"How?" she pressed.

He nodded. "Chaos, uncontrolled, could destroy anything in a five-league radius, along with the Harvester. That is why I stress to train you, and we will do so here, where the consequences are minimal."

This realm was hauntingly beautiful in its own right, and she couldn't believe she had never known of it prior. "Do the other Gods come here?"

"No," Sekar responded. "Chaos has granted me access here. No one can enter at will; one must be given permission by her, and even I must ask every time I wish to enter. Anyone who enters without Chaos's approval will be crushed, their lifeforce disintegrated into nothingness. Gods included."

Syra raised a hand and touched her chest. "But me . . ."

"Chaos is aware of you," he answered. "She knew of your arrival in advance, knew you would need to be trained—remember, she chose you to serve her. That is why you can stand here without any issues. If you were not welcomed, you would be dead by now."

"Oh."

Sekar reached for her arm. "No need to worry." He tugged her hand away from her chest and squeezed it, but only slightly, as if to prove she was really there. She let him, too caught up in the shock to be annoyed. "Here, you can exhaust your abilities, practice whenever, or harvest enough energy to destroy the living. Make it burn, destroy everything, whatever you desire, but it will always regenerate to its original form." The God let go of her hand, which she let fall back to her side. "Shall we begin?"

The panic she'd felt prior to his arrival returned. Syra was a bundle of nerves. "Where do you even start? What do I do?" She turned her hands around in front of her, studying the lines that traced across her skin and told the story of her life.

"When you master your abilities, you can do endless things here. For me, illusions are what Chaos granted me, so I can change my surroundings to become anything I want, even memories." At that, Sekar stepped forward and raised a hand. He did not flinch, nothing about him changed, but in a rippling flash, the illusion began. The ground gave way to the lapping waves of a lazy sea, the otherworldly sky transformed into the crystal blue she knew so well. She even saw some seagulls flying by. In the distance, a ship sailed, its red flag raised. Syra looked down to see the sandy beach her boots were sinking into. No more horned mountains or orange sand; not even the metallic scent of the Gray Realm reached her.

Sekar stood there with her and smiled, clearly pleased with himself. "This is the coast along Helyna Falls, just on the south side of Eiyrǎl. Dragon Riders used to come here as part of their training, and they would have to identify the song that the waves created when they lapped against the shore. It's an old tune." Sekar glanced her way and then moved his hand just slightly.

The scene cracked. All around her, lines cut through the image, and the reality he had built shattered into a thousand pieces without a sound. An arrow whizzed by her head, heat brushed her skin, and the sky turned gray and red as fires leapt upward. Soldiers raced by, their once-polished armor now dented and covered in ash. Her eyes fell on the crestless, red-armored soldiers, their swords raised. As she beheld them, a new figure appeared, walking alone. His black armor was a bold comparison to the surrounding carnage, along with his crimson gaze and pale blue skin. In his hand was Death's Sword, drenched in gore.

It was Sekar in the form of the Guardian she had come to know so well. Kar.

Syra stepped back, stunned at the scene unraveling before her, and felt her boot hit against something. She turned, and her knees went weak. Her foot had landed on the hand of one of the dead.

"A memory. This was during the Diyrǎllian Massacre," Sekar told her as they watched him in his Guardian form step up to a lone man. He was unperturbed by the violence. "Hm."

Again, he flicked his wrist, and the world around her folded in on itself before she could see the rest of what happened.

A bitter wind whipped at her clothes now, and she crossed her arms as her hair was torn from side to side. Snow. It struck her face hard, and she looked down to avoid the blizzard coming at her. Something moved beneath her boots, and a large eye appeared, slit-like and brown. It blinked lazily at her but did not move.

"Uh—"

"One of my dreams," he interjected. "Nothing more."

And then, like sand caught in wind, the eye disintegrated, along with the rest of the snow and ice. The harsh orange sand of the Gray Realm reappeared. The red sun and the jagged horn mountains felt comforting after so much swift change. Syra had known Sekar was powerful, but seeing him in action was a different story. She felt like an ant next to him. Here was a God who had centuries of experience over her—he could do anything he wanted.

"Master your power," he announced next to her, "and the world is your playground."

The ground began to shake violently. Tremors jarred her bones, and she snatched Sekar's arm to keep herself steady. Ahead, the ground bulged upward. Sand fell away, and the stone that had been underneath—how deep, she did not know— emerged and tumbled. But underneath, she watched as rock arose. It grew larger, taller, stretching to the sky. The ground broke away with a deafening roar as the mountain burst through and continued onward until Syra could no longer see the peak or the land beyond. The mountain blocked everything in front of her, and it would take quite the walk to make it to either side.

Syra's mouth fell open as she looked between the mountain and him. Yes, the God of Dreams was powerful. Terrifyingly so. If this was what he did for fun, then she feared what he did when he was angry or had a point to prove.

Sekar removed his hand. Syra let go of him, steady but suddenly aware of her own actions. In a moment's notice, she'd latched on to him. Love and hate danced on a thin line, but she was mostly disgruntled with his smugness. She didn't have to ask him to know he enjoyed it.

"Now, it's your turn."

She motioned at the mass wall of rock that now protruded upward. "Am I supposed to replicate that?"

"No, it's an illusion." He shrugged. "Although if you do that on your first try, I would be impressed."

The tone of his voice suggested sarcasm, and she raised a brow in response, trying to bury her exasperation. "What should I do?"

They turned to the open landscape ahead, where the orange sand was cast in shadow. "Anything. The goal is to start small. Remember, it comes from here—" Sekar pressed his finger into his chest. "Much like harvesting any energy, you shouldn't overdo it. Chaos is already an exhausting force to manage . . ." The God frowned. "Are you familiar with Dark Energy?"

She nodded. "Some. Zarek taught me a little bit about it when he trained me."

"Ah." Sekar leaned in now, seeming entertained. "And did he train you on harvesting?"

"Yes." Syra crossed her arms and eyed him defensively. "He's the only one who has so far, so don't be cruel. You certainly didn't teach me anything when we traveled together."

Unbelievably, he laughed. "Then you didn't learn a thing while we were together," he replied, and gestured outward. "Go."

His answer didn't make sense. "What do you mean—"

"*Go*," he pressed, smile gone, eyes cold. There was no room for debate, and it was clear that he was upset.

Syra licked her lips and looked ahead. Whatever he was angry about was a conversation for another time. If he squirmed, then good—it meant she had caught him by surprise, which was a rarity. The God, despite everything, had felt he had taught her *something* on their travels together, even if wasn't swordsmanship or energy harvesting.

"Okay," she mumbled to herself. Syra let her mind go blank. She shoved the fleeting thoughts aside, put herself into an empty chamber, and slowed her breathing. If Zarek had taught her anything, it was that harvesting energy took concentration, and she couldn't do that with her head full of concerns, worries, and questions. Chaos, she assumed, was the same basics.

She became acutely aware of the buzzing. It was all around— the very air she inhaled was so charged that it hummed with a life of its own. How had she missed that? Syra was supposed to harvest the Chaos from within herself, not draw upon the energy around her, like with Light Energy. Her mind focused inward, trying to identify anything that felt like energy.

Time continued on while she stood there, motionless. Sekar did not press or rush her. He remained quiet, which helped. She could feel the slight movement of energy shifting inside her, but grabbing it was proving more difficult than she realized. Every time she got close, ready to pounce and manage it, it evaded her with one swift motion.

Patience. A virtue she was quickly losing as she became more and more aware of how long she'd been standing there. Her thoughts grew muddled and she clenched her jaw, refusing to say anything, eyes locked straight ahead.

"Frustration will not speed up the process," Sekar observed, breaking the silence for the first time. He was watching her closely. "You've never been the most patient person." She couldn't tell if he was amused or annoyed.

Syra let an exhale escape between her lips but refrained from saying anything. Instead, she poured herself back into grabbing ahold of that energy. It was moving quicker, avoiding her at every turn. Syra felt like a predator hunting prey—desperate, enraged, foaming at the mouth—

There it was. She had it. And just as her mental fingers wrapped around it, the heat of the force overcame her entire body at once. Syra stumbled backward and looked down at her hands, expecting to see them consumed by flames, but they weren't. The hum was loud now, a constant in her ears, and she shook her head to try and rid herself of it.

"Chaos accepts you," Sekar told her. "That hum will lessen as you gain more control."

She looked at him. "Do you hear it?"

"No, but I know the sound." He gestured in front of her. "Do something now. I won't tell you what to do, because it's different for everyone. Follow your instincts. From there, we can begin to determine your strength."

Syra raised an eyebrow at him. "Strength?"

"Gift," he clarified. "Your strength will not be the same as mine, or Helyna's, or Greve's."

"Ah." She understood now. The strength or gift was what she would be known to do, what Chaos had deemed her worthy of. Syra let the air in slowly, relying heavily on the sound of her heartbeat to steady herself, which was nearly suffocated by the hum. What would she do? What *could* she do?

The answer was simple: anything.

Raising her hand, she brought it to rest midway and let her thoughts wander. So many things she wanted to do, but none quite struck her interest or spoke to her. The humming was incessant, borderline annoying, but she used it to keep her head free of other unnecessary things. As she let the force of Chaos fill her mind, she saw memories flash. Memories that were out of chronological order, in disarray. She focused on the smallest details, the quick, passing moments in the grand vision.

Suddenly, she was staring at the broken wings of a dragonfly. The wings were crumpled, pieces torn out, and the small creature lay lifeless on the dock before her—once vibrant with life, now pale and dusty. The poor thing had been dead for quite a while, and Syra was impressed that nobody had stepped on it. The dock was flooded with people of all types, their steps against the wood a hollow melody atop the waters lapping underneath.

Warmth flooded her fingers as she reached for the little creature, feeling the silken texture of the wings. A flash of faint white light crossed the small figure, and a searing pain ripped up her arm and through her own body. Syra stumbled backward and onto her ass. Terror demolished all sense of logic as she desperately tried to get herself under control. She was stomped on, kicked; she could feel the bones crack underneath the immense force—

"*Syra.*" Sekar's voice was in her ear, and it was hot. Something jerked her up, and when she blinked, she saw the orange sand and the grayish sky. Above her, the God's expression was numb. No surprise, no furrowed brows, nothing. Agony still razed her, but it was pulsing in waves, synchronizing with her heart.

He picked her up with ease, and she closed her eyes. She still felt like that little insect. If she slipped away now, it would all be gone and she would never have to worry again.

"Chaos is pure, raw, and destructive energy," Sekar said, leading her somewhere. She wasn't too concerned about where. Her head lolled, and exhaustion suffocated her. The scar on her wrist itched profusely, close to burning, but she couldn't bring herself to alleviate the discomfort when she could hardly move. "If you do not control it, it will kill you."

The air shifted, turning chilly and dead. Her body landed on something so soft, so delightful, that she relished the instant comfort. "Focus on your breathing, Syra," he continued.

Fingertips brushed themselves through her hair, warm. "Don't fall asleep just yet."

Her head started to spin so intensely that she squeezed her eyes shut harder and gripped the sheets. Weightlessness; a never-ending sensation of falling. That was how it felt. A pounding headache stabbed her as the spell settled. She wanted to sit up, ease the torture, but she couldn't gather any strength to do so.

"You're experiencing one of the consequences," Sekar explained, but his voice felt leagues away. "Learning how to manage Chaos takes practice—*boundaries*," he emphasized. She felt a hand press against her forehead. "You will feel sick when you wake. Do not push yourself."

A soothing sensation washed over her, and she relaxed. Her head stopped spinning, the pain ceased, and she felt an intoxicating pull to slumber, as if she had stayed up all night. The world shifted around her between slow blinks, and Syra found herself staring at the plain ceiling of her chamber back at the Infernol. Her body was settled nicely on the soft bed, and in the corner, a single lantern burned. The deep confines of sleep pulled her in without hesitation.

STARVED FOR PEACE

The pain in his core came in waves, much like how the sea would crash over the delicate sand of a beach. Cyrus clenched his teeth and lay there, cheek to stone, watching the dungeon door for what felt like an entire season. It had been two days since he'd gotten here—two days since he had first been drugged. Meals came, but they were hardly anything to be impressed by. Stale bread and pungent, watery soup that could be days old and provided hardly any substance—no meat or vegetables, just broth. Already, his body lashed out in various ways—tongue parched, muscles aching, stomach twisting and retwisting, over and over, as it warred against the poison inside him. He could not drink water for fear it contained the drug, and he refused to eat anything.

The guards had ceased forcing water down his throat, only done it the once. He wasn't sure why.

Cyrus tried over and over to reach out to Sozar, but he had little luck. Whatever they had given him was powerful, for he had not been able to even sense the dragon, despite not ingesting anything further. In Geral, which felt like so many centuries ago, the drug had worn off quickly, but this was different, and it worried him.

What if he could never reach Sozar again? Sure, maybe he could see the dragon and even run his callused hand over the soft and hot scales, but to sense as the dragon did? He wasn't sure that would ever be granted to him again.

Dreams had come and gone in fleeting glimpses. While it had only been two days—marked by tracking the passing guards—he had felt less and less himself. Perhaps it was the side effects of whatever they'd given him, but thrice now, flashes of light had appeared above him. Nothing big, nothing long, but they startled him nonetheless.

He would twist his head and stare at the ceiling, only to find himself gazing upon a void. Strange and nameless beasts would pour out of the chasm before turning to dust just as quickly, their roars mute. Heart pounding, he'd lick his dry lips, and then he would slowly lower his head back to the cold stone. Hallucinations were deemed a bad omen amongst the Diemon people, for it was believed they were cracks between the realms of the living and dead; Soul Speakers were taboo for this very reason. That was what he had been taught growing up—the boys he'd bunked with all spoke of how the dead would come and snatch away anyone who paid them any attention.

Cyrus inhaled the musty air, no longer tasting the sea. Funny what happened when the charm was no longer there. If he didn't know any better, he would have said he particularly hated the sea, because it had done nothing for him but bring him here.

Then there was Leonzo to consider. Had the man with the red sigils all over his body known something like this would happen? Leonzo had spoken so fondly of his mother that it seemed outrageous. Leonzo, who waited for him on the outskirts of Jasper Village along the Gulf of Beritisian in just two cycles' time, must have trusted her just as her own son had.

He grimaced. The thought of her did nothing but force bile up. Cyrus had spent a long time alone. Even when he was in the orphanage, finding friends had not been a gift of his. Taking Leonzo's word on the promise of this working had been gullible, and he understood that now. Hope had been what he'd clung to as he'd flown across the world, but his mother had squashed that. Now he had to live with this decision.

It felt pathetic to just lie here and wait, but he had no other plan. There was no clear answer as to where Sozar was, and he had no idea the way out of here. He was a Dragon Rider without the ability to energy harvest and without a dragon. His sword was gone—had it really ever been his to begin with? The metal had called to him like an old lover, but who was he to take it when it had belonged to Evander?

Perhaps this was his punishment for such an unfair crime.

Steps caught his attention and dragged him out of his spiraling thoughts. Perhaps for the best.

"You two are dismissed." The voice came from beyond the dungeon, and he tensed. There was an exchange of low voices, and then echoing steps—two pairs receded, and another pair grew closer.

Cyrus forced himself upright and felt his body protest—ribs hurt, muscles lit up, head swam—but he leaned against the wall behind him. There was no way he was going to look as dead as he felt to this visitor.

A light illuminated the walls ahead, but it took Cyrus longer than he wanted for his eyes to adjust before he saw the king's son standing there. Alaric held a lantern in one hand and an apple in another. He wore a purple jacket that was embroidered in gold with a white undershirt—too nice for down here. Rings decorated his left hand, and a gold necklace hung about his neck.

"Care for a visitor?" he asked in that thick accent.

Cyrus glared. "No."

Alaric slid the metal lock to the side, the sound horrifically loud, and swung the door open. The hinges squealed, making Cyrus wince again, but the prince didn't react as he stepped inside and hung the lantern up.

In the sudden light, he felt abnormally exposed, but he did not want to look weak in front of this man.

Alaric tossed the green apple at Cyrus, who instinctively caught it. Chains rattled and his wrists burned as the metal scraped against open wounds and bruised skin. The mere sight of the fruit made his mouth water.

"Eat it," Alaric ordered.

He couldn't. "Is this your new way of trying to keep the drug in me?"

"No." The prince shook his head. "You must be starving."

Cyrus eyed him. "Hard for me to trust the son of the man who has me here."

"I know." Alaric walked over and sat down on the slab of stone that served as Cyrus's cot. From this close, he could smell a number of spices off the prince. "But I am not my father. Eat."

A drawn-out silence followed. A few things crossed Cyrus's mind at once—he could eat this and die, or ingest more of the drug, or Alaric was being honest and this was simply an apple.

Cyrus had seen the way the son had eyed his father. And so, he took a bite. The fruit was sweet and tart and rich with juices. Some of those juices went rogue and raced down his chin, which he wiped with a swipe of his hand. It had to be one of the best apples he'd ever had.

"Consider this a peace offering," Alaric said quietly. "I am not here to be your enemy."

Cyrus didn't reply right away. He couldn't. He ate the apple in its entirety, unable to stop until he was nibbling at the core. His stomach knotted in discomfort—having starved for that long, the food actually caused pain rather than relieving it— but his mind felt sharper, although still leagues from his reach. With nowhere to drop the core, he set it down next to him and inhaled deeply. If he was to die by an apple, then at least he could say it was good.

The prince didn't say anything while he ate the fruit, and for a fleeting second, Cyrus felt empowered. Alaric was waiting for him to speak, and he made sure to drag this moment on until it was making him itch.

"You can leave now," Cyrus said at last. "There's nothing to talk about."

Alaric didn't budge. "I know you don't trust me. I'm not asking for that. I'm asking for you to listen."

"Is that why you sent the guards away? Because you want to confess your darkest secrets to the prisoner? Not interested."

The prince's lip pursed. "There is another Dragon Rider," he stated. "My father believes you Riders threaten his reign. He wants control, and he thinks he can leverage you against the other."

Cyrus nodded. "I have met the other Dragon Rider. He's the one you should be worried about."

"The prince of Saveen was bred for war," Alaric replied. "My father believes Dameon is building an army to raise against him."

The news struck him like a frigid wind. "The prince of Saveen?" Dameon hadn't revealed his heritage. Why?

Alaric nodded. "Aye. You didn't know?"

He shook his head. "He wanted me to join him, but I refused." The memories of that last stand-off crashed over him. There had been a look in those eyes that Cyrus had recognized—bloodthirsty and determined to see the world to its knees. The same look he had seen in the king of Geral.

"My father believes you were sent here by Dameon—"

"I pledge to no one," Cyrus cut in, angry.

Alaric raised a hand. "And I wasn't saying so. It has been centuries since Dragon Riders roamed the skies, and I doubt the first two to show up are going to form an alliance. That was the days of the Rider Federation, and even then, they managed to burn their own city to the ground."

"So what's this about?" Cyrus motioned at the prince. "You came here to apologize for your father's actions? To appease some guilt you have for what he's doing to a Dragon Rider? Or is it something else entirely, Alaric? Have you sought me out in hopes of talking me into a pledge to your father so that I might live?"

Their eyes remained locked, and Cyrus could see a storm of emotions passing through the prince's pale gaze. So much to say, but so much unsaid. An entire story that Cyrus might never know.

Most of all, he saw a prince who hated his father. Here was a boy raised under the thumb of a ruthless king. Whether there were scars to show, he didn't know, but he dared to believe there were. The callused knuckles on the prince's hand told Cyrus that he had spent many times punching something or someone—an outlet for built-up rage—and his lack of reactions to anything Cyrus said was a telltale sign that Alaric had faced many outbursts from his father and had learned to internalize everything.

"Who are you?" Alaric asked.

Startled, Cyrus furrowed his brow. "You didn't answer my question."

"And you haven't either. Who are you?"

Annoyed, he snapped, "A Dragon Rider. You know that."

Alaric leaned forward and dropped his voice. "Are you?"

"What's that supposed to mean? Have you come here to harass me?" He shook his head. "My eyes are a clear sign, everyone knows that. What of my dragon? Have you harmed him?" Cyrus yanked against the chains to make his point clear. "If you've done anything—"

The prince stood and cut him off with a wave. "My father's reign is unstable, and he knows it. Saveen and Barnǎl have already threatened once to remove themselves from the Creitón treaty because my father has acted out of bounds in the last four summers. He's intercepted imports to Saveen on several occasions with claims that he is trying to protect the country, but the other rulers doubt this, as do I." Alaric inhaled deeply, the sound cutting through the tension between them. "If they so please, Saveen and Barnǎl can retract all loyalty to our city and squeeze us out of a territory. This would end my bloodline."

"And why would I care about this?" Cyrus asked, tone sharp. He wanted to strangle the prince.

"Because if Delion falls and the treaty ends, this country will fall back into the old ways—murder, war, and grappling for world power. No matter how far you run, Sea Flyer, you will have to face the music at some point, even if you loathe the tune. The choices you make from here on out will either destroy or save the Vore World. Have you ever heard of Ghrynál?"

Mute, he shook his head.

The prince nodded. "It is the belief that every action creates a different path. My choices here will forge something different than if I had not shown here today. It is from the traditional beliefs of Vorelians and literally translates to 'the path forward.' My mother was a firm believer in this, despite my father's refusal to acknowledge our family's ancient beliefs. Her persistence that his violence would carve a hideous future for us led to her death." The last words came out barely above a whisper.

King Raj had killed his wife.

It was horrific, but Cyrus didn't care what the political tensions were in Creitón, didn't care about this prince's sob story. In fact, it only reinforced his belief that Delion was nothing but a home to backstabbers and betrayers. Sure, he felt for the prince—his own father was a horrible person, just like Cyrus's mother—but the sympathy ended there. He just wanted to leave.

"So you see," Alaric continued, "the choices you make now will impact tomorrow. If you had not eaten that apple, a different path would have been forged, but you ate it, and now the path has been altered. Neither of us know what that path may be yet, but I want to hope it is in our favor. Do you understand?"

Cyrus's thoughts were racing, but he nodded. He had never heard of Ghrynál before, and he was certain the prince knew that. Sorréle was the youngest country of the Vore World, and that meant many older systems had not been integrated into the cities there. Questions of the afterlife were silenced, history of the Vore World was monitored, and energy harvesting was taboo.

"Your dragon," Alaric said. "He is fine."

Cyrus leaned forward. All other thoughts ceased immediately. "Where is he?"

"Here," he answered. The prince approached the door but left the lantern. "He has killed five soldiers already. Burned them alive. Nearly killed my father too when he tried to get close." Alaric chuckled, the tone sinister. "A shame he didn't. Would make this all much easier, don't you think?"

Alaric turned his gaze toward Cyrus, but he didn't reply. Pride swelled his chest. Sozar was not easily persuaded, and to think he was in these halls somewhere gave him a renewed sense of hope. The dragon was fighting, and that meant he should be too.

If the prince of Delion anticipated an answer, he did not wait for it. He stepped out and closed the door, and the metal once more cried out against the hinges. Cyrus watched as Alaric slid the lock back in place and flashed him one more look, which hinted at a thousand different things.

Alaric was planning something, and Cyrus was unsettled to be part of that plan, even unwillingly.

In the silence that followed, he listened. The guards did not come back.

MAD LIKE THE CROW

Clouds hugged the distant mountains in the northeast, directly behind him. Moisture clung to Morei's tongue, hinting at a storm brewing. Hopefully they wouldn't get stuck out in the rain. He loathed being bogged down by wet clothes.

Many of the Caster men he was surrounded by did not speak at all. Never in his life had he been around such quiet soldiers; men like these were usually loud and obnoxious. At least in Geral they had been. Many times the commander had rolled his eyes at council meetings—well before Morei was even king—when his soldiers were brought up. It was well known that while Geral soldiers were rowdy, they were the best.

Morei blinked. Boris's face was in his head, and he needed it out. He gave a good shake, and once the image shattered, he was satisfied. This was not the time and place to be living in the past. He needed to be focusing on the present, not consumed by a past he couldn't change.

Several of the Caster men glanced his way during the ride. He did not return their stares, always keeping his head forward or down—when they wanted to, they would make the first move. Morei knew better than to speak first. To them, he was a criminal; to them, he was to be spoken *to*, not with.

As the sun dipped lower and dusk painted the landscape in orange hues, the group made camp for the night. They situated Morei next to a man about his age, who was working on getting the fire started. Others pulled supplies, like blankets and waterskins, and another grabbed his bow and trudged outward to find wildlife for food. For a moment, he thought about offering to use energy to hunt—it was far simpler coaxing a rabbit or two out from their burrow than to find where the little furry things might be hiding. But he withheld. In time, he would.

So, he watched the soldier cast flint against steel to ignite the sparks needed for the fire to come alive. A beard concealed most of his face, his eyes were the color of hazelnuts, and his skin a soft honey brown. Droplets of perspiration decorated his brow, and Morei became acutely aware that it had to be incredibly hot underneath all that armor. That soldier probably wanted to lie down in snow, not start a fire.

After a few harder strikes, a spark burst forth and smoke rose from the pile of brush. The soldier quickly shoved it toward the larger sticks and blew on the smoke. Flames sprouted to life and grabbed the nearest wood. Satisfied, the soldier grinned and glanced Morei's way.

"Always keep my flint handy," he told him, and stuffed it back into a pouch. "Been through a storm or two when I didn't have it, and that was brutal."

Morei nodded. "My father taught me how to light a fire before I was six."

The soldier raised a brow. "Before six? You were taught early." Then he shrugged. "Guess I can't say I'm surprised. You being royal blood and all."

"We traveled much more back then," Morei said. "My father was worried that if we were ever ambushed and I escaped, I wouldn't know how to keep warm." He shrugged, although it was tough to move even that much with the chains. The memory of his father lingered, reminding him of simpler times.

Underneath the fading sky, the little blades of grass that teased his legs and hands were cold compared to the heat of the day. Sitting here like this brought him back to the days he used to run out from the Geral palace and sit in the desert sand when he was a boy. It was so incredibly hot, but he loved it. The tiny pebbles would cling to his exposed skin, burning to the touch, while he listened to the world. Wind, insects, even the occasional larger wildlife that could bear the merciless terrain. He always came back with a burn, and his mother would scold him.

He was preparing to say more when several soldiers approached and fell quickly into conversation. Morei cursed silently, reminding himself that he had to be patient. Gaining their trust and friendship would not be a quick process, and he would have to be strategic in how he connected with them. They were soldiers—brutes, built for war and loyal to their city. Morei would have to leverage that. If he could have their trust, he could utilize those exact things when he took Caster for himself.

All in time. First, some simple conversation.

Morei stared at the fire. Dark Energy's presence was stronger now, the life of the flames feeding her. Last night, they had forgone a fire, having traveled much of the night to make progress and only resting a bit just before dawn. Tonight was the first time he had stared at the heart of Dark Energy since the night he had mercilessly murdered his own people in rage.

Rage fed by her; rage fed by the people, by the *Gods*.

It all seemed rather trivial now, what he had done. As he sat here, touched by the force that had driven him damn near mad and would still do so, everything he had done felt leagues away. Here he was, east from Gamer's Village, far from Geral's hands, listening to the crackling of flames as they devoured the wood.

Ah, but wood did not satiate the ever-expanding appetite of Dark Energy. Death did. Morei could hear her begging, teasing at the corners of his mind, asking for a soul to feast on.

All these men surrounding him had no idea that he could kill them with just a thought. If he allowed Dark Energy to fill him, to turn his limbs cold and carve a deeper hole in his mind, he could burn them all alive. The screams, the blood . . . Ah! Wouldn't that be a sight to behold? A king, shackled, while his keepers writhed on the ground. The thrill of it all was too much.

"It's not rabbit," someone said, "but I managed to catch us a few kahls."

"Those don't have any meat," another retorted, and sat down with a huff. "Might as well as have left them to dig."

The soldier who had started the fire waved them off. "Skin them and let's cook. It's better than nothing. Commander?"

An older man, tanner than the others, nodded slowly. "Aye. Get it going while the fire's hot, boys."

Morei hadn't had a kahl since he was a youngster. The rodents lived underground most of the time, but they came out to hunt for mice. The short hair, sharp claws, and tough skin meant they could dig almost anywhere. Their meat was gamy, sometimes even pungent.

As two got to skinning and prepping, the soldiers started passing around three waterskins filled with ale. Morei wasn't sure where they'd carried them, because he certainly hadn't seen them prior, but he assumed they must have been stored on the horses. The soldier next to him took a swig and, in front of everyone, offered it to Morei.

"Want some?"

Morei refrained from showing the surprise he felt. Many of the others raised a brow, but some looked indifferent. The commander eyed him with disdain. That would be the toughest man to appease, he figured. Convince the commander and he could convince the rest.

"Sure." Morei reached for the waterskin with both bound hands and took a swig. The warm ale tasted like shit, but he didn't let it show. After all day in the sun, he couldn't deny how refreshing it was to quench his thirst with anything. As he swallowed, he passed it onto the man to his right, who took it without a word. "Thanks," Morei said.

That single action was a huge breakthrough. He snuffed his excitement and fell quiet, waiting. A few comments were passed back and forth as an awkwardness settled over the group. Morei could practically taste it on his tongue—rotten. Someone was bound to break the tension, or so he hoped. It surely wouldn't be him.

Eyes darted about, fingers intertwined with one another, bodies shifted from side to side, small talk was long dead.

"All right!" The two in charge of prepping the kahl stepped up. The trio of dead rodents were impaled and bloody. "Who wants to hold these while they cook?" Several hands rose, and the soldier passed them about before he got between a pair of men. They all slowly started twirling the rodents over the flames.

A horse snorted from behind Morei, and the soldier to his left finally broke the silence. "So . . . Is it true?"

He raised an eyebrow. "Which part?"

The man opened his mouth, but before he could say anything, another piped in. "The part where you eat hearts."

Now *that* got Morei's attention. He couldn't hide his astonishment. "Excuse me?"

"Yeah," said the one to his right. "They say you eat hearts and kill women for fun."

"All right." The words left his lip before he could stop himself. For once, he was the one caught off guard. "Neither are true, although I appreciate the creativity."

That got a few to laugh, and the tension eased some. It was a massive breakthrough—exactly what Morei was hoping for. This was a good sign. When he killed their king, he needed men like these to vouch for his . . . compassion.

The soldier to his left cleared his throat. "My name's Harrison."

"A pleasure." That was a kingly response.

"Lanz," the one to his right said. "Commander Edwin is the one with the permanent scowl."

Edwin raised a single eyebrow in acknowledgement but didn't say anything. Maybe that was just his personality; Morei didn't put much worry into it. Names were offered around the group of eight soldiers, the commander included. Morei made sure to repeat each one to himself and note anything in particular that was unique about the soldier. The last thing he wanted to do was ask for any of them to repeat their names—he was no king if he could not recall a handful.

"Uh—" Lanz shifted in his seat and tested the kahl he was cooking. He retracted his fingers and shook them out with a hiss. "Is the story about you bathing in blood true?"

How outrageous! Morei scoffed and showed his gloved hands, damn the chains. "That is repulsive. No."

"What about the battle with Diemon," Harrison said. "Were you really on the battlefield with your men?"

Morei nodded without hesitation. "Of course. I was not raised to hide in my palace in times of war." Now, he licked his lips, ready to take a risk. "Does your king do so?"

The question was direct, a challenge. Morei knew it was dangerous. He could either ostracize himself even more by insulting their king or gain their affection. There was not an in-between, and the men certainly wouldn't all agree one way or the other. He just hoped the majority of them leaned his way.

Commander Edwin broke the awkward silence. "King Drexis has health issues that prevent him from joining us."

Morei nodded slowly but he kept his eyes pinned on the other men. Some glanced toward the commander, while others looked down. It was a lie. Or some version of one, but he was in no place to press for more information.

"That's a shame," he replied, voice low. "I know what it means to the men to be on the field. My council loathed me on the battlefield, begged me to stay aside, but I could not. I refused."

One of the men grunted—Otis, he believed, another one with a constant scowl. The soldier had broad shoulders, built to swing axes wide and for long periods of time. A brute if he had ever seen one. "Ain't no king brave enough to look his enemy in the eye."

"Why?" Morei asked.

Otis shrugged. "Their riches are far more important. You kings would rather be fat and happy than face a sword."

Morei gritted his teeth and took a deep breath. This was a man raised to believe kings like Drexis were the only type of ruler. But it wasn't easy for him to hear that, not after everything he had done for the citizens of Geral. And then they turned their back on him still.

"Sword to sword," Morei offered. "See if I'm as fat and unskilled as you think I am—"

"No," Commander Edwin interjected, hard. "Those chains will not come off."

Otis flashed his commander a savage glare. "We can tell the king his prisoner died in a bizarre accident."

"It'll be your body we carry to Caster," Morei retorted, "not mine."

The words were out faster than he could stop himself, the taste of copper thick on his tongue at the idea of dragging his blade across this man's neck.

The response he got was not what he'd expected—the other soldiers' eyes went wide with thrill. Bloody thrill. They wanted to see the fight, wanted to place bets and see if Morei was exactly who they had come to know through tall tales. Their reaction was so astonishing that he momentarily forgot all about Otis.

"Enough." Commander Edwin raised his hand to emphasize his words. "We have a job to do, and I will not stand before the king to explain why half my men are dead or why his prisoner—an ex-king, mind you—is dead. The kahl, is it ready?"

"Here." Lanz handed him his impaled and now cooked meat. "Take what you want." The others carefully pulled at pieces, while Edwin tore a leg off after a good twist and handed the spear back to Lanz. After some hesitation, Lanz reached out with the meat toward Morei. "Hungry?"

Truth was, he was starving. His stomach had long stopped growling and just hurt. Food had been sparse since leaving Gamer's Village, and it would likely remain that way until they arrived at Caster. Why these men hadn't restocked their supplies on the way out, he did not know, and he couldn't ask. Yet.

Morei shook his head. "Go ahead. I'll have whatever is left."

Otis's eyes rolled, even as he sank his teeth into an arm and tore the meat from the bone. Morei ignored him. But he couldn't deny his absolute need to end this soldier's life.

And he would. That was a promise.

Rodrick grabbed the impaled kahl, and as he plucked a few pieces of meat, he asked, "Can you use magic?" The soldier had one blue eye and one brown—a unique trait that Morei had never seen before.

He cringed.

"What?" the man asked.

"Energy," Morei corrected as nicely as he could. "Don't use the term magic—it's improper."

"So . . . can you use *energy?*"

It wasn't even worth telling Rodrick that he was saying it all wrong. Properly, it was harvest or manipulate. One couldn't *use* energy, because that implied energy could be absorbed and changed, altered, when it couldn't.

"Yes," he answered. "I can."

"Oh." Harrison took a swig of the ale in the waterskin. "Do you— Can you, like, make grass move and stuff?"

Morei refrained from grinning in absolute amusement. "To an extent, yes. It depends on what form of energy you call on to do that work."

"Wait." It was Jude. "There's different energies?"

"Well, yes." Morei raised his brow. "You didn't know that?"

Most of the men shook their heads. How— Morei halted himself. This was the culture of Caster. The city had been built on violence, not intelligence. He doubted any of these men had even picked up a book in the last ten summers to simply pass the time. They all seemed rather curious to know more, though, so he stole a quick glance at Edwin. The commander remained stoic.

Morei started cautiously, tip-toeing around the concepts of Light and Dark Energy, studying Edwin all the while. But as he continued and the lecture turned into a discussion with the men, he stopped caring. These men were intrigued—even if Otis sat there with a constant scowl, the man didn't look away. So much that felt basic to Morei turned out to be the spots he had to backtrack on to ensure the men all understood even the foundation of *what* energy was.

He found himself enjoying it. The time ticked by, the fire grew lazy and settled, and the night grew taller. A moon hugged the horizon, and the world shushed as the critters all bedded down for the night. An occasional moth flew by, but out in these rolling hills, night critters were not common. There was no guarantee of water or shelter.

The night was filled by "oohs" and "ahhs" in response to Morei's speech. He motioned when he could, remembering that he was still chained, but by the way these men hung on every word, it was like he wasn't. Maybe that was true to some extent. Mentally, these men were engaged and treated him like an equal, but physically, he was the prisoner and they, his keepers.

They asked questions, gave opinions, and even shared things that he deemed odd, like "My sister had a friend and I swore she could use magic." But Morei welcomed it all. He was passive about sharing his own opinions on any matter, molding himself to the mindset of these soldiers. What was important was making them all feel heard, understood, and like he was grateful for what they had to say. So he played along, even poked fun when his questions couldn't be answered.

As the night progressed, he found himself more comfortable, more certain that the decision he had made when he left Geral was the right one. The men around him didn't think poorly of him, they were just uneducated, and that meant they made piss-poor decisions and had false assumptions. What they needed was a king who wasn't afraid to get his hands dirty.

THE DEAD ARE WATCHING

Syra was fine. Or so she kept telling herself as she meandered through the halls of the Infernol. The Gray Realm haunted her. It was only the night before that she had stepped foot in a world so unlike the Soul Realm and living. The experience had changed her, and now she was struggling with the concept of what was real and what wasn't. Sekar had brought her back here and then disappeared, dumping her in her bed.

People passed by, but when they tried to say anything, she just kept walking. The ringing was incessant—could nobody else hear it? Syra's legs were weak, but she forced each foot in front of the other, on a mission that she could hardly find the strength to speak about.

She was trying to find the dead girl.

The young thing had been staring at her when she had awoken. There was not a doubt in her mind that this spirit was a result of what had happened in the Gray Realm, and now the girl wanted her attention. A giggle and a twirl later, she had bolted right *through* the door. Syra, confused and disoriented, had shot out of bed and chased after her, determined to figure out what the spirit wanted to tell her. Somewhere in these halls, that little girl was waiting for her, expecting her, and Syra couldn't let her down.

Left, right, left, right. Syra couldn't decipher how many halls she'd scoured or how many times she'd been down the same one. Some people stared, and some avoided her, but only once had someone tried to stop her, asking if she was all right. Syra had simply pushed the woman aside and kept going. Her breaths were frantic now, quick and uneven, and her stomach twisted in knots.

The incessant itch of her Zyulë Bond scar was maddening. She had already started to scratch it without thought, resulting in immediate regret. A flare of pain burned her arm when she did that, so now she was stuck living with an unsatiated itch that made her want to scream.

There she was. Syra spotted the brown hair and the playful smile stretched across the girl's face as she darted down another hall. "Wait!" But she was gone in an instant.

"Syra?"

She ignored the call. Not now. She had to find that girl. If she didn't—

A hand latched on to her arm and spun her around. Zane was staring at her, his pale blue eyes wide. The soldier's expression twisted into some form of shock as he furrowed his brows. "What's going on? Are you all right?"

"I'm fine," Syra answered, strained. Getting a full breath of air suddenly felt impossible. Her lungs constricted, her heart beat faster, and her head spun. "I just . . ." She backed up until her spine met the wall and then slid down with far too much speed. Her ass struck the ground hard, forcing the air from her. Vision narrowing, she put her head into her hands and shut her eyes.

"You're not fine," Zane told her. "What— Never mind. I need to go get Zarek."

"Don't—"

"Too late," Zane snapped. Already his voice was leagues away.

*   *   *

Syra blinked. The sheets that should have been covering her were kicked aside, her skin drenched as if she had submerged herself in a cold bath. Visions of the sand and the orange sky from the Gray Realm flashed across her mind. It felt like she was being pulled there—a tug here and there that made her want to close her eyes and hope she could leave all this behind. The Infernol, obligations, the politics, all of it. In the Gray Realm, Chaos smothered her in comfort. She could be anything she wanted there. Here, she felt a void in her chest that hadn't been there before last night. It was cold, and hollow, and it made her grimace. The ringing in her ears had ceased. Her head pounded, and she reached up to rub her eyes.

Then she heard a giggle.

"What . . ." Her mouth was dry, her voice raspy, as she sat up and stared at the little girl who now stood at the end of her bed. The soft pink fabric of her dress was translucent. One wrong blink and she might disappear altogether.

The little girl clasped her hands together and twirled again, but this time she did not run. When she was done, she faced Syra once more and beamed. "Do you like?" she asked. Her voice was an echo.

Syra nodded, obeying the direction of this conversation. "I do."

"Mother got it for me before . . . before I left her." The grin slipped slightly from her face. Her brown eyes were huge, as if expecting something from Syra.

"I—" Syra licked her lips, trying to find the right words. She didn't know why this was happening or what she was supposed to do. Frankly, she couldn't tell if she was living some vivid dream or if this was real.

The little girl suddenly twirled again. When she stopped, she asked, "Do you like?"

Syra stared, momentarily speechless. It was possible the little girl was stuck in a loop, reliving specific moments over and over, and Syra just happened to be exposed to one. Slowly, she nodded. "I do," she repeated.

"My mother got it for me before . . ."

This time, she didn't finish. Syra mumbled, "Before you left her?"

The spirit's head snapped up, and those big brown eyes stared at her. In a deathly whisper, she said, *"We're always watching you."*

Syra leaned forward on her bed, intending to get closer, but when the girl took a step back, she stopped. "Excuse me?"

"Are you going to save my soul?" the spirit asked.

She opened her mouth to answer, and then the door opened. Syra tore her gaze free from the little girl long enough to see Zarek coming into the room. At her shocked expression, he halted.

"Are you all right?"

Syra looked back only to find the little girl gone. It hadn't been a dream, and for some reason, that made it worse. The door closed with a bang, and the Guardian was next to her in a heartbeat. "Are you all right?" he asked again, sterner.

She relived the passing moments with the spirit, trying to put it together. Sekar had told her the realm fracture would cause strange things to happen, but whether this was what he meant because of her exposure to the Gray Realm, she had no idea. We're always watching you. No doubt those words tied into what she had been told a dozen times already, that she was the Light Bringer. It did not bring her peace.

She couldn't shake the dread that what she'd just experienced was a warning. That Shevana was coming for her.

"There was a little girl," Syra whispered, and looked up at Zarek. "She was here."

"Just now?" He sat down on the edge of her bed, watching her intensely, perhaps expecting her to go running off again.

Syra shook her head and looked at her hands. Each finger stared back up at her, offering no answer. "She told me they're always watching." She thought back to the woman she had seen in Jared's home in the Nighthunter Federation. It had been so long since that incident that she'd thought it would never happen again, but she was wrong. The dead always knew where to find her.

"Syra." The sound of her name pulled her attention back to the Guardian sitting next to her. "What happened?"

She swallowed, knowing what he meant.

"You were determined to seek Sekar's guidance with your gift, and then the next thing I know, Zane is frantically telling me you're trying to find a dead girl. His words, not mine." He reached out and took a hand from her lap, giving it a squeeze. "You do understand that no matter what's happening, my loyalty is to you, right? I don't particularly like that God, but I surely will hate him more if he's done anything to jeopardize your safety."

Despite it all, Syra snorted with amusement. Zarek didn't apologize, not like normal people. What he'd just said was his own way of telling her he was sorry for how he had treated her. Guardians were complicated, that much she had learned, and Zarek was no exception. Reading his actions and words was a skill learned, not granted. To have him say that to her meant the world. Right now, she needed friends.

"Last night," she finally said, "Sekar took me to the Gray Realm."

Zarek's brow rose, and it all came out in a torrent. She told him how she had felt there and how she felt now that she was back in the living world, and how she suspected the interaction with the spirit was some sort of result from her exposure with Chaos. Syra spared no expense in also telling him Sekar's words about how Chaos worked with each Vore God. She told him all this because she trusted him, and she also trusted his words, whatever they may be, and she wanted him to see that Sekar *was* trying.

When she fell silent, Zarek took both his hands and rubbed them over his face. He looked exhausted. "You could have died," he told her.

That hadn't crossed her mind because . . . well, because she had been with Sekar. Despite all his actions, she hadn't once doubted him when he brought her there. "But I didn't," she countered as gently as she could. "I need to learn somehow."

"I know," he replied, and looked at her. "If I ever see him again, I'm going to punch him. His claim for forgiveness is through you. You do see that, yes?"

Syra didn't want to be the one defending Sekar. It felt all wrong, especially when she was still learning to forgive him for what he had done to her. Yet the words still escaped her tongue. "He may be the only chance we have at restoring the Soul Realm. You've said so yourself that he was always far more invested in the Soul Realm than any other Guardian. I'm the key to it all, aren't I?"

The Guardian nodded. He knew she was right.

"I know what's happening is outside of my scope," he said. "Sekar's knowledge on Chaos and his ways of training you will be more than I could ever offer. But please be careful. You're all the Soul Realm has. You're all we have."

The weight of his words pressed heavy on her, and she nodded. "I know," she whispered.

"Get some rest." Zarek stood and walked toward the door. When he reached it, he added, "Lock the door behind me, Syra. I came here originally to tell you there's a riot starting down in the south, where the soldiers are. Keryn is down there now trying to ease tensions, but I'm not sure how long it'll last or if it will get worse."

Syra felt her stomach sink. It was because of her. "Are we safe here?"

Zarek's hesitation was the only answer she needed to hear. "We're not, are we?" Syra sighed and looked about the chamber. "Is there any way we can leave?"

"And go where? The world isn't safe. What's happening in here is happening out there."

"A small town," she offered feebly. "Somewhere where we can disappear." There she was again, trying to run from her problems. Syra almost laughed at herself but refrained.

"Keryn told me that he hasn't made any progress with the Lirallian," Zarek continued, perhaps more to himself than to her. "Everyone is pointing fingers, and he's been forced to groom records himself to try and come up with any leads."

She shrugged at his words, her mind still on the political mess of the Infernol. "Did he say anything else?"

Zarek's expression softened. "All he told me was that the men were growing antsy with talk of storming Raveer."

What he didn't say and didn't have to was that the people were divided over Syra. Her mere presence was causing an uproar, and for a moment, she wondered why she bothered trying to fit in at all. All Syra ever did was cause problems. If someone didn't die, then it was rejection. Sure, she had a few people here and there, like Irsilla—she wondered where the lady was now—but they felt so few and far between compared to the sour moments like now.

As he left, Syra did as she was told and locked the door behind him. Her legs moved mindlessly between the door and the bed, and as she sank back down, she was more certain than before that if she didn't master her newfound abilities, she would end up dead, one way or another. The Infernol was a mess, and she couldn't shake the severe disappointment of it. Zarek had to feel it too, even if he didn't outright admit it. If Dryl was here, he would certainly be enraged to know Keryn had let it get this out of hand. The Infernol had been built to protect the Vore World from realm-altering dangers, like the Lirallian Empire, but she was now certain that this organization was falling apart. Possibly, she concluded, because of her.

Syra sat there for a long time, just thinking.

DUST AND STONE

tone had texture. Cyrus had spent the better part of the night tracing his fingers over grooves he had never felt before. His thoughts had finally silenced, but not because he had given up or because he felt there was no way forward.

It was because he was thinking. Feeling, sensing. All of it.

Everything around him had a life of its own, a world within a world. He could hear the scuttle of insects, the distant laugh echoing from the hall where a guard likely stood, and he could also hear his own heartbeat, slow and steady.

It was raining. He could tell because there was a crack in the stone to his right in the ceiling, just over the cot. Water dripped freely and had now pooled on the stone slab, which told him he was underground. Cyrus listened to the constant drip, but he wasn't annoyed by it. It brought him a strange sense of peace. He used the sound to track time and to disconnect from the chaos going on around him. An opportunity to reevaluate his situation.

The metal links around his wrist were tight enough that he couldn't slip them off, but that didn't mean he could find another way. There was a story he'd heard once about a prisoner who had been taken by the Ferguson queen. She'd had him locked away and told him that to be free, he would have to turn on his own king, to which he refused. The prisoner had broken his own thumb and joint to slip out of the bonds and run away in the middle of the night.

Cyrus looked at the metal and the tight grip on his wrist. It would not budge enough to slip his hand through, even with a drastic step like that. But . . . He ran his fingers over one cuff and found a groove deep enough that he paused. A key went there. Which meant if he could find something on the ground thin enough, he could try to pick the lock.

Cyrus began to run his hands along the rough texture of the ground once more. It was cold to the touch, and he moved slow, feeling out every part he came across. He couldn't make it to the door—the chains forbid that—but he made it halfway and that was enough. Along with touch, he used his eyes to map out anything that looked like it could be of any use, but even with the light from the lantern—how long had that been going now?—he found nothing.

Cyrus tried to swallow his frustration, to promise himself that luck could not be this poor for any prolonged amount of time, but even then, he couldn't get the lump of rage to go back down. So, in one impulsive act, he lashed out at the wall. Knuckle met stone, and the jar of the impact reverberated all the way up his arm.

The pain came second. Cyrus reeled and withdrew to look at the damage. Blood poured from open gashes along the knuckles, and he couldn't close his hand without excruciating discomfort. Tears of anger burned his eyes. The heat from the gore rushing out reminded him of the everlasting chill in this dungeon, and a shiver raced through his body.

If he couldn't get out by breaking free from these chains, then he was as good as dead.

Cyrus leaned over and cradled his head into his hands. Stone buried itself into his knees and elbows, but he didn't care.

He couldn't care. A world was out there, and he was stuck in here like some fool.

His fingers dug themselves into his hair. He was daring himself to pull, yank out whole tufts, anything to feel in control. Being alone in this dungeon was madness.

He could not stay here, would not. Cyrus felt a roar building in his chest. It was accompanied by something else—an urge to tear the stone in two. He wanted to pound his fists over and over into the ground until it gave way into nothingness. Damn the repercussions, damn the world, damn it all. He wanted freedom.

Over and over, he told himself to be quiet, but it was like something else had possessed his body. A power surged through him—a promise—and turned his blood hot. It tore through his limbs like muscle and bone were nothing and traveled all the way up his torso, until it reached his head. Then it stopped, and pressure started to build at an immense pace. It needed an escape, or he was certain his head would explode right here and there.

His jaw clenched; his teeth ground into one another with cracking force. His fingers dug deeper into his head like he could break right through into his skull.

And then he couldn't take it any longer. The fury exploded, and he roared into the stone. A reverberating crack echoed through the dungeon, and a chill engulfed his entire body. It was a different kind of chill—one that Death herself would be responsible for. Her ice-cold fingers trailed all the way down his back until his spine convulsed inward and he collapsed onto the floor, exhausted and dazed.

All his energy was gone in an instant, and he felt his head spin. He could hardly lift it without feeling like he might throw up. The ground was too cold to the touch, and he shivered from the contact. Waves of hot and cold crashed over him—one moment he was trembling, the next he was gasping for air. But as he moved his hands about, trying to find any sort of comfort beyond himself, his fingers struck a hard and jagged edge that had not been there before.

Cyrus moved his head a little at a time until he could face whatever it was he was feeling, and then he felt the air leave him. There was a crack in the stone floor before him, running from wall to wall, and it was deep.

Somehow, he knew that he had done this.

Cyrus tried to crawl forward, but he couldn't. His muscles refused to work, and from somewhere he heard the loud echo of boots. They were coming for him. Delion would be angry, and he had no way to protect himself because he couldn't even find the strength to lift his head. His breaths came in short bursts, his heart raced so sporadically it hurt, and a tingling sensation wiggled about in his toes and fingers.

The piercing cry of metal met his ears. They were here. He could not look up or greet them. A boot stared at him, round and slick with a fresh shine.

"What's going on in here?"

Cyrus couldn't find his tongue, but it didn't matter. A kick to the ribs was enough to tell him that they didn't care what he said.

"Sir," another soldier said. "Look."

From where he lay, Cyrus knew they were eyeing the crack that he'd created. Mumbles slipped between the men, and then he heard: "The king will want to know about this."

"Go," one ordered. "Well, Rider, anything?"

Cyrus licked his cracked lips. "Make sure he knows I'm not paying for it." Despite his exhaustion, the words still came out dripping with sarcasm, and that brought him some pride.

If they heard, they did not reply. Footsteps echoed once more as he laid there. He would have tried to get up, but he sensed that any movement would elicit a further beating. He closed his eyes, listening as the men stood there, awaiting instruction. It seemed they were stunned and without direction, which he used to his advantage to rest after what he'd done.

Cyrus wasn't sure how long he waited, but when he opened his eyes again, he heard the distinct sound of approaching boots. Someone coughed, and the words that followed could mean nothing but trouble.

"Grab him."

WARY OF MONSTERS

The sun was intense. Morei had managed to get Harrison to flick his hood over so that the heat didn't bother his face anymore. His blue eyes were sensitive to the sun's rays, something he had learned quite well as a boy when he dared to look at the sun once or twice. Back then, they'd call the sun Rauna, the name of an ancient queen who, as legend told it, fell in love with a God, Zyne. Their love had resulted in the betrayal by her citizens, who believed she had struck a deal with something sinister. In a rage, the people killed Rauna, which angered Zyne so much so that he lit the entire city on fire. His love was so deep that he tore the city from the ground and thrust it into the sky, creating the sun. But it did not bring Rauna back like he'd hoped, so he took all the energy of his lifeforce and threw himself into the sky, becoming the moon. Forever, he would chase Rauna, determined to prove his love for her by giving up his physical form.

It was a tragic love story that Morei had grown up believing. As he has aged, though, he no longer looked at the moon and sun the same. The legend was older than Sorréle itself, and nobody actually believed the sun and moon were Rauna and Zyne. Myths kept the culture alive, and reinforced tales about how Gods came and went in Drügalism.

Now, shaded by the cloak and on the steed he had endearingly named Grumpy—to himself, of course—they were making decent pacing today. The men were quiet, as always, and kept to themselves, only exchanging words when necessary. Although compared to their liveliness last night, he was beginning to wonder if the problem wasn't the men but their commander. Perhaps Edwin was far more ruthless than he let on—a silent dictator, which was worse than the obnoxious and loud ones.

That didn't align with the commander being willing to let Morei talk last night, but he was still trying to put the pieces together.

On several occasions, the men stopped and stretched their legs. Lanz and Harrison seemed the most perceptive and accommodating to Morei, which he appreciated. They helped him down, let him walk around, and then helped him get back on Grumpy. There was little chat, but that was fine. Morei used the space to observe.

Ever since they had passed a dead stump that protruded from the ground, the men had grown a bit wary. They were jumpier, checked over their shoulders, and their faces wore constant frowns, as if in intense concentration.

Nothing felt different to Morei. The endless field of grass and dirt patches went as far as the eye could see but ahead, just to the left—northeast—he could see the faint outline of something. It was still too far away to determine what exactly it was, but he could only assume they were coming up to the territorial marks for Ferguson and Caster. That would certainly make them anxious, especially if they were at odds with the Silk Family.

As the sun passed its halfway point and soon settled just above the horizon, Morei couldn't take it anymore. Curiosity was killing him, and he finally managed to get Harrison's attention after a few failed attempts. The soldier's horse was leading

Grumpy, so it had become a matter of making just the right bit of noise to catch the soldier's eye.

"What is this place?" he asked. He kept his voice low, suddenly aware that there was no wind. Everyone could hear him.

Harrison licked his lips, a nervous gesture. "You don't know?"

Morei shook his head.

"Um." Harrison ran a hand over his face. "This stretch of land has a history to it . . ."

"The dead live here," Rodrick answered. "Nothing good ever comes from these parts." He blinked and looked ahead once more.

Morei didn't understand. "Tell me more—"

"You feel that?" It was Lanz, and everyone suddenly stopped. The horses' ears flicked, the tails swished, and the entire world fell quiet.

Too quiet.

Morei swallowed, feeling his throat constrict. The force he was struck with consumed him. This was no ordinary energy. This was something more, something far above his understanding. This wasn't supposed to be happening. He was supposed to be in control, always, and his thoughts scrambled as he tried to think of anything that could explain what was occurring.

Yet he could not shake the familiarity. This was the same force he had felt that night outside of Gamer's Village.

"We should keep—" Commander Edwin froze, eyes wide. He was looking behind them, and one by one, everyone else followed suit. Morei felt his heart skip a beat in anticipation as he spun the best he could on Grumpy while still chained.

He saw it immediately. The mound of dirt spit out rocks and grass as it sped toward them. It moved fast, the cause of the disruption wide—possibly as expansive as the Sorréleian River at its widest, which was about half a league. It would be upon them in no time at this pace.

"Greve, give us strength," someone mumbled, but Morei didn't turn to see who had spoken. Never in his life had he been witness to such power. Even his body could sense it.

"We need to move," Lanz ordered. "Move!"

The horses bolted, jarring Morei back into their reality. He nearly fell, repositioning himself barely in time before the steeds all broke into a full gallop. Morei crouched in his seat, tightening his core muscles and squeezing his legs to Grumpy's side to keep from falling. They raced, continuing onward. Horses snorted, the pounding of their hooves deafening, and the wind tore at his clothes and hair, ripping the hood off.

It wasn't long until he could feel something else—the deep vibrations that shook the entire ground that they rode on. Edwin raised his hand suddenly, and the men all slowed. As Morei looked about, heart racing, he saw that everything had gone still.

He opened his mouth to speak, but no words came out. There was no doubt he had felt that vibration. It had been so loud, so powerful. Surely someone else heard it?

"Where is it?" Otis gasped, as if he'd been the one running. "Where in the Gods is it?"

"I don't know," Rodrick whispered. He swung his horse around, its body rising and falling, nostrils flared. "It was there . . . just a moment ago."

A quick succession of words to his left told Morei that Lanz was praying.

"What was that?"

"Evil, that's what that was," Harrison answered. "I ain't ever seen anything like that before."

Edwin grumbled something inaudible and pulled at the reins of his horse. "Let's save the discussion for when we're back. Let's keep moving quickly. We're close to home, men."

"But what if it's following—"

Morei blinked, then blinked again. His head felt weird, his mind too far from his reach for his own comfort. A sliver of logic screamed they needed to run, but another part of his mind—one far more in control—wanted to lay his ear against the ground.

Boom. Boom. Boom. He could hear the heartbeat, slow and steady, as it filled his mind.

It was beneath them.

Grumpy was the first to react. He reared up, and Morei's entire body lurched backward. He fell just as the ground behind him exploded. His back landed against protruding pebbles and rock, gouging right into his shoulder.

The others bolted. Some were on their horses; others had grabbed reins and were running, but he heard the recognizable scream of a dying man. Dirt fell over him, along with clumps of grass, and he rolled over into a fetal position to cover his head from any larger debris. His mind was in shambles, and his only instinct was to protect himself from the immediate threat.

When the dirt stopped falling all over him, he realized just how hard he was gasping for air. Not even on the battlefield with Diemon had he been so out of breath, so scared. It didn't feel good. Morei was never one to admit that something had the best of him, but this was one of those cases, and as he opened his eyes, he realized he was no longer in the sun's path.

If he'd been a praying man, now would have been the time to do so.

Shouts came next, once the ringing in his ears faded— again, he hadn't realized because it had happened so fast. Morei didn't know what they were saying, but he was acutely aware that there was something over him. The beating heart was loud, and it felt like his mind was being ripped in two. Morei groaned into the ground and then coughed and spit, dislodging dirt that had managed to wiggle its way between his lips and nose.

"Morei!" Harrison screamed. "Run!"

He moved to stand—and felt the shifting of whatever was over him shake the ground.

"Morei!"

He gasped. Sheer terror. It had been a long time since he had felt this way, and he needed to leave as fast as possible. Morei scrambled, dragging chained hands through loose dirt. The gloves felt sickly hot, his cloak too clunky, but he moved as fast as he could. He could see the men a bit farther back, torn between honoring their duty of keeping Morei prisoner and tempted to leave. He took one step, two steps, and then paused.

In the silence that followed, a series of clicks filled the gap. The noise drove a dagger into his chest. The beast was huge.

His mind raced—at least the parts he still had control over—and he started teasing the edges of Light Energy. Morei would test this creature first, try to distract it long enough to get away without drawing on the darker force, but a large leg met his eyes. It had tiny hairs protruding all over, encased in a tough, tan-colored armor.

Slowly, too curious to run now, he turned his eyes upward.

The giant pincers were the first thing he saw, stretching wider than he stood. A dozen beady black eyes blinked, some larger than others. They were staring at him.

Exterior armor, some kind of shell, covered the creature, and at least ten legs were apparent—all identical to the one he'd seen with the hairs. As the creature lifted one, he saw tinier claws at the end, likely used for digging. The razor teeth that jutted out from the mandible were a yellowish black.

Morei was dwarfed by the creature, at the mercy of it, and could no longer find the ability or desire to run. His knees became weak, his arms weighed too much, and he collapsed before the beast. The creature clicked again in a series of patterns and tilted its head. If this was how Destiny saw his end, then so be it.

Slowly, it got closer. The pincers almost touched him as it moved its head from side to side. The shell exterior grated against itself, creating a rhythmic noise that soothed his racing heart.

A powerful presence pressed against his consciousness. Morei inhaled sharply and tried to retract, but the presence seized his mind and squeezed. He convulsed, attempting to grab a full breath of air, but couldn't. The presence wiggled its way deeper, sorting through his memories like they were nothing. Fleeting, sudden, and without order. There was no rhyme or reason to this beast's method, but each memory exposed had emotions attached to it that Morei had spent many summers trying to forget. Anger, sorrow, torment, excitement—on and on it went, and he felt like he was being tossed around in a sandstorm.

The world faded around him as he was forced to face this unsatiable wrath and torment. Morei could hear the bloodcurdling screams of dying brethren. Pincers torn free, legs ripped off, and swords thrusted into his abdomen over and over. The images were fleeting, but the emotions were bold, as if this beast were screaming into his ear.

His mind was suffocating, his lungs squeezed so tight that he could no longer fill them. Morei's eyes stared up at the horrifying creature as it continued to shift its head antennas lazily moved by an unseen wind. Those dark globes remained locked on him, and he could almost see himself in their reflection. A dying man.

The power of the energy that consumed him was too much. The sliver of him that remained screamed in terror as he felt the very essence of who he was being torn away by the gust that devoured him whole.

TROUBLED TENSIONS

A knock broke Syra's focus on her hair. She was braiding it for the fifth time, finding peace in the action. So much had happened, and in such a short time. She'd seen the Gray Realm and then seen a dead girl, a spirit. She could not rid herself of it, like a sour taste on her tongue.

Time. Syra needed time. She was a Vore God now, and that meant she needed to master her abilities. It had only been two days since she'd been to the Gray Realm to train with Sekar, but she felt like they were wasting time not being there every waking moment. A deep urgency bubbled just below the surface, and she found that sleep had started to evade her. Instead, she'd lie there awake, thinking about everything that could go wrong if she didn't master Chaos.

The living realm would be devoured—the fracture would split wider and wider until the Soul Realm spilled forth and suffocated the Vore World whole. Beasts would break through—or maybe they already had—and rampage the living. That didn't even include the demons, like the Honuyál, that could use this to their advantage.

A knock again. Syra blinked and stared. She'd forgotten entirely the door was there. "Who is it?"

"Your knight in shining armor," the voice called back. Zane.

She smiled at his comment. "Sure," she muttered, and jumped off the bed.

When she opened the door, there he was, the man who had given her refuge on the Raveer ship and had stood by her side with no other reason than that it was the right thing. His ice-blue eyes beheld her there, and she realized his blond hair had grown out. She couldn't remember when that had happened.

"Your hair," she told him. "It's different."

Zane pushed her aside and entered with the elegance of a commander who had a lot to say in little time. The faint scent of ash followed him as if he'd been working with fire, and she wrinkled her nose. He had come a long way from the man who had rebelled against his own city and traveled across the rolling hills with them.

When she closed the door, he asked, "How are you?"

"Good to see you too," she remarked, and crossed her arms. At his raised brow, she relented. He had been the one to find her wandering the halls, after all. "Fine. Better, actually. Amazing what some sleep can do." A lie, but she didn't want him asking too many questions about what had happened.

In truth, she didn't want him to worry about her. She was growing tired of having everyone concerned about her.

Zane eyed her. His tan belt stood out from his gray outfit, along with a sheath that held what appeared to be a new sword based on the simple handguard. It was a nice build; she could tell by the polished metal.

"Syra," he started, then tried to smile. It looked forced, and he quickly dropped it. "This"—he motioned to the world around them—"is what I'm used to. Stone, sweat, and blood. I was bred for war. Had a sword in my hand by the time I was five, fighting enemies by nine. My blood knows this world, but what I saw with you . . ." He shook his head. "That was outside what I know. You gave me a good scare. I'm just glad Zarek was nearby when I found you."

Syra nodded. She appreciated his concern, and clearly he needed to say his piece.

"Has that been happening a lot?" he asked.

"Only that one time," she answered. She couldn't tell him that she'd been taken to another realm to harness Chaos. He knew much of what was going on with her now, but he'd kept a lot of distance as of late, and she feared it was because of exactly what he'd just hinted to. This was outside his world. Zane found comfort with a sword in his hand, not with energy or speaking to the dead.

Zane made a sound in his throat, a half attempt at an acknowledgement, before he ran his hand through his hair. "I came here to check on you, but I also wanted to tell you about what's been going on with the Infernol."

"Oh?" Syra was glad to change the topic.

"The men and women talk a lot. They say things about Keryn, those two Harvesters with the dead eyes, and they talk about the future of this place." He took a deep breath. "Many don't agree with Keryn anymore. They think he's acting on his own accord rather than for the entirety of the Infernol."

"The meeting we had," Syra said. "He wants to take Raveer." Zane had been there, but it felt important to restate what had been disclosed.

"And he's already instructed that we prepare for a departure." His voice was low now. "There are a lot of people who disagree, though. People are turning on each other left and right. Some think we need to remain where we are; others agree that we need to expand our resources. Can't say I'm surprised—everyone here is a rebel of some sort."

Syra nodded. In truth, she'd had no idea that Keryn had made that request. The last she'd heard, it had only been to talk. There had obviously been more once they left. Zarek had been upset and dragged her out of the meeting after accusing the Infernol leader of knowingly allowing Lirallians to move in on Junok.

"Do you think . . . Keryn wants war?" she asked Zane. When he tilted his head at her, she continued. "Keryn turned a blind eye on Liral when they moved in on Junok. Why is that? All I can think of is that he's seeking war, he wants—"

"Or he *is* the Lirallians' agent," Zane mumbled. "Think about it—and I mean no disrespect to the Infernol by saying this. Liral is a giant, and we are an ant. Our resources are fantastic for what the Infernol has done, but nothing can compete with undead soldiers and possibly Henry Junok leading this. If I were Henry, instead of sparing the resources to fight, I'd collect allies. It would be the fastest takeover this country has ever seen."

Syra opened her mouth and then closed it again. This was not the discussion she'd anticipated having, nor what she'd expected Zane to say. He'd had his concerns prior to coming here. "You don't think he's just trying to use Raveer for resources? If the Infernol was trying to go up against Liral, they'd need more soldiers and allies. Raveer could be that."

"You heard him," Zane countered. "The Infernol wants to take Raveer while the city is at its weakest." He dropped his voice and narrowed his eyes. "I've lived my entire life doing this. This isn't a siege to do the right thing, this is domination. If the Infernol was as genuine as it states its cause to be, why wouldn't Keryn just send a letter with some men to the king? Showing up with an army isn't what I call a good first impression."

Syra didn't reply right away. She'd been so caught up in her own problems that she hadn't even considered how it all sounded, but Zane was right. If Raveer was still recovering, the city could never defend itself against an army. This was like sneaking up to a soldier and striking them while their back was turned.

Still, she wanted to exhaust all possibilities. "What if Keryn has information stating King Matthieu is working for Liral and that's why he's moving against Raveer?"

Zane turned and started to pace between the large bed and the lounge area. She watched him go back and forth a few times, his eyes down, lost in thought. Finally, he shook his head. "No, I don't think so. I met Matthieu several times, and while he's cruel and has his own chamber for torture pleasure—please don't ask for details—he's proud. He wouldn't make a deal with anyone, even if there was a blade against his neck. If the city falls, he would fall with it."

Honorable, yet she knew Zane rebelled against the city because he disagreed with some of the practices. That was not the point of the current discussion, though. The more she thought about it, the more she wondered if Zane's suggestion was right. Keryn was the agent. Maybe Henry had promised him safety if Keryn utilized the Infernol in Liral's favor. Regardless of whatever false promise Henry had made—because she doubted he would uphold any deal—that did not change their reality.

"Does Zarek know?" she asked.

"Not that I know of. He seemed pretty set on the idea that the Infernol would leverage Raveer strictly for resources." Zane eyed her. "The Guardian doesn't know everything, despite what his ego might say."

Syra cracked a smile, even with the weight of conversation on their shoulders. Zarek did have an ego. "We need to tell him. I can come with."

"No," Zane said firmly, stopping in his tracks. Those pale eyes drilled into her. "The people talk about you, Syra. It isn't safe. When I left the south side, the tensions were at a boiling point. Zarek's down there, and I don't think it would be safe for you to stroll into that environment. People are antsy. They're looking for a reason to strike."

"And you think I'm that?" she pressed. She'd suspected the political unease was in part due to her, but Zane had just confirmed her suspicions. "Why not you? Why not Zarek? Why me?"

Zane shrugged. "Your name is what people know, not you. You're *the* Syra who took off with the Demon Killer from Caster. That's what people say down in the south end. Some think you've got yourself mingled with Henry—it was his blade, after all." His voice turned solemn. "I know it's not what you want to hear, but that's the truth."

"That's ridiculous," she snapped. "I don't even have that thing with me anymore."

Zane looked apologetic. "They seized us outside of Raveer because they wanted you. Not me. Zarek's a Guardian, so it's easy to say he was a part of the reason to get to you." He sighed and planted his hands on his hips, as if he'd been wanting to say all that for a while.

Syra stared, unsure of where to even go from here. "Did the people say that?"

Zane nodded. "I spoke to one of the men that apprehended us a few days ago. Said Keryn wanted the redhead. That was all."

Her heart sank. She'd tried to stay low here and only interact with people like Keryn when summoned. It wasn't not like she'd run around yelling at the top of her lungs that she was Nala's daughter or that she was bound to Chaos. But it appeared her name carried stories with it—and assumptions.

Dryl had given her the ring to ensure she was safe, and perhaps the Guardian had left the Infernol with different beliefs in its intentions. Obviously, that had all changed.

"I'll tell Zarek myself, and we'll come back here to talk to you about next steps," Zane said. "Does that sound like a plan?"

She looked about the spacious chamber, which now felt more like a dungeon. "Not like I have a choice, do I?"

Zane approached her. "Don't worry, Syra. We'll get this sorted. If we've got to take off tonight in some mad dash through the mountains, we'll do it. You hear me?" He placed his hands on her shoulders and met her eyes. He was like a brother to her, even though they had met on a whim.

"It's good seeing you, Zane. It feels like it's been too long."

He gave her shoulders a good squeeze. "I haven't been the best at checking in, have I?"

"I haven't either."

A smile spread across his face, as if he'd just heard something funny. "Here we are, in a mountain, leagues from any home we've ever known, and we can't even find the decency to check in on one another. What ever happened to the simple times?"

She laughed. "You mean sleeping on a boat?"

"Obviously." Zane retracted his hands and reached for the door. "Try and get some rest, yeah? You look like shit, and I don't mean that to be rude. You just look like you haven't slept in days." As he turned the handle, he paused and raised his brow. "Try and not chase any dead girls while I'm away, yeah?"

They had spent enough time together for her to know when he was being playful. "I'll try," she replied with a smile. "Go to Zarek, tell him our thoughts, and come back as soon as possible."

He nodded. "Deal."

As he left the room, Syra tried to shake herself free of the stress. She'd come to the Infernol believing that she could find refuge here while she trained, but she was standing in the heart of a very dangerous situation. If Keryn really was working with Liral, she was far closer to Henry Junok than she wanted to be. And she still didn't know Sekar's relationship with the once-believed-dead leader. Maybe Zarek had been right—maybe she'd been a fool to accept Sekar's help.

She made her way over to one of the chairs and sat down. She needed to keep herself busy or she'd go crazy waiting for Zane to return with him. Her mind raced, and she swore that little girl lurked around the corner, waiting to laugh at her for not seeing this all sooner. Syra didn't want to be alone, not when she felt so vulnerable, but at least she had a weapon. Death's Sword. And once she could harvest Chaos with ease, she'd never be in this situation again.

She reached over and picked up a book—one of the few left on the table for guests. It was on the history of Diyră. If only it were on the Infernol, although she couldn't say she expected any physical books on an organization that had spent the better part of its existence a secret. Still, maybe she would find something between the pages that could offer any sort of insight into them.

She leaned back and started reading. If she left tonight, it would be quite some time before she could sit with a book again.

TO FACE THE DRAGON

yrus couldn't keep his feet under him. The soldiers were dragging him, yanking his shirt and pushing him forward. All about, the stone walls glared down at him, but he hardly had time to see where he was going. His throat hurt from the scream earlier, and every time he spoke, it felt like he was going to cough, but the Delion soldiers didn't seem to care. They threw insults, annoyed that the stone floor had been cracked. They'd already told him he would get a new cell.

When Cyrus tried to ask questions, they shoved him. Once, he had fallen on his hands and knees, and the two men had grown furious and kicked him. It was as if they were releasing every single morsel of resentment onto him, as if their entire lives had been made for this moment. He tried to bite his tongue, but he was becoming more and more irritated. This was wrong, and he was done playing victim, even if it got him killed.

Cyrus lashed out and felt his elbow connect with the nose of the soldier to his right. It cracked under his strike, and the man roared in pain. The one to the left reacted immediately and drove the hilt of his sword into Cyrus's stomach. The impact forced the air right out of his lungs, and he hunched over, gasping. When he saw the upright soldier's fist heading his way, he ducked and heard a slew of curses as those knuckles met stone instead of him. Cyrus smiled, albeit weakly, before a boot crashed into his ribcage.

Something hot landed on his cheek as he rolled over, and he wiped at it. It was red, and he glanced up to see one of the soldier's face smeared in blood.

"You look far more charming," Cyrus complimented. "Red suits you well." The discomfort in his ribs molded into a sharp cry as he shifted his weight, and he grimaced. Hopefully not a broken rib, but it wasn't like it mattered anyway. Cyrus had asked for this, wanted it. Being locked in a cell, even if only for a handful of days, had been driving him mad.

The left soldier lunged for him, and Cyrus was too slow. A hand wrapped around his throat and shoved him against the wall. His head slammed into the stone, and the grip tightened. The bloody-nosed soldier leaned in and spat, "You have no idea how much I want to kill you right now."

Blood decorated Cyrus's face with a warm brush. He tried to shift but found he couldn't move without the hand digging itself into his throat. Wheezing, he swung at the soldier, but his fist never connected. Instead, it was caught by the other, with a bone-breaking grip.

His lungs were begging now. The air was growing thinner, and he couldn't get a full breath. "Don't . . ." Cyrus tried to tell them no but couldn't. His thoughts scrambled, instincts racing—he couldn't die. Not here, not now. This was not how his story was supposed to end.

The soldier leaned even closer, their noses almost touching. Those dark eyes were savage, primal, as if before him stood a beast, not a man.

"You got something to say?" the soldier hissed. "Not so strong, are you?"

Cyrus was screaming, but nothing was coming from his throat. Where was the power he had felt back in the dungeon?

He tried to reach outward for anything, but his mind was shrinking as the air ceased altogether.

"Jon," the other soldier cut in suddenly. "The king wants him—"

"Damn the king," Jon snapped. He curled his upper lip and squeezed harder. "I'm—"

"Damn the king?" a voice rang from somewhere to the left. "Should we tell him that now?"

Jon's grip released, and Cyrus slumped down to the ground. He took as deep of a breath as he could with the pain. That was too close. Relief washed over him in hot waves.

Jon took a step back and raised his hands. "He struck first."

"I don't care who struck first." Another soldier came into view. His blond hair was tied in a bun with hard lines around his eyes and mouth. "You had an order."

"Commander—"

"You're relieved." The man unsheathed his sword and right before Cyrus's eyes cut into Jon's neck. It was not a clean beheading, far from it, which made the entire gruesome scene worse. Jon's head was half on, spitting blood outward across stone. The other soldier did not react as his body fell to the floor.

The commander wiped his sword on the tunic of the dead man. When he sheathed it, he looked at them both and said, "We're late."

Cyrus nodded and stood. That was not a man he wanted to annoy. He hadn't even flinched. How many had he killed prior like that? Cyrus had reeled over killing Evander for moon cycles, ashamed, and this man would probably not even think of Jon by supper.

Together, they walked in silence. Cyrus kept his distance from the leader. His throat was bruised, and he involuntarily reached for his neck on several occasions to rub it, anticipating feeling indentations, but there was nothing. He eyed the soldier who walked next to him, who returned his gaze at least once but otherwise kept to himself, clearly afraid of the commander as well.

It wasn't until they reached their destination that Cyrus blinked. The commander unsettled him, and he'd halfway presumed the man would shove the same sword used to kill Jon into him. The door was cracked, and the commander pushed it open. Cyrus already knew exactly where they were. The feeling was sudden, overpowering, and he felt his knees weaken.

Sozar was here.

Chains scraped, and Cyrus pushed himself forward, no longer caring about any of these men. Lanterns hung everywhere, illuminating a massive room. It was so large that he couldn't even see the other side, but he didn't have to. In the center, wrapped in chains larger than Cyrus, he beheld his best friend.

The chains stretched from either wall. Metal cuff links so wide that he couldn't fathom a single man hoisting them were wrapped around Sozar's legs. The dragon looked unharmed physically, which relieved him—he'd been expecting to see torn wings, bloody skin from where scales had been ripped out.

One of Sozar's massive, fiery eyes blinked and beheld Cyrus, the dragon lifted his gigantic head. Cyrus poured himself into their mental link, hoping to feel *anything* from the dragon. But there was only silence. Sure, he'd known he was being force-fed a drug that snuffed out his abilities, but he had hoped that the close proximity would change that.

He didn't need words to understand what was being conveyed. They were alive, they were here.

"Only fitting that the Rider face his dragon when interrogated," a familiar voice announced. Cyrus whirled around and saw King Raj standing there, dressed in a blue silk robe that would've looked more appropriate at a royal dinner party. This man's intense need to wear fine clothes even in the dirtiest of places annoyed Cyrus to no end, though he hadn't quite realized it before. Next to the king stood Alaric, dressed far more simply, like a servant rather than a prince. His eyes were unreadable, his expression stoic. If he was surprised by any of this, Cyrus couldn't tell.

"Original punishments for Riders and their dragons were conducted in the same room," the king continued with a matter-of-fact tone, as if this were all natural for him. "It was believed that the closeness of the two weakened resolve and made the punishment more . . . fulfilling." He spread his hands wide. "Shall we begin?"

Hands grabbed Cyrus and shoved him to his knees. Sozar snarled and pulled at his chains to no avail. Cyrus wanted to reach out to the dragon and beg him to stop moving. This was not his battle, and Cyrus felt ashamed that Sozar had been dragged into something because of him. They were dragon and Rider, but that did not mean Sozar should be punished because of who Cyrus was.

He could not communicate at all.

There had to be an Energy Harvester somewhere nearby, someone who was responsible for causing this. A fist landed across his jaw and his body lurched sideways before a soldier grabbed him and forced his body upright once more.

The king glared down at him. "Who sent you?"

Cyrus worked his jaw. If they thought hitting him was going to have any influence, they were wrong. He had been beaten so many times already, it was all starting to blend together. "No one," he murmured. "I came on my own."

Raj stepped forward and grabbed the collar of his tunic. Alaric kept his hands clasped in front of him, eyes unchanged. "You work for Dameon, don't you? You two got some big plan to overthrow this country?"

"No," he gritted out. Alaric had asked something similar, but now Cyrus wondered if the two had even spoken. He was annoyed that they would assume he would bend the knee to

Dameon at all. Just because the other Rider was a prince did not give him immediate rights to rule.

A slap. The impact stung, and Cyrus blinked to clear his head from the jarring strike. "You want to know why we're here today?" the king asked. "Desperation can make a man do a lot of things. We've withheld you from your dragon, chained you, beat you. Old ways of Rider punishment, so that we can get you to talk." He leaned forward, breath rancid and hot. "So if you think I won't throw you back in that dungeon and starve you for the next moon cycle to get what I want, you're a fool. I ask again: what are your intentions here?"

Cyrus chose his words with care. The king was a second away from killing him, that much was clear. Raj wanted a reason to spill blood. "I was abandoned by family and grew up alone. My only intention was to find my mother—"

"Who turned you over like you were a thief," the king cut in with a smile. "Isn't that sweet of her."

Cyrus didn't reply. He knew better. Raj was right, but he could not bring himself to confirm that out loud.

Behind the king, Sozar kept one eye focused on them. The dragon appeared docile, weak even if that was possible. Was there some kind of spell? Perhaps they were starving him to keep his strength lowered. He was so *tired* of people taking advantage of him. The bitterness bubbled in the pit of his stomach—people had continued to use him, or try to, and Cyrus was sick of being Destiny's toy. He needed to start taking control of his life.

Raj tugged at his shirt, and the motion forced his eyes back on the king. "Was it Morei Geral who sent you? Is he behind all this?"

The name startled Cyrus. Had the Geral king's name traveled all this way? "How . . ." He blinked.

The reaction earned him another punch, though not nearly as painful as the previous. Maybe he was just growing used to the pain.

Raj was in his face, spit flying. "You heard me. Don't feign surprise. You think that fools me? You think—"

"Father." Alaric's voice was stone. "I don't think Geral wants anything to do with you."

The hold on his shirt released, and the king turned to face his son. Even facing the wrath of such a monster, the prince did not flinch. "Do not interrupt me. I have no tolerance for such disrespect."

Alaric did not move.

Raj turned to face Cyrus, and the corner of his lip twitched. "If you don't intend to speak—"

"That's because I don't know anything," Cyrus interjected.

The king raised a hand and jutted his chin out. "Send in Gandel."

The prince walked off to the door they'd entered through. Cyrus watched but he kept one eye on the king. Power was intoxicating, and he sensed Raj drowning in it. Here was a man who would do anything to show the world what he was capable of, even at the cost of his own men. But Cyrus was focused on Sozar. The dragon huffed, and after so long together, Cyrus knew that whoever Gandel was, Sozar was familiar with him.

He tried to extend his mind again, hoping to brush against the dragon's, even faintly. He poured every single part of him into the act, feeling his muscles strain from the attempt. Surely, this close would give them *some* sort of advantage to connect. There—

It happened. Faint, but Cyrus let out an audible gasp, too stunned and relieved to care. The look in Sozar's eye told him everything he needed to know. Cyrus felt and heard all. A hundred emotions passed through him at once: fury, sorrow, confusion, agony, and more. He saw as Sozar roared and blew fire, slaying three soldiers at once. But behind the fallen men, another stood—Gendal, the Energy Harvester.

The memory faded, and he remained where he was on his knees, mouth agape.

This Harvester had done something to Sozar. Who could harm a dragon, even if they believed they were doing the right thing? Perhaps he was scared of King Raj, or maybe he truly thought Cyrus was working with Dameon and Ashtir and felt the duty to protect his city and king. But that did not excuse it.

Cyrus would kill Gendal. The thought was so sudden, so violent, that he felt like a bystander to his own body for a fleeting moment. The emotion consumed him. Such rage was unlike him, yet here he was, prepared to do anything to prove his loyalty to Sozar. Even take another's life.

"Gendal will help get things moving," the king stated. "You can save your breaths. We'll let the dragon speak for you."

Cyrus yanked his arm, testing the soldier's grip. Suddenly, nothing mattered anymore. "What are you going to do to him?"

"Nothing that will concern you," Raj replied. "Gendal is a master of the mind, and his extensive research in dark practices makes him a weapon."

The Energy Harvester said nothing as he stepped up next to the king. He stood slightly taller; he was bald and had a deep tan, and piercing amber eyes. Silent, obedient, the king's pet.

"You will *not* touch him," Cyrus insisted, as if he had any say in this matter. At this point, all he could do was plead, demand, beg, anything. He needed them to understand that he would do something terrible if they took this any farther. "I will not—"

The king slapped him so hard his teeth hurt.

"Gendal," Raj whispered, "do what you need to do." The king's fingers wrapped around Cyrus's jaw, and he glared down at him with a look of repulsion. "Maybe then we can get our Rider to talk."

"As you wish, Your Majesty." The words were devoid of any emotion. Perhaps the Energy Harvester didn't feel anything at all.

The king was still standing in Cyrus's line of sight, grip tightening, blocking his view. "I want to see the look in your eye when your dragon shrieks," Raj muttered, voice hardly audible. "There's nothing quite like it."

White-hot fury poured through his limbs. Cyrus's breath turned shallow. "Don't touch him," he seethed. The next words came from a place so deep in his core that he could hardly recognize himself. "I will kill you."

"That's rather touching. We are blinded by what we want the most."

"Please. You've got this all wrong. We never came here for trouble. Surely you must see that by now?"

King Raj regarded him for a moment. In the heat of it all, the stare felt eternally long. "No."

The sound of chains moving met his ears, and his heart skipped a beat. He would not let this happen. He had made a promise many cycles ago to protect Sozar at all costs. He had rebelled against his own city and fled his home country. Many nights he had lain awake when Sozar was no bigger than his arm, promising to be his protector, to defend Sozar if the dragon could not defend himself.

Cyrus watched the corner of the king's lip twitch. "Still don't want to talk?"

A bead of sweat rolled rogue down Cyrus's cheek, cold in the humid chamber. "You've proven you're determined, I'll give you that, but my respect ends there. Why would I give you any sort of information if you hurt Sozar? What's the gain here?"

Raj didn't even blink. "Listen, Rider. Isn't that what you lot are known for?" He let go of his shirt and spit on the ground next to Cyrus. "None of this would happen if you only told me about your deal with Dameon. Power, hm? World domination? What is it?"

"It's none of that—"

The sound came first. A guttural scream that Cyrus had never heard in his life. It tore the air apart, clawed at his senses. Panic erupted in his chest as if it were his own life at stake. Sozar's agony radiated through every part of him. There was nothing quite like the sound of a dragon in pain.

He tried to get air but couldn't. The agony tore through his lungs, and he gawked at Gendal as the man's expression remained completely void. Did he not feel any emotion for what he was doing?

Raj knelt next to Cyrus as Sozar's scream died off. "Have anything to say?"

Words barely formed on his tongue. "I'm not who you think I am."

"Hm. Shame." He stood. "Again."

Sozar's tail smashed into the ground, shaking stone and stirring dust. The soldiers next to him tensed as the dragon's roar came out somewhere between anguish and fury. It hollowed out Cyrus's mind, and his limbs went cold. Sozar's once-stunning eyes glazed over with a strange green hue. Sozar shook his head violently, jerking chains, and started to whine.

"Stop this!" Cyrus yelled. Gendal didn't even flinch. The only indication that he was a living, breathing person was the tic in a jaw muscle as he concentrated on the torture.

Raj didn't even look his way. Cyrus didn't know what he could possibly say to prove to this man that he was nobody. Not even his own mother wanted him. Why would Dameon? Sozar's whines grew sharper, ear-piercing, as Gendal continued. Cyrus reached out mentally, trying to get to Sozar in any way he could, even if just fleeting like before, but a barrier blocked him.

He started gasping for air, his entire being overcome with anger. He was a *Dragon Rider*. He was not to be shackled like this, forced to watch his dragon being tortured. Just as these men felt they had a duty to their city, Cyrus had a duty to protect Sozar.

The scene unraveled fast. The dragon's shaking escalated, horns and scales scraping against the massive chains. Sozar screeched so loud that Gendal finally jerked back, along with the soldiers next to him. King Raj seemed to be the only one still entranced as the dragon began yanking and stomping. The green hue steamed upward from his eyes, and Cyrus realized the horror.

Gendal was burning the dragon's eyes.

This was it. This was his breaking point. Violence was not Cyrus's friend, it never had been, but times were different now. The man who had left Sorréle was not the same who had arrived at Creitón. He was tired of the world beating him down, and he was ready to prove to everyone, himself included, that he would do anything to keep this dragon safe.

Cyrus roared and surged upward. The strength was immediate, born out of the determination to put an end to the Energy Harvester. Every action came without thought. Cyrus ripped his arm free from one soldier and punched the other. The man's nose cracked under his knuckles, and he did not wait to see the reaction before turning his attention to the king. Raj barely had time to react before Cyrus shoved him aside like he weighed less than a bag of flour.

He ran. Time slowed all around him, as if Destiny herself was proud of this moment. She watched him take the ten paces needed to reach Gendal, whose head whipped around to see him coming, but it was too late. Sozar's teeth flashed, his claws grinding into the stone, as Cyrus slammed himself into the Energy Harvester.

He started beating Gendal. The man raised a hand, but Cyrus was too quick and harsh. He punched his eyes, nose, jaw, mouth, skull, everything. Nobody would touch Sozar. *Nobody.*

His vision blurred, his thoughts molded into one single word: *revenge.*

A force tore him free from Gendal, but he kept punching the air. When it was clear he couldn't make it to the Energy Harvester's face, he turned his attention to the nearest person and swung. His fist connected with the king.

Raj's face contorted, and he ripped free his blade. Cyrus froze.

A moan came from his right, and he looked down to see Gendal's face unrecognizable, bloody. He glanced at his knuckles—they were covered in gore. Shame and guilt should have rampaged through him then, but all he could feel was *pride.*

Cyrus tried to swallow that unnatural feeling, but it lingered on his tongue, like a foreign food. The crashing reality of his actions squeezed in from all around.

"Beat him," the king ordered.

Cyrus tried to duck but couldn't. A boot landed on his ribcage, then a punch to the head, and then another boot. Over and over, he tried to deflect. There were three soldiers on him, and he couldn't defend himself from every blow. He landed several hits, but it was not enough. Adrenaline fading, he couldn't keep up as his body grew weaker and weaker. Each strike sapped his energy; each punch sucked the life out of him more and more. Cyrus *hurt.*

Something warm filled his mouth—blood. Cyrus spit and coughed, trying to crawl his way to freedom. Blood splattered the stone beneath him, and another kick to the chest forced him over. No longer could he move. His vision was slipping from his fingers quicker than he could fight it. The soldiers weren't stopping. Each hit numbed him a little more, and his lungs burned with an icy fire that consumed him whole.

And then, just like that, it ceased. Cyrus felt warmth engulf him, and he tasted the pungent flavor of blood on his tongue.

PART 2

"You seek power, but I seek to end all fear."
~ Vorelian Scrolls

A SEA FULL OF WRATH

The smell of salt met his nose, the sun kissed his skin with the fierceness of a warrior, and the sand was hot to the touch as Morei shifted about. Here he was at the coast of the Merrél Sea. Never had he seen the ocean before, and he found his eyes drifting across the vast blue horizon. It felt endless. Peaceful.

He dragged his legs up, wrapped his arms about his knees, and inhaled. If he could, he would bask in this moment for eternity. Already, his mind felt clearer, sharper, and—

Syra.

Morei turned in his seat and saw her there. Sitting criss-crossed, her green tunic contrasting deeply with porcelain skin and fire-red hair. She smiled at him, freckles and all. "Welcome back."

Morei could only stare. Not because he was surprised, but because this felt real. As real as him pacing the halls of Geral, galloping on Sunny with the wind in his face; as real as it felt when he drove a sword through the heart of an enemy.

"Is this a dream?" he asked.

The lapping waves sparkled under the sun's rays and soothed his soul. Although he appreciated the water before him, nothing could come close to the crunch of sand after so many summers in the Hazar Desert. Syra's expression twisted, her eyes now distant. "I think so," she answered. "I don't know how or why, but the last time we met—"

"I couldn't shake it," Morei interjected. "I remember."

"So . . . it was real," Syra whispered, and looked at the sea. "I didn't want to believe it."

Morei's mind was racing. So much he wanted to say, do, ask, but he couldn't quite grasp what was happening. They were here, in some sort of dream, but it was real. As vivid as his waking life was. Morei Geral was sitting on the coast of the Merrél Sea with Syra Castello. The girl the world wanted.

Where did he begin? A hundred questions surged at the forefront of his mind. When he finally had some control, he asked breathlessly, "How?"

Syra turned to him. "I'm not sure how to explain, but . . . I'm not who everyone believes I am. I've changed. I've become something—" She raised her hands to gesture as she spoke, but it seemed she was struggling to say the right thing.

Morei took a leap. "Light Bringer?" Based on the way she looked at him, he knew he was onto something.

There was a surge of thrill and desperation in his chest. He had so much to say, but he wasn't sure how much time he had left or if he'd see her at all again. This was their second meeting, and it was obvious that there was no rhyme or reason. It was sporadic and unplanned. More specifically, it felt that his survival was based on these interactions.

Syra's smile was fleeting. "I suppose I should tell you I died."

And she did. Morei listened without interrupting, but he could hardly pay attention. A deep sensation filled his chest— he didn't feel safe. With his back turned from the land, he felt as though an enemy could walk up at any point and stab him. Morei turned, stared, certain he heard footsteps approaching, but there was no one.

"What are you going to do?" she suddenly asked.

He dragged his fingers through the hot sand, coming back. "Why do you care?" Morei wouldn't share his intentions with a stranger. No matter how often he'd heard her name, he still did not trust her. Everyone had a motive—he just hadn't learned hers yet.

"Because there's a reason we keep seeing each other," she pled. "Maybe we're supposed to help each other—"

"Why?" Morei asked, cold and defensive. This woman knew nothing of what he'd been through. "The world wants me dead. How do I know you're not like the others?"

"I don't want you dead."

"Yet," he corrected.

For that was his destiny. No matter how hard he wanted to do the right thing, no matter what he sacrificed to make the people safe, everyone always turned on him. There was not a single person he had met who had not learned to hate him. Even Emerald despised him because she could not gain anything from him, save for the seed she'd stolen.

When Morei left Geral, he left his forgiveness behind. No longer would he rule passively but with a merciless hand. If the world wanted the Demon King, they would get it.

"Morei." Syra turned to him. "Look at yourself. Is this who you want to be?"

"The last time I took advice, my throne was taken from me." Morei wanted to shake her—shake the innocence from her. The world was vicious, and to survive, one had to act ruthlessly. If she could not understand that, then she did not grasp the fundamental reason for his choices.

"I'm what the world has made me to be," Morei hissed. "And in time, you will be too."

The ground shook. Clouds sprouted with unnatural speed, blocking the sun, as the ocean grew violent. It all happened so fast that Morei barely had time to react as ice-cold rain pelted the back of his neck and face. He blinked and tried to stand, but the wind was growing too powerful. He tried to reach out and grab Syra, to tell her to stop whatever madness she had ensued, but her eyes were wide with terror.

She didn't know what was happening. This was not her doing.

Morei stood—and came face-to-face with the Dark Lord.

Sekar was not smiling. His dark eyes were colder than a winter storm as he tilted his head at Morei. The rain did not strike the God, somehow. He was completely dry. "You aren't supposed to be here," Sekar said.

Morei clenched his teeth and shot a glare at Syra. She wasn't smiling, but he saw the recognition flash through her green eyes—she knew this God. This had all been a façade to get him alone, cornered. He turned his eyes back to Sekar. The first time he had seen the God, he had been paralyzed in fear, but not now. "You've got the worst timing, did you know that?"

Sekar looked amused. "Still as snarky as the night we met. Tell me, how's Geral? Oh"—those lips turned into a grin— "that's right. You massacred your own citizens and then fled like the coward you are."

"You made them turn on me." His clothes were soaked, and the chill grabbing his bones was relentless. "You wanted to take everything from me and for what? For entertainment?"

"Then tell me this," Sekar whispered, and stepped forward. Despite all the noise around from the sudden storm, Morei could hear the God's voice as clear as day. "How did it feel when you killed them? Oh, don't tell me." Sekar took one step forward. "It felt *good*, didn't it? So good, in fact, that you can't stop thinking about it, can you? You were born to kill, destined to be cruel, Morei. No need to keep secrets between each other."

Morei seethed. This fucking God had taken everything from him. Energy surged through his limbs, turned his innards icy, and he didn't shy away as the voices rampaged his mind at once. Morei summoned the Dark Energy in an instant, and the fire burst alive in his hand. The bright light between them drove Sekar's eyes down to the flames and there was no denying the sheer astonishment that etched that all-too-handsome face.

In the God's moment of hesitation, Morei flung the fire.

He awoke with a start, gasping. Clothes soaked and skin wet with sweat, he rolled over and coughed violently. His body heaved until he threw up bile all over the grass. The sour stench filled his nose, and as he reached to wipe his mouth, he found his wrists shackled.

"What—"

Then he remembered.

Morei remembered the creature, the running, the absolute power that the beast had fed his mind until he was literally suffocating. Panic filled his chest. Was he alone? Left for dead? The night was upon him, the stars blocked by clouds.

"You're alive!"

He turned and saw Harrison staring at him, along with the others. The fire was long dead, smoldering. He could only make out the faces of Harrison, Rodrick, and the commander, Edwin.

Despite the vomit, his mouth was as parched as if he'd traveled through the Hazar Desert. Morei tried to move, but his head swam and his body ached all over. "How—where are we?"

"Just outside Caster territory," Rodrick answered. He ruffled through a few items before producing a waterskin. "Thirsty?"

Morei sat up slowly, careful not to drown in the fierce dizzy spell that threatened to consume him. When he was certain he would not black out, he reached for the water. As he lifted it to his lips, eager to wash away the sour taste, he paused.

"Ain't water, I know," Rodrick added with a shrug. "Figured you might want something stronger."

And he did. Morei took a swig of the alcohol—a clear and pungent brew that tasted like moldy cheese. In different circumstances, he would have gagged and asked for a finer quality, but now, he was just grateful these men had come back for him.

That meant something. They had a duty to bring him to King Drexis, but they could have just have easily fled in terror—he knew quite a few who would have done that in the face of something so ancient. When he'd finished a second gulp, he handed it back, and Edwin tucked it away again.

They stared at him, as if they expected something more.

"I don't know what happened," Morei said. It was a lie. He could not risk losing what little faith these men had in him by telling them. If they came to fear him, he risked everything. "One moment, I was standing there. The next, I'm here." They did not need to know how that beast had ravaged his mind, how he had come in contact with such pure power, and how he had just encountered the Dark Lord and the most wanted woman in Sorréle.

"The beast left after you collapsed," Harrison whispered, and shook his head. "We've never seen anything like it."

Morei bit the inside of his cheek. That creature, whatever it was, had invaded every part of him and then just left? He didn't like that. Everything felt out of his control. The only thing he could control was this conversation, and as the men sat there, eyeing him with either uncertainty or reverence—he couldn't tell—he swallowed. "How long have I been out?"

Commander Edwin answered without emotion. "You've been unconscious for three days."

THE COLOR RED

Sekar's hands were on her. He shoved her back with a glare. She stumbled but still had her footing. They were back in her chamber, next to the chair where she'd fallen asleep. The book she'd been reading lay on the ground, face down.

At this proximity, he towered over her. The God was furious. That dark gaze of his twisted into an animal's as he hissed, "How long have you been seeing him?"

It had happened too fast for Syra to gain any control of the situation. Her dream with Morei had been *real*. The first time, she'd believed it was just particularly vivid, a part of what Sekar had talked about as a side effect of the realm fracture, but it was more than that. Countries apart, and they'd somehow found each other. She reeled with that revelation, regardless of how cruel he had become. His words still clung to her like mold— they'd been so bitter. But there they were, sitting side by side.

"Syra," Sekar cut in, glaring. "How long?"

She blinked. "Twice, I think."

"You think?"

"Yeah. The first time, I thought it was just a dream. I was on a beach, and I asked him to tell me what it was like to die." The words that came out of her mouth sent a chill down her back, and she saw recognition flash across those eyes of Sekar's. He'd been the one to shove the Demon Killer into her chest, after all. "But when I saw him this time, it felt different. It felt so real. Even he thought so."

Sekar inhaled sharply and turned away from her. His shoulders tensed as he ran a hand over his face. "You need to not make a habit of that. Morei Geral is a threat, and he will hurt you. This is a man who slaughtered his own citizens because he felt like it. His ailment makes him unstable, and no matter how nice you want to be, he'll still find a way to kill you. He's extremely dangerous."

"And you're not?" she scoffed. The words came out fast, without thought, and she watched as he turned to face her, clearly unimpressed. Sekar was serious, and she shoved down her irritation. If this God was worried about Morei, then she had cause for concern.

"When I asked you if you'd been experiencing anything out of the ordinary because of the realm fracture, you said dreams. Yes?"

She nodded. "I'd only seen him once before that, like I said. Before that, the dreams were just vivid moments of me talking to royalty, sharing food, that kind of stuff. It's why I thought this was just another." Syra recalled the way Sekar's expression had shifted when Morei had summoned fire. "Did you know he could harvest Dark Energy? Is that why you say he's dangerous?"

Power like that . . . Syra couldn't imagine what it was like living with it. She'd been exposed to Dark Energy only once, from the very sword she now carried. Just thinking about it made her uncomfortable.

"I knew," Sekar answered slowly, "but I didn't think he had any power like that there."

"What do you mean?"

"There are boundaries in dreams to protect the person having them, no matter how real"—he looked at her pointedly—"they become. You two were the dreamers, so a part of your consciousness should have been inaccessible, such as harvesting energy. Yet, he did. Likely because of the fluctuating energies from the fracture. It's all I can assume."

Syra's head spun. "And this was only possible because of me?"

"Your connection to Chaos," Sekar clarified. "You're far more sensitive to the realm fracture than a normal Harvester." Shaking his head, he looked visibly disappointed in her, as if any of this had been her choice. "If you ever see Morei again, I need to know about it. He will be your downfall if you're not careful."

Mute, she reached down and picked up the book, then placed it back on the table, hoping the mundane action might ground her a bit more. This all felt so out of control, and she knew Sekar was upset, which made it worse. This was not something she'd actively done, yet now that she reflected, she couldn't stop thinking about the words between her and Morei, or the way he'd looked at her when Sekar showed up. The God said he was dangerous, and she believed him.

She looked over at the door as she did so, wondering when Zane and Zarek would be back. She had no idea how long she'd fallen asleep for, but hopefully they'd return soon. Knowing there were tensions in the south of the Infernol, where the majority of the soldiers were, made her uneasy. This whole place felt like a disaster waiting to happen.

"You haven't been honest with me," Sekar mumbled, but after the silence it felt like a roar.

"And you haven't been honest with me," she shot back. Syra was tired of the back-and-forth—he constantly considered himself in control. He had just shown up in the middle of a dream, even if it was real, and abruptly ended things. "The last time I saw you, you were hauling me out of the Gray Realm. You show up in my life after what you did to me and try to salvage things by offering to train me. How charming, Sekar. Really."

The God crossed his arms, his expression stoic. He neither looked angry nor annoyed. Her heartbeat was loud in her ears. She knew that look better than anyone. When he had tested her in Raveer, like a predator playing with its prey, he'd worn it as well.

"You assume I'll apologize," he said, eyes unwavering. "You think I have any sense of remorse for what's happened. But I don't." Sekar scanned the chamber as if studying it for the first time. "My only regret is having felt anything for you."

Syra opened her mouth to make a snarky remark, but he raised a hand and halted her.

"You need me," he said, although his tone suggested otherwise. "You stand there, proud and ignorant to just how desperate the world is to eat you alive. If I hadn't interrupted that dream when I did, you risked your safety. Chaos, even bound to it, can devour you. Exhibiting power as you did without understanding the consequences could get you killed."

Syra held her tongue. She was so tired of him always having the upper hand, but she couldn't argue his points. She didn't know Morei or how to control Chaos like Sekar did. Watching him stand there as he did now, so confident, she wondered if that persona came with so many centuries with this kind of power, or if Sekar had always been this way, even as a mortal.

"I don't *need* you," she bit back, crossing her arms. His expression twisted in surprise, as if he'd not anticipated such words from her. "Don't give me that look, Sekar—"

He turned his head away and held up a hand again. The action was so abrupt, she froze. Sekar was calculated; he didn't act sporadically. A flush rippled through her body, and she swallowed, feeling dizzy. She tried to remain standing, even as her body swayed and she reached out to the chair next to her. Her lungs felt on fire, her vision narrowed, and when she looked up to the God, she found that he was gone.

She blinked, gasping. A hallway. So much fucking gold. It was atrocious, a blaring statement of power. A desperate cry for authority and respect.

Syra shook her head, feeling her stomach twist violently. When she blinked again, she saw the chair and lowered herself into it. Panic rose in her chest, but along with it came rage from an unknown source.

The world around her narrowed as her vision went gray, then black, and her mind went blank. She held her head in her hands, fighting back the intense waves of nausea that washed over her. When she opened her eyes, she didn't see the table anymore.

So much fucking red. They were everywhere, like bees in a nest. There'd better be a good reason for all of this. He was a God—*untouchable*. And now, Henry had just violated the one rule they'd ever agreed on: don't meddle with his life. They'd had an arrangement, and now this resurrected corpse wanted to overstep for no other reason than to prove his growing power.

Syra wheezed. Her lungs felt like they were closing in on themselves.

A face glared at her, contorted in fury. Red markings decorated his sickly pale skin from his neck to his hands. He was dressed in a black robe and had the most vivid, ice-blue eyes she had ever seen. A familiarity that tugged at her could not be ignored.

They looked just like Morei's.

"What was that?" Henry Junok screamed. The sea of red that surrounded them—followers who had committed generations of their name to his resurrection—stopped what they were doing and looked, but Ku'sar did not even look their way. His frigid gaze was locked right on Sekar's.

"I have called for you two different times and you've ignored me," Henry continued. "Where were you?"

"Busy," Sekar remarked, and raised an eyebrow.

When Henry did not reply right away, Sekar said, "Something on your mind, oh great Ku'sar?" He eyed the reanimated corpse, for that was what he was. Henry should have died, and there were times when Sekar regretted ever keeping the bastard alive. He was the result of a risky ritual, a blood bond. Several dozen souls had been harvested to grant him a new chance in life.

Syra was on the ground, throwing up next to the table. Bile and spit were all that came up as she heaved and tried to gain a full breath of air. Tears blurred her vision and her braided hair.

Sekar felt strange, like he wasn't alone. The scar underneath the fabric—the Zyulë Bond—burned, but he refrained from scratching it, so as to not give it away.

"My spotters have informed me that a Dragon Rider approaches," Henry announced.

Sekar crossed his arms. "The white dragon?"

"Yes."

"And what do you plan to do?"

"Enslave him." The answer was simple, final.

Syra coughed and spit, her strength waning. She crawled back up and pulled herself into the chair, shaking. The putrid smell of bile met her nose, and she tried to distance herself from it. Her head felt heavy, and she leaned over the arm of the chair, dazed. She lay there, gasping and staring at the wall. She didn't want to return to whatever was happening to her. Syra was desperate to regain her composure, but her mind felt like it was being torn in two. When she blinked, she found her vision shift back to the red palace.

Henry had a blade. Dipped in black and with rubies embedded in the hilt, the Demon Killer was a weapon that could never be mistaken. Sekar had taken it, used it on Syra, but he had quietly returned it without ever hearing a peep out of this corpse. Now, the weapon was turned on him. If Henry thought this was the way to kill a God, he was quite wrong.

The sea of red had left, receding back into the depths of the palace where they could not bear witness to what was now unraveling. "Your sister told me I was a fool for trusting you. Is this true?" The blade was only a hand's width from his neck, the blackened metal mockingly bright under the light.

"Do it," he whispered.

Henry didn't move. "What did you say?"

His blood was hot, his patience evaporated. "Do it," he repeated, louder.

Syra gasped. Her mind returned to her, and she found herself back in the familiar Infernol chamber.

Chills racked her body. She lay there, her head pounding, as another wave of nausea rushed her. This time, she managed to keep the bile down at least. Syra didn't think she could move if she tried. One arm hung over the edge of the chair, and she blinked, eyelids heavy.

Her mind wandered, but it was sluggish. What had just happened? She tried to make sense of it, but she couldn't. Questions moved like sludge through her head. She didn't understand Sekar's motives or whose side he was on. Zarek might have been right—he'd earned the names Dark Lord and God of Darkness for a reason. They had left with so much unsaid, and her mind raced with what she'd seen. Sekar had come directly to Henry Junok, and his thoughts had blended into her own. There was no simple explanation for that. Sekar had been so furious, his emotions still clung to her senses even now. Did he know she'd seen some of his encounter with the false god?

It also felt like the entire ordeal with Morei and their interaction remained unresolved. She had no idea what to do if she dreamt of him again, or how to stop it. If he was as dangerous as Sekar warned, she was safer not engaging with him at all.

Not while she was still learning. Morei was dangerous—anyone who could harvest Dark Energy was—and she felt like a fool thinking she could befriend someone who was clearly so driven by sinister purpose.

As she lay there in that awkward position, she strained her ears. Zarek and Zane would be back soon, or so she hoped. She didn't want to be alone. Not anymore. But there was only silence.

When she had the strength, she would clean herself up. For now, she waited.

THE PRINCE WHO WANTED MORE

"Drink." Cyrus heard the command but didn't act. Couldn't. His thoughts were so far away, his head pounding with a ferocious snarl, and his body felt like he'd been trampled by a hundred bison.

If he could sleep for the next century, he would. All he needed to do was reposition himself. His right arm felt like it was being dunked in a pit of fire.

"Drink."

Whoever was pestering him would not go away. If it was Gendal, he hoped the Energy Harvester was close enough that he could gouge his eyes out with his own thumbs.

The thought gave Cyrus enough energy to open his eyes. His eyelids were heavy, and it took several blinks to take in his surroundings. Stone, metal, dreary—the common traits of the dungeon. But it was Alaric who caught his eye. The prince was kneeling before him and holding a waterskin up. There was a new laceration across his left eye and down to his cheekbone. The skin puckered, a grotesque pinkish red around the cut.

"Drink."

Cyrus realized the command was coming from the prince. He looked down at the waterskin and gave the faintest nod. He was ready. Alaric raised the skin just a tad, and he was able to take a drink of the crisp and cool water. It was so refreshing; he hadn't realized how thirsty he was until he had swallowed. Cyrus took three more large gulps—damn the discomfort his body cried with—and felt his stomach fill with the newfound delight. Never before, even after the life-threatening gashes to his legs, had he been so grateful for water.

When he was done, Alaric pulled away and sat on the ground with a sigh. There was a plate of breads and cheeses next to him, which Cyrus eyed. The prince shrugged. "It was all I could get."

Cyrus licked his lips. He had to look like utter shit, because he sure felt like it. "Why?" His voice croaked, and he found that even speaking made him grimace.

Alaric looked between the plate and him. "What my father did was wrong. I don't need anyone to tell me that."

"Is he dead?"

The prince scoffed. "Yes, and I earned this"—Alaric motioned at the gash—"because of it."

Cyrus shifted to get comfortable. The act seeped the little strength he had, and it took every piece of him not to turn over and go back to sleep. "He struck you because of it?"

Another man dead at Cyrus's hands, and this time, he wasn't even ashamed of it. Did that make him a monster? If it did, then he didn't want to know how men like King Raj or Morei Geral slept at night. It stunned him how little remorse he felt for the atrocious end he had brought to Gendal—there was no guilt, sorrow, or even regret. If he could face the man again, he would only wish to be cleaner about the kill.

The Energy Harvester had harmed Sozar. That made him an enemy and the *real* monster. Yet that did not change the underlying worry that hung in the air: King Raj had wanted Cyrus to kill Gendal in some cursed game of his, to prove something. Cyrus didn't know what. All he knew was that he had acted on a hunger to take control back of the life he was being tossed around in. As he sat there, reliving those feelings, he felt the smallest familiar feeling of guilt. Sure, he was glad Gendal was dead, especially for what he had done, but knowing that he may have died as part of some larger plan gave Cyrus pause.

He swallowed and motioned for the plate with a weak finger. The prince understood and pushed it toward him. He grabbed a piece of white cheese and took a bite. The chewing was slow, but the flavors were pungent, bold, the texture creamy. It reminded him of goat cheese, though not as sharp in flavor.

"Yes," the prince said. "I confronted him after you passed out. Told him what he got he asked for, and that's when he did this." He shrugged. "Not the first time."

Cyrus continued to eat. He was certainly not looking for someone to back him up, and he couldn't help but wonder if this was all just for show. Perhaps Alaric thought if he faced his father enough, he would earn Cyrus's trust. But Cyrus had been beaten into believing trust was not something that existed. Everyone he had come to trust in had betrayed him in some way. All except Sozar.

"Charming," Cyrus whispered, and grabbed a piece of bread. It was still soft, fresh. "What is your goal, Alaric?"

The prince nodded as if he'd been expecting this question. "What's happening is not right. Delion was never meant to be a city where not even a Dragon Rider could enter without fear of losing his life. Creitón was built on unlikely agreements with pirates, distant kings . . . even Saveen had an ongoing arrangement with the Guardians of Death for centuries." He paused and looked away. "We are supposed to be a country with an open border treaty—anyone can enter without fear of harm. It's why the pirates stay here, why they prefer to call these waters home, because the other countries don't have that."

It all made more sense now. "So, you are in disagreement with how your father rules."

"Yes. Not even the council will face him for fear of his wrath. The last councilmember to tell him he was breaking traditional law was killed on the spot."

A tyrant ruling Delion. No wonder the soldiers were ruthless—some of them were probably terrified that if they didn't act, they would lose their life. People would do terrible things if it meant staying alive. He should know.

Regardless of it all, Cyrus was appreciative of Alaric's kindness. The prince despised his father, resented his ruling, and wanted to make things right. Alaric was constantly going behind King Raj's back to pick up the pieces he had so carelessly tossed aside.

"Do you want to see your dragon?" the prince asked.

The question hung in the air between them. Cyrus could no longer taste the bread. Everything had stilled or gone numb. His thoughts raced, and he opened his mouth to speak but realized he was still chewing, so he swallowed. "The guards—"

"I've sent them away. It's only us down here." Alaric glanced at the door. "We are in a separate part of the dungeon, which was dedicated to—"

"Dragon Riders," Cyrus finished. It was obvious, really. The place where Sozar was held had clearly been built to hold dragons twice his size. No other creature he was aware of would need it. "So much for open borders, hm?"

Alaric sighed. "I do not condone the actions of my ancestors or my father. Most old cities have dungeons made to hold Dragon Riders. Toward the fall of the Rider Federation, many Dragon Riders went rogue, created deals with rulers against their oaths, and this created tension between Riders. If one did not pledge himself to, say, the king of Saveen, he was considered an enemy. You get the idea." Alaric stood and held his hand out to Cyrus. "Eiyrǎl has them too. Diyrǎ, possibly. Sorréle was too young a country, founded just after the fall of the Riders."

Cyrus refused the hand, using the wall to pull himself up instead. The prince didn't move at first, but when it was obvious what Cyrus was doing, he withdrew. "You said you met Dameon . . . How was he?"

At first, Cyrus didn't reply—couldn't. It took every bit of strength to get himself upright without help, and he could feel the cold sprout of sweat along his brow. Muscles shook, bones ached, and his chest felt like it was going to cave in with each breath, but he managed. He was determined to. When he was finally facing Alaric eye to eye, he answered. "He was cruel when I met him, hungry for violence." The bruising along his face thundered with a vengeance now, and he blinked several times. "Why does it matter to you?"

Alaric shrugged. "I grew up with him. He and I are the same age, just about twenty-eight summers. Dameon was my best friend for many, many summers until one day, he just stopped being one. He withdrew, grew hostile whenever I tried to contact him, and when I showed up one day, only seventeen, his father threatened to have me killed."

That came out of nowhere. "I thought with the cities . . ."

The prince waved him off. "Nonsense. There was once a time that the territories blended among Saveen, Delion, and even Barnǎl. The kids would wander between; annual markets would be held in each city with the entire country's people invited. I was raised during that time. Princes and princesses gathered outside of borders—" Alaric paused and motioned at the door. "So much to say, but so little time. Let's go while I know we are still safe."

Safe. In other words, his father might get a wild idea and come down there. It meant that the king was still wandering the palace halls at this very moment, which made this entire plan incredibly risky.

Cyrus hesitated, thinking about Raj. He wanted to see Sozar, to promise they would be okay, but he also knew the consequences if they were caught. Alaric seemed to sense this and offered a faint smile. "Give me a sliver of trust, Rider. I am simply trying to do the right thing."

"Doing the right thing may still get us both killed. Have you thought that maybe Raj made me kill your Energy Harvester?" It came out as a whispered plea.

The prince regarded him before asking, "What would my father prove by losing his greatest asset?"

"I'm asking you that."

Alaric nodded. "My father believes people are disposable. If that was his intention, then he did so to prove his power and control over his soldiers, as well as you. If you sit here and think on it, then he got exactly what he wanted. He wiggled his way right into your head, and now you'll question yourself. Is that what you, a Dragon Rider, want? To be beholden to a king like that?"

Cyrus stared at him, wondering why once more a man like this would be willing to risk so much to prove that he was not like his father. He remained wary.

"You underestimate my disdain for my father," Alaric observed. "He'd be dead before he knew it." With that, the prince walked out of the dungeon and motioned for him to follow.

Cyrus was too amped on the idea of seeing the dragon to question further. If this was the opportunity, then he was willing to take the risk. It had been too many days since he had spoken to Sozar, and he was going crazy not being able to communicate. They had been given a fleeting moment; all they needed was time and proximity.

"Your powers . . ." Alaric trailed off as they walked, as if searching for the right word.

"Aren't reliable," Cyrus finished, and glanced toward the man. He had forgotten all about the cracked stone—it felt like so much had happened in such a short timeframe. "What happened was the first time that's ever happened. I came here, to Creitón, to figure out why I haven't been able to harvest energy. Nothing more."

Their boots echoed along the hall for a short time. "Why here? What was here that you couldn't find somewhere else to do that? Doesn't a proper Energy Harvester train someone up and coming in their abilities?" Several heartbeats passed. "Did it have to do with your mother?"

"Yes." Despite what she had done, he felt little for her at this point. Part of him thought that paying her a visit would give him some closure after what she did, but on the other hand, he wanted nothing to do with her anymore. She had been a dream, a wish, that was all. "I have spent the better part of my life alone. When Sozar hatched for me, I realized I had these abilities but I could not tap into them. I have been searching for answers for more than four moon cycles now, and I was promised them here."

"And here you are."

"And here I am," he echoed. "I spent so long running from the world, Alaric . . . The Dragon Rider who wants nothing to do with the world, and yet the world wants everything to do with me." Those were Zorya's words, when she had learned of his intention to leave. Guilt squirmed in his chest so violently that he stumbled before regaining his composure. He hoped so desperately that she was okay.

"So," the prince interjected, and motioned to the right. They turned down the hall. The walk was becoming more familiar now. They were close to Sozar—he could feel it. "Let's say you discover your abilities and achieve what you set out to do. What then?"

For once, Cyrus was ready for that question. "I embrace what I am."

A moment of silence. "And that is?"

"A Dragon Rider."

Alaric nodded as they came to a stop before a door. He met Cyrus's gaze with his own dark eyes. "I don't know who you are or what you've been through, but I do know something: the love you have for this dragon, Sozar, goes above anything I've ever seen. Do not make me regret taking you here, Rider. As you've trusted me this far, allow me to trust you, even if just for this moment."

Cyrus paused. There was no need to ask for clarification. Despite the drug still in his system and his honesty, the prince believed that once he reunited with Sozar, they would flee. Even if that was his plan, even if he wanted to shatter the stone that had been confining his dragon and bring this city to its knees for what it had done to Sozar, he wouldn't. Such terrible violence was not in his nature, but the thoughts still lingered—ugly, loud, and hateful. This was a side of himself he was not accustomed to, and the emotions that ravaged his body made him uncomfortable. This was one of those times he wished he could communicate with Sozar to ground himself. The dragon always knew what to say.

"Do I have your word?" Alaric pressed.

The question broke Cyrus from his spell.

"Yes." He nodded and swallowed his thoughts. Whoever this prince was, he had been kind thus far, and they already had a mutual agreement on how they felt for King Raj. The risk was still there that the prince would betray him, and he would be a fool to ignore those gnawing concerns that this was all part of Raj's greater plan.

Yet he had a good feeling about Alaric, just like he'd had with Zorya. Cyrus needed to trust that feeling.

The prince nodded, and with one final motion, he opened the door and let it swing wide.

Every bit of self-control Cyrus had carried leading up to this point vanished, and he bolted inside. The dragon was in the center of the room, like last time, chained and shackled to the ground. Sozar lifted his head and made a loud snort—his greeting. Flashes of what had happened trickled across his thoughts, but Cyrus hardly acknowledged them. A man had died here by his hands, but he didn't care. For once, he felt proud to have defended the dragon.

"Sozar!" He skidded to a halt and placed his hands on the dragon's neck and jaw. The hot scales alighted his senses, and he gasped. A force surged through him and turned his blood ice cold. His mind went blank, and his worries ceased. The room around him dimmed. The dragon's humming reverberated across his mind like rolling thunder, and Cyrus was engulfed in affection.

Then it faded, and Cyrus blinked, stunned. He stared at the dragon, meeting one fiery eye. The pupil dilated. Sozar let a large puff of smoke out.

You are safe. The words came from Sozar, relieved.

"Yes," he mumbled, and ran a hand along the dragon's neck. Sozar was growing bigger—his neck was now thick and hard to wrap both hands around. "I'm here." His mind raced—all this time, they couldn't communicate, but now they suddenly could. What had changed?

Touching the dragon had unleashed something powerful between them. It was because of Sozar's ancient lifeforce, that Cyrus had no doubt of. But how, why . . . The questions buzzed in his head like a swarm of bees.

You did something, the dragon stated. *I felt it.*

Cyrus ran his fingers over a sharpened scale. *I cracked stone. Raj was furious with me.*

He could hear the dragon chuckle across their link. So much shared in an instant. Cyrus let his emotions be flooded by Sozar's, and vice versa. They told each other everything without ever saying a word. Images passed across one another's mind—countless stories, flashes, and all sorts of sensations that could never properly be conveyed in language. He understood Sozar and the happenings, what Gendal had done to him, which further justified his rash beating of the Energy Harvester. Gendal had used dark practices to break into the dragon's mind, to cause pain. He had tried to extract information from Sozar but without success. Sozar had nearly ripped Gendal's head off when he'd ventured too close in frustration, and when that failed, he'd burned the nearby soldiers to death.

That made Cyrus smile.

"I've never seen a dragon." The voice interrupted the spell. He had completely forgotten about Alaric. As he beheld the prince, Cyrus remembered that they were still in the dungeon, still prisoners to Delion.

Alaric stood a good ten paces away, clearly nervous. He knew of Sozar's fire. At any moment, the dragon could burn him alive.

"Not the most conventional way," Cyrus replied, and got his fingers under a scale at the base of the dragon's neck. He scratched, and Sozar rumbled with satisfaction. His mind felt *alive*. For too long it had been dead and desolate, but with Sozar's presence connected with his own again, he could think properly. "The drug given to me, what is it?"

"Indül," the prince answered. "It's a flower harvested from the forest just beyond Venkar City, south of here. The Indül flower was used as a torture tool in the age of exploration, when seamen would return without telling where they'd been or what they'd discovered, so rulers invented a way to make them talk. High doses of the toxin can be fatal, but just the right amount can render a man useless and riddle him with hallucinations, making him vulnerable. You were given a concoction of the Indül flower and suppressant to reduce your abilities—assuming you could harvest—and remove your connection with your dragon."

Sozar blinked and huffed. Already, Cyrus knew what he was thinking. "You know a lot about it."

Alaric took a deep breath and looked about as if hoping to melt into the stone beneath his feet. When that didn't work, he returned his eyes to Cyrus. "That's because I was the one to make it. It is my specialty."

Don't, Cyrus warned Sozar. *Let him talk.*

Useless, the dragon snapped, and tilted his head. *My fire could reach him. I should burn him alive where he stands.*

"Did you do it willingly?" Cyrus asked.

"Of course not." The words were out of his mouth before Cyrus had even finished the question. "My hand was forced. My father was over my shoulder. If I had not done what he had requested—"

"He would have killed you." It all made sense, but that didn't answer the main question. "You despise him, yet you do not act against him. Why?"

Now Alaric looked like he wanted to run. His fingers twitched, and he would not stand still. The prince's Adam's apple rose and fell as he swallowed, and he touched the gash on his face but did not flinch from pain. "Does a bird leave its nest if it never learned to fly?"

The question went unanswered. Cyrus could sense remorse from Sozar and felt it bubble up in his own chest. Alaric had never acted against his father because he was afraid of what lay ahead if he did so. He did not know what life was like without the ominous presence of the wrathful king always hovering over him, did not understand the lifelong damage this man had wrought on his soul. He had learned to live under his father's thumb, and every time he wiggled out just a bit too far, he was punished. The scars were proof.

"I do not seek sympathy," Alaric continued. "I have lived this life long enough to know that I could have changed it plenty of times, but I did not know how." His expression darkened. "What would the country think of a city that was ruled by a son who killed his father, hm? The rumors already circle—that my father has summoned demons and made deals with the Dark Lord. Things of that nature. If I killed him, they would turn on me, cast the shame on the only son of a monster. That is not how I want the world to see me, Rider."

Cyrus nodded and shifted his hand under Sozar's jaw, where the skin was exposed. He scratched the soft, leathery surface without much thought. "If you time it well enough, the world might see you as a hero."

"I've already thought of that," the prince replied, and clasped his hands together. "Here I am, confessing to you my deepest secrets—my overwhelming desire to end my father's reign. That was not my intention, Rider. I brought you here so that you may see your dragon without the disastrous presence of my father—or anyone else, for that matter."

The prince was hiding something. Cyrus wasn't sure what, but he could tell Alaric was uncomfortable. For now, he would let it slide. "Thank you," he said. "For everything."

Alaric nodded. "If it's any peace to you, I didn't like Gendal either. He was a brute."

That made Cyrus laugh, though it was a bit forced. "So, what now?"

With a gesture toward the door, Alaric answered, "We play the game my father wants to play. I will work on a solution to getting you out without outright treason, but I cannot do it overnight. You must be patient with me." His shoulders rose and fell, and he hesitated. "I will do everything in my power to keep you and Sozar fed and peaceful. No more beatings or harassments. If my father wants answers, I will volunteer to do it, and that is when you will see me."

To wait felt like suicide. "Why?"

"I will need the council's support prior to me acting. They will have to have some awareness of my intentions, but it will have to be a delicate conversation. I cannot risk the wrong member learning of my motives—some still put their faith in my father's ways. But if I can garner the support of at least half the council, I can have the political strength for what I will do next."

Sozar blinked and turned his large head to eye the prince. Alaric swallowed at the direct eye contact, even as Cyrus asked, "And that is?"

"I plan to kill the king."

SPLINTERED MIND

It had been five days since Morei had seen Sekar. Five days since he had harvested energy in the illusion that he had thought a dream. He hadn't seen Syra either in that time, and he was relieved. She was a danger.

He'd been certain the God had been done screwing up his life after killing Emerald, but he was wrong, and now he had Syra to worry about as well. He could not deny the control Sekar had over the entire illusion, either. It both unsettled and invigorated him. This wasn't scrolls and age-old documents that some distant king had signed off on, these were energy-oriented, realm-altering concepts that his studies had not covered. Concepts well outside mortal knowledge.

No Man's Land was long behind them. It was unreal to think how much Morei's life had changed. A cycle ago, he had been the Geral king, and now he approached the grand wolf city on the sea. He had crossed Sorréle for this. It was unbelievable to finally see his future. Ahead was the birth of a new era.

Despite all the excitement from the soldiers around him to return to their home, he could not shake his own thoughts. It had been supposed to be straightforward: leave Geral, be intercepted by Caster soldiers, and then come here to fuel a war that would destroy his former city. But now, it was messy. Now, he might not be able to hide from those like Sekar or Syra. Something bigger was happening.

But he did know he was not the same man he once had been. Morei wasn't ignorant. Something was changing in his thoughts, the way he considered things, the way he wanted to act. Impulses were increasing, making his fingers twitch at the slightest justification to draw blood. It had been progressive. The day he marched onto the battlefield with Diemon, he had started to lose a part of himself.

And the day he looked that beast in the eye, his mind had fractured. Too strong was the force—the Chaos—that had surged through him, along with those memories of emotions. They still clung to his senses, occasionally rearing up so large that the air was ripped from his lungs. Morei found himself withdrawing at times, succumbing to the voices that never ceased. He'd listen now, unable to control them like before, and they had quite the tune. They entranced him in a way that rivaled summer rain on a hot desert landscape.

When he snapped back, he would blink and take in his surroundings. It felt like, at times, whole afternoons would go by before he came to from his spell. The men wouldn't say much, although Harrison often handed him a waterskin to drink from, insisting he stay hydrated. The sun was brutal, and as the humidity spiked, they sweat constantly, even if they did nothing but sit on the backs of their steeds.

Commander Edwin stared at him—a lot. It was quite clear the commander still did not approve of Morei. Other men, like Otis and even Lanz at times, followed, sharing whispers and glancing back at him. To them, he was an anomaly, a bad omen. Everything about Morei was meant to destroy. And now, Caster soldiers were bringing him, the traitor and murderer, to face their very own king. Of course it sparked confusion and uncertainty.

But he still had a couple of supporters, like Harrison and Rodrick. Nobody outright said what they thought of Morei, especially after the incident with the beast, but they didn't have to. He could pick up on the small behaviors here and there, like how Lanz tried to avoid handing anything directly to him, as if a mere touch would set the soldier aflame. Or how Harrison always seemed to be concerned with Morei's wellbeing. While he had made progress, a division had become apparent after their encounter. Some thought he was attracting bad luck, while those like Harrison and Rodrick seemed to revere him.

"When the king is ready, he will summon you," Harrison said as they rode. "We are approaching the city, so—"

"There will be stares," Morei cut in, softly. "I know."

A horn sounded from the walls of Caster—soldiers announcing their arrival. Rodrick pulled a blue flag with a gold howling wolf from a pouch and began to wave it in the air. Another signal to confirm that they were indeed Casterian soldiers.

The horn sounded back.

Morei refrained from smiling. It had been a long time since he had heard such a call. As king, he'd grown used to the sounds of oncoming and ongoing travelers, deafened even by the redundancy of it all. But now, so long since the last Geral call, the sound traveled all the way to his bones and filled him with warmth.

He loved it.

As they neared, Morei studied the stone architecture of the wall that surrounded the city. That was something he was not used to—Geral had not gone so far as building an entire encompassing wall. To do so foretold not only of violence, but of distrust among the citizens and royalty. Small settlements spotted the left and right side of the main city—the outer portion, where the less fortuned lived. Though by the looks of it, he would opt for outside the walls too. If not for the view, then for the freedom it offered. The idea of being locked away and unable to see the world around the city felt rather claustrophobic. In Geral, he could look out of his palace and see leagues upon leagues of land.

The stone was of high quality—the Caster family clearly took pride in their work. Among the thousands of bricks that made up the wall, many were engraved with intricate designs and patterns: wolves doing various activities, and even Old Tongue sigils on a few. There were gold embellishments along the gates with a howling wolf atop each side, facing each other. The gates were iron, the metal bars as thick as Morei's arm—impenetrable. Above, Caster soldiers stared down from their walkway, lips curled up in ugly snarls.

"You're back," one announced, rather unenthusiastically. "And you brought *him* with you."

"King's orders," Harrison replied, although Morei was sure that was obvious.

"Open the gates, soldier," Commander Edwin ordered. "Or I'll have your head."

"Commander—" The voice stopped, even as the soldier's eyes were going wide. "Apologies, I did not recognize you."

"The beard will do that," Edwin retorted. "Open up. I am in need of a bath."

Morei remained expressionless, even as his eyes darted between the two. How had a soldier not recognized his own commander? Every soldier of Geral had known Boris, and Drew once he had taken over.

Apparently, there was a major gap between the soldiers and leadership.

A deep groan echoed over the land. The gates were being opened with levers, and they all waited until the space was wide enough to allow comfortable passage. The horses moved steadily, and Morei held his breath as the gates gave way to the city by the sea that he had learned to loathe.

It was not as hideous as he anticipated. Homes with gray shingles lined the outer edge, and as they came closer to the center, where the palace lay, residencies gave way to shops, markets, all sorts of goods to be bought. Some of the people were garbed in rags and others in fine fabrics, and many of all castes stared without manners.

They probably believed him a cannibal, a heart-eater, that he bathed in the blood of his enemies. Some must even believe he and Sekar were working together.

He was a monster to these people.

For once, Morei was glad of it. There was nothing to prove. Here, he could simply be. The rumors were true, the crimes had been committed, and there was no point in denying any of it to prove that he was the son of a peaceful king. Morei was what the world wanted him to be. There was nothing more freeing than that revelation.

Their travel took a long time. The city was large, and the streets extremely crowded as people clambered over one another to get a good look at him. He kept his face devoid of emotion, but he didn't hide behind the hood of the cloak or drop his eyes. As they rode, he locked eyes with anyone who dared to.

As they approached the second wall, he looked ahead. The sun was cresting behind the palace, lowering as the afternoon dragged on. It would be dark soon; the shadows from the tall outer stone wall were already long. A chill clung to the air despite the glow that still kissed his skin.

Two soldiers stood at the smaller gates. These carried the carved metal wolves as well, identical to the first pair, but the gates did not have to be opened with a lever, only a simple hook. Odd.

Perhaps the gates and stone walls were a representation of power and fortune, not of distrust. Morei would have to ask to find out more. A lonesome hook lock like the one on the gate ahead could be opened by a simple flick of the wrist. The only hassle would be taking the two soldiers out, but any Energy Harvester with basic training could do that.

There was a lot more to this all than he'd realized. Perhaps fear kept people at bay, but fear of what? Of a mad king who'd lost his mind? The citizens of Geral hadn't been afraid to turn their backs and hurl insults at Morei, despite the knowledge of what he was becoming and his ability to harvest Dark Energy.

The gates opened without word, just a few nods in passing. Morei, again, was stunned. This was unlike any structure of armed forces that he was accustomed to. Caster men did little speaking. They assumed, and turned a blind eye more often than not. It was a miracle this city was still standing.

Morei felt a deep sense of purpose. There was a lot of work ahead, and a lot of answers to find, but what lay before him was something he could control. He would make this city into one the likes of which the world had never seen before. No man, God, or beast could or would reach him here.

He would be untouchable.

A DANCE WITH DESTINY

It was the sliding of metal against its sheath that alerted Syra first. She tensed in the chair. She'd managed to clean herself up, along with the half-dried bile she'd left on the floor—not her finest moment—and she'd been waiting for Zarek and Zane, hoping to have them back by now. It was late, but there had been no word or knock to suggest their return.

She knew the sound of a sword from anywhere.

Syra didn't trust her own breath, afraid the noise would manage to reach whoever was on the other side. She eyed the lock—it was in place. Beneath it, she saw slight movement as the handle was tried.

Death's Sword lay on the chair next to her, sheathed and waiting.

"Come on out, redhead," a voice called. A familiar voice. She'd already dealt with this one before—he'd spit at her.

She held her tongue, hoping they'd think wasn't there. Or maybe Zarek or Zane would show up before anything got out of hand. Her heart was in her throat, hammering away.

"You still got that sword?" another called. Toothless, no doubt. He'd been interested the first time too. "I bet I can get a lot of coin for that one."

"Shut it," the first snapped. "You talk too much."

Syra reached for the weapon, the leather cool to the touch. Her mind wandered, searching for anything that could help her, but unless she was suddenly able to summon up Chaos on a whim, she was out of luck. Her ability kept slipping from her mental grasp, a chase that she couldn't win. Worthless. She was absolutely worthless in the face of danger.

"We just want to talk," the main one continued. "Think we left on the wrong foot last time. We wouldn't want to upset the . . . *Fräurune.*" The name came out with such mockery that a shiver ran down Syra's back. Zane's words flashed across her mind from their discussion. He'd been worried about her coming to the south end of the Infernol, but it seemed they had found her.

More knocking. "Come on, Syra, we know you're in there," Toothless said. A rustling noise, then scratching on metal. She stared hard at the door—they couldn't open it without unlatching the lock, but now she wasn't so sure. The only thing she knew was that she needed to hide. It felt far safer than standing here. If that meant going under the bed, she would.

Syra slid across the floor on her bare feet. The bathroom was too spacious, with no obvious hiding corners. There was the walk-in closet, though? She paused halfway to the bed, feeling it too obvious.

They were attempting to break in. She wasn't sure how, unless they knew how to saw through metal, but she didn't like it. If there was an Energy Harvester among them, even one with little talent, they could get that door open. Syra tightened her grip on the sheath and ran across the room. Quiet or not, they were coming in.

Syra shoved herself behind the door, using the dark to shield her presence, and slowly unsheathed Death's Sword. The metal came into view. Even in the shadows, it managed to glint from some unseen light. Adjusting her grip on the hilt, she set the belt on the ground and waited.

She followed Zarek's instructions and slowed her breath. It would do no good to be hyperventilating if these people broke in. Syra focused on the weight of the sword, adjusted her feet so that she was already in a fighting stance, and strained her ears.

There was an awful silence. The sound of her own heart was too loud for her comfort, and she tried to peek out between the crack of the door to the main area, but she found nothing. She wished that she believed they had just given up, but she knew better. There was not a single piece of this that made her feel good. Syra was ready to tear her eyes away when she heard the metal latch slide back. Shifting her gaze, she finally found a narrow view of the door and watched in horror as it opened.

Four men came in—two she recognized from the previous incident and two she didn't know. Only Toothless had his sword drawn, but it was the main one who made her hesitate. He appeared to be listening. The tilt of his head was a dead giveaway, and while the other men moved out of view, he stood there, eyes down. He was the Energy Harvester, and he was sensing for her lifeforce.

As brave as Syra was trying to be, she could not still the shake in her hands. When she'd been on the ship with Zane, things had felt uncontrolled but far easier to cope with, even though they'd been leagues from land and there was an Onye onboard. Right now, she felt like a cornered animal preparing to be slaughtered.

She'd tried to think ahead, but she was right where they wanted her to be. Syra had stopped praying a long time ago. She did so now—prayed that Eazon, the God of Luck, would shed her some sort of fortune. She didn't feel like a Goddess, the Light Bringer, Fräurune—whatever the world wanted to call her—she felt like Syra. Helpless, scared, and hoping she could run her way out of this problem.

Holding her breath, she blinked and refocused her attention. She couldn't see anyone. Syra tried to swallow the immediate panic, hoping not to choke on it, and to readjust her angle from the narrow gap to see more. As she shifted, a large brown eye came into view.

"Cozy in there, ain't it?" he said.

Syra reacted fast, slamming her shoulder into the door to close it. She saw a hand come into view to try to stop it. An agonizing howl broke out as his fingers were smashed, but Syra didn't care. She jabbed with her sword, and the person retracted with bloody cuts, though not without a shove back against the door. She stumbled back, losing her footing, and tried to push herself against it again, but she was outnumbered, outweighed.

An arm stuck out around the door, and she lashed out with the sword, watching the metal glide right through the skin. Another yell, but it was no use. The door opened, and Syra found herself standing before the four men. Toothless had managed to bear both assaults. His right arm was bloody, but he looked as determined as ever. The Harvester tilted his head.

"We just want to talk," he told her. "All this discussion about a Lirallian floating around, and we can't help but wonder . . ." He paused for dramatic effect, although it did little for Syra. He was obviously used to being in control of situations. "If you were working with Liral?"

At that, two lunged for her. Syra drew up her sword just in time for a hand to come down on the sharp edge. The one to her left stepped back, clutching his lacerated hand, while the other grabbed her. Instinct took over, and Syra punched him square in the face. Knuckles met cheek, and her hand was flooded with pain from the impact, but it caused enough surprise for the man to let go.

The cold touch of a blade against her throat. She froze in place. Syra's eyes scanned the group. The one standing behind her was their leader. She'd been too caught up defending herself from the other two to see him shift around her.

"Grab the sword," he ordered. The one Syra had punched reached over and started to pry the blade from her grip, but she resisted. The flat of the dagger pressed against her neck, hard. "Let go."

If they wanted to talk, so be it, but she didn't believe it was all about that. No, this was planned. When the other had Death's Sword and was admiring it, she asked, "How's the south side doing? Did a riot finally start?"

That caused a cold laugh. "Glad you took notice. It's got everyone busy down there."

She would have nodded if not for the blade against her throat.

"Garett, you ready?" Toothless asked.

Ah, so his name was Garett. When he pushed her forward, she had the instinct to shove an elbow into his face, but as if he were reading her mind, he latched one arm around her own and forced it behind her. The muscles in her arm strained, and it felt like her bone was going to snap in half at the slightest give.

"Just talk, huh?" she said out loud as they headed toward the hall. The awkward hold on her made it difficult to walk with ease. They were too close, and his sour stench consumed her with each inhale.

"It'll be just a chat if you tell us what you know," said Garett.

"Know what?" she snapped back, and nearly tripped as they picked up the pace. The Infernol was massive and usually full of people, but the hall was eerily quiet.

The riot had been a ploy to get to her.

Toothless looked over at her, still brandishing her sword like it was his new prize. "Who you're working for—"

"I'm going to stab you," Garett cut in. "Just shut it. You do best when your mouth is shut." His words were hot with annoyance; she sensed tension between them all. She wondered how long they'd been planning this, and whether or not they would really just let her stroll free at the end of this. They wouldn't, of course, but she just hoped to figure out her next plan of action before Garett got too comfortable with the blade.

She licked her lips. "So—"

Garett yanked her arm, causing her to hiss in pain and stumble. The blade against her neck scraped under her jaw, where the skin was thinnest, and she felt the familiar pang of blood being drawn. The three other men glanced over but kept walking without a word. It was clear they didn't want to question their leader.

"Quiet," he told her. "I'm not in the mood for games."

She wanted to snap back that she wasn't either, but she knew a real threat when she saw one. Garett was itching to prove his point, and she bit her tongue. Warmth trickled down her neck, slow and steady.

Her thoughts raced. If she yelled, Garett would cut her neck open. If she shoved him off, the blade would dig right into her skin. That didn't even take into account her arm being pinned behind her back. If she got free, she'd run, but she wasn't even sure where she'd go. These men likely knew these halls better than anyone.

They passed most of the sleeping chambers, then the galley. Syra trained her eyes on anything that looked familiar, but the only thing she could distinctly recognize was that everything was made of stone. She had no idea where they were going.

The walk was short-lived—too short. It felt like they had just left when they came upon a door. She'd been so worried about how she could get free that she hadn't spared a chance to consider who would actually be behind this. Yet even before one of the men pushed the door open, she already knew the answer.

Arik stood in the center of the grand room. His face, despite the commotion, remained devoid of any emotion. As he greeted them with a simple blink, her eyes fell on Keryn. Anger welled inside her.

He stood there behind Arik, only walking around when the doors behind her closed. The intricate and colorful pattern on the polished stone floor made her think this place had once been a room for some sort of authoritative figure. It was certainly large enough, but now that everything had been removed, a distinct echo that filled the room as they approached.

Nobody else was here—not even the other twin—and Syra wasn't sure if that terrified or relieved her.

Keryn's eyes barely met her own. "Drop her, Garett. She isn't going anywhere."

The man who had held her so tight shoved her forward like she was nothing more than a fly on his shoulder. Her knees hit the stone hard, but she used the force of the throw to get to her feet and lay hands on Keryn. The leader's expression twisted in surprise.

Arik stepped forward and, with a single sweep of his hand, sent her sprawling. Her elbow hit the stone with bruising force, followed by her hands and shoulder. Syra, momentarily dazed by the sudden fluctuation of energy, remained still.

"Are you done?"

Keryn's voice dripped with annoyance. Carefully, she rolled over and stood, not wishing to show how uncomfortable she was from the fall. Her elbow throbbed, but she didn't touch it as she took two steps forward and stopped. Sword or not, Syra would put up a fight, but she needed to strategize first. Arik would make it far more difficult to act against the Infernol leader.

And then there were the four men. Syra internally cursed—too many to fight by hand. If only Chaos could come easy to her. Now was the time she needed it most.

But when she reached for that force again, she saw Arik's face twitch. His gray eyes met hers. He knew.

As if to confirm, Keryn took control of the room. "No point in these verbal games, Syra. Arik has told me you possess

Chaos, and as far as any of us are aware, only a God can have that. You've been living here, right under my nose. I'm not quite fond of secrets, you know. They tend to fester."

Zane's words hung over her, and she eyed the Infernol leader and then Arik. The Energy Harvester would have known days ago that she possessed Chaos if he could sense it, so why now? And it didn't make sense that only one of the twins was here—she'd never seen them apart until today.

She threw caution to the wind. "I'm glad we're here, Keryn. I've been hearing some things about you." Her calm tone caused the Infernol leader to hesitate. "Rumor has it that you've got a deal with Liral?"

Keryn stared hard in return. A vein bulged in his neck, and she swallowed. Nobody moved. She'd felt confident saying it, but now she wasn't so sure it was a good idea.

"Quite the rumor, Syra. Did Henry tell you that himself?"

She snapped, "That's the best you can do?" She was buying time. For what, she wasn't entirely sure. Arik seemed the only real potential she had at getting out of here—if she could get him to see her side. It didn't seem anyone was coming for her.

Keryn clasped his hands together and offered a slight amused smile, as if he found her remark funny. When he spoke, his words were cold. "Arik, please."

Syra felt the energy shift before she saw it in action. The Energy Harvester's gray eyes were the only thing that gave away his motive as he turned his attention on the four men. Without warning, they all dropped to the floor. Death's Sword clanged loud, and she grimaced at the impact it took. She stared, but when she saw not a single chest rise or fall, she returned her gaze to the two men left.

"Thank you. The tall one annoyed me," Keryn said to Arik, then looked at her. "You must be careful with what you say. Words like that could cause quite an issue if they reached the wrong ears."

Syra opened her mouth, stunned, but he waved her off. "Don't. There's no need. I've never been fond of verbal wars. They bore me." He took a half step forward but then paused. Perhaps because he didn't wish to get too far from his protector. Syra refrained from saying more. Keryn had exactly what he wanted—just her.

"This is going to go one of two ways, Syra. You're either going to stand by my side or you're going to cause quite a mess to clean up," Keryn said softly. "The Infernol can use power like you."

She raised her brow. "You mean Liral?"

He regarded her. "The Infernol is still the Infernol. Regardless of where we gain allies from—"

"I'm not serving you or anyone associated with Liral," she cut in. "Is Arik not enough for you?" The Energy Harvester blinked.

Keryn continued, unperturbed. "I've been informed that there is a war coming, and it will be the greatest one this world has ever seen. If we are to prepare and survive it, we need to gather resources, make allies, and put our trust in one another. I would hope that to be you. The people here could use . . . a little *faith*."

It all sounded fantastic in theory. Until she put Liral in the mix. "Did Henry tell you to say that? Was that his grand speech? Or did he have a sword to your neck when he made you pledge fealty to him?"

The tension shifted a bit. Keryn looked frustrated. Arik still stood like a stone statue.

"Well? I'm waiting for an explanation." She recalled the vision with Sekar and the brandishing of the Demon Killer. She hadn't seen the lead-up that would cause Henry to draw up the blade, but she suspected the false god—Ku'sar—didn't need much of a reason to do so. He was unstable. She'd gathered that much.

"If—" Keryn coughed then, voice strained. He frowned and reached up to touch his chest, rubbing it. "I . . . um . . ."

Syra's jaw slackened as a mist materialized behind the leader. As the mist thickened, Keryn's looked to turn to stone, skin paling. Arik's expression showed the first real emotion that she had ever seen on him—shock.

Sekar stood behind Keryn, a head taller. The Infernol leader's body lurched backward as the God's eyes dropped and yanked his arm back. "Hm," Sekar breathed, and yanked harder. Keryn staggered again. This time, his eyes glazed over, and a trickle of blood fell from his mouth. The Infernol leader's gaze dropped to Syra as his head rolled. Then his knees buckled, and he slumped to the floor between them.

In the God's hand was a spasming heart. His black glove dripped with crimson, coating the ground with Keryn's blood. He was dressed in red, but there was a clear splatter of blood across his neck and arms.

"I don't believe he'll be needing that anymore," Sekar mumbled casually, and dropped the heart on the floor. He removed the gloves from his hand and tossed them on the body before turning his attention to the Energy Harvester.

Arik looked physically shaken. Syra stared as the man dropped to one knee, stuttering, "Never . . . Never in my life—"

"Did you think you'd see me?" Sekar laughed, his voice bouncing off the walls. "I'm flattered." A single twitch of the God's finger was all Syra saw. Arik's neck twisted and snapped. The Energy Harvester dropped to the ground with a final thud.

She hadn't anticipated seeing Sekar here, not so soon after everything. She couldn't tell how she felt. Everything felt so raw still, unfinished, and that didn't even include the strange vision they'd shared. She wanted to punch the smug look off his face, as if he'd planned even this entrance. There was hardly anything that surprised him, and even when the Demon Killer had been directed at him, he'd asked for Henry to kill him.

"Dance with me, Syra."

She swallowed and blinked. She'd hardly noticed him approach. Six bodies lay strewn about the floor, there were unsaid words still hanging in the air from their previous encounter, and he wanted to *dance*. No, she wouldn't twirl about like some maddened maniac while the Infernol leader lay dead. They had problems—immediate problems—to deal with.

"I hardly think now is a good time. We have stuff we need to talk about."

There was a gleam in his dark gaze, one of passion and thrill, a devious combination for a God like him. "Dance with me," he repeated slower. This was not a request, but a demand.

She crossed her arms, appalled. "You just murder—"

"I will not ask again."

They stood there, eyes locked. Syra wanted to challenge him, argue, anything to make sure he knew just how annoyed she was that he would show up at random and not address what had just happened. Yet her gut told her to accept. Sekar was here for a reason, and whether she liked it or not, she'd have to play by his game for the time being. While she was grateful that he'd shown when he had, she could not find herself to thank him. His timing was always coincidentally impeccable, and that got under her skin after the hundredth time.

Still, she reached her hand out, and he engulfed it with his own. He drew her in, placing his other hand on her waist in a simple form. Syra laid her own against him, and when he smiled, she said, "Is this really what you want?"

In answer, Sekar took the first step forward, and she followed.

A silence fell over them, and Syra remained tense as they moved. She hadn't danced in many summers, but the steps came easily to her. It was customary for many to know simple dances like this one—a step forward, a step backward—for festivals, and she sensed Sekar knew that.

But as her eyes landed on the bodies behind them, she felt her breath catch. This all felt so wrong, so out of her control. She didn't understand the point, and while she was nervous about his intentions, she also knew him well enough to say something. "Sekar—"

"When I was mortal, I danced frequently," the God whispered. He sounded like the man she'd first met. Kind, considerate. Not like the one who had just ripped someone's heart out. "The empire held many festivals and royal balls, and I was always in attendance. In those days, the people found any cause to hold a celebration."

They took another step forward. Syra turned her eyes up to his, studying him. She knew he was centuries old, but at the mention of an empire, she realized how little she knew of who Sekar really was.

"They say a dance can tell you a lot about a person," he continued. "How their muscles move, the tension in their shoulders, where their eyes settle. You look to the dead, yet I don't understand why. They were going to hurt you, Syra. Do you feel sympathy for those who wish to take everything from you?"

She raised her brow. "Of course not."

"Then don't look," he insisted. "They are not worth your time."

But they were. Didn't he realize that? The Infernol leader lay dead—that alone would cause an uproar among the people. If they found she was tied to any of it, she would be killed before she made it to her room tonight. Zyulë Bond or not, there was no protection from someone who snuck up and shoved a blade into her back. Her mind couldn't rest. Not now. They had a massive problem on their hands.

"What happened wasn't supposed to," Sekar said as he led her. "I knew you were there—I could feel you, like an itch I couldn't get rid of. If you think I have an explanation, I don't."

Now her attention was on him fully. "I could hear your thoughts too."

That seemed to catch his interest. "Really?"

She nodded. "Do you think it has to do with the fracture?"

"Possibly. The Bond could affect it as well."

It was unlike Sekar to not have an exact answer, and she fell quiet, thinking. He didn't seem upset by any of it. Frankly, he seemed unconcerned. The dance slowed, their steps more leisurely, but they did not break. She wondered if the God found comfort in this, if that was the cause for his demand. She hadn't seen what happened between him and Henry, but now she wondered if he'd returned because of it.

Syra could ask a thousand questions, pry for information on Henry Junok. Sekar might relent. But it all felt meaningless—the most dangerous person was the one right before her.

"Will you ever betray me?" The question hung in the air, untouched between them. Syra waited, watching for any reaction, but his face did not change. There was no need to expound on what she meant. He worked alongside Henry Junok, the man who now possessed the Demon Killer and had once asked for her. The danger with Keryn, the Infernol, and everything else felt leagues away. Sekar had shown commitment at times, but he was unreliable at best. Seeing his interaction with Henry, even just those moments, made this all too real for her.

His grip tightened on her hand, and they stopped moving. Sekar cupped her face with his other. "I will not break our deal."

She wanted to ask more—it was hard to believe him fully when he'd already done so many horrible things—but the creak of the hinges from the door opening caused her to pause. The look on Sekar's face contorted into complete disbelief. She anticipated Henry Junok himself to be walking in with that look, and her nerves flourished as she turned to face the next problem.

But it wasn't the false god. It was a Guardian dressed in a tattered cloak with a normal sword on his hip. He walked slowly, his crimson eyes scanning the bodies. When he finally met Syra's astonished look, he slowed to a stop and nodded.

"You've made quite the mess," Dryl said.

THE KISS OF DEATH

It had been seven days. Seven days since Cyrus had seen Sozar and spoken to Alaric. He had been locked in his dungeon the whole time, forced to piss in the corner and ration his water. Soldiers came to drop off food and occasionally a new jug, but that was it. The portions were small, but it was safe to eat. Cyrus had determined that after the first time he'd eaten and still been able to communicate with Sozar. It also meant Alaric had kept his word—even if King Raj was ordering it, the prince was not drugging any of his food or water. There were no more beatings.

By the third day, Cyrus's pain was finally lessening. His wounds were healing, his headache had receded, and the swelling in his face had gone down significantly. The new cell he had been moved into after cracking the stone in the previous one had fewer leaks, so he was able to sleep on the dingy cot. Although it wasn't anything comfortable, not sleeping on the ground gave him the slimmest bit of peace. Most nights, he just lay awake— his sleep pattern was all messed up. He was too unsettled to slip into a deep sleep, so he napped.

He and Sozar spent a large portion of the time trying to figure out the surge of energy he'd been able to harvest. It was a massive push forward in understanding himself, but it left significant questions. The most prominent was why he had been able to do such a thing when he had a curse that should've blocked his ability. Sozar theorized that the intensity of his own emotions had overrun the strength of the curse, but Cyrus wasn't sold. There were plenty of times Cyrus could say he'd felt similar. No, this was something abnormal. What had happened wasn't supposed to, yet now it was all he could think about.

If he could replicate it, maybe then he could confirm that he was able to harvest energy. The ability was clearly there, just volatile in his grip. Already, four times, he had tried to harvest, to call upon the energies around him, and the attempts had all failed miserably.

You try too hard, Sozar had finally said. *The summoning should come easily.*

Cyrus scoffed into the dark—he had lived without light for two days now. *Care to explain what happened when I touched you? How you were able to reconnect with me without a problem?*

The dragon grumbled his response. It had been an ongoing thing between them. Sozar thought maybe it had to do with his age and maturing, but Cyrus believed his own energy harvesting had a direct link to how the dragon manifested energy.

So they did that, over and over, theorizing on what-ifs and grand possibilities about what it could all mean. Cyrus no longer felt a vacant void when he tried to harvest energy. It was all there, just out of reach, like mist slipping right through his fingers every time he tried to grasp it. Leonzo had not come up, but the man weighed heavily on Cyrus's mind—they had made a promise to return on the third moon cycle, and if they did not leave soon, he feared they would not make it. It seemed like such a minuscule problem compared to everything going on, but Cyrus was the kind of overthinker that would make any of the Vore Gods mad. He obsessed far too much time on every topic, like King Raj, Alaric, energy harvesting, Leonzo, the future of the dragon eggs . . . on and on it went. The points were clear, the direction obvious, but he couldn't stop thinking.

Yesterday, it had occurred to him that they hadn't seen any women as of yet. Not even those who brought the food were women—only the soldiers ventured this way. He wondered if there were any women who worked in the palace above him.

That brought him to Zorya, which then brought him to face the one regret he truly had: leaving her behind to face whatever Dameon and Ashtir had planned. More and more, he wanted to hope that the Dragon Rider had been bluffing to scare Cyrus into confession, but he couldn't shake the fear that Dameon had done something unthinkable. The Razan princess had been the first person Cyrus could trust in this scheme life called fate, and he'd thrown that away like it meant nothing. Maybe he should have brought her with him, but then what? She'd be here, locked up with him, and he would have failed to protect her in a whole new way.

Stop it. Sozar interrupted his spiraling thoughts. *You have done nothing but worry about what you cannot control. Don't you grow tired of all this?*

Cyrus repositioned his arms behind his head, propping himself up. There hadn't been any chains either, which he was grateful for. It had given his wrists time to heal. Whatever Alaric had done, he had at least convinced the soldiers and his father that he was not a threat. Probably because King Raj still believed him to be drugged.

Then what should I do? Cyrus countered. *Call out to the dead and converse with one of them instead?*

Summoning the dead is not a topic to toy with. The dragon was displeased with his humor. *You should try energy harvesting again. I think you're close—*

Cyrus sat up. Boots in the hall. Someone was coming.

He listened. This was outside the pattern he had grown accustomed to. Cyrus had gotten good at predicting their arrival, and he wasn't expecting anyone for quite some time. If his tracking was right, it was the middle of the night.

Cyrus tensed and waited.

The person walked with far too much certainty for his liking, as if in a fit of rage or all out of patience. When the boots finally came into view, a lantern floated above them, showcasing their shiny, polished black leather and buckles. As well as the wearer.

King Raj.

Stubble lined his jaw, unlike Cyrus's, which had turned into a beard days ago. There were circles under the king's pale hazelnut eyes, a telltale sign he had not slept, and his eyes looked like they belonged to a savage animal, not royalty. The king's hair was messy and unkempt, and his clothes were wrinkled. He slid the lock open to the cell door slowly, letting the screeching metal fill the gap between them.

"Greetings, Rider."

Cyrus swallowed but did not reply. There was no point. Sozar's presence loomed in his mind, as if the dragon were hoping to burst through right here and tear off the king's head.

King Raj hung the lantern on a hook, this one on the right side of the room. It cast just enough light to make Cyrus dread looking the king in the eyes—he could see their disdain. "I've come to chat."

He nodded but held his tongue. This was a violent man and not one he wanted to act irrationally with.

The king approached his cot. Cyrus recoiled. The man noticed and smiled, then sat on the stone. He clasped his hands together and looked right at Cyrus. "You've put me in a predicament, you know." The king waited for a response, then continued. "You killed my Energy Harvester, which is grounds for immediate execution. Did you know that? I'm sure you did, but you were brave. So very brave. My soldiers and staff are still talking about it, despite my orders. They can't help it. The Rider who killed Gendal—that'll be a story for quite a long time, won't it?"

Cyrus took a deep breath, letting it seep out through his nose. The slightest movement felt like a trap, so he remained as still as possible. His thoughts circled back to his initial concern about Raj urging him to kill Gendal, and he wondered if the king knew his thoughts. Perhaps Alaric was right, and Raj had wiggled himself right into Cyrus's head, exactly what he wanted.

King Raj continued, smooth and calculated, as if he had rehearsed this. Maybe he had. "My son, who thinks he's so clever, continues to protect you." Cyrus's blood turned cold. "I know you're not receiving the drug, and I know because of that, you've likely reconnected with your precious dragon. You don't need to answer that—I'm not a fool—but I am curious on one thing. If the drug has worn off, what keeps you here? Do you prefer to be a prisoner, Rider?"

Now, he had to speak. "No."

"Ah, I was worried you had lost your tongue." King Raj chuckled, sending a shiver down Cyrus's spine. "So, what keeps you here? A Dragon Rider who willingly stays a prisoner is no honorary thing."

He's baiting you, Sozar warned suddenly.

But Cyrus knew that. It was clear the man was trying to rile him up, get him scared enough to say something he shouldn't. Or maybe he was fishing for information on his son. That thought pressed itself on the forefront of his mind. The king was here trying to gather information on Alaric—to see if Cyrus knew anything or was willing to speak against him.

Cyrus licked his lips. "You speak as if your concerns lie within your council. How would I know this answer?"

Now, King Raj grinned wildly. "You have experience with royalty, don't you?"

There was a motive. "What brings you here? To speak poorly of a son you already despise or for something else?"

Raj's face twisted. "You're so eager to prove your worth now, but when I arrive as I have now, you don't act, just sit there, reeking of fear. If I didn't know any better, I'd say that makes you a coward."

He didn't need Sozar to tell him to be quiet this time. A lifetime of receiving insults from the boys in the orphanage had made him aware enough to recognize the tactic all too clearly.

"You've flown for quite a while," the king continued, "but you fail to fly with purpose. Don't you grow tired of it?"

"No," Cyrus snapped. "I'd rather fly alone than for a purpose that does not define me."

The man clasped his hands but kept them on his lap. That cold smile was plastered on his face, like he was a part of some horrifying tale that Cyrus was about to be victim to. "So . . . what *does* the great Sea Flyer desire?"

He inhaled deeply, noting the faint scent of body odor, but whether it came from him or the king, he wasn't sure. It had been so many days since he'd actually bathed. The idea of cleansing himself and taking a large gulp of water passed through his mind. He licked his lips, acutely aware of how dry they'd become. He was sure he looked less than bold to this man, but that didn't sway his values.

"I want peace," he said as confidently as he could.

King Raj laughed. It was a full-belly one, tears rolling with it. It was the kind that made Cyrus want to disappear right into the wall. When the king straightened, he wiped at his left eye. "You are such a fool," he muttered. That face quickly turned stoic again, but his eyes told Cyrus everything he needed to know: the king was a monster.

"There's a war coming, and if you don't choose a side, the dead will snatch you up when you're not looking. So, tell me, what is that you desire?"

Cyrus swallowed. It was all falling together, but the frigid grasp fate had on his heart right now made it difficult to move without a pain shooting through his chest.

The king could obviously tell, because he leaned forward and narrowed his eyes. "If you pledge yourself to our cause, you will be absolved of all your crimes, but if you fail to do so . . . Hm." He curled his nose. "You smell like shit."

Cyrus reacted before he could think, like he was possessed by something else again. This time, though, as he lashed out in some attempt at bravery, he was immediately overcome with fear. He struck out, slamming his palm into the king's head. The force of the impact made Raj curse and jump up, while Cyrus stumbled from the cot, keeping his back to the wall. He eyed the king as the man cursed and glared at him.

"Is that your answer?" he demanded, so loud that Cyrus cringed. If soldiers were nearby, they would have surely heard the commotion.

He was right. Footsteps started filling the hall, along with a few shouts, but the king did not tear his gaze away from Cyrus. It was like looking into the eyes of a starved animal—one wrong move and the beast would strike. The only problem was that he already had. If King Raj hadn't wanted him dead before, he did now.

"You will never earn my respect or loyalty," Cyrus told him.

The guards showed up then, but they paused once they saw the king. Cyrus would have in their place as well. The way this man stared at him, the hunch of his shoulders, the curl of his fingers, and his snarl would have caused pause in even a God. King Raj had officially snapped.

"Chain him and take him to the whipping post," the king ordered, and then a wicked grin seeped across his face. "And bring me the spiked whip." The man looked back to the soldiers and then to Cyrus once more. The next words that came out were filled with venom. "I want him to face his dragon when I whip him."

DRENCHED IN PURPOSE

Morei had expected a lot of things upon his arrival. He had anticipated being tossed into a dark dungeon, starved, and beaten. In the same breath, he had also expected to be hauled right into the throne room to face King Drexis. If he'd been in charge here, that was what he would have done—get the confrontation over with. If the Caster king was so mad, Morei expected to be handed the brunt of whatever he had in mind.

What he hadn't expected was to be escorted toward the great throne chamber and then told to wait.

He'd been left with Rodrick and Harrison after some discussion between the men. The two selected to stand with him came as no surprise. He quite liked them, despite all the hassle and uncertainty. They were easier to understand. The others, while predictable, were harder to connect with, and that had grown tiresome. If he was going to wait, he'd rather it be at the hands of those he could strike up some sort of conversation with.

The humid air clung to his skin, unbearable with the cloak on. Sweat dripped down the back of his neck, offering no cool reprieve. Yet when he looked at the two soldiers, they did not look uncomfortable. It was a different kind of heat than he was used to. Desert and sea heat were two different beasts, and it would take some time adjusting to that.

They stood where citizens would stand if they had appointments with the king. There were some backless stone benches nestled up against the wall, but that was it. In Geral, there would have been a table with drinks available for those who waited. Morei was certain that Drexis did not want to give the impression of hospitality.

The hall was made of solid, polished white marble, just like everything else. Another sign of power and riches, he presumed, but that did not waver his respect for the architecture. Silver and gold columns held the ceiling up, gold veins crossed through the marble in a sporadic design, and the floor beneath him was broken up routinely by detailed gold wolves. When he stared at the one he stood over now, he realized the design must have been achieved by pouring melted gold into the carving before sealing it with a gloss.

Impressive. Geral had never done anything like that.

At the end of the hall to his left, he saw several staff members pause and glance his way before exchanging words and disappearing. When he looked to his right, he saw a soldier quickly walk by at the end of that hall, not even sparing a glance.

Based on the lighting, he knew the day was growing old, but he hoped to have this matter taken care of before night fell. He was eager to see Drexis once and for all.

"You, uh, ever see the sea before?" Harrison asked.

Morei was grateful to have him start the conversation. "No. Only in literature."

"Some people love it, others get as far from it as they can," the soldier remarked with a shrug.

"And you? What do you think of it?"

Harrison looked to weigh that for a moment. It occurred to Morei then that none of them had even bathed, and while he couldn't be surprised about himself, he was surprised that there hadn't been an opportunity for these soldiers to at least freshen up. Their armor was dusty, their hair greasy and beards unkempt. He knew he didn't look any better, but he was supposed to be the prisoner. At Geral, there would have at least been a handoff between the soldiers who'd traveled and others who were well-rested.

"It's water," Harrison answered. "I forget it's there."

"So true," Rodrick commented. "The only time you remember is when there's a storm. The surges we get from the sea can be nasty sometimes."

"There was once a time when the port was submerged," Harrison added, then waved it off. "But that was a long time ago."

Morei listened with interest, enjoying the ease with which they spoke. It was the first time he had felt so comfortable since leaving Geral. Regardless of the chains on his wrists, he felt like they were three friends having a casual chat. Of course, being able to talk like this helped him gain their trust more too, so the interaction served several purposes. "In Geral, there's always been talk about pirates and the dangers of cities with ports. Is that true?"

Rodrick scoffed. "Far from it. I've lived in this city my whole life—that's thirty-three summers, mind you—and we've never had a pirate attack."

"We do get visits though," Harrison commented. "We've got trades with a few of the clans. Crazy what they do. I wouldn't ever want to spend my days on those waters. I'd go mad."

They fell silent. Morei stared at the double doors ahead of them. More specifically, he eyed the great howling wolf that was carved into the massive gray slab of wood. He tried to will it open—hoping that Drexis would summon them now—but that didn't happen. After the travels, his feet were starting to grow sore from just standing here.

Morei couldn't wait for a bath.

Footsteps danced through the hall. A staff member was making her way by, holding a basket of freshly cleaned cloths. Dressed in simple attire and with her dark hair braided to the side, she kept her eyes lowered as she passed. Morei wondered if she averted her gaze because of him or because she wasn't supposed to make conversation with anyone. She soon disappeared.

In normal circumstances, Morei would have gladly stood in silence, but he was anxious, and he also wanted to keep these men talking. It kept him distracted. Morei could feel the urges flaring—the knowledge that he would soon have his way with Drexis was making him fidget. Patience, he reminded himself. Patience. The upcoming moment meant so much to him— revenge, rebirth—and it couldn't come fast enough.

"So," Morei said, "any idea when he might summon me?"

Harrison looked at him with quizzical eyes. "You in a hurry to die or something?"

Morei raised his brow. "You think that's what he intends to do?" It didn't surprise him one bit. Actually, he'd anticipated as much, but he wanted to hear what the soldiers had to say. It would tell a lot about what they thought of their king.

Rodrick snorted. "Whoever—whatever—you are, I don't think you're a fool." *Whatever.* The word stung, but he didn't let it show. It was a rightful thing to say because all they knew was what they saw and heard about him. The soldier looked up at him with that dark gaze. "You did something to that beast. I don't understand it."

"Rodrick," Harrison warned softly to his left.

But the soldier continued. "I believe you know more than what you say. The others want to dismiss it because of superstitions, but I don't. *Sir*"—the word came out desperate—"they want to tell the world you've come to rain blood from the sky, but I don't know what to believe. Part of me wonders if driving a blade through your heart here and now will spare us. The other part of me wants to drop to my knees and ask for your forgiveness. So what should I do?"

Morei, for once, was speechless. He had misread the soldier, perhaps both of them, and now he wasn't sure what their motive was, save to stay alive. Was that all this was? Their attempt to stay alive by befriending him? Morei didn't need friends, had worked alone and would continue to do so because nobody could entirely be trusted. But there was something with how this situation had shifted that left a sour taste on his tongue. It felt like he had been misled, and that rubbed him the wrong way.

He couldn't blame them, though. If their roles had been reversed, Morei would've done everything in his power to befriend the most dangerous person. These men were simply watching their backs, and acknowledging their motive gave him a much bigger advantage.

Without looking either in the eye, he whispered, "If someone came into your home and killed your wife and children, would you seek justice yourself or would you leave it to the court?" Morei didn't know if these men were married, but he was willing to take a bet at least one of them had a partner.

Rodrick cleared his throat, his answer shaky. "I'd kill the man myself. Our court is unreliable."

A city built on violence. Morei would weaponize it to gain the loyalty of these people. As he started to answer, the undeniable hook of a lock being undone radiated through the entire hall, and both men stiffened. The shackles on his wrists clanged together as he watched one of the doors open.

Two more soldiers stepped out—one with blond hair and the other with dusty brown. They both appeared devoid of emotion. "The king will see the prisoner now," the one on the left said as they approached.

"Ah." Harrison nudged Morei forward, even though he was already gladly approaching them. He anticipated Rodrick and Harrison to follow, but they remained stationary. As the two new soldiers latched a hand around each of his arms, he nodded. "Evening, gentlemen."

They didn't reply, but their grip tightened.

This was it. This was the moment Morei had been waiting for since the day he left Geral. If he wasn't careful, he'd find himself smiling, and that would really unsettle everyone. He didn't want to scare them too soon.

With a deep breath, he wiped his expression of emotion, kept his chin up, and entered. A prisoner would enter, but a king would exit.

DAMNED FOR POLITICS

yra's body went numb. Her heart hammered, and she could do nothing but stare for what felt like an eternity. The world became unreachable as she beheld the one person she'd expected never to see again. The rain from that day felt cold on her skin, the scent of blood thick in her nose; she relived that last bit over and over. Dryl had given her the belt, Death's Sword, the ring, and the note. It felt like he'd been the sole reason her life had progressed, and she'd known she would do everything she could in his honor.

She'd had to accept his death, even if she regretted every moment leading up to it. Syra had told herself over and over that the Guardian had planned it all, even death. She'd told herself that to find some sort of peace. But now he stood before her—alive.

Sekar spoke first. "You're alive." Still, he looked as shocked as Syra felt, and she couldn't tell if he was relieved or terrified to see the Guardian standing there. It wasn't like they'd left off on good terms.

Dryl met him at eye level. So many times they'd shared that same look when Sekar had been concealing himself as a Guardian. It looked like an entire conversation passed between them. As old as they were—having seen the world and the things they had—Syra realized that there was probably little that could ever be said to right wrongs.

Finally, Dryl pushed the hood of his cloak down, revealing shaggy black hair—a look she was not used to. He had always kept it short. "Your eyes haven't changed," the Guardian told him.

"I came for you," said Sekar. "You were not there."

Dryl pushed passed the God and approached Syra then, who still hadn't moved. She'd expected a lot of things, but she hadn't anticipated Sekar's relief—or his words. Yet Dryl pushed him aside, eyes locked on her own, and beheld her for a long while.

"You've changed," Dryl told her. "I didn't expect it all to happen in such a short time, but here you stand, reborn as a God. Tell me, have you harnessed Chaos?"

Maybe Syra had expected him to bring her into one of his hugs, or maybe she'd wanted an apology for believing he was dead. Yet he was greeting her as if business was normal and Keryn wasn't lying dead on the floor next to them. As if he hadn't just jumped right back into her life with no warning.

"She's come a long way," Sekar answered for her. "But still much to learn. Chaos comes differently for each God."

Syra opened her mouth and then closed it. No, she realized, she'd wanted a hug. Not this.

"Do you have the ring I gave you?" Dryl asked.

Numbly, she nodded.

"Good," he replied. "It'll be required for the next part."

"What part?" she asked. Her voice was barely audible to her own ears.

The Guardian motioned to the bodies. "The Infernol leader is dead. I suspected his involvement after I heard some stories from exiled Infernol members, but it seems Sekar was one step ahead of me. Unfortunately, that causes an issue with the politics. The council will be fighting to get their voice heard for a chance at the title. There are people I'm sure were working with him in the Infernol who we'll have to locate and remove. That ring will guarantee me leadership. It was the original Gonsín's ring, and it was bestowed to me by him for the possibility of this day—when the Infernol lost sight of its original purpose."

Syra stared. The words went in one ear and out the other. She'd carried that ring believing it was her key to safety. When Keryn had looked at it, he hadn't said anything to her—had he known?

She looked at Sekar. "Did you know?"

The God gave the slightest shake of his head. "When his body wasn't there, I suspected he might have managed to get out of there before Henry's followers showed, but I was never able to confirm."

"What he's trying to say is he missed me," Dryl observed with an obvious tone of humor. "He couldn't stay away after dealing with me for all these centuries." His expression grew serious as he looked over at the God. "What you did back at the Nighthunter Federation was cruel."

Sekar regarded the Guardian. His words were hardly audible, but they carried a level of certainty that could not be argued with. "We made a promise to keep Syra safe. I have upheld that, regardless of who you thought I was then."

"And yet you still manage to cause problems, wherever you go."

Syra held a hand up. Damn the politics, the mess they were in, all of it. She didn't want to hear it—she wanted proper answers. "Dryl," she managed to say, "you left. You were stabbed, bleeding out, and I was terrified." Annoyance bubbled up in the back of her throat—she felt like these two were treating this like all one big joke, like they didn't care just how significant this all was. She turned her attention to Sekar. "All this time, you thought Dryl could be alive? When I asked you the first time, you didn't tell me that."

"What good would it have done for me to tell you my thoughts on that when there was no way to know for certain? I am not his keeper, although he wishes I was."

"Cut the sarcasm," she snapped, irritated. "The three of us"—she gestured—"were it for a long time. I expected more from you. Honesty." She emphasized the word, hoping he picked up on her insult from their previous conversation. He'd wanted to accuse her of not being honest? Well, two could play at that game.

He showed no response, save for the single blink.

Done with him, she turned her attention to Dryl. "I have spent almost every day thinking about you, believing it was my fault you were dead. Instead, you were off exploring and now you show up acting like nothing's wrong." Her voice rose, and she felt her cheeks turn hot. "Do you all think this is a joke?"

"No," Dryl shot back, crossing his arms. "I didn't come back for you because I couldn't. The Infernol politics are in shambles, but so is the Soul Realm's. I needed to disappear so that I could research and collect information without looking over my shoulder."

"So you faked your own death?"

"That part was real. The Lirallian I ran into had a blade forged with a deadly toxin. It would have killed a mortal man, and when I saw you—" He paused, his expression relaxing. "I did think I was going to die."

"And the *Leangé?*" Sekar asked, cutting into the moment. At the mention of the book that belonged to the Soul Realm, she stiffened. She'd found it in a drawer in Jared's home. Not the most clever hiding spot for a Guardian, now that she looked back.

"Taken. I'm assuming it's in Liral."

"I was unaware," Sekar replied, and rubbed a hand over his neck. Blood still splattered his sleeves and parts of his neck.

"I know you're upset, Syra," Dryl told her. "I know you want to scream, punch me, whatever, but I need you right now." He pointed at Keryn. "What we do next will either cause the Infernol to collapse or unite, but I cannot do it alone. Your support and confidence will persuade people."

She bit her tongue, feeling the familiarity of Zane's words surfacing. "The people talk about me. They don't want me here—a lot of them. They think I'm some sort of bad omen."

"That's the work of Keryn," Dryl countered. "He likely had his people spread false things about you. Anything to cause enough division to make you seek his council."

She couldn't share his confidence. Her eyes landed on the bloodied body. "He wanted me to work with him."

"Who wouldn't?" Dryl remarked with a chuckle. He walked toward the bodies, pausing when he saw Death's Sword. He picked it up and examined the metal. His fingers ran the length of the font engraved along the blade. *For you I stand. For you I fall.* Syra had memorized those words.

She studied him. He was different. The Dryl she'd known had been more passive, selective about his actions, even when he was certain. He'd always been so calculating in his words. It felt like she was speaking to a stranger, and maybe she was. Maybe she didn't know Dryl like she'd thought she did. Or perhaps her own changes had shifted her perspective.

"This is the story," Dryl said. "Syra was never here—safer that way. These men got into it—we'll call it a political disagreement. Unfortunately, Arik here turned on his leader, and a fight broke out. I discovered them, having just returned from a trip."

"People will challenge your authenticity, given the death of the Energy Harvester," Sekar pointed out. The God had managed to come up right next to her. "These men couldn't have killed Arik."

"Fair point," Dryl replied, and eyed the Harvester's broken neck. "You didn't make this one easy, Sekar. Nobody will believe me if I say I broke the man's neck. Not a break like this."

Sekar shrugged. "Call it a tragic story. Arik was so devastated at the loss of his leader and guilt-driven from his actions, he didn't hear you approach."

Dryl shook his head, but she saw a faint smile. "Always dramatic," he observed. "His sister?" His eyes fell on Syra then. "Was she here?"

"No," she said. "I thought it was strange."

"It is, but we'll use it to our advantage. The twins wanted different things—she killed him and fled."

"And I'm the dramatic one," Sekar remarked.

"Let me do the report," Dryl offered as he approached them. Death's Sword looked so flawless on him, like an extension of his own arm. Syra realized then how large the sword was for her frame, yet she'd been carrying it around and training with it. The weapon, while heavy, was one that she liked, but it was no longer hers. The owner of the sword now stood before her. "I'll deal with the ramifications, clean-up, all of it."

Sekar nudged Syra, and she looked up at him. "He lives for this," the God commented, clearly amused. "When Shevana kicked him out of the council, he made the Infernol so he could play king for a day whenever he wanted."

The brotherhood between these two was undeniable. It was like they'd never been apart, like Dryl hadn't just learned the Guardian he'd befriended was a God. In fact, his response to it all had been so calm Syra wondered if he'd come to know this all prior to his arrival. On top of it, these men had spent centuries working together in the Soul Realm. After so much time together, there would be a bond there thicker than stone. The story that Sekar hinted to was one she'd never heard of before, and it made her realize how little she knew of the Guardian.

Syra didn't understand any of it. The reality she'd become so accustomed to felt like a façade. Everything was changing in an instant, and she either had to get on this horse and go or be left behind.

She knew they didn't have all day to catch up, not with Keryn lying dead. Someone could barge in at any moment. Zarek and Zane would be looking for her. By the Gods, Dryl's brother was here.

"I must return," Sekar said. As he stepped around her, his eyes did not leave hers, as if he hoped to tell her something. "I will return tomorrow evening."

She knew what that meant—training.

Syra nodded, but she couldn't find the right words to say. The confrontation over Morei still hung over her, along with other things he'd said to her. He'd promised he wouldn't betray her, but the complexity of what existed between them felt bigger than those words.

She watched as his physical form turned to a black mist before that too evaporated.

"You know, Gods can usually carve portals with the use of Chaos," Dryl explained. "The purity of the energy cuts right through space and realms, but leave it to Sekar to turn to mist."

Syra turned to face the Guardian, who granted her a kind smile. She wanted to laugh with him, but even that felt too soon. "Here," he said, and offered the sword.

Frowning, she shook her head. "That's yours."

"But I want you to keep it," Dryl insisted. "It may save your life one day."

Begrudgingly, she took it back. The familiar weight gave her comfort. "If you change your mind—"

"I won't."

They stood there, face-to-face, and she felt an awkward pang wiggle itself into her chest. She'd spent so much time dreaming of different outcomes if the Guardian had fled the

Nighthunter Federation with her, but this was not one of them. She was beyond relieved to see him, though, and to know that she still had him to guide her. Deep down, she'd always blamed herself for his death, and she'd learned to burden that guilt, as best she could.

She resorted to the one thing she could wrap her head around. "Your brother is here." The words felt foreign on her tongue. "He'll be grateful to see you."

Dryl looked startled. "Zarek?"

"He showed up after we thought you died. Zarek came looking for you. He wanted to right the wrongs of what he'd done."

The Guardian nodded but didn't reply. His eyes turned downward, lost in thought. She wondered what he was thinking about—she knew the brothers hadn't had the best relationship.

"Where is he?" Dryl asked.

"There were some problems in the south side," she replied. "He was down there helping manage it. Fights, a riot, that kind of stuff."

"I never thought it would come to this." If he meant this entire situation with Sekar or Zarek, she didn't know. "You should go. Get back to your room. When I call for you, bring the ring. I need to get this reported—preferably with Bane before word spreads—while we still have the upper hand."

Syra nodded. Betrayal, anger, relief, it all had melted away. She wasn't sure what she felt anymore. The Infernol was now in Dryl's hands, so long as everything went to his plan. He obviously knew everyone already, which didn't surprise her. Zarek had told her enough for her to understand that the Guardian had essentially helped build this place from the ground up. Still, amid all the unknown, a strange sense of peace settled over her.

As her steps carried her to the door, she didn't look back.

A SAVAGE DESTINY

ragged, beaten, and yanked down the hall, Cyrus could not get his feet underneath him for long enough to fight back. The soldiers were following orders, even as the king ranted. King Raj was telling him of all the torturous acts taken upon dragons back when the Rider Federation was falling.

Like how they would drug and chain the dragons before pulling out their scales one at a time. It sometimes took days before they heard a dragon scream—it was a sound that many said even the dead Gods could hear, and it echoed long after the dragon was killed. He said that when Cyrus was rendered barely conscious, he would make death a blessing by driving a blade into the dragon's eyes, one at a time. And when the dragon was blind, he mused, he would cut his wings.

Blood poured from Cyrus's nose; the soldier to his right had slammed him head first into the stone wall. His head swam, but he continued to struggle, even as he was practically thrown into the one chamber he'd been desperate to return to.

Sozar growled at their arrival, his voice rolling over the walls like thunder. Chains moved, and Cyrus barely had time to look at the dragon before he was kicked in the ribs. The boot was familiar—one could only grow used to the giver of pain by learning the quirks, like how King Raj's boot curled up at the tip and burrowed itself into his chest. Blotches filled his vision, and he swallowed, tasting blood on his tongue.

"Make sure he can see his dragon," the king demanded as the soldiers grabbed his arms and hauled him up. Already, his strength was waning. The beating on the way here was taking its toll on him, exaggerated by the little food and water he'd been receiving. Sozar strained, but the chains held. That metal was made for holding dragons twice his size.

Cyrus's hands were strapped to a wooden post that was nailed horizontally above his head, and he leaned against the vertical frame in front of him, resting his head against the worn wood. It was cold to the skin, and he blinked slowly, watching the dragon.

Then he smiled. *Funny, isn't it?* Cyrus thought out loud for Sozar to hear. *I spent all this time trying to protect you, and I still failed.*

The dragon's response was loud, his snarl making the soldiers flinch. There were no words, just emotions—hot, white fury—that flooded his mind from their bond. He knew Sozar was angry at him for saying such a thing, but even angrier for what was happening.

Fire erupted from the dragon's jaws, covering the ground around him as he tried to melt the metal, but it would not even grow red. It was molded with some immense power to refuse a dragon's fire.

If they had the ability to render a dragon flightless and defenseless, then Cyrus was certainly bound to die.

His shirt was torn free from his body in an instant, a knife cutting through the fabric along his back. The cold kiss of the blade nicked his skin, just enough to make him flinch. Cyrus tried and failed to make any progress with the leather restraints on his wrists. The humid, chilly air of the chamber caressed his exposed skin.

"Your Majesty," a soldier said from behind. "The whip."

"Ah, good."

Cyrus's heart was racing as he prepared himself. Fear had her claws deep in his chest. It would hurt, of course, but he hoped it numbed or he passed out before it became too much. There was only so much his body would be able to take.

The horrid touch of the whip dug itself into his back without warning. The immediate agony that seared through his back came as such a surprise that a cry left his lips without permission. His body tensed, his arms strained against the straps, and he tried everything in his power to shy away from the weapon.

"I think it works," King Raj commented with a satisfied tone, as if testing leather in a shop. "You still stand by your decision, Rider?"

He nodded without thought, eyes locked on the dragon. Cyrus would rather go to his grave than agree to anything this fucking animal had to say.

"Shame," the king replied. "I saw so much potential. Think of all we could have done together, but you choose to die like a coward."

Again, he struck, and again, Cyrus cried. The agony of a spiked whip was horrific. Hot blood spilled down his back. The spikes tore apart layer after layer of skin until muscle was exposed, and that was a different kind of pain all together. Cyrus's cries turned into guttural screams. He could not contain them as the whip grew fiercer, hungrier.

Sozar watched, a fiery yellow gaze focused right on him. It did not blink, would not move anywhere else. The dragon was feeding him with his own lifeforce to keep him strong and taking the pain that he could. While the dragon couldn't take away the physical pain, he replaced the emotional pieces with grand adventures of flight and warmth, trying to keep his thoughts far from the horrifying reality of this crime. It helped some but could not remove the traumatizing agony his body was enduring.

His back must have been splayed open like a butchered animal. Blood had seeped into his pants and down his legs. The post that his head was shoved against smelled thickly of metal.

A door slammed open, followed by a shout. The incessant beating of the whip ceased, but it did not give Cyrus relief like he hoped. Instead, the pause gave his body the opportunity to spasm from the sheer agony of the injury. The pain amplified, his thoughts grew heavy, and he was certain he heard footsteps but could not find the strength to move his head.

Unconsciousness wavered just on the point of stealing him away, but the sharp hiss of the whip yanked him back into this reality. Internally, he was begging for it to end. This was too much—he should have been dead long ago.

But Sozar was still feeding him with strength—strength he no longer needed nor cared for. Strength that this dragon needed, not him.

Let . . . me . . . go, he insisted. It was almost cruel to see Death's reach but still not be able to feel her embrace. His thoughts were fading, even as his heart beat furiously from the added energy.

The whip struck the side of his face, whether by accident or on purpose, he didn't know, and he didn't care enough to react. Muscles laxed, his head spun, and he was growing increasingly sluggish, even as warmth filled his body.

A soldier came into his line of sight, his face twisted in horror, a blade in his hand. He was shaking his head, blood splattered down the left side of his face—likely Cyrus's. The soldier said something, and Cyrus realized he couldn't hear. There was a deafening ringing in his ears.

Suddenly, the thrashing stopped, and King Raj was in front of him. The whip hung in his right hand, coated in crimson and gleaming with an unquenchable hunger under the light. The king lashed out and started beating the soldier with so much force, the man didn't stand a chance. Caught between striking the king he was supposed to be loyal to and the frozen terror of the unraveling situation, the soldier fell to his knees just as Raj unsheathed his sword and slid it across the front of the man's neck. And just like that, the soldier slumped over, head hardly attached, blood pouring, and King Raj flashed him a smile.

Then he repositioned his blade and started to approach, his steps too slow and too calculated. His eyes didn't leave Cyrus's as he grabbed his hair and pulled his head back at an uncomfortable angle. The tip of the blade brushed against his neck, cold.

Never had Cyrus been so relieved at the thought of dying.

Another blade came into his line of sight. It was so quick that Raj couldn't react. His face twisted in surprise, even as the metal embedded itself into his chest. The king's sword faltered, nicking his skin with a sting he couldn't even feel from the roaring pain of his back. Then Raj stumbled backward and dropped his weapon, grasping at the hilt of the dagger.

He tripped on the dead soldier, falling, yelling something Cyrus could not hear. Cyrus watched, certain he was hallucinating all of it as Alaric came into view and knelt over his father. The prince started to beat his father with a series of frenzied punches. There was soon blood on Alaric's knuckles and forearms.

And still, Sozar did not take his eye off Cyrus.

He was growing wearier. No matter what the dragon was feeding him, he could not—did not—want to feel anymore. His eyes opened and closed, his head rolled to the side, and when he tried to breathe, he found he no longer felt the need to.

A KING OF WOLVES

The throne chamber was smaller than Morei had anticipated. Not that it wasn't grand, but given the outrageous number of polished gems and tapestries and the halls, he would have expected even larger. It was a bit smaller than Geral's, but still quite spacious. A ridiculous blue-and-gold rug ran all the way from the entryway to the thrones—one for the queen, who was absent. Come to think of it, Morei couldn't remember the last time he had heard of the queen of Caster. Was she dead?

That didn't matter. What mattered was the old man who sat on his throne, dressed in royal blue—a large silhouette of the howling wolf embroidered on the chest in silver—with a scowl that could have cut ice. The shirt was clearly for formal events, perhaps even what he had worn on his wedding day, and King Drexis had found it fitting for this occasion.

The Caster king stood at Morei's arrival. Next to the throne stood another man—a chancellor, he presumed. The man was middle-aged, with dark hair tied in a high bun, stunning tawny skin, and amber eyes. Strikingly similar to Ezra's, he realized, which didn't bring him peace. He grimaced—too many memories were tied to the man he'd left behind as king.

The wide shoulders of the chancellor hinted at a number of summers swinging a sword. Impressive.

"Hold," King Drexis ordered just as Morei came within ten paces of the dais. The raised stone slab he stared at was intricately painted with thousands of running silver wolves. It was quite the artistic touch to an already ostentatious room, with the throne chairs and their hand-carved wolf-head arms.

The soldiers still held him, tenser now, their grips bruising. It was clear they were uncomfortable.

King Drexis grinned but did not move. "Your neck. Is that from whatever ailment eats at you?"

Morei did not reply. There was no need.

"You are more hideous than I could have ever imagined. Isn't he, Rhys?" He motioned at the chancellor, who gave the slightest nod, which satisfied the king.

Again, he held his tongue. Better to look resolved than to put up a fight.

Drexis clasped his hands together, the sound echoing across the silent chamber. Nobody moved, save for the Caster king as he paced the dais—his safe place—and spoke proudly. "When Sorréle was founded nearly 780 summers ago, the major families—Caster, Diemon, Ferguson, and Geral—were already at odds. The tension of the Great War, the failing politics of Diyră, and shifting cultural expectations drove many arguments as the four families chose their preferred locations. Despite all this, they did not want war. They had lived it and fled from it already. So the Royal Treaty was signed and put into place as a promise that would protect upcoming centuries of prosperity— and to some extent, it worked, didn't it?"

If Drexis expected an answer, he didn't wait long enough to hear it.

"The families all chose their values. Diemon even went so far as to exploit children and mine in the dangerous mountains so that they could trade gems not found anywhere else. But Geral . . ." He shook his head, and the smile finally slipped to reveal the horrid monster underneath. "Geral went to the farthest reaches of Sorréle, on the cusp of land that no man has gone to and returned safely from, and for what? So you could remain in possession of a land that half the world had forgotten about? And as if that wasn't enough, Geral decided to forge weapons—not as a pastime, but as your primary financial income. Your entire economy is built off weaponry—off *war*, Morei. Let me make that clear. Your family has craved blood-shed since the day they sailed off from Diyră and landed here."

Drexis paused in front of the queen's throne and tilted his head at Morei, as if seeing something for the very first time. "Did you know your grandfather nearly rode the entire army of Geral in a fit of madness up against my city? Probably not." And it was true, Morei had never heard of that. There was no documentation or evidence to suggest so. "You probably didn't know that your great-great-grandmother was a witch, either. She was burned alive by her own husband as a way to appease the citizens and keep the peace."

Again, Morei did not know. His stomach twisted in knots as a hundred questions stormed his tongue. He had been raised, as the prince and heir, to know his lineage and everything about it. Why was this man telling him things that no one else had?

"I know these things because I have spent a lifetime collecting information from all over the country, from every family. I have ears everywhere, and my mother took a particular interest in Geral when I was only a boy. She befriended a Geral princess, and they exchanged letters, and soon stories. My mother documented them all, so that I could learn from them, because there would be a day when Caster would have its chance to reign. And it seems that time is now."

Rhys's eyes never wavered from Drexis. The king took one step off the dais and onto the rug. "Here is the sole heir, the last of the Geral bloodline, chained before me." He grinned madly, like a boy given his first sword. "I have waited for this day for decades. Chancellor!"

Rhys's chest rose as he came to life. "Yes, Your Majesty?"

"Sword," the king ordered without taking his eyes off Morei. "I think this little show is over, hm?"

The chancellor did not say anything but proceeded to step behind the throne and produce a sheathed weapon. The encasing was a beautiful silver leather with engraved wolves. The sword's handguard was shaped into what looked to be teeth, like a wolf's mouth prepared to snap shut on the neck of an enemy. As Rhys handed it over to the king, Drexis unsheathed the weapon to unveil metal that was tinted blue when the light hit it just right. Despite the circumstances, Morei could not help but appreciate the craftsmanship of the weapon.

Another step toward him. King Drexis showcased his sword. "Impressive, isn't she? I had her forged with metals harvested from the Releuthian Mountains—a gift from Queen Reaza. Before you killed her, of course." He glanced Morei's way and then took another step forward. "Do you have anything to say? Any last words?"

If the Caster king could stop talking for more than a moment, he would hear Morei's racing heart. It slammed itself against his ribcage with a ferocious pounding, like a caged animal desperately trying to break free. His skin was damp along his nape, spurred by the nerves of excitement that made the air taste a little sweeter. Even his mouth salivated like he was an animal.

He licked his lips, acutely aware of how dry they were. Drexis was waiting for him to say something. "What will you do once you kill me?" More time, more opportunity for the grand Caster king to close in on him.

All he needed was a few steps.

"Hm"—Drexis flashed him a sinister grin—"I'll rally my troops and set for Ferguson. Best to start there, right? They are the closest. It would be foolish not to seize the city first." The king took several steps forward and motioned at the guards. "Put him on his knees."

Hands shoved him down. Morei's knees met the rug with a jarring force that radiated all the way up his back, but he refused to let it show. The less he spoke, the better.

"Move away now," the king ordered. He was only five steps away, and he motioned with his sword. "Don't want to lose your heads too in the process, eh?" Drexis laughed—shrill, maddened—and Morei cringed as the sound grated against the stone walls. If his wife was dead, it was for good cause. That was a laugh that would send even the bravest men to the Afterlife.

Morei saw the men move away in his peripheral vision as Drexis tested the sword. He swung, controlled, at an angle. "I think I'll come at it from the left. Seems to be the best for me." His eyes sparkled with a hungry malice. "This is it, Geral, any last words?"

Another step forward. It was now or never.

Morei took a single breath. In it, he felt the current of Dark Energy devour him at once. The power surged through his limbs, chest, all the way down to his fingers and toes. A coldness enveloped him—perhaps the touch of Death herself—as he listened to the voices that now screamed in his head for his submission. It had been a long time since he had felt this *alive*, as if he had consumed the hearts of a hundred men.

It all happened too fast for Drexis to react. Morei forced the energy into the cuffs, shattering the metal into pieces. The chains fell off just as he lurched forward and wrapped one hand around Drexis's throat while he grabbed the sword with his other. He pried the weapon from the king's hands with far too much ease—perhaps Drexis was still stunned and trying to catch up with what was happening—and brought the metal up to meet the corner of his eye.

Soldiers rushed forward in a frenzy—all four of them, a pitiful number—but Morei could sense their lifeforce and feel the open borders of their minds. Such arrogance. Without moving, he seized all their minds in one swoop and forced them to still. It didn't take much effort, not when he was summoning Dark Energy to do the bidding.

Take them! one of the voices begged. Dark Energy was starved for a soul—she always was.

Morei refocused his attention on the king—no longer was he smiling, and that brought him joy. Drexis's eyes were wide, his cheeks flush. Up close, Morei could see the stubble that decorated the king's jaw. He sniffed—the man stank with fear.

"In all your arrogance, your desperate plea for power, you forgot one little thing," Morei hissed. "I'm an Energy Harvester."

He tried to speak, but all that came out was a wheeze.

"What was that?" Morei asked, and squeezed a little harder. "Will you threaten me? Tell me I'll never get away with this?"

Drexis was now turning red all over. His eyes—once so blue and bright—were bloodshot. "Stooo—"

"As you wish," Morei cut in, and let go. The king dropped to his knees, coughing and gasping. He spit all over the floor as Morei circled him, adjusting his hand over the sword. It was quite heavy—more of a decoration—but it was balanced, and he found it easy to maneuver.

"You are a king who has spent his lifetime hiding," Morei told him. Drexis tried to get up, but Morei forced him down to his knees with a swift burst of energy. As he wrapped around the king, he saw the soldiers staring, bodies still his to do with as he pleased. "Tell me, oh great king, what should I do now?"

"You're—" The king shuddered and rubbed his neck. "You can't just take my place. Is this what you intend?"

Morei smiled. "It's a part of what I intend. But why shouldn't I?" He brought the sword down to face the king, the point just over the bridge of his ugly nose. "You think your people will protect you? Demand retribution for a king who has taken everything from them?"

"You've lost your mind," Drexis spat, but he did not move under the weapon's glare.

There was so much he wanted to say, do, all of it, but at last, Morei couldn't resist the urge that was growing in him. The urge to make Drexis suffer. He stepped forward and latched a hand into the king's gray hair, forcing the blade against his neck. The skin broke, and a thin line of crimson ran down and stained that precious fabric.

"You took *everything* from me. You turned everyone against me, so that you would have to force my hand. Do you think I would really not come for you?"

Despite it all, Drexis managed a faint smile. "You did that all yourself." The words were final, full of resolve, as if he had been wanting to say it for days.

Morei didn't waste any more time. He knew it was dangerous—to split his mind up between men as he had already done—but he wanted Drexis to scream. Morei drove the portion of his mind that was still his into the king's. The boundaries were flimsy, and he easily cast them aside. He didn't want to sift through memories, he wanted to elicit pain. So he did the one thing he could do—he gave Drexis his own. Down to the night he was abducted and killed, the fall that nearly broke his legs when he was ten, and everything afterward. Every bit of his agony was forced down Drexis's throat in a concentrated poison.

The king screamed.

Morei watched as he tried to squirm free, to do anything. His hands tried to latch on to the blade, but in his frenzy, he sliced them right along the edges. Morei didn't want to end there, despite the warning signals in the back of his mind. Shards of the Caster king's mind inevitably slipped into his own, tainting his thought process, never to leave. Foreign emotions reared before being squished by his own—terror choked out by hatred, anger stomped out by a savage need to see this through.

Slowly, he fed the Dark Energy her meal. The power surged through the king's body, tearing apart muscle and bone like they were made of dust. Vessels popped, organs combusted, and before he knew it, blood seeped from those blue eyes that had once been so proud and vain. Drexis was hemorrhaging now—the blood was leaking out of anywhere it could.

Morei watched with delight as the king began to choke on his own fluids. The end was near, and he retracted his mind, but not without the haunting wisps of Death trying to cling. Caught up in the moment, Morei had waited too long to pull away, and he blinked in realization as he let go of Drexis. The body slumped to the floor in a puddle of blood as he narrowly avoided the pull that souls felt when it was their time to go.

He stared at the body that had once been the Caster king. Good riddance to finally see the parasite dead.

A noise caught his attention, and he turned to see the four soldiers standing there, mouths agape, unmoving. Not because of him, he realized, but because they were utterly stunned. When had he let them go? Morei realized he couldn't remember. He had been so caught up with Drexis that he had failed to remain in control of these men.

It was a mistake he would not make again. The only thing that had kept him safe was their sheer terror that this torture would be visited upon them as well.

Morei inhaled, acutely aware of the copper scent that now filled the air, along with the urine as Drexis's body relieved itself in death. "Gentlemen," he greeted, voice low. "You have a choice to make, and I advise you to think carefully before you speak."

"I assume you mean me, as well," a voice came from behind. Morei turned his head to see Rhys approaching. Slowly, the man started to clap, the sound radiating the entire room. In all this, the chancellor had not moved or acted, only observed. It was why Morei had forgotten about him—Rhys had not been a threat. "What a show," he complimented, and came to stand next to the soldiers. "Never have I witnessed such power in action, *Your Majesty.*"

Morei raised an eyebrow in judgment. "A loyal chancellor, I see."

"Oh no," Rhys quickly said, "only by family lineage was I given this title. My father before me, his father, his father's father, and so on. Our family has served the Casters for as long as the city has stood. That did not mean I respected him."

Morei was unconvinced. "You think me foolish enough to trust you?"

"No," Rhys answered. "But you are foolish if you do not utilize me in the steps that follow."

A door opened, and all eyes turned to see an older woman quickly approaching, face scrunched in fury. "Drexis, how many times do I . . ." She stopped and closed her mouth, holding the dress up so that she would not trip.

"And this is?" Morei asked.

"Mistress," Rhys answered. "Lady Genesa. She holds a place on the council."

"Ah."

The soldiers still barely reacted. Morei was beginning to believe that while they had been trained to fight, they had never seen a dead body before or watched someone die. A matter he would have to address later.

"What's . . ." Lady Genesa looked between them all, her eyes going wide. "What's going on?" she stammered. Her shoulders remained straight, her chin up, as if she refused to show Morei how she really felt. Commendable—people coped differently in the face of fear.

Rhys motioned at Morei. "This, Lady, is your new king." The chancellor looked at the soldiers. "Can I trust you to clean this mess?"

"And get rid of the rug," Morei added. "It's hideous."

That made Rhys laugh. "That it is."

Morei approached the woman, who took several steps backward, as if he might lunge for her. "How long have you been on the council, Lady Genesa?" She stood nearly his height, but her doughy eyes and narrow face made her appear smaller.

"Over two decades," she whispered.

"Good. That means you have plenty of sway. When is the next meeting?"

"T-tomorrow."

"Even better," Morei replied and offered her a smile. "I ask that you inform the rest of the council that Drexis is no longer with us. A shame, really. Don't you think?"

A test. Morei wanted to see how she responded.

After a long pause, Lady Genesa finally shook her head. "No . . . Your Majesty. It is not."

Morei nodded, satisfied. "Glad to hear it. And may I add." He stepped closer, and this time, she didn't move. He took her hand into his own and raised it to his lips, where he gently kissed the skin. She was trembling. "I will not be cruel unless forced to do so, so please do not make me act against you."

As he let her hand go, she nodded. "Yes, Your Majesty." He could hear the faint certainty in her words. If there was one thing he could count on, it was that people were terrified of dying. And he was betting on the fact that Drexis had been a terrible king, too. Put those two together and he had a chance of winning these people over at an exceptional rate.

"Go on now," Morei ordered gently. "Do not hesitate to find me if there are any questions."

She did as she was told—even closed the door as she left.

Morei turned back to Rhys and the soldiers. "Is there anything I should be informed of immediately?"

"Um—" the soldier to the far left started—the blond—and then stopped himself before glancing at the other men for approval. They nodded. "There's a festival in three moon cycles."

"The Festival of Seasons," another added. "It's our rebirth celebration for the coming summer. It's highly regarded here."

Morei nodded. That was not what he'd meant, but he appreciated their forthcomingness. "Chancellor?"

Rhys stepped forward and looked to be struggling with something. He glanced about, as if anticipating someone might come running in. "There is," he muttered, and got closer. Whatever it was, he did not wish the soldiers to hear. They had finally started to clean the mess up, grabbing the body first. One of the men unlatched the sheath from Drexis's belt and laid it aside. Morei was pleased—he was still holding the sword, and they had enough awareness to consider that he might need it.

When the chancellor was close, he finished, "A daughter."

Morei raised his brow in surprise. "A princess?" He kept his voice quiet, matching Rhys.

The chancellor looked troubled. "Not so much. You see, Drexis wrote her off, seeing her as a threat to the throne."

"So she's no longer here?"

"No, she is. She works as a staff member. She's . . . been silenced. Nobody knows she's the daughter of Drexis."

"Interesting." This would need to be addressed. "Does she know?"

Rhys shook his head.

"Anything else?" Between what he had already observed about the soldiers and the city's dynamics and now this, he was stunned. Geral looked relatively easy to rule compared to the political mess he was walking into.

Rhys pursed his lips. "As you are aware, we are a port city and therefore do business with ships. This includes pirates." Morei kept his expression stoic. His words with Harrison and Rodrick were tumbling through his head. He knew of pirates, and he also knew just how dangerous they could be, no matter what the soldiers said. "Drexis originally signed a deal with the Red Queens, but he has recently failed to uphold his end. I assume we will be hearing from them before the summer about this. They are quite . . . well, they don't care about titles and all."

"Ah." Morei nodded and eyed the soldiers. The summer was a ways off, but that would give him time to learn about these Red Queens and any other of Drexis's failures. As well as to initiate some changes to how this city was ran. "Your men"—he changed the subject, needing to address a handful of things at once—"they did not act when their king was being killed. Why?"

Rhys stared at him for a long moment, and as he finally spoke, he frowned. "They're afraid of you."

And there Morei had it. In the span of a cycle, he had crossed the country and overthrown Caster with no army. But it had come at a gruesome cost—the trust of the soldiers. That was something he would have to prioritize if he intended on being successful.

Or taking over Sorréle.

WAR AND SALVATION

Last summer, Syra wouldn't have expected to find herself hunched over a Vore map in the Mourale Mountains, standing next to two Guardians of Death, planning for the Infernol's future. But most of all, she couldn't believe Dryl was here. He still was an anomaly, and her mind was struggling to grasp that he stood here now in the flesh.

At least she had a drink with her. Syra couldn't believe how relieved she was to have the mug of hot tea. It tasted like citrus and mint, and it quenched her throat.

Her emotions were still scattered, but a little sleep had worked wonders, even if it was just a nap. Even better because there had been no dreams. Dryl and Zarek were here now—they looked almost like twins, although she noticed Dryl's crimson color was a shade lighter. And it was easy to tell them apart by their Marking and behaviors. The Marking on Dryl stretched higher on his neck than Zarek's, whose own covered the majority of his arms.

She didn't know what Zarek knew. When he'd entered right after her, he hadn't said anything about what had happened. Certainly, Dryl would have told him about Sekar and everything, but if he had an opinion on it, he did not share it now.

Dryl leaned over and snatched up his dark ale just as the door behind them opened. The chamber was the same one she'd been in with Keryn and the council, the one with the large table. Her elbows rested on the cool parchment.

"Bane," Dryl greeted. "Good to see you."

The commander nodded. "Gonsín," he greeted. The man did not know of Syra's involvement, or that Sekar had shown up. As far as the commander knew, it was exactly what they'd planned—Arik had killed Keryn in a fit of rage, and then Eva had killed her brother before fleeing. Dryl stumbled upon the remaining bodies after. It was the most feasible story.

As far as she knew, there was nothing official yet—this was an informal, secret meeting. Dryl was not formally titled yet, as he would have to face the council and earn their vote. These people would have questions, and Dryl wanted to be as prepared as possible by understanding the current condition of the Infernol.

While she'd missed the initial greetings, Bane looked quite at peace with the situation. Syra had experienced only a fraction of the political problems, but the commander's attitude suggested that he wasn't surprised by Keryn's death—maybe even relieved. Dryl already had the ring on his pointer finger, and it felt odd seeing it there after having held on to it for so long. She'd tried to speak to him when she'd first arrived, but he'd said little to her. The Guardian was on a mission, his thoughts solely focused on what they were preparing to speak about. But it still bothered her—she felt like she was owed some sort of better explanation than what he'd left her with.

But at Bane's large presence, she waited for word on Zane. The man had disappeared. It didn't make sense to her. He had once been a Raveerian commander—Zane couldn't just go missing. There was no sight of him the last they'd heard, and she feared he was among the few dozen dead from the riot. Bane had gone down to the south as soon as possible to give orders and bring back any information he'd been given.

When he looked her way, he gave a single shake. "No sign yet. They've only just started identifying the dead."

She nodded, disappointed. A yes or no would have given her closure—this just kept her waiting. Syra tried to swallow her guilt, unable to shake that this might be her fault.

Dryl shifted the mug over the northern side of the map. "Bane, I need a report on the current status. Nobody knows yet, yes?"

He shook his head. "No word about Keryn's death."

That felt odd to her, but she'd been raised to sell fish, not run a city in the mountain. And frankly, she knew well enough that she wouldn't be standing here hearing any of this if not for the two Guardians.

Zarek shifted. When she looked at him, he gave her a small nod. She so badly wanted to ask what the two brothers had discussed once they'd found each other.

"Good. We'll worry about the formal announcement once we wrap up. Bane, I have Syra with me because she will be an incredible ally. You and I have shared many summers together, and I wouldn't move forward without bringing this up. I understood Keryn had concerns about her, though." Dryl spoke with such ease that she hardly noticed it was her he was talking about. When the commander looked her way, she blinked and tightened her grip on the warm mug. "Do you?"

Bane was silent for a moment, clearly taken by surprise. Syra hadn't expected the discussion to go here—she'd known Bane would arrive, but he'd not shown any hostility toward her. Dryl seemed to feel this needed to get out in the open, but he wouldn't disclose why she would be an ally, which she appreciated. Not that she expected the Guardian to tell the world she was bound to Chaos, but it did reassure her.

The commander shook his head. "Keryn's concerns were not mine. If you trust Syra, then I do too."

Syra took a deep breath, relieved. Bane's behavior made sense now too. He and Dryl had a history, and she wondered then where Bane had come from. Was he a commander who had rebelled against his own city? Or was he part of a family who had lived in this mountain in secret for decades?

"Good—we'll need your help to persuade the people of that. Any report on Eva's whereabouts?" Dryl didn't miss a beat.

"None. She's vanished." Bane leaned forward on the table, and Syra realized just how exhausted he looked. She'd only spoken to the commander a handful of times, and most of it had been in passing. "I have scouters out now. Bounties will be sent out tomorrow morning."

There was nothing fantastic about the idea that an Energy Harvester like Eva had fled. If she was as powerful as her brother, Eva could do some serious damage if she wanted. Perhaps the Harvester had caught wind of her brother's death and ran. Although Syra thought it was unlikely, given she hadn't been with Arik, and nobody knew of his death yet save for the people in this room.

"Are there any other Energy Harvesters?" Zarek asked then. "Perhaps someone strong enough to search for her lifeforce?"

"Bane?" Dryl directed the question to him. "It's been quite a few summers since I've been here."

The commander shook his head. "We have several, but they are nowhere near skilled enough for that kind of search."

"Hm." The Guardian stared at the map. Syra took the opportunity to have a drink, finding the liquid still hot. "The concern about Keryn and his alliance with Liral. Have you made any progress with identifying any supporters?"

Bane shook his head again. "I've got several men grooming reports and names, but when I was down there, they hadn't made any discoveries. They'll continue overnight, though."

"Thank you," Dryl said. There was a gap where nobody said anything. Syra couldn't help but feel the Guardian's urgency, as if he were on a time limit. Or perhaps this was normal for rulers to do.

Dryl cleared his throat. "It's also come to my attention from some documents I was reading in Keryn's study that there is to be movement against Raveer?"

Bane nodded. "Keryn wanted to gather more resources that way. He felt with Liral having shifted and taken Junok, we needed to increase our numbers and resources, although that was before we knew what we did. We began preparations, but with everything that happened, it has not been completed yet. I have seconds-in-command already identified, but I know some of the men were not quite fond of the idea—"

"We'll do it." The words were final, and Syra felt her jaw go slack. She'd expected him to pull back all preparations, not support it. Even Zarek looked surprised.

Bane stood there, motionless. "Really?"

Dryl nodded. "It would be a death trap to allow Liral to seize these cities while we remain in our mountains. You don't think Henry doesn't know about our location? If he had Keryn in his hands, then he knew exactly what the Infernol was planning. Overthrowing Raveer was likely part of a bigger plot for the Lirallian Empire. Henry was going to use Keryn and then toss him aside."

Syra's original assumption had been right. Dryl *was* a different person. The man she'd left behind at the Nighthunter Federation was not the same one who stood here. He knew something that they didn't. Or perhaps he'd seen something.

"Taking Raveer may still lead us right into Liral," Zarek countered. "You say that under the assumptions Henry doesn't have people there already, waiting for the Infernol to arrive. They wouldn't know Keryn was dead."

"I've got a plan," Dryl said, and turned to Syra. His rich gaze bore right into her own. Those were the same eyes she'd come to know so well, but he felt like a stranger. "Do you understand?"

She did, but she couldn't nod or speak. Dryl wanted her to utilize Chaos for whatever he had planned for her. That was why he'd asked how she was doing with harvesting. She wanted to ask but knew Bane had no idea, and it had to remain that way. Although she wasn't sure why now, not when Dryl intended on making a public display of her. That thought rubbed her wrong. The idea that Dryl had come back just to utilize her as a weapon turned her hollow—and angry.

"Sounds risky," Bane commented with a sigh. He didn't pick up on the hint Dryl had dropped for her. "The council will want details if you intend to persuade them. A few were adamantly against storming Raveer, so that won't help your cause."

"I'm confident I'll earn their trust," Dryl promised. He flashed the ring. "This is my key. Ian sealed this ring with a blood ritual—his words are bound to the gem. I know the Old Tongue sigils to reactivate the blood ritual and have them read aloud so that the council can hear for themselves the original Gonsín's request for me to hold the title."

"You've been carrying that with you for all these summers?" Bane asked, sounding genuinely curious. Syra was too—she'd hauled that ring all over the place, with no idea of the power it possessed. Frankly, she'd had no idea that such power existed. Blood rituals had been taboo to discuss growing up, considered a part of dark practices, so her knowledge of them was slim to none. Either way, she was intrigued. There was so much she didn't know.

"Times have changed," Zarek warned. "I don't think you'll walk in there and just be handed whatever you want. People's motives are far different than what they were three or so centuries ago."

"One step at a time," Dryl replied. "That's all we can do. If there's pushback, I'll cross that bridge. For now, I have all the information I need to comfortably face the council."

Everybody stood there. Syra felt like she was standing on the edge of a cliff, dared to jump. Dryl had exposed a part of a plan she knew nothing about until this moment. She wanted Bane to leave so that she could confront the Guardian once and for all on the matter of what he intended to do with her. Liral or not, Dryl had insinuated Syra would just agree to whatever it was.

Her focus was locked on the Vore map, staring at the wavy lines that represented the sea. Her eyes landed on the Grave of the Sea, and she recalled the mentions of that place when she'd worked Caster's Port. A few ships docked there that had come from that far south. Their men spoke little, and when she asked once about their travels, she'd been hushed.

Syra picked up her mug and took a drink, trying to keep herself busy so that she didn't say something she'd regret. Right now, her tongue felt loose, her patience fried after the recent events. She still couldn't shake herself of Keryn's lifeless body and the way Sekar had held his spasming heart. That was not an image she would forget anytime soon.

"Can I ask you something?" Bane asked. She looked over to see that the commander had crossed his arms. He looked visibly uncomfortable, and his eyes were on Dryl.

The Guardian nodded. "We've worked together for two decades on and off, you know you don't need to say that."

The commander's next words came out far less certain. "The realm fracture . . ."

Dryl stared, waiting.

"What are we going to do about that?" Bane continued. "They say it's just some crack hanging there. Does it—will it get wider?"

Dryl sighed and dropped his head. Syra stared—they all did—waiting for him to say something. The air tensed, and it was clear then that this was what Dryl knew. Syra leaned forward. The more they knew, the better they could prepare.

"Dryl," Zarek pressed. There was a tone there that suggested even he was uncomfortable with the silence, which put Syra on alert. "How bad is it?"

"I was north for most of my travels," the Guardian replied. His expression was solemn as he looked around the room. The previous urgency and charge in the air from Keryn's death and the secrecy of the meeting evaporated. "Volkeri Island is inaccessible. The fracture has already provided beasts the ability to cross into this realm, but that's not what I'm most concerned about." He let his eyes wander to the map, and his pale blue fingers hovered over Volkeri Island. "I didn't cross The Shade because there were Cer'hans in flight, and I didn't have my blade, but it was unnecessary. From where I was on the north tip of Diyră, there were already signs that the ailment that has destroyed the Soul Realm is seeping across this one. Volkeri Island is unrecognizable, The Shade pungent with the same deathly smell as in the Soul Realm, and the rock blackened."

Syra had heard them discuss this once long ago, but they'd only said it *could* spread to the living realm if not addressed. She felt the air torn right out of her. The fracture accelerated the process, but it didn't change the fact that beyond the politics and soldiers, the Vore World was going to have much more serious problems to deal with.

"The ancient beasts of this world have stirred," Dryl continued, "in response to this fracture. If they've not made themselves known yet, they will."

"Then what's the point of this all?" Bane asked, motioning to the map. "Talk of war and strategy, but we've got bigger problems. Things my men can't fight." Syra watched the older man's face twist in disbelief. He had worked alongside Dryl for so many summers—the commander couldn't be entirely blind to what was beyond the living realm.

"Do you think someone like Henry Junok will stop simply because there's an extra obstacle to overcome?" Dryl countered politely. "We still don't know entirely why this fracture exists. It could be his own doing or something else. I have to do more research, but we have time." At that, he looked at them all fully again, confidence restored. Syra wanted to hold on to that same feeling, but she couldn't. There was something harrowing in knowing that they could not get the upper hand or catch a break, and that they didn't have time. She'd spent the last few moon cycles trying to stay alive, and now they were scrambling to keep the world alive.

"For now, this information does not leave this roo—" A knocking interrupted them. Frantic, irregular.

"Hello?" The woman's voice sounded out of breath, muffled from the door.

"I thought you said nobody knew," Zarek started to say, but Bane was already approaching.

Syra looked down at her mug. The dark liquid stared back up at her, reminding her that she'd hardly drank anything all day. It was one problem after the next, and she couldn't remember the last time she'd eaten properly. Maybe yesterday. When she looked back up, ready to deal with whatever was next, she saw Bane exchanging words with someone out of sight. conversation was quick, and he closed the door.

When he looked back, his face was grim. "It's Vic. He's turned up, but Elaine tells me there's a problem. She's been trying to find me and Keryn since he arrived." The dead Infernol leader's name came out so causally that he could have passed as being alive. He walked over and snatched his mug up and downed the rest of the ale.

"Vic Resanson?" Syra clarified.

"The very same," Bane mumbled, and set the mug down.

The man Dryl had sent her to find all that time ago. Hearing his name now, after so much else had occurred, gave her whiplash.

There was hesitation on Bane's end. He looked at Dryl directly, and those once-fierce eyes softened. "You should come. Elaine said there's something wrong with him, and between you and me, it doesn't sound good—they say he looks sick—but he may have information we could use."

Syra didn't know how close he and Vic were, but based on the devastated look on the Guardian's face, she could only assume they were friends. She reached over to try to comfort him, but he moved his hand and motioned to the door.

Zarek shuffled him and Syra forward. When Dryl looked back, his brother said, "We're coming." No room for debate.

Bane was already at the door. "Let's go," he insisted. "I don't want word reaching anyone else yet."

Syra moved, although reluctantly. She would have been quite satisfied just disappearing for the rest of the night. Things were moving fast, and seeing Vic felt unnecessary—he'd only been a task because of Dryl, but the Guardian was here now. Zarek seemed to think this required everyone's commitment, though, and she was in no mood to argue with a Guardian.

Bane ushered them out of the chamber and into the hall, then motioned for them to follow. Elaine must have shared Vic's location. Dryl and Bane took the lead.

Zarek walked beside Syra, clearly lost in thought, but she nudged his arm for his attention. When he looked down at her, she asked as quietly as possible, "Is this necessary?" She hoped he understood that she meant everyone going.

The Guardian nodded and matched her voice level. "Lesson number two, always stay curious. The more you know, the better prepared you are, even if it's something as possibly mundane as this."

Syra rolled her eyes. Not because she didn't agree with him, but because he'd really just turned this into a teaching moment. He hadn't used that tone on her since they left Jasper Village, and she thought they'd outgrown that. She shook her head and wished she'd grabbed that tea now.

In the same tone, he said, "I know what happened."

Syra stole a look up at him, and she wasn't surprised to see that he didn't appear at all satisfied by what he knew. Then he turned his gaze ahead and fell silent.

SCARS OF A TRAITOR

Cyrus should have died. No man, no matter how power-ful, could withstand the brutal bite of a spiked whip for that long and live. The blood loss would have robbed him, if not for the shock his body underwent after the twentieth strike. Tendon and muscle had been ripped and shredded, his spine exposed just along his neck where the skin was thinnest, and nerves severed by the sheer brutality of the whipping.

Yet, he lived.

Sozar had ensured this by flooding the Rider with everything he had. Cyrus still recalled the energy that had flooded his limbs when he'd begged the dragon to let him go. Starved, Sozar had not had the immense strength needed to fracture the cursed chains, which had been molded with the blood of a dying dragon over a thousand summers ago. It would have taken far more than physical strength to break those chains—it would have taken the energy that Sozar flooding his Rider with to do so.

Sozar had given a piece of his own lifeforce, the very essence of what defined him, to Cyrus. It was this act alone that had kept him alive.

That did not mean the Rider was okay. He was far from it. Upon Alaric discovering his father's extremely sinister rage, he had resorted to the only thing he had taken from his father:

violence. The prince had thrust a blade right through the chest of the king of Delion. When Raj had fallen, Alaric had resorted to beating the man, even if he was just a corpse by then, and sat there for a long while before the two soldiers who had been there slowly approached and asked what they should do now. When they spoke, it broke Alaric out of the stupor, and he quickly ordered Cyrus to be removed from the whipping post and treated.

Cyrus didn't remember any of that because he'd passed out, but as he drifted in and out of consciousness later, the dragon showed him by passing visions between their link. In those glimpses, Cyrus had felt Sozar's relief—but guilt, too. He felt he had let Cyrus down, though the Rider had tried to remind the dragon that they couldn't have changed the outcome. On the brink of death, he'd felt the cold tendrils of the void pulling him downward until he could no longer recall his own body. In and out, he slipped between a space that promised peace and back into a world of pain, where Sozar would always be, feeding him visions of what was happening and with promises that everything would soon be okay. Yet the distance between him and Sozar grew. Alone, he wandered along the blurred lines of death and life, finding himself embraced by the peace of Death's embrace on more than one occasion. Her touch was so enticing that he considered returning by his own free will, but he halted.

There was a call he could not place, but it was there, telling him to stay.

And so he did, unsure why or for what.

It would take the hand of a powerful Energy Harvester and healer to keep Cyrus alive, but even that would not stave off the scars that would come with such a terrible injury. Sozar promised him he was in good hands, but even in his compromised state, he tried to yank himself free of his restraints. When a hand pressed itself against his back, he lashed out, then succumbed to exhaustion.

It would be several days before he fully awoke again.

* * *

Cyrus startled awake. He tried to move but found himself restrained on a cot. The leather straps were wrapped around his ankles and wrists, his back facing upward, which meant he was lying on his stomach. He yanked, but a searing pain erupted along his back that made him groan. Tears sprang to his eyes. Blinking, he tried to see where he was but found his line of sight blocked by a torso dressed in blue and black.

"Easy, Rider," the voice assured. "You're healing."

"Let me go—" Cyrus moved again and felt the harsh snap of skin breaking along his skin.

A presence shoved itself into his mind, stalling his movement. *Still yourself.*

The warmth, the affection. Cyrus blinked repeatedly, finding himself overcome with the dragon's arrival. He stopped moving, trusting Sozar's instructions.

"You need some more time," the man told him. "I've been doing everything I can to accelerate the healing process, but you are in no shape to move. Not yet, anyways."

Cyrus tried to speak but found his tongue unreachable. He wanted to ask about the restraints, to say he didn't quite trust anyone who would strap him down.

"They are helping you heal," the man told him. "If I hadn't done this, you'd still be far worse than you are now. I can't risk you opening your wounds moving about in your sleep."

Cyrus did his best to relax, although doing so while face down on a table with his ankles and wrists strapped was no easy feat. Like hanging cattle and telling them to relax before slaughtering them. Distrust and unease gripped him, but he couldn't do anything but lie there, guided by Sozar.

The stranger seemed to sense his resolve. "Fate has not been kind to you, Rider. It never is to those who wish to change it." Something cold bathed his back then, and the muscles tightened, but he felt no pain this time. "The traditional medicine practices used on Riders was a combination of leaves and petals found in regions of the Beutóne Mountains—these had properties that were not seen anywhere else in the Vore World. A touch of energy and we could practically bring back the dead." The stranger laughed at his own words. Whatever he was doing, Cyrus couldn't tell anymore with how numb his back had become.

One of the man's words struck him. *We.* "You . . . That was so long ago." He passed his concern to Sozar, but that dragon did not share the same, although he would not give Cyrus any clear answer, and he didn't know why.

Sozar only told him, *You have nothing to worry about.*

"Have you ever heard the story of Kera, the first Dragon Rider?" the man asked suddenly. Cyrus heard the creak of wood as a chair was settled into, and he thought he could turn his head to get a better view of this stranger, but he didn't. The man had strategically sat behind Cyrus.

Annoyed, he said, "Have you ever considered that an introduction might give me some peace?"

A low and barely audible chuckle. "In time, Rider, but not today."

Cyrus held his tongue, sensing Sozar's urge to not say anything snarky, but he did manage the slightest grimace—his lame, invisible attempt at showing his disdain for that answer.

"Kera was the daughter of Queen Oanez, who was the dominant ruler of Assane. Back then, tribes held elections to identify their next leading ruler, and then those that didn't get elected would stand in as what we know as councilmembers.

This constantly kept politics changing because every ten summers, a new ruler and council would be elected. As you can imagine, this gave room for war." There was a pause and the sound of some shifting before Cyrus heard the familiar noise of a mug hitting a table.

"Assane wasn't really what we know it as today. Centuries before the first Saveen ship would ever land and erect what we now know as Jasper Village. The people in Diyră then were the leftovers of a crumbled empire. The Vorelian Empire. That's another story, but from what the ancient Gods used to say, it was a rather peaceful time."

Cyrus let out a large exhale. "Why are you telling me this?" Who was this stranger, and how would he know this story? In all his summers growing up, never had he ever heard or even known anyone who had this kind of knowledge. Kera was a myth. No ancient text even had that story.

The man continued, his words dreamlike, distant. "Kera wasn't happy with her place. She saw the pattern of war, understood that eventually, Assane would devour itself, and she tried to say something to her mother. She was beaten and bound, punished for her beliefs and tied to stakes that were left out in the sun and rain. Oanez wanted her to starve, more caught up in her power than the love for her own blood."

Another drink.

"And then it's said that when Kera was ready and willing to die, a Guardian of Death showed up. He took her away and gave her the only gift he could give for such a heinous crime: a dragon egg. The Guardian told her that if she was as pure as she wished to be, the dragon would hatch. And thus, Cyrus, the first Dragon Rider was born."

A long silence followed. The story struck such a chord with him—a child tossed aside and left to die at the hands of someone who was supposed to love her. He was so moved by Kera's story that he couldn't stop reliving the story in his head.

It would have taken incredible bravery to do what she did, and instead of dying, she was granted the biggest gift the Vore World had ever seen—a dragon. And instead of dying, Cyrus had been granted a new life by this stranger.

He licked his lips, the skin cracked and dry. Cyrus wanted to keep the conversation going, especially now that he couldn't feel anything from the injury. "How do you know this story?"

The chair groaned and screeched as the man stood. Cyrus felt panic grab him with cold fingers—he didn't want him to leave. Not yet. "Don't go," he pleaded.

"You have to rest," the stranger told him, "and I am needed elsewhere." The sound of receding steps halted. A door opened, the hinges in dire need of being oiled again. But there was a pause, drawn out over what felt like a century as Cyrus realized he was still strapped here like an animal. "All Riders were taught that story when they were trained. It was a story about resilience and courage to go into the unknown, guided by nothing but a belief."

Then the door closed, leaving Cyrus stunned in the silence.

Time could not pass quickly enough. Questions danced about in his head, and he became aware of the hum between him and Sozar. The dragon was more at peace than he had been since they left the depths of the Releuthian Mountains and crossed the Ashen Sea. In his heart, Cyrus knew that whoever this stranger was, he was going to come face-to-face with him eventually. And truthfully, lying here now with his cheek pressed into the stone, he wasn't sure he was ready. This was someone who was not only powerful but very, very old.

A PACK OF BEASTS

It was safe to say that Morei had caused a mess with his actions. He knew killing the king would create an immediate divide—people who hated Drexis and people who thought Caster blood should remain on the throne, even if it was merciless blood. Word traveled fast, and soldiers and staff members talked. It had been less than a day, so much of the city did not know yet, although by dusk they would. Right now, most of the staff members knew, along with the palace guards and the council. The first moon cycle would be stressful. If anyone wanted him dead, they would act soon.

Morei slept in the room that had once belonged to Drexis. It wasn't really sleep, though. He remained awake most of the night, utilizing the room to keep safe and to wait out the night until the council meeting. He listened all night to the hall outside the room. Once, he heard footsteps approach and stop before going on their way, but nothing else. A guard? Perhaps. He would have to learn the schedules of the palace staff and soldiers.

The faster Morei learned, the safer he would be. No matter how much power he showed, anyone could slice his neck open in the middle of the night.

His primary concern was the chancellor.

When Lady Genesa had left and the guards had pulled the body and removed the rug, Rhys had taken Morei on a quick tour. It all had a similar feel to Geral, but for Morei, it was a way to better understand the man. He paid attention to Rhys's behavior, the way he spoke, whether or not he made eye contact, and how he explained certain things when asked. Did he withhold information, was he wary on sharing politically confidential things, and so on. It seemed, at least to Morei, that Rhys was complicated, both eager and cautious to speak to him.

Peter had been extremely giving. The old chancellor hadn't had a bad bone in his body and was often quite transparent in his approach—whatever was best for them. It was why Morei and Peter had gotten along so well. Morei had taken advantage of that, grown accustomed to the ease with which conversation flowed between them. That was the way the dynamic should be between king and chancellor.

This was different. Rhys was guarded, yet excited. The chancellor shared information when asked but he was always quick to add, "That has been the way," or "I don't believe in this approach." Rhys, as Morei was quickly learning, was extremely opinionated about matters. It was both a blessing and a curse, a delicate dance of determining whether or not the chancellor had the citizens' best interests or his own at heart.

Rhys was power hungry, that much was obvious early on. His discussion on finances and strategy made it quite clear that he had studied the surrounding countries, knew the current kings and queens, and even the pirate fleets to the south in Creitón. When asked about his own experience on the battlefield, Rhys explained that his family had a long heritage of commanders and battle strategists—distant brothers, grandfathers, and so on. This was on top of the number of chancellors that had served Caster from this family. Simply put, Rhys came from a family that was well-informed of the world, royal politics, and war.

The chancellor carried himself as such. Which was why Rhys was wary of Morei, and rightfully so. He had been raised in a family that saw change as both a threat and opportunity. It was Morei's job to prove to Rhys that he was an opportunity to get exactly what they both wanted.

Power. Strength. Domination.

Morei hadn't considered it like that, not until he had spent the evening alone in his chamber. His new chamber. Upon arrival, Morei had requested the staff change the silk sheets and clean it—he did not want one piece of Drexis, save for the sword that was on his hip. He would hang this one up, most likely, and then retrieve his own, which he knew was in the weapons chamber that all soldiers had access to. It was probably hung up somewhere, collecting dust. The sheath needed to be oiled again to keep the health of the leather up to royal standard. Maybe a fresh blade sharpening to ensure the edges were clean. That didn't even include the custom clothing he would need done, to have his closet full of royal clothes and everyday wear.

So many tasks.

Right now, he stood in the middle of the chamber, dressed in the same clothes he had worn upon arrival. They stank, filthy, and he wanted to burn them, but he had nothing else to wear. The cloak he had worn was on a nearby chair—thankfully, this had taken the majority of the dirt on his travels. The Lirallian Ring was in his pocket, always near, and Drexis's precious sword was attached to his hip. For now, it was the only weapon he had. Morei had freshly shaved, using the bathing room that was attached.

One thing was clear: Drexis had an ostentatious taste in decorations. The whole quarters were over the top. Tapestries with vivid scenes hung all about—scenes of battle and conquering— along with gems fitted into everything and anything. Even the hairbrush had bright blue sapphires. The marble floor, which was white with gold veins, had a giant golden wolf engraved in the center of the room, howling to an unseen moon. Frankly, Morei was surprised that the pillows didn't have gems sewn into them.

He'd found a small terrace behind a wall of tapestries, discovered it during the night when he was searching the giant chamber for anything of interest. The terrace looked like it hadn't been used for ages; the stone railing was cracked and the furniture out there was old and shaggy, destroyed by many seasons of storms.

There were small signs everywhere that Drexis had let go of reality. The bathing room was barren, save for a handful of essentials, and even the tub was dirty. Morei had spent the better part of the evening cleaning it before using it to rinse himself. Towels for drying were nowhere to be found, so he'd resorted to standing there until he was dry.

A knock interrupted his thoughts. It was time.

Morei approached the door and looped a hand around the wolf-head knob, which was frigid to the touch. He opened the door and found Rhys standing there, dressed in green and black, hair still up in a bun, with a maid to his left. She was petite, with blond hair and big blue eyes, and looked no older than twenty. Her clothing was simple.

Glancing at the chancellor, he raised his brow. "Greetings," he acknowledged, and then turned back to her. "You must be the head maid?"

"I brought her here because I assumed you would like to address the chamber," Rhys explained before the woman could reply. "Drexis was not . . . organized, by any means."

"No," Morei agreed, and motioned for them to enter. He kept one eye on the maid, noting how she seemed to look everywhere but at him. "I have a few things in mind already." As they entered, he motioned at the tapestries. "These must go. All of them. Half the furniture, like these chairs"—he pointed at the two chairs, which were vivid gold and covered in sapphires—"must go. I nearly threw these over the terrace last night."

A snicker. Morei turned back and saw the maid covering her mouth, but her eyes gave away her amusement. "They are hideous, aren't they?" he asked. He hoped to gauge her opinion on him—she either loathed or accepted him. No in between.

"Yes . . ." She glanced from him to the chancellor and back. "Your Majesty," she added.

He nodded, satisfied. Another supporter. "Then it will be all the better to toss them. The patio—I would like it redecorated, cleaned, and fixed. I quite like spending evenings outside. The bathroom should be stocked as well." Morei shook his head, realizing the immense work that lay ahead. "Everything. Just address everything here. I want it to look brand new and not like some madman lived here."

Rhys ran a hand over the nearest tapestry, which was covered with dust. "These have been in the Caster family for nearly four centuries."

"If you have a better use for them, then by all means, but they will not remain here." Morei motioned at the lady. "I also need the palace's seamstress. Drexis's clothing does not fit, and I find it a bad omen to wear the dead king's clothes. Can she see me today?"

She nodded. "I'm sure we can make that arrangement. When would you like her to see you?"

He waved her off. "I'll come to her. She should anticipate me before high noon." Morei looked back at the chancellor. "I'm assuming the council meeting should not take the entire morning, correct?" He was determined to put these staff members at ease by being as accommodating as possible wherever he could.

Rhys blinked in surprise. "Well . . . I'm sure they will have plenty of questions about, you know, what's happened and all."

"The most important matter is the documentation of my title," Morei replied. He expected as much, and he was eager to see how this council behaved. "Let's hope they don't insult me with their questions—I tend to have a low tolerance for fools. Madam"—he turned back to the maid—"how should I address you?"

With a curt nod, she answered, "Madam Rose is quite fine, Your Majesty."

"Thank you, Rose, for attending to my needs on such short notice," he told her. "Chancellor, are we ready?"

"We are."

At that, they exited the room, leaving the head maid to fetch her staff and begin the cleaning. Morei trusted the work would be done, but that didn't mean he would ignorantly reenter the room without first checking for any traps, whether physical or energy-based. He hoped he wouldn't find any. If he did, he'd have to kill Rose, and he found her quite charming and sweet.

Here he was, giving orders as the new king of Caster. There were nerves, sure, especially since he didn't know who to trust, who might kill him, and so on. He also didn't want to say the wrong thing, but he was far more at ease being in a role he had been born for than traveling on horse in the middle of the country.

It struck Morei then how strangely similar his and Ezra's paths were. Ezra had accepted the title as new king to a city long standing. They were both gifted Energy Harvesters, and they both shared a passion for doing what was right, no matter the cost. They'd certainly agreed on a lot of things when he was still in Geral. He wondered how the man was doing. More importantly, he wondered what Ezra thought of him after this time. He gave himself a sliver of hope that Ezra didn't hate him, and that maybe one day, the king would understand why he'd done what he had.

As they headed down the hall, Morei took the opportunity to address the one matter that he felt was the most important. "The daughter. Has she been informed of Drexis's death?"

Rhys cleared his throat. "She has."

He'd expected as much, but knowing that she had no idea that the man was her father made the entire situation a bit tense. Essentially, he had just killed her father, and now he intended to request she accept her title, if she desired. Morei didn't anticipate there to be much love between them once she learned of her heritage, although one could never be too sure. Until she proclaimed her loyalty to his cause, though, she was a possible enemy. If she accepted his offer, he had a better chance at earning the entire city's support—she would be the Caster blood they wanted. It was almost too convenient.

The chancellor dug into his jacket and pulled out a scroll. It was already untied. "This has been under my protection since I took over for my father."

Morei unrolled the parchment as they walked and took a quick glance. It was a royal death certificate for Isla Caster. It was signed by both Drexis and a woman named Talia, whom he presumed was the queen and mother. The document stated that the child had died during birth. "This was to be used in case Isla ever stepped forward to try to claim a title. I found that outrageous since she doesn't even know, but Drexis was paranoid."

The political mess of this place—unbelievable. "And your thoughts on this?"

The chancellor shrugged. "Sometimes things are better left unsaid. Would it do more harm than good to present this to Isla, who has spent an entire life thinking she was abandoned?"

Morei eyed him. An answer like that suggested Rhys had more to say.

"Old Caster tradition states firstborns to be boys," Rhys continued. If he sensed Morei's unease, he did not let it show. "A girl is bad luck and a sign of a failing kingdom, or so the old stories say." The chancellor took the document back, rolled it up as they walked, and tucked it back into his jacket. "Drexis and Talia were ashamed their first was a daughter. They told the people the child was lost, but they couldn't completely give her away. So, she remains here, believing she's an orphan."

"So she was just dropped off with the staff?"

"Sort of, yes. Isla was handed to the staff as a newborn, explained to the maids at the time that her parents were dead and the king had done something favorable by offering a home and life in the palace. Imagine the thrill the staff had at such kindness by their king and queen." The last sentence came out in a mocking tone. "Unbeknownst to anyone, it was their own blood they had rejected."

"Interesting." He rolled up the parchment and handed it back to the chancellor just as they passed a group of soldiers, who did not acknowledge their presence. Morei took note, as it could possibly mean they were against him taking the throne. Either that, or they were afraid. When they'd passed, he asked, "Have you met her?

"Yes," Rhys said, and tucked the parchment into his jacket. "Quite lovely woman. Perhaps a little meek, though. Seems she's afraid of her own shadow at times."

"Nothing we can't work through," Morei observed, eyeing the man. It was obvious by the way Rhys swallowed that he was not in support, and Morei wanted to know why before they arrived at the council chamber. "Why don't you support this?" Best to be direct. He didn't need to explain himself.

The chancellor scoffed. "I mean this in no offense—"

"Spare me," Morei interjected.

"The people want a male heir. That has been the Caster way since the founding of this country. Do you know how many royal daughters have been drowned at birth because the king and queen were ashamed? You haven't lived here. You just showed up yesterday afternoon and think you can do whatever you want. You think you can be a hero, right? Give Isla the life you think she deserves in the name of honor, and suddenly everyone is one happy family and supports the king?" Rhys shook his head. "Caster doesn't work that way, Your Majesty. Maybe in Geral, but not here."

Morei could taste the tension in the air. Sure, the chancellor was willing to stand by him as he navigated these new politics, but seeing this side of him made Morei wary. He wasn't sure he could trust Rhys, and those words reminded him that he needed to watch his back with this man. Rhys's influence mattered, though—a good reason not to kill him.

"Do you think I've ignorantly strolled into this palace thinking I can earn everyone's support?" Morei challenged. "Or do I threaten your control?"

The chancellor gave him a sideways glance but did not speak.

They were fast approaching the chamber. "Tell me, *Chancellor*, what life do you think Isla deserves?"

Rhys wasn't used to this kind of power. Perhaps Drexis had granted him decision-making rights in his spiral, or maybe Rhys had gotten used to working alone. Either way, Morei knew the man was weighing his next words carefully. And he should. Morei would make his way through ruling this city just fine without him if his hand was forced. He could get knowledge elsewhere.

As they stopped before the double doors, the chancellor spoke tensely. "We have a saying here in Caster. Anyone can captain a ship, but it takes a crew to run it. Do you know what that means?"

Morei regarded him without saying a word. Best to let Rhys think he'd got the final say for the time being, but Morei was already letting his imagination run a bit wild. A little scare would do this chancellor good.

Rhys continued, oblivious. "It means that just because you think you can steer the wheel doesn't mean you know anything. The crew does. *We* do. Listen to what your crew has to say, Your

Majesty, or you might find yourself in waters you don't know how to steer out of."

Morei stood there, holding the chancellor's gaze. He wanted to see how long it would last before he flinched, and he waited until the man next to him shifted his eyes to the doors. A part of him wondered if the chancellor regretted speaking so openly, but only time would tell. "We should go in," Rhys informed him.

"We should," Morei agreed, and waited for the chancellor to open the doors. He could have done it—in Geral, he would have—but he wanted Rhys to. After a few heartbeats, Rhys obliged with an annoyed look.

Morei was struck with an intense smell of alcohol, and his nose wrinkled. He saw a large round table with the Caster wolf emblem carved into the center of it. The wood was a rich red, polished, the most well-loved object he had seen thus far. The twelve chairs were half-empty—only six members sat there, and they had kept their space from where Morei would be presumed to sit. Lady Genesa sat the furthest back, withdrawn. The largest chair was silver, with a gold cushion to sit on. Along the high back ran silver vines that stretched to the top. No wolf or clear representation of Caster colors.

It had to be the ugliest thing he had ever seen.

In fact, it was so hideous that he just stared, appalled. He made no effort to hide his expression as he slid the chair back, grabbed the next one over—a nice and simple one, like the rest—and sat in it. The wood creaked and groaned from his weight, revealing the chair's age. Nobody spoke, but as he got settled and Rhys sat to his left, Morei took a quick chance around, observing everyone.

They were all older than he; they had likely been on this council for quite a few decades. That was both good and bad. Good in the sense it meant there were family lines attached to the title of councilmember—these people likely knew everything about Caster and more. Bad because that also meant they would not be so easily persuaded by him. They would be either stuck in their ways or so fed up with the late king's authority that they no longer cared about law and royal politics.

He let the silence sit, comfortable with waiting. Morei liked to use these moments to watch people's behavior. Fidgets, shifts, anything to give away someone's true emotion. Silence was the song of the heart, and he was a master of the tune.

The man straight across from him shifted and leaned forward on his elbows, revealing tan skin covered in ink. The councilmember was about twenty summers older than Morei, his piercing blue gaze haunting, and his short brown hair was cut close to the scalp. He had a fierce scar over his left cheek and across his lip, and when he spoke, his voice was that of thunder.

"Have you come here to make a mockery of this city?"

Morei noted how the others looked to the one who had spoken. Perhaps he was the unspoken leader of the council, much how Lord Rodrick had been before he killed the man. "I've come here to resurrect this city to what it once was."

The woman next to the man and Lady Genesa scoffed. She was hardened by age and politics, but underneath all the lines, he could tell there had once been someone beautiful. "Perhaps Geral is much more . . . flexible, but not us. Death does not scare us."

Another Lady Dail, he presumed. "Death doesn't scare me either," Morei replied, and smiled. "Now, if we've got the petty remarks out of the way, why don't we get down to what's important." He laid his hands on the table and made eye contact with each of the members in turn. "Your city is in political shambles. Crime rates are so high, it's the only thing the surrounding cities know Caster by. And your previous king was so dead set on suffocating the future of this city in his deteriorating mental state that he'd rather stare at generational-old tapestries than lead the citizens."

"All right," Rhys murmured.

He noticed eyes glance at the black veins that decorated both of his hands. He let them look and make whatever judgment they wanted to. Soon, the lead councilman met Morei's gaze once more. "You want us to back you in your seize of Caster." It was not a question.

"Good things await Caster," Morei remarked as calmly as he could. "What happens next will either be with or without you all."

Another man scoffed—Morei really needed to learn their names. This one was a bit younger than the first, his dingy brown hair falling just past his ears. He had wide shoulders, and the chair looked too small for his frame. A bit of scruff lined his jaw. "What is your interest with this city?"

"To slaughter its citizens?" the woman remarked. Her scowl was monstrous. "Don't act like we are ignorant. Word spreads fast. We know what you did to your own people before you *ran*. What's to say we haven't sent a letter to King Ezra already to inform him of your whereabouts and intent?"

The sound of that name made him cringe, but he did not let it show. All he could hope was that Peter was guiding Ezra appropriately. If so, the chancellor would have told Ezra that raising an army to march to Caster for Morei would result in devastating results for the Geral troops, which he didn't want to be responsible for.

"If you intend for me to kill you now, I can. My hope was to come to a compromise, a deal, where we could all gain something." The words came out clipped, harsh. Before anyone could say more, Morei continued, "You ask what I seek, so let me tell it to you all. Caster has an advantage that no other city in Sorréle does—direct access to the Merrél Sea. The city not only has a port but manages all imports and exports. Everything we could ever need is at our fingertips. We could set sail tomorrow to any country, or we could become self-sufficient in everything:

food, weaponry, clothing, war." He inhaled. "Sorréle is a failing country. Centuries ago, the Royal Treaty pacified the families, but it is quite clear that there is a power shift happening. Geral and Diemon have already fought, and Queen Reaza is dead, replaced by her daughter. Geral is weak after the recent battle and hardships, with a new and malleable king leading them." He didn't wish to speak of Ezra so poorly, but the words came out far easier than anticipated. Morei was angry, and right now, he saw the Energy Harvester-turned-Geral as nothing but an obstacle.

"Ferguson is and has been nothing but a quiet and meek family since the day it staked its claim along the Dark Forest. The city hardly has an army worth scoffing at, and as I'm sure you are aware as much as I, recent summers of trade have been decreasing significantly from the Silk Family. This is either because the family wants nothing to do with the surrounding cities anymore or because the city itself is failing, but we don't know that because the Fergusons are private—too private."

When no one spoke, he was satisfied. It meant he had their attention. "Caster, by all means, has every opportunity to become the most powerful city this country, perhaps even this world, has ever seen. I didn't come here to play politics, I came here to build an empire."

"And we are to be your puppets," the woman said.

"You can be the key to the empire," Morei countered. Scanning the table, he met each set of eyes once more. "You all have something unique to offer, something that I don't have—experience, knowledge, expertise. A crew to a ship. Am I wrong?" He leaned on what Rhys had told him. Despite how much he wanted to stab the chancellor, it was right for the moment.

Nobody objected. Rhys eyed him, picking up on exactly what Morei had just done. "If your intention is to sit by and watch the world go by, then the door is behind me."

The man with the braided gray beard looked unsatisfied. "You come to stake a claim to a throne that you know nothing about. The Caster family has bloodlines all over the world, married into royal families and ruling to this day. You think you can be granted this throne without a fight?"

Morei stared hard. "Your name?"

"Lord Varun."

He regarded the councilmember for a long moment before he replied. "Lord Varun," he began, not quite fond of the name. "I would expect as much—you can sail anywhere from this port. If I was a young prince, I'd have traveled too. If there are distant cousins or immediate family members that are out there, I'd love to connect with them." His tone dripped with a challenge—he was not afraid. "I'd be more than happy to share my dreams for the Caster name."

Lord Varun tapped his fingers on the wood. "Your tone does not escape me, Geral."

"Good," he retorted, and straightened. "Then you should know I'm serious. If we must pay off people to keep this city from falling victim to a familial political mess, then so be it. We all know what happens when too many family members try to get their hands on a title." He waited to see if he had to explain himself. Historical cases of family wars and feuds for the crown were everywhere across the Vore World. The case of Kalic was infamous. Over nine hundred summers ago, Kalic had been prepared to hand the throne over to the firstborn son from the aging king and queen. However, the younger brother murdered the heir beforehand and tried to take the throne for himself. The disaster caused a familial war, and left five out of the eight Kalic royal family dead. It took decades to recover.

"I don't see any of you trying to take the throne, no?" He gestured around the room. "Please, I'd love to see who thinks they have the ability to rule as I will."

This time, it was Rhys who shifted, though he remained silent. Morei still took note of the movement. The council exchanged looks. If he had to stand here until the next full moon to make his point, he would. When they had stopped, he nodded.

"If you are in agreement that Caster has the potential to be the most powerful city ever seen, then do I have your vote to act as king to the people and council?"

Morei knew he had them, or at least the majority. They had been dealing with a mentally deteriorating king, a man who had succumbed to a grotesque world of unreachable needs—Drexis had long outlived his worth. The council was tired of it, and he hoped that by playing this card, he could gain the foundation of their trust. More importantly, if he could get them hungry for a future they could all agree on, then he didn't see why they wouldn't support him.

The main councilman with the tattoos—Lord Varun—nodded. "All right, you have my curiosity. But I cannot ignore the question that's on everyone's mind. Why Caster? Why not do this with Geral, your home?" He gestured at Morei now. "You certainly have far more history there."

He could not lie his way through this answer. Morei had dealt enough with councils and politics to know that there were plenty of times to spin lies, but not like this. These people, staring and waiting like starved animals, wanted something to sink their teeth into; they wanted vulnerability.

He would give it to them.

"I have spent the last season trying to prove to those people that I had their best interest in mind. I marched onto that battlefield with Diemon for no other reason than to stand next to my soldiers and declare my loyalty. And all the citizens could do was blame me for the city's hardships. So no, Geral is no longer my home. Geral is now an enemy, and one I will take great pride in turning to ashes."

There was no point in stating more—that answer should do. What good would it be to start talking about Gods and the murder of Emerald?

"Hm." A councilman leaned back and crossed his arms, his black mustache well loved and curled at the corners of his upper lip. "What do you expect now?" His voice hinted at a strange accent, not from there.

Morei was glad to see the progression in thought. "First things first, document me as the new king of Caster. There is no need for a coronation ceremony—I think it's safe to say nobody here is in the mood for celebrations. Second, I want a list of all appointments that were upcoming for Drexis, along with a list of all things Drexis was involved in. With that, I will also require a list of items and discussions that require my awareness, whether Drexis was involved or not. I suspect all contractual agreements are in your study?" He turned to Rhys.

The chancellor nodded.

"Good. Then I expect to be provided insight on which contracts are ongoing, which are out of date, and any that were made without Drexis's knowledge." Several eyebrows went up, but Morei's sole intent was to see if the chancellor squirmed— he knew the man had been acting outside the entire council's and king's knowledge. It reeked off him. "If I was a council and that was my ruler," Morei observed, "I would have acted without his knowledge. So I expect to see whatever contractual agreements were made without Drexis's knowledge, no matter how big or small. I need to know where Caster has her hands. The more I know, the better we can act."

"Right," the black-bearded man replied. "Then you are also aware of the Festival of Seasons?"

Morei nodded. "I am."

Rhys spoke up. "The ruler—in this case, you—is expected to have the first dance. It is tradition. Usually, a king has a queen and this is no issue."

"The ruler also gives some sort of speech," Lord Varun added. "Something grand. In passing summers, Drexis would bring in a performer or even utilize wild animals as some sort of show."

Morei nodded, understanding. "So I have three moon cycles to prepare something grand and to choose a dance partner. That is no problem." Already, he had something in mind. It was risky, but he couldn't shake himself of the idea.

"Am I to assume you will use the same study?" the chancellor asked.

"Yes."

"Then I shall bring the document to you this afternoon for the official title transfer. Council"—he turned his eyes on them—"do we have your blessing and support in this?"

And so Morei Geral, ex-king and traitorous murderer and prophesized Demon King, became king of Caster. The council agreed, wholeheartedly. Their eagerness to see this through surprised him. He'd expected there to be arguments, perhaps a death or two, and even a threat, but he had not anticipated taking Caster to be so . . . *easy*. It was as if Destiny had forged this moment out just for him.

Each name would be signed on the title transfer: Rhys, Lord Cayden, Lord Malachi, Lady Yara, Lady Genesa, Lord Eli, and Lord Varun. Then Morei himself to acknowledge that he consented and would uphold the duties being given to him. It was the same kind of document that Ezra had signed, and this was now all too fitting only a little over a moon cycle later.

So much had happened, so much had changed, but Morei was right where he wanted to be—where he *needed* to be. He could feel it in his bones, as certain as the wind was when a storm was fast approaching.

THERE ARE DEMONS IN THE HALLS

Elaine was fidgeting next to the door when they arrived. She was a fierce-looking woman with red hair that was cut short to her jaw. When she saw them, she paused. It was clear she hadn't expected the group.

"Is he in there?" Bane asked, ignoring her puzzled look. When she nodded, he said, "Good. Stay out here and don't let anyone in if they come snooping around."

When she opened her mouth, the commander added, "No questions, Elaine. If anyone asks what you're doing, you tell them I'm in here with a possible prisoner." It was a lie, but the woman didn't even hesitate to nod her head.

"Understood."

Syra offered a small smile to the woman, who barely returned it—she looked shaken. She had no idea who Elaine was or what rank she was compared to Bane, but there was an obvious level of respect between them. Still, one more person to consider, to keep an eye out for. Syra had been much more comfortable with just the four of them.

The others hardly hesitated, opening the door. She wished she could be as confident as they were.

The first thing she noticed was how dark it was. There were two lanterns burning on either side of the room, closest to the books and chair that sat toward the back. There was a figure tied to the chair, hunched over. The man was snoring, loud, and his chest rose and fell in sporadic fits. The clothing, from what she could see, was wet—black leather shone where it wasn't torn—and as the man slowly lifted his head at the commotion, Syra inhaled sharply.

Black splotches covered his skin, along with a spidery network of black veins that devoured the right side of his face. The spots that weren't covered in the ailment were puffy and angry, red. His eyes were a pale white—the entirety of them—and when he turned toward them, he opened his mouth to reveal yellowish teeth and a blackened tongue.

"Welcome," he greeted. His voice grated over her nerves, raspy. "Nobody will talk to me."

Zarek leaned in and cupped a hand over her ear. "Stay curious," he muttered. If he thought he'd get her to laugh, she didn't. When Bane had said there was a problem, she didn't think this was what he'd meant—and based on his expression, he hadn't known it either.

"Vic," Dryl greeted calmly as he approached. "My friend, you don't look so well." He stopped several paces back, not getting too close. Syra stood back with Bane. She didn't want to get close either, but the Guardians didn't seem perturbed.

A grating sound echoed through the room, and she realized it came from the man in the chair. "Vic's not home," he said. "Can I give him a message?"

Syra crossed her arms, alarmed, but she tried to keep her emotions internalized. When she looked at Bane, she could see that he was keeping a stoic expression, but when he met her eyes, she realized they felt the exact same way. They wanted nothing to do with this. Whatever was happening was far beyond their understanding. If she could melt into the wall behind her, she would have. This was not a soldier with an injury—this was supernatural.

The demon arched his neck upward, breath hitching as his entire body shuddered. The room remained silent as the man convulsed several times, arms and legs straining against the rope, before he relaxed once more. When he raised his head again, blue eyes stared back at her.

"There are—" The man coughed violently, splattering his legs with a reddish-black sludge. It could have passed for coagulated blood, but she wasn't sure. "Demons," he huffed. "They are everywhere."

Still, the Guardians did not approach, even as Vic's gaze searched both of them desperately. "Dryl? What's going on here?" His voice shook, and Syra's heart twisted at the sound—he was absolutely terrified.

"What happened?" Dryl asked, taking charge. Zarek rested a hand on the hilt of Death's Sword, and she noticed the latch of the sheath undone. The Guardian was prepared to draw at the slightest notice. Vic was restrained, but based on the Guardians' distance and Zarek's movement, this was a much more dangerous situation than they were letting on. She took a half step back, and Bane followed.

The man's chest was rising and falling faster, his breaths louder, harder, struggling. "They took the crown. It's gone. *Gone.*"

Syra tensed at that. Roman had said something about a crown when they'd talked about Vic. She wondered what Roman would say and do now if he was faced with this. Maybe he wouldn't bat an eye, but she wanted to think that he would have been up there with the Guardians. She blinked, unsure why her thoughts had gone there.

Dryl waved him off. "Don't worry about that. I'm more worried about what happened, Vic." But she noticed Zarek glance at his brother.

Vic sounded frazzled. "Take that blade and shove it through my heart. Please—"

"I need to know what happened," Dryl insisted, harsher. "Where did Keryn send you off to?"

Breaths turned to wheezes, which then evolved into a grating, guttural sound that clawed its way down Syra's back. Vic's body convulsed again, and Zarek wrapped a hand around the hilt of Death's Sword but did not draw. Dryl laid a hand on his normal blade and took a half step away from Zarek to protect himself if the Guardian drew. She watched, noticing how the brothers worked so seamlessly together.

Arms strained against the rope, and the man smiled maniacally, revealing those yellowed teeth. "Vic's not here anymore, Death Seeker." He coughed again, and more of that sludge came out, sliding down his chin and into his lap. A sour smell filled the air, and Syra wrinkled her nose. "I don't think he'll be back," he added with a mocking tone.

Zarek spoke. "You are from Volkeri Island or no?"

The demon did a dramatic neck roll to turn his attention to the other Guardian, despite the brothers standing so close. "I come from Ashýon, your favorite place."

Syra knew that term, and she watched the brothers' shoulders visibly tense. "Charming," Zarek replied. "I haven't given the place a visit since your kind destroyed it."

"You should," the demon remarked.

"I think I'll pass this time around."

Dryl's hand shifted just the slightest, and Zarek fell quiet. Again, seamless. There was a lot going on, but she was impressed by the way the two worked together. It reminded her of Sekar and Dryl when they'd all traveled together.

"The crown," Dryl said. "Where is it?"

"The Soul Realm is doing much better these days, wouldn't you agree?" the demon taunted. "I quite like the purple sky."

"The crown," Dryl pressed.

The demon only gave him an amused stare. "Are you worried, little Death Seeker?" He laughed, but it sounded somewhere between a choke and wheeze. "I'm eager to see what this world will do once it's *ours*."

His face changed first. She watched as the sickly looking skin hardened and the eyes turned gray. The smile stilled, the sludge still dripping from the mouth, and the demon stopped moving. Cracks appeared along the skin, and before her eyes, the entire face caved in on itself. The ropes loosened, the clothes falling now that there was nothing inside them, and they all stood there, staring at an empty chair and a pile of dirt.

Bane shifted first. "Is he gone?"

Dryl looked over at Zarek before approaching the chair. His fingers ran through the pile, sending more dirt to the ground. Then he picked through the clothes.

"He's gone. I'm assuming he's returned to the Soul Realm."

Zarek loosened his grip on the hilt but did not latch the sheath. He eyed Vic's remains. "He was apprehended by these demons." The statement was confident, devoid of doubt. "I'm sorry," he added. Those words sounded foreign to her coming from Zarek, but his eyes were trained on his brother. "I know he was a friend of yours."

Syra licked her lips, feeling like she'd turned to stone herself. She and Bane had hardly moved through that entire endeavor, and her neck muscles were stiff with tension. "Roman had said something about a crown." The words caused everyone to look at her. Dryl had no idea who she was talking about. "He was Vic's father. We met him on the ship heading out of the Nighthunter Federation. Why is it so important?"

"Rül'Cril," Zarek said, and looked her way. "Henry forged three powerful relics during his initial reign. The Crown of Gods, and it was named that because it has the ability to control any beast. One wouldn't need the help of a God to do so."

She raised a brow. "Like what Sekar did outside of Raveer?"

Dryl frowned.

"Long story," Zarek told him, "but there was a Firóle involved. To some extent, yes, just like that. But the relationship between Sekar and Yalana was different. This crown would take away the beast's ability to think for itself. They'd essentially be enslaved to the bearer of Rül'Cril."

She nodded, not liking the sound of this. "And you think . . ."

"Yes," Dryl answered. "The Ashýon region in the Soul Realm is home to many, many beasts. If that crown has managed to get back to whoever their master is at this time, we could be facing significant consequences for both this world and the Soul Realm."

"But what about Henry Junok?" Bane asked. She felt bad for the commander. He'd been thrown into this mess. Syra was no expert, but Bane hardly had enough exposure to these elements to be comfortable. The idea that there could be some demon army to deal with made her want to crawl out of her own skin.

"It appears we have two primary concerns," Dryl told them. "Henry Junok and the resurrection of the Lirallian Empire, and the possibility that Rül'Cril could be used in the Soul Realm. There's no way for certain that we know, though. The crown could have been intercepted. Demons aren't very loyal."

"That's comforting," she observed. Zarek chuckled.

"One step at a time," Dryl echoed from earlier, but his eyes landed on hers. "Let us deal with the Soul Realm, Bane. That's what we do. Your concerns are with the soldiers and what you can control, and that's me." *Us.* Syra knew what he meant. Her bloodline was tied to that realm. What he meant was that this would fall on her, one way or another.

"I can do that," the commander agreed. He looked around the room again. "I will take Elaine with me, and we'll return to the south side and see what it looks like. Is there anything else you need of me, Gonsín?"

Keryn's death hadn't even been made public, and the commander was already calling Dryl their leader. It stunned Syra how quickly people could change and how fragile loyalty really was. It made her appreciative of those who had not turned their backs on her.

"Just keep this quiet," Dryl told him. "Zarek and I will clean this up."

"What about me?" Syra asked.

Zarek's look told her not to challenge this. There was a reason they wanted to be alone and talk in private, but she couldn't help but feel left out. Then again, perhaps they had personal matters that still needed to be discussed from earlier. She kicked herself for assuming the worst in these Guardians after she'd just thought about loyalty.

"Right," she said before anyone else could speak. "I'll head on back and do some things." Not that she had any idea what, but she didn't tell them that. For the time, she would take the opportunity to bathe and maybe grab some food from the galleys.

There was nothing she could do about the next part, after all. Dryl would stir up a political storm with Keryn's death announcement and his intention to take over. If there were disagreements now, she was sure there would be more, and she didn't want to be on the receiving end of any devious plan, like Garett's. The best she could do was wait out some of it by staying completely separate from the mess. If they needed her between now and tomorrow, they'd come for her. Zarek always had a strange sense on where to find her.

But that didn't solve Zane. She looked up at the commander. "If you hear anything, please let me know."

He nodded but said no more. Syra took that as her cue to leave. The commander motioned to the door, sensing her departure. "Let me walk you back to your room."

There would have been a time when Syra would have said no, but it was far safer to have someone like him escorting her back. Given the uncertainty with the Infernol, it was safer always having an extra person around. If Dryl trusted the commander, she would too.

When she glanced Dryl's way, he gave her a single nod.

Syra took one last look at the pile of dirt where Vic had been. Her life was so strange, and she wasn't sure when it would ever slow down. As their steps carried down the hall, she knew exactly where to go to find a little peace.

She'd need her fur blanket and some snacks, maybe a book. Syra rolled her shoulders. One step at a time.

IT TAKES COURAGE

yrus's movements were slow, deliberate. With the help of the maid—the first woman he had seen since arriving in this palace—he was able to dress himself. The scabs were stronger; the skin had healed at an accelerated rate that allowed him now to stand and move, but only barely. The pain remained. Any sudden movement and he would be gritting his teeth on the ground.

It was manageable, though. Cyrus was so grateful to be up by his choice, nobody else's. When word had reached Alaric that the Rider was up, he had been sent an invitation for dinner. Dinner! Cyrus had not expected to be spending his first evening awake and alive having dinner with the new king of Delion.

"Let me help," the woman pressed, and pushed his hands aside. She picked up the hems of his shirt and began buttoning the fabric in place with far more speed and precision. Cyrus hadn't been paying much attention, and with his slow movements, she'd probably thought he was incapable of buttoning his own shirt. He allowed her to do it regardless.

"Thank you," he managed to say. Speaking had come last for him. Not because his tongue was injured, but because he had lost the desire. Cyrus knew he needed to talk—he anticipated tonight's dinner to be full of conversation—but he dreaded it. His heart was no longer into the games and sparring. He wished to seclude himself for days on end and think. If that meant he didn't say a word until next season, then so be it.

When he had first received the invite, Cyrus had nearly refused. It was Sozar who had insisted he go. *There is an energy in these walls,* the dragon had informed him. *It is ancient.*

Not entirely sure what that had meant, he had relented and accepted the offer. Sozar sensed something that Cyrus could not, and it was only right that he fulfill the wishes of the dragon to investigate the origin of this feeling. After all, Sozar had saved his life.

Again.

I don't understand why I can't feel anything, he told the dragon.

Sozar snorted. *You are healing. If you could feel anything, I'd be surprised.*

Cyrus rolled his eyes, agitated at how little he was grasping right now. He knew he needed to be patient with himself, and he also knew that if he said anything, Sozar would tell him the exact same thing.

So he refrained from replying, but he knew the Sozar could sense his discontent. Three days ago, he'd been chained and whipped. Now, he was dressed in a blue silk shirt and preparing to go have dinner with the king. Cyrus was beginning to believe his relationship with politics and royalty was far from healthy, yet he still felt the tendrils of excitement wrap around him. They were accompanied by uncertainty—if Alaric asked him to pledge fealty, he'd refuse. No amount of torture would sway his opinion on the matter. Cyrus refused to pledge himself to any ruler.

"Your hair." The maid's voice cut in. "Lean over, please. You're just too tall."

Cyrus smiled and did as requested. Her fingers flitted through his bright blond strands, pushing and shoving them in place until she was satisfied. With her help, he'd also shaved his beard prior to this fitting. That had been the best part so far of this entire process—getting rid of the itchy and dirty hairs on his face. It wasn't the look itself, it was what the beard represented. His time as a prisoner.

"There," she finally said. "Do you need anything from me?"

Cyrus straightened and met her gaze. She was older and reminded him of the lady who had run the orphanage that he'd called home for so many summers, except she was far kinder than Miss Hans. "I'm fine," he replied, and dipped his head in respect. "Thank you for everything."

She nodded, satisfied. The maid hadn't given him her name, and that seemed intentional, so he hadn't asked. In fact, nothing about her was welcoming in that sense, so he had refrained from asking her any questions. She simply had done what she was ordered to do. Her actions were bold, her eyes hardened by summers working for King Raj. Who knew how many murders she'd seen at the hands of her previous ruler? Death changed a person—it was one thing to cause it, but it was another to bear witness.

The maid turned and motioned at the door. "The soldiers will lead you to the private dining chamber," she told him. "Ah, don't forget your belt." She walked over and picked up the leather, which had replaced his old one. The sheath that held the Rider's Sword had been freshly oiled and complimented the new leather spectacularly. This new belt was gray with engraved bones along the smooth leather, and on the edges, darker leather was braided to reinforce the strength of the belt. It was stunning—and a gift, although Cyrus was certain it was more of an apology.

Sorry my father almost killed you. Take this.

That thought almost made him laugh. In a dark and ironic sort of way.

The maid didn't let him strap the belt on. Instead, she wrapped it around his hip and fitted it to his size before slipping the strap through a hole in the leather and tucking in the extra piece underneath a loop. She took a step back, studied him, then did another quick adjustment before she clapped her hands together. Cyrus knew better than to intervene with a woman who had a mission.

"You're done. Go. I cannot keep the king waiting with my fretting."

At that, Cyrus nodded and left, thanking her once more, but she just waved him off. It was her job, she insisted.

When he stepped out into the hall, now a guest and not a prisoner, he sucked in a breath at the sight of the soldiers. They were dressed in their greens, helmetless, though they still wore their chain mail, greaves, and braces. They looked prepared for war, which was not something he was used to. Even Geral's palace soldiers hadn't been this armed and ready, and Morei Geral was a ruthless king.

"Greetings, Rider," the one on the left acknowledged, and motioned down the hall. "This way."

Cyrus fell into step between them, but he couldn't walk as fast as he wished. They were forced to slow their pace, and he was relieved when neither mentioned it. The word about having a Rider chained and beaten had gotten around the entire city, as Cyrus had come to learn, and he knew people had questions, but no one overstepped. In the depths of his mind, he wondered what his mother thought. Did she feel guilt for her actions?

I hope she does, Sozar said. *I hope she is drowning in it.*

His words were filled with hate and rage—something Cyrus was also feeling. The dragon was not one to show so much emotion, but then again, this entire trip here had been full of firsts. He swallowed as they turned down a hall, passing several maids, who greeted them with nods. He was the center of attention, which he despised, but there was nothing to do. Alaric had insisted he be led by soldiers. The new king wanted to prove a point that the Dragon Rider was untouchable, and it was working.

The soldiers did not speak the entire time, which was fine by him. He was not in the mood for unnecessary conversation, and he was still quite wary of them. He knew these men were not the same ones who had managed the dungeons, but that gave him little peace.

Sozar remained quiet after that. The dragon just listened, his presence constant, but when they stopped in front of the door to the private dining chamber, the dragon's excitement grew. It bled over into his emotions, and Cyrus could feel the deep sense of thrill—there was something here.

"The king awaits you," the soldier on his right said. "We will be out here."

"Thank you," Cyrus replied, and laid a hand on the cold door handle. It was curved upward, like a talon, and when he studied it more, he realized it could have passed for a dragon's claw. Interesting.

The soldiers didn't move. Cyrus raised an eyebrow at the one on his left, who held an expression he had not seen on a soldier since he'd become a Dragon Rider. Shame.

The fat pause brewed between them all. Finally, the soldier opened his mouth and spoke softly. "The men . . . Not all of us condoned what happened. We extend our apologies on behalf of Delion."

Cyrus could not deny the sincerity of the words. He looked at the other soldier, who offered the slightest nod.

"In these halls, you're safe," he added.

"Thank you," Cyrus replied, and he hoped they understood just how much he meant that.

Without further ado, he opened the door and stepped inside. The smell of baked goods filled his nostrils, and his mouth immediately watered. It had been days since he'd had a proper meal. Plates of all kinds filled the short, narrow table.

Meats, breads, fruit, cheese, several decanters of wine. And at the table, two men.

One was Alaric, who stood immediately upon his arrival. Dressed in royal garments, Alaric could not have looked more like a king. Silver and green complemented his skin tone and eyes, the shirt was embellished with the family's crest on the sleeves, and several silver rings decorated his left hand. One caught Cyrus's eye. The chunk of red stone in the center of it was big enough to cause serious harm if it met anyone's face. Some kind of family heirloom, no doubt.

Even as Alaric greeted him, Cyrus's eyes fell on the other man who sat there.

He had blond hair that was a bit shorter than Cyrus's and somewhat darker, and a scar stretched down the right side of his face, cutting straight through a silver eye. Silver. He wore a contented expression. He did not get up upon Cyrus's arrival, just sipped his wine. Dressed in black and blue, he did not need to introduce himself, because Cyrus knew who this man was.

He was a Dragon Rider. He was the man who had saved Cyrus's life.

He was Hyle, the God of Courage.

THE WHITE ROSE

Drexis's study turned out to be the most organized space in the palace. Rhys had guided him there, and once he was alone, he had set to work sorting through everything he could get his hands on. This was what Morei enjoyed—the politics, the feel of parchment against his fingers, the processes that made running a city so complex. He had been born and raised in it. This, right here, was home.

The study was quite large—larger than his own. A terrace, high above the city and the wall, overlooked the sea, and chairs and a table sat in the center of the room, likely for meetings and discussions. Behind the massive desk, with legs carved to look like waves and boat scenes carved and painted on the top, there had to be at least three hundred books. To his right was the door to the hall, and to his left a table with glasses and an empty decanter, along with shelves of safekept items. Things like a list of all active criminals, ship reports, imported and exported goods, sea captains and their crews, and so on. The active criminals list was bizarre—something like that would never exist in Geral. Criminals were identified and punished, of course, but this was different. Next to each name was a price, along with a quick note of how they worked best. Drexis had been utilizing these criminals for secret work.

The warm wind ruffled his clothes, bringing with it the smell of the sea. Morei wanted to take it in, but he couldn't. Time felt precious, and finally being back where he belonged, a king, was fueling his urgency to gather as much information as he could.

He was due for the seamstress soon, but he was hoping to do some digging and then address Isla prior.

Morei opened the desk drawers and sifted through them. Little antiques, like a smooth rock and even flint, were in the first one, along with ink and a quill. In the next drawer, he found a scroll and snatched it up. It had to be important if it was here and not on the shelves. He leaned over the desk and unrolled the scroll, which was damaged along the bottom corners, but the image on it was clear.

It was the bounty sketch of Syra.

For a moment, he stared. How strange it was that the king of Caster had this in his drawer. Morei set it aside and reached back in. If the sketch was in there, then perhaps he could find something else about Syra.

He dug out a small, folded paper from the bottom. It was soft to the touch, well used, and the parchment looked like it had been wrinkled in a moment of rage before the reader had carefully straightened and then refolded the letter. The handwriting was clean, straight, and easy to read despite the wear and tear.

What he found was both shocking and fascinating.

Syra's father had been a spy for Ferguson. He had spent many summers living in Caster, employed by the palace and collecting information for the Silk Family. The father had been caught in a restricted area of the palace—a place Morei would have to go snooping for—and sent home on a warning. However, Drexis had grown suspicious and requested that Rhys keep an eye on him.

When the Demon Killer was stolen one night, Drexis had immediately been informed, and he'd acted against Syra's father. *We'll make it look like an accident*, the author of the letter wrote, who Morei now realized was the chancellor. *A fire that killed the daughter and father. Shame, right?*

A thousand things raced across his mind. The most wanted blade in history had been stored away in possession of the Caster family for who knew how long, then stolen by Syra's father. Why? Perhaps to return to Ferguson—a complicated task for a thief and spy—but her father was already being tracked, and so he was caught.

But that didn't add up. If Syra's father had made a living out of spying, acting so boldly did not align with managing to stay under the radar for so long. Had he wanted to be caught?

"Huh." The word came out in an exhale as he laid the letter down. If Rhys had written this, then perhaps he knew more than he was letting on. It felt like Morei had walked right into an intricate web of secrets. This didn't even include the idea that there was a restricted area in the palace. He wanted to know what Drexis had been hiding there, and more importantly, what Rhys knew.

The door opened, and Morei blinked and looked up. In walked the chancellor as if on cue, guiding a beautiful woman dressed in staff garbs. She had been scrubbing, that much was clear, based on the wet fabric around her knees and the grunge on her hands. Her near-white hair was clipped up, but rogue strands had broken free to frame her round face. She was petite, her frame was hidden in the baggy clothes, but Morei didn't need to look twice to know that underneath all that was an hourglass figure that had been molded by countless summers of hard work.

"Your Majesty," Rhys acknowledged, and motioned at the woman. "Isla Caster." At the name, he saw her tense, and he wasn't surprised. She hadn't woken up expecting to be told that her whole life was a lie.

He nodded. "Thank you, Chancellor. You may leave."

"That is not advised—"

"Your previous king may have been a coward, but do not forget who I am or what I am capable of," Morei warned, and met the chancellor's gaze. Everything from what he'd just read was conveyed in that single stare, and he saw a muscle in the man's jaw spasm. "Your concern is appreciated, although I find it extremely unnecessary, given the circumstances. Go."

He was not foolish. Rhys wanted to stay because he was curious about what would be said. While a king often had his chancellor as a bystander and witness, there were certain situations that did not benefit from such a presence.

Besides, he wanted to observe her by herself. How she acted around him when no one was watching, how she spoke, all of it. Underneath all that garb could be a dagger poised for him, and if they were alone, she might be more likely to act on her impulse to lunge and stab him.

The chancellor worked his jaw, and a heated silence passed, so quiet that Morei could almost hear the crashing waves despite the distance. Or maybe he was imagining it all.

Then Rhys relented. "As you wish. I will be outside."

"Thank you."

As the door closed behind them—begrudgingly—Morei inhaled the salty air and beheld Isla. "I'm sure you are a bit overwhelmed." He motioned to the table, where a decanter of red wine sat. "Something to drink?"

She shook her head. "Oh, no, thank you." Her words sounded strained, nervous.

Morei wanted to put her at ease, so he walked over and poured himself a drink. The sound of the glass was loud in the silence, and he lifted the drink to his nose and sniffed. It was rich with cherries—a classic wine. He'd had to request Kendell's

Milk be brought in. As she stood there, he watched her eyes take in the chamber. Specifically, the details of the desk. He took that as an opportunity.

"Beautiful, isn't it?"

She nodded.

"Royalty always has a way of being over the top. I'm sure it looks ostentatious to you."

That elicited the faintest of smiles. Good. He knew she was nervous, and anticipated that she might not know what to say. No matter, he would get straight to the point then. Morei took a drink, letting the pungent liquid roll down his throat and into his stomach. This had to be the best thing he'd had since leaving Geral.

He lowered the glass and approached her slowly. Her blue eyes jumped to him, and he smiled at her. "There is no need to worry, Isla. I brought you here so that you could decide what you wanted to do."

That got her attention. "What do you mean?"

He twirled the liquid in the glass and stopped before the desk, a few paces shy of her. Best to give her space. The last thing he wanted to do was make her feel uncomfortable. "Rhys has told you that you are of Caster descent. Your blood is royal, and it would be cruel of me not to make that known to you."

She looked incredibly uneasy, as if a shift of the wind might send her running. He couldn't blame her. Based on her attire, he wasn't even sure she had ever walked these halls. This was clothing meant for the lowest levels of the palace. "There was a death certificate . . ."

"Forged," Morei clarified. "So that Drexis and Talia could cover themselves when people asked what happened to the baby. Did Rhys show you this?"

She nodded.

"Good." At least the chancellor had had the wherewithal to do that, even if he wasn't in total support of this decision. "I would give you my condolences for killing Drexis, but I suspect he meant nothing to you."

This time, Isla chuckled, and that relieved Morei but also surprised him. Perhaps she had a sense of humor. A dark one, which he liked. She had hardly spoken, but it didn't matter—he was already growing fond of the potential. He saw in Isla a woman who could run the world if she wanted to. Morei had been raised in royalty, molded to identify types of people without them ever having to say a word. This woman before him had the traits of royalty despite never having spent a day as a member. She was quiet, which meant she was a listener and observer; she stood straight and kept her hands clasped, expectant for whatever came next. She might have been dressed in rags, but swap them out for an embroidered dress and she would look like a painting.

He let his eyes wander the massive study. Not a speck of dust on the furniture, and he welcomed the breeze from the open terrace. Silence could tell a lot about a person, so he took his time broaching the next part, observing her from the corner of his eye.

Isla remained motionless, matching his stoicism. She would be perfect.

"I am aware of Caster traditions. It was brought to my attention that firstborn girls are considered bad luck, which was the reason you were abandoned. But you should consider yourself lucky, Isla—they could have drowned you."

He set the drink down on the desk and looked at her fully. "You have a choice, and I will not tell you which way to choose. You can walk out those doors right now and pack whatever is yours and leave this city. I would not blame you, especially after how you've been treated, and I would be glad to offer you enough coin to last a lifetime. You'd never have to work a day in your life again, and you could go anywhere, marry whoever, and live however you wanted."

He gestured at the room. "Or you can stay here and embrace your heritage. You are pure Caster blood, and I cannot take that away from you. You would be reinstated with official documentation as the princess, the fake death certificate destroyed, and you would have a place on the council." He raised a finger, knowing what she might ask. "You have a lot to learn, and in no shape or form do I suspect you to act as a queen, but I do want to teach you where I can. I would be more than willing to teach you the politics and swordsmanship needed to be a successful ruler. You would act as a voice, have a place in the royal palace chambers, and be granted all rights as royalty. The only caveat to that is that you must sign a contract acknowledging me, Morei Geral, as the king, and that despite your bloodline, you will not attempt to seize the throne from me."

Isla looked a bit shocked now. She had been so good at hiding her emotions up to this point, but the veil had fallen. "You would make me a princess?"

"Well, of course," Morei answered. "You're royal. It is your right, if you choose to accept." Had she not heard the first part? He blamed nerves.

Isla bit her lower lip. "And if I choose to leave?"

"I'll have a horse or ship ready for you, to go in whichever direction you choose," he replied.

"Wow . . ." Isla fell quiet and dropped her eyes. "I feel the Gods have granted me a gift."

Morei held his tongue. She had no idea what the Gods were capable of, and she probably didn't want to know.

"If I accept, what happens?" she asked, and looked at him again with those wide blue eyes. Eager eyes.

Morei tried to hide his excitement—this was what he'd been hoping for. The citizens would be far more accepting of him with Caster blood by his side. There was also the matter of the Festival of Seasons, but he was getting ahead of himself. "If you accept, I have a document prepared for you to sign that has already been signed by the council and chancellor, as well as me, approving this induction. Given you are Caster blood, we had to adjust the document to reflect that." This was not a case like Ezra, who had been a commoner inducted into the Geral name. Morei could still remember that day as clearly as the back of his hand. Ezra had been so eager, as eager as Isla was now, but he'd been determined to discuss matters with his mother.

"To be frank, Isla, I went into this discussion unsure where you stood, so if you agree, I would inform Rose and make sure the royal chamber was set up for you immediately. Clothes would be prepared too—they would be custom-fitted for you. Lily is quite good at that, and I'm sure she could have something done before sunrise tomorrow." The head seamstress was spectacular. With everything going on, she had been a breath of fresh air. "Once you were settled, I would have you summoned immediately to attend to any plans I had. The faster we initiate this, the quicker you can learn. That is"—Morei looked at her pointedly—"unless you wish to leave Caster."

He wanted to give her this chance. He might be merciless, cruel; he might have a list of murders under his belt, but he was always determined to do the right thing. This was one of those times where he was set on doing what was right by the Caster name—the name he now represented—and it started with the woman before him. He could not start his reign in a bed of secrets and lies.

Isla sighed and rubbed her hands together. "I want to . . . but I don't know if I am what you want."

"Who says I want you to be anyone?" Morei countered, surprised. "The only thing I need you to be is eager to learn. Everything else will come with time."

That seemed to solidify whatever was going on in her head. "Okay," Isla stated with far more confidence. "I want this.

I'll sign your document too. I have no problem doing such a thing . . . It's not like I have any experience in this anyways."

Morei smiled, glad to have done something right today. "By next summer, you will be an expert. It comes fast to those gifted to rule." He raked his eyes over her, not hiding his delight. "I sense that will be easy for you."

That earned a double take. "How do you know?"

He shrugged and picked up his drink. "Just a guess."

Isla's chest rose and fell, as if she had just taken the biggest breath of her life. Her eyes glittered with excitement, and Morei felt it too. He was even more thrilled with the opportunity this presented. Multiple opportunities, actually. She could become an exceptional asset.

"Why don't we get Rhys called back in here and set things in motion?" Morei asked. "So that you can be in your chamber by this evening. I'll summon you tomorrow."

"That sounds wonderful. Thank you, Morei—um, Your Majesty."

Isla looked embarrassed, and he waved her off. "Nonsense. Formalities are only for public appearance. You're a princess now, Isla—you may call me by my first name."

"Okay."

Morei was amused. People got so odd with formalities. In time, she would come to realize that. In time, she could be a queen. Morei certainly wasn't looking for marriage—far from it, especially after Emerald—but that did not mean Isla couldn't have her own throne. An empire would require far more rule than a city, and he hoped that she would be exactly what he needed to see that through.

What happened next would alter the future of the Vore World. Morei had no doubt about it. This was the start of his plan, and it was going exactly how he wanted it to. Isla had been a surprise, but a welcome one. She could be exactly what the people needed—the epitome of compassion.

Potential, he reminded himself. This was a woman with a world of potential.

WEATHERED FOR THE WORST

The cave still offered the best sanctuary. She was away from the world, the noise, and all the drama. While her chamber was nice, Syra couldn't go back there, not yet. With everything she knew would undoubtedly happen once Keryn's death was publicized, she didn't want to be anywhere near that disaster. Up here, the only things she needed to worry about were the position of her blanket and the wind.

The sun had been up for some time; she'd been able to watch the sunrise before dozing off. Next to her lay that book she'd originally picked up about Diyrằ's history, an almost empty mug of water, and bread and cheese. The fur blanket had been a smart call on her part. While there wasn't a cloud in the sky, the weather was still cooler. Now that she was awake, she snacked and watched the trees sway, tousled by the wind that hadn't yet reached her. Birds came and went. A few had landed and been startled by her presence, but she tore off a few pieces of bread. If she was lucky, she could get a few birds to nibble so she could watch them.

By now, Dryl would be deep in the mess of whatever political storm he'd brewed up. He would either be speaking to the council or preparing to. Zarek would be somewhere close to him, she was sure, perhaps driven by a guilty conscience to stand by his brother's side after abandoning him for so long. Syra knew how haunted he'd been when he believed Dryl dead, so she was happy the two could work through whatever they needed to. But by now, she also knew that if Zane wasn't identified as one of the dead, then he was missing. Right now, as much as she wanted to be courageous and find those answers, she couldn't move. She didn't want to.

Right now, she wanted to be Syra. The girl who used to disappear by finding a secluded spot on the beach to think.

She knew Dryl wanted to leverage her. She also knew that the Soul Realm needed help. Syra had gone into all of this understanding that eventually she would have to make decisions without knowing the consequences, but she hadn't been prepared for the severity.

If she turned her back on the Soul Realm—or worse, failed to secure it, as the Guardians so diligently reminded her of—the entire realm would be lost. Worst yet, there was a fracture on Volkeri Island that Dryl had confirmed to be ravaged by beasts. If she didn't succeed in what was expected of her—taking over the Soul Realm and restoring it to its former, prosperous self— the Vore World would be destroyed too.

Tonight, Sekar would show, and he would train her again. There was no denying any longer just how essential it was that she master her abilities. Destiny was catching up to her at an exponential rate, and she either had to be prepared to face these problems head-on or die.

And Syra really didn't want to die. She hadn't come all this way to be left for dead.

She snorted and reached for more bread and cheese. Piling on a few slices, she shoved the whole thing in her mouth and chewed. Eventually, she'd have to return to her chamber and prepare for Sekar's arrival. Her hair was still braided, but it was a mess from the events of the last day, and she wanted to at least freshen up, if not for anyone but herself. There was nothing like a bath to restart the day.

But . . . she didn't have to wait for Sekar, right? Up here, away from the world, she could still practice some of her harvesting. Nothing extreme, but she could get used to the idea of it and how Chaos felt moving through her. If she could grasp the force, that was.

She closed her eyes and let her lungs rise and fall several times in a slow, deliberate manner. Focusing on the wind, she cleared her mind. It was just like the basics, and that she could do. Zarek had taught her that much. Then again, she realized, she'd ended up in the Soul Realm by accident a few times because of her tie to it. The realm hopping hadn't happened in a while, but ever since she'd been bound to Chaos, it had been extremely difficult to even harvest a little energy. It felt like she was learning to walk all over again.

She peeked one eye open—a bird with vibrant blue feathers landed on the edge of the cave and tilted its head at her. It took one hop toward her and then fled with a flutter of wings.

Focusing on herself again, Syra remembered the pebble Zarek had given her. He'd told her to focus her attention on it and feel its lifeforce. She took that same mentality and directed it on her own lifeforce. She traveled further into herself, mapping out her own bones, following the flow of blood, listening to the beat of her own heart as it slowed. Her lungs rose and fell, her ears stopped listening to the wind, and her mind felt *free*.

Syra searched, grabbing at the tail of Chaos here and there. It was there, and she now was certain that to harvest it, she needed to first catch it. Chaos was energy at the end of the day, and if she could harvest Light Energy using this method, she could do the same here.

She stopped after the twelfth try. She wasn't frustrated, but a sudden idea had come to her. Syra was so focused on chasing it that perhaps she was doing it all wrong. Chaos was uncontrolled. It was intelligent. It thrived in a realm outside her own because it was simply too powerful for its own good. *Her* own good—Sekar's own words echoed in her mind then.

Chaos would come to her.

So she stopped, and in her mind, she stood there waiting. All around, Chaos flourished at the sudden halt of her chase. She felt like she was being encircled by a fierce wind, yet she did not feel any pull on her clothes or hair. She remained motion-less, sensing that Chaos was intrigued. Mother had chosen her, but that did not mean she could call upon the force without first gaining permission. It all made sense now.

Chaos turned her limbs hot, but Syra did not draw away from the sudden heat. The energy raced up her arms and legs, ravaged her chest and throat, and she did her best to remain still. Air came in stifled gasps. This was what Chaos wanted, and so Syra would give herself over.

And then it stopped.

Syra's breaths returned to normal, and she thought she heard a flutter of wings again. She sniffed the air but found it thick with what smelled like mold. Confused, she opened her eyes, and saw the purple sky staring back at her. She was high up in a cave, but the stone around her was slick with black slime.

Movement far below caught her attention. A giant beast with leathery wings and a long snout shuffled through a pile of bones on the ground there. Almost the instant she saw it, the beast turned its massive head toward her. From here, she couldn't see the eyes, and she didn't need to. It knew she was there.

"Oh, shit." As the beast launched itself into the air, she shoved herself backward and slammed her head into the stone.

Syra opened her eyes. She was staring at the familiar blue sky. The fur blanket lay across her legs, and a bird took off with a piece of bread as she stirred. This was the cave she knew.

Yet the pain in the back of her head proved that what had just happened was real. Syra reached up and felt the spot, bruising already, and there was something wet as well. When she drew her hand away, she saw black slime on her fingers.

She stared, bewildered. She should have been terrified, but she wasn't. Syra didn't fully understand the extent of her abilities, but she did know one thing: she'd just gone to the Soul Realm and back. She stared at her surroundings, anticipating at any point that she'd see that flying creature coming for her. But it couldn't reach her here.

The old Syra would have turned inward, uncertain. The new one wanted to scream at the top of her lungs with triumph. She'd done that. Nobody else. And she wanted to tell people, but she knew she couldn't. Not yet. Dryl and Zarek would be busy with the Infernol, and they would have questions she couldn't answer yet, like if realm hopping put her in any real danger. And why had she gone there and not anywhere else?

Syra checked the sun. It was still early afternoon, which meant Sekar wouldn't be around for a bit, assuming he came mid-evening. That couldn't come fast enough.

Antsy, she snatched up her mug, book, and blanket. She left the bread, knowing the birds would eat it, and took off down the narrow tunnel. The sooner she got back to her chamber, the better.

A GOD'S SMILE

There was a God in the same room with him. There were no instructions on how to act in the presence of a deity, no right words to say, nothing. But Cyrus was not scared. The unwavering silver gaze of the God of Courage gave him peace, despite the whirlwind of surprise. The journey that he had been on up to this point suddenly all made sense, no matter how difficult some parts had been. A part of him was in awe that a Vore God would make himself known to him, of all people—Dragon Rider or not—and another, smaller voice wondered why.

Cyrus stared for a long time, even after Alaric greeted him. The words went in one ear and out the other. He opened his mouth, then closed it. He hadn't prepared for this, and he was grateful when Sozar took the lead.

Greetings, Rider, the dragon said. His voice carried between the two men with ease, and Cyrus watched the expression on the God's face shift from content to pleased. *You have come a long way for us.*

That elicited the slightest curl of Hyle's lip. *It is you who has come a long way, son of Aythen.*

Cyrus's mouth fell open, but no words came out.

Aythen was the dragon the stories told about. She had gone mad with rage and abolished the Rider Federation after her

Rider, Vikter, had been killed. It was she who many believed had been the last dragon to fall, about eight hundred summers ago. So little was known about the Rider Federation because most of the documentation had been destroyed in the Great Fall, but Cyrus knew of Aythen. Almost everyone knew of the dragon responsible for bringing an entire city to its knees. To now know that Sozar was the son of Aythen, though, it was enough to cause him pause.

He had discovered Sozar in the mines of Diemon, not in Eiyrăl, where the Rider Federation's remains resided. How a dragon egg wound up a country away had always been a question of his, but now he knew Aythen was responsible. Perhaps she had fled with Sozar's egg and hidden it, or maybe Sozar's egg was one of many that Vikter and Aythen had placed in hopes of ensuring dragons would not go extinct, well before the Great Fall and the Rider's death. The latter thought was hopeful, even foolish, but now he wondered of the possibility.

There were so many questions, some he knew Sozar shared. The dragon's emotions stomped over his. Shock being the strongest of them all, and he couldn't say he was surprised. They had traveled across the Vore World and never once had Cyrus stopped to consider that their journey would give Sozar closure on his own heritage. The dragon had simply accepted that he may never know. Cyrus too.

"What did I miss?" Alaric asked.

Hyle smiled—it was a smile that could have passed as cynical. "We are getting acquainted." The God motioned with his hand. "Please, sit. I am sure you are starved."

He was, but his appetite felt nonexistent compared to his overwhelming. A God sat before him, and he had just called Sozar the son of Aythen, the last dragon. Still, Cyrus walked over and lowered himself slowly into the chair, feeling his injuries as he did.

Hyle noticed. "That was the best I could do," he told him from across the table.

"You . . ." Cyrus tried to speak, but his words were failing him.

"Under different circumstances, I could have fully healed you, but there are certain . . . shall we say rules, with energy healing." Hyle reached for his wine. "You are a Dragon Rider, I am a God. We are bound to different energies. Chaos serves me as much as I serve her, but she does not serve you, despite your dragon's connection to the ancient force. Healing you with Chaos would have killed you." Hyle took a drink now. "I had to get creative with my harvesting to aid you the best I could."

Alaric, sitting between them at the head of the table, leaned forward on his elbows. "Cyrus . . . you died twice on that table. Your heart stopped beating, and it was because of Hyle that you are alive. The injuries you sustained should have killed you then and there, but—"

"Sozar," Cyrus finished quietly. "He kept me alive."

"Dragons," Hyle hummed, his eyes growing bright. "They are extraordinary, aren't they?" His words turned inward, his face showing no sign. *Sozar fed you an immense amount of energy, and while he kept you alive in that moment, his energy imbalanced your lifeforce. You could not remain alive without additional aid these last few days, so your dragon has been feeding you continuously. Between his energy and my harvesting, you are alive.*

Cyrus kept his face still as well. Sozar broke in. *I did not sense you.*

Centuries of practice, Hyle replied without hesitation. *Eat. Alaric is watching.*

Cyrus reached forward and picked up a piece of bread. "You are king." The words were calmer than he planned, and he was pleased to see the man appeared to have no concerns. He didn't show any indication that he sensed there were words being passed between the dragon, Hyle, and Cyrus. Best to keep it that way.

Alaric grabbed a slice of white meat from a nearby plate. "Yes. It's been a tense few days."

"Thank you." It seemed that was all he was good at saying today. "You saved my life."

The king paused midslice on his plate, holding a knife in one hand. "I did the right thing," he whispered. "My father was cruel. He would have killed you, and I could not fathom the idea of him taking the life of a Dragon Rider."

Hyle raised his brow. "But you could accept him taking other innocent lives."

The fork clattered on the plate, causing Cyrus to flinch. "I did not and do not condone what my father did."

"Yet, you were only brave enough to act when it suited you best. *Courageous*," he mocked with a smile. "I am not insulting you, King, just observing."

Slowly, Alaric picked up his silverware and continued to eat. Cyrus took the opportunity to do the same, choosing with care which items he wished to experiment with first. After days of not properly eating, he anticipated a stomachache after a meal like this.

Cyrus wasn't sure what he had been expecting. Maybe for Hyle to be a bit more respectful—although who was he to assume a God owed anything to a king? More specifically, a Dragon Rider turned God. There was no one Hyle would serve, save for his dragon.

There had always been questions about whether or not the God of Courage wore the eyes of a Rider intentionally or by right. It seemed those rumors were settled now.

In that perspective, Cyrus could relate with the God who sat across from him. The scar had been with him a long time, that much was obvious, based on how the skin looked—raised and slightly discolored, a little grayer than the surrounding porcelain. He had so many questions, but he followed his gut instinct, which was to not say anything right away. Let the God lead the conversation. Alaric was doing the same.

Alaric did not invite him, the dragon observed. *This meeting is because of Hyle.*

That made sense, considering how Alaric was acting—he was clearly uncomfortable, but just a bit more acquainted with the idea of a God in the same room. Cyrus had gone his entire life thinking these deities were, for lack of a better word, untouchable. In fact, he'd gone so far as to believe they weren't even real.

They ate for a long while in silence, which he was okay with. It allowed him to gather his senses and thoughts, to adjust to the idea that he was sitting across from a Vore God.

It struck him almost as funny. Who could say they'd done that?

The wine was helping him settle his nerves, as well as numb the discomfort from his back. The injury was not entirely thrilled with him sitting, so he continued to drink. The buzz would help him manage. Not the most ideal approach, but with Hyle sitting across from him and the king of Delion to his right, Cyrus needed a drink or two. Or three.

Finally, Hyle leaned back. He hadn't eaten much, deliberate with every bite. He dabbed at his mouth with the cloth and then reached for the decanter of red wine, pouring a healthy amount into his glass. "Tell your cooks this is phenomenal."

In all his thinking, Cyrus hadn't even thought about the actual *taste* of the food. He was so caught up, he'd just eaten it. An act to pass the time, not an act of enjoyment. He looked at his plate—how much had he even put on there? His stomach was stretched, his mind still telling him he was starved, but he pushed his plate aside and grabbed a cloth as well. "The food is delicious," he concurred.

Alaric nodded and took a bite of a pastry. Cyrus had no idea when those had arrived. As the king chewed, Hyle turned his attention to Cyrus again.

"How much do you know about the Rider Federation?"

"Um—" He searched his thoughts, surprised by the question. "The Rider Federation was responsible for managing politics, was home to the Dragon Riders, and Aythen and Viker were the last to fall."

Hyle nodded, but his eyes said he wasn't satisfied. "Sad to think such an empire would become only a fragment to the Vore World after such little time," he commented, and took a drink. When he set the glass down, his silver eyes flashed with recognition—amusement, perhaps. "Vikter was stubborn. So stubborn, in fact, that he started a political war, or encouraged it." He smiled. "The war was already there, but he exploited it. You remind me a lot of him."

Cyrus stiffened, unsure if this was a compliment or not.

Hyle raised a hand from the table. "You are so stubborn to prove your point that you refuse to choose sides." The God shrugged. "What you don't realize is everywhere you go, you bring a war. Your very existence elicits a primal response among people, one they cannot control."

In Cyrus's head, he added: *No matter what you do, you will always be feared by some.*

Cyrus shook his head. "I don't want people to die because of me, because of what I am," he insisted. "I've been on the run since Sozar hatched to protect him, because every time I think I can trust someone, they have underlying motives."

Hyle leaned forward now. "So stop running." The statement was loud, the meaning bold. The God did not have to explain himself, yet he did. "Sozar chose you to be his Rider, so start acting like one. The people"—he gestured as if to encompass the world—"will always see you as a Dragon Rider, but if you never see yourself that way, you will spend a long life running.

You have the power to change the world, Rider. Not anyone else. If you don't choose a side, a purpose, Destiny will do it for you. And you do not want her deciding for you what your purpose is."

Alaric hadn't moved, the glass lifted but nowhere close to his lips. Cyrus had half a mind to ask him to leave, because he felt like he was being exploited—this conversation should have been private. "You're a God. Why can't you do something about it?"

"Chaos," Hyle muttered through clenched teeth. "I serve her, no matter how much I wish I didn't have to. It's because of her I can't intercede. I cannot interrupt how Chaos chooses to court Destiny. You can, I cannot. The Gods are required to stay out of anything that could harm Chaos's control."

He swallowed. "Control?"

"The realms are all interconnected by Chaos," Hyle continued. "Gods cannot intervene with anything that could potentially destroy the realms. I cannot show up to the Soul Realm and kill the Guardians, because doing so would upset the order of Chaos. Everything is balanced—or is supposed to be. All I can do is influence and guide, and if something is threatening me, and therefore Chaos, I can act. My job is to help protect Chaos and keep the balance of energies, not to upset that balance. Does that make sense?"

It did, although Cyrus had a hundred new questions already.

"You feel the weight of the world is on your shoulders," Hyle observed, "yet you know nothing about what's going on in the world because you're too busy proving your point that you want nothing to do with the world." A cold smile crawled across his lips. "The world wants everything to do with you, but you want nothing to do with it."

Zorya had said those words, and based on Hyle's expression, he knew that. If Cyrus had shared the Razan halls with a God and never known about it, that was unsettling. Was it possible that a God could live side by side with the very citizens who worshipped him and never make himself known?

"If you ask the right questions, you can be the most influential person this world has ever seen," Hyle pressed. "Or you can be another story."

Cyrus swallowed again, a lump in his throat. "What do you know?" he asked. It was time to play by the God's rules.

That made Hyle smile. "You learn fast, Rider. Where do you want to start?"

He knew Hyle already anticipated what he was about to say. "Zorya."

Alaric, of course, had no idea who she was to him. The king of Delion sat there, as still as a statue.

The God tilted his head. "When you left, Dameon and Ashtir flew to Razan and killed the king. Zorya now rules with her mother."

Cyrus closed his eyes, humiliated. He was ashamed, full of guilt, angry at himself for turning his back on her. Deep down, he had begged to whoever could hear him to spare that family. Kyllian was no hero, but he loved his daughter dearly, and Cyrus felt directly responsible for his death. It was a blow to the chest and shattered the veil he had placed over himself—he had gone all this time in a false belief that everything was okay, that he had not left a trail of misfortune behind him.

When he opened his eyes, Hyle was still staring at him through that hideous scar. "What else?" Cyrus asked.

"Morei Geral has seized Caster for himself and intends to take the entire country." He said it so matter-of-factly that at first, Cyrus didn't grasp the meaning. "He will be a force to be reckoned with once he asserts himself as Demon King, which will be soon."

Cyrus licked his lips. "How do you know that?"

"I know a lot of things," Hyle answered. "The question is whether or not you want to know them too."

Of course he wanted to know. He nodded.

That satisfied the deity. "My brothers and sisters, the Gods you know, have begun to take sides in a war that is coming. Some will support you; others will stand against you. While we cannot directly interfere with whatever Destiny has planned for the living realm, we can be influential in how those things happen." Hyle regarded him for a moment. "Like how Henry Junok possesses the two dragon eggs you found in Razan."

Cyrus's heart seized. He blinked once, then again.

Alaric finally moved, his expression going from curiosity to horror in an instant as he set his glass back down and leaned forward to stare at Hyle. That was a name that no king or queen wanted to hear. Nobody wanted to. Henry Junok was the owner of destruction, leader of the Diyrăllian Massacre, and had erected one of the most merciless empires in Vorelian history.

And if he had the eggs . . . then . . .

Cyrus felt like he was going to be sick. His stomach knotted. Nausea struck him like a galloping horse, and he couldn't find his breath. At once, he felt incredibly hot; the sensation blossomed in his chest and seeped into his limbs.

A loud clang broke the spell, and Cyrus looked over to see Alaric raise one hand, while the other adjusted his plate and silverware. He had struck the ceramic, and now he looked humiliated to have their eyes on him in such a tense conversation. Cyrus wished he was in the king's shoes, so that he could absolve himself of all these horrific feelings—guilt, shame, embarrassment, and the burden of the world on his shoulders. It was in these moments that he wished he could return to simpler times, when the world didn't place so much expectation on him.

"You didn't know," Hyle continued, drawing Cyrus's attention back to the crushing present. "Who would have thought

Henry would have come for you?" He laughed, although Cyrus wasn't sure what was so funny. "He took advantage of your desperation, of your . . . *stubbornness.* You didn't want to choose a side, you wanted to do the right thing, and now he has the eggs."

Sozar interjected. *How do you know this?*

Hyle replied aloud. "My job is to keep the balance, remember? If I don't know what's going on, then I'm not doing my job." He snatched up his glass and took a drink. When he set it down, he smacked his lips. It seemed he was the only one having a good time. "Making a deal with the most powerful Energy Harvester to date was not entirely the best idea you've had," he commented, and laughed. "Helyna told me everything."

Cyrus didn't bother asking about Helyna. His mind was still on Leonzo—on Henry Junok, who had tricked him. "What do I do?" he asked.

"What do you want to do, great Sea Flyer? You can't be everyone's friend. Sooner or later, you'll have to make an enemy."

Shaking his head, he replied, "If I would have known . . ."

"It doesn't matter now what you wished you would have known. All you can do is make a decision based on what you know now, so I ask again: What do you want to do?"

Cyrus was quiet for a bit, trying to find the right words to convey how much he wanted to right his wrongs, but also how much he wanted to do the right thing. He knew he couldn't say that—Hyle would likely stab him for it. The God didn't strike him as someone who focused on the *right* thing, rather what best suited the world. He would slaughter an entire city if it meant fulfilling the obligations he was assigned to. If Hyle lunged across the table and drove a blade right through Alaric's chest, it wouldn't have surprised Cyrus.

He found himself stuck on one phrase that repeated over and over in his head. It encompassed everything he wished, needed, and wanted to be.

"I want to be a Dragon Rider."

For the first time since they had sat, Hyle smiled wide—a true smile, filled with genuine pleasure. It was exactly what the God had wanted to hear, and Cyrus had never been so relieved.

The tension in the room shifted. Cyrus wondered if everything up to this point had been a test. The God had been feeling him out, and Cyrus almost shivered at the thought. Hyle didn't strike him as someone who gave second chances.

"I asked you earlier what you knew about the Rider Federation," Hyle said, pulling him back to the conversation. "You answered everything as I suspected. What you'd never have been able to know was that the Rider Federation fell with the belief that there would come a time for them to rise again. This time, with a new leader."

Cyrus had no idea what to say. What Hyle was suggesting was impossible. He stole a glance over at Alaric, who looked like he had turned to marble once more.

"The eggs that were preserved were, as you probably came to figure out, to begin a new era of Dragon Riders. But it was so much more than that. The Rider Federation entrusted the future Riders—people they knew they'd never likely meet— to carry on the name and order. The fallen city was never cleared, because the surrounding cities pledged never to touch it. That was the responsibility of the new Riders. When the time was right, a new federation would be erected in the same place. Everything that was meant for you is still there, amid the rubble. What was destroyed can be fixed, and special ceremonies were completed to protect the most important artifacts and documents. These would only be revealed to the Rider who was destined to lead the new federation. I believe that Rider is you."

"What about Dameon?" The question came out in a whisper.

"Why would the fate of the Rider Federation be placed in the hands of a man who has spent his entire life having the world handed to him?" Hyle asked, and reached over to grab a handful of berries. He leaned back and kicked his legs up, popping a few of the berries into his mouth. "Dameon is destined to choose wrong. Not because I know his future, but because I spent lifetimes working with other Dragon Riders like him. I can recognize a nasty one when I see one. Perhaps one day he will come to realize his tendencies, but until then, he will continue to choose wrong."

The answer still didn't satisfy him. "How can you be certain I'm the one for this? What about the other eggs? They will eventually hatch and choose their own Rider."

"Maybe," Hyle countered. "If Henry does not make them mindless beasts, that is." He smiled as if he had just told a joke, and ate a few more berries. Cyrus didn't find it funny, and neither did Sozar. "When the Rider Federation fell, it was left in my hands to protect it. I have spent centuries walking among the fallen buildings and palaces, looking for any sign of life, but the city will not reveal itself to me, only to the Rider chosen to resurrect it. That was a part of the promise made prior to its downfall. It's only fitting that the son of the dragon who tore the city to shreds would be the dragon to lead the rise. Vikter wouldn't have wanted it any other way."

"I don't think I'm capable of leading a charge like that," Cyrus confessed. He could hardly keep his head above water just caring for himself and Sozar. The idea of being responsible for a city, let alone other Dragon Riders, was overwhelming.

"You don't have to decide today," Hyle said, "but you will one day." He stood and picked up his drink, berries in the other hand. "Vikter thought he wasn't capable of leading anyone either, but he ended up being one of the best Dragon Riders this world has ever seen. The only fault he ever had was that he wanted to believe the world could change."

With that, he walked over to a side door and left. Cyrus had no idea where it led to. This had been one of the most bizarre interactions in his life, yet it had been fulfilling in ways he could not describe. His thoughts wandered. His emotions felt scattered, but he couldn't shake the resolve that settled in his soul.

He was a Dragon Rider.

The sigh from his right caught his attention. Alaric was pouring more wine in his glass and shaking his head. "I don't know about you, but I will be drinking very heavily for the rest of the night."

Cyrus stared as Alaric downed the glass in one gulp, then placed it down and topped it off again. After everything, drinking felt reckless. It also sounded freeing.

He raised his glass to his lips and took two big gulps to finish off the drink. The king topped it off without a word and then raised his own glass.

"Here's to what will undoubtedly be a fantastic friendship," Alaric announced, and they toasted. He didn't know the new king as well as he'd like to, but Hyle had clearly dragged him into this for a reason.

They drank freely. Conversation passed easily, and they even continued to eat. More pastries showed up. Cyrus couldn't remember when all the food had disappeared. It had been so long since he'd stopped trying to be someone that to let go like this was liberating.

Sozar gave him space. At least for tonight, he was in good hands.

FRACTURED DREAMS

Morei's vision changed quicker than he could take in his surroundings. He saw fire and blinked, then felt the ground shake beneath him as the buildings crumbled. He ducked, inhaling the pungent smell of ash and smoke. Morei started to cough violently from the assault, and he turned to run.

Destruction. Everywhere.

The sky was black, only visible by the rich orange glow of the flames that devoured everything in sight. He could not get his feet under him; sweat coated his brow, turning ash to grime. He tried to pull on Dark Energy, but he felt nothing.

Morei stumbled over debris that he swore hadn't been there, and then he looked at his hands. His skin was . . . untouched. Normal. Devoid of the black, spidery veins he'd grown so accustomed to. Devoid of power. Morei tried to tap into Light Energy, but he couldn't do that either. Panic blossomed. Screams crushed his logic. There was nothing he could do to protect these people, to stop the destruction of this city. A city that had been under his rule.

Things were happening too fast, and he felt the world slip from his control. Morei scrambled over broken stone, which cut through his palms. One of his boots got stuck in between the rubble. Morei yanked and felt a fiery pain shoot up his leg, but the foot did not budge. He shoved his bloodied hands against the stone to move the piece, with no luck.

"Give me a break," he hissed at the stone, frustrated. He needed to get out of here. There was nothing he could do, nothing he could change.

People rushed by him and did not stop to help. He was about to yell for their assistance when his eyes landed on the two figures in the distance. Cloaked, they approached slowly.

In the light of the fire, he could see red hair. And the pale blue skin of a Guardian who walked by her side, loyal. This was *her* doing, her destruction. That revelation seared through his head with agonizing force. His heart slowed, his breaths turned erratic, and perspiration drenched his skin with that realization. She had brought the end of times to his reign, and she would not stop here. He knew it as clearly as he knew how to swing a sword.

Morei gasped and shot up from his seat. Looking about, he found himself alone in his chamber, in a chair. To his right, a drink sat, half-empty. The silence that filled the vast room was deafening, and he took care to scan the entire room, suddenly feeling very vulnerable. Morei couldn't remember falling asleep, but when he looked down, he saw himself dressed in the first clothes he had been given by the seamstress. The blue fabric had already been halfway sewn when he arrived, just needing some quick adjustments to meet his measurements. It originally had been intended as a shirt for Drexis.

The lanterns still burned bright, granting him proper visibility. He sat up slowly and rolled his shoulders. The way he'd fallen asleep had given him a kink in his lower neck, and he rubbed it with a hand.

Morei was shaken to his core. Evil. That dream had been evil. The hollow feeling in his chest proved that. Syra leading the charge, the destruction of his reign—and of the world. That thought settled deep into his mind. His life had been consumed with so many unexpected and unexplainable events, and she was one of them. Syra Castello was a bad omen. Morei had never been one to be superstitious, but he was growing warier of her by each passing day. And if she could potentially threaten his rule? That made her an enemy. No matter what she told him, he couldn't trust her. Not when Sekar was involved.

He couldn't help but wonder if all this time, he'd been misled intentionally. The interaction in Geral with the spirit had startled him, and he'd believed he was supposed to find her. But what if that had been a trick? A way for her to latch on to him and drown him, strip him of everything he was working to reclaim, steal from him any future that he had control of?

No, he could not trust her. She was a threat.

A whisper from behind caught his attention, and he spun around. Nobody was there, but he wasn't satisfied. Quietly, he stood and approached the bathroom. The light illuminated the space, but he scanned the entire chamber. He had to be certain he was alone. Energy was just a short reach away, and his sword was on his hip. Morei had also retrieved his dagger to keep tucked away in his boot earlier too. Despite it all, he felt ill-prepared to face whatever was here.

No matter where he looked, there was nobody. Morei searched every crevice, corner, and hiding spot he could think of until he was satisfied that what he'd heard was a figment of his imagination, although that did not ease his nerves at all. His muscles tensed with a preparedness to fight at any given moment, and even his fingers twitched to draw on his weapon. He forced himself to stand by the small table and breathe slower.

This was all in his head. It had to be.

Another whisper, this one as quick and strong as a gust of wind, passed by. Morei spun, nearly striking the table with his leg and losing his balance. "What is this?" he demanded into the open space.

No response, but had he expected one?

He waited, and when nothing happened, he reached for his glass. It was all in his mind. Perhaps a consequence of the dreams with Syra.

There was a lot he could handle, but he did not enjoy the unknown. This was beyond his scope of understanding. If this was how Dark Energy consumed her prey, then he could not say he was surprised to see the end so near—dabbling with a force that not even the Gods would touch was a dance he was not skilled enough to master.

Yet he tried. Addicted to the rush, the power, all of it, but he was arrogant if he thought himself above Death's reach.

Morei raised the glass to his lips and took a long drink. The burn of the liquor was strong, and he grimaced as it seared his throat and stomach. If he could have four more of these drinks, he might be able to sleep—

"*Morei.*"

He spun around and threw his drink at the source. The glass smashed into the wall and shattered with a deafening sound. "Stop!" he screamed.

Inhale, exhale. The air came out ragged, hard, as he stared at where his drink now covered the ground. This was all wrong. It shouldn't be like this. Morei had worked too hard to take this city only for it all to be stripped from him by the grace of madness. Not yet.

A knock on his door broke the trance, and he turned his head. Morei waited, trying to discern if this was all in his head or real.

Another knock.

Cautiously, he approached the door. Part of him wanted to yell and demand that whoever was there go away, but another part was curious if this was real. He didn't want to be so caught up in the illusions that he ignored something important. When he got to the door, he cracked it.

"Who is— Ah, Isla." Morei weighed opening the door a bit more but decided against it. "What do you want?"

The woman was dressed in a white robe that fell to the floor. Her blond hair was braided to the side, and she looked like she had been asleep not too long ago. "I heard a yell and wanted to see if you were okay."

"I'm fine. You can return to your room."

But she didn't move. Great, she needed something. Morei couldn't go a single day without the world needing something from him. It came with the title, and he fully accepted that, but now was not the time. "I'm not in the mood for talking," Morei told her. "Unless the city is burning, I don't want to hear it."

"Who were you yelling at?" Isla asked, voice low.

"Nobody," he shot back, annoyed. "Do you need something?"

"So, you were yelling." The statement was not a question. She shrugged. "I just wanted to make sure you were okay. I was roaming around because . . . well, because I couldn't sleep. The room is so big, and it makes me feel—" Isla blinked. "Goodnight, Your Majesty."

She turned to leave, padding along the hall in what appeared to be wool slippers. Almost like a ghost, her steps were so light. Isla had made a living being nobody.

Morei closed the door and locked it once more before turning back to the empty and cold chamber. The broken glass on the ground did little to calm his frayed nerves and spiraling patience. He wanted to scream and force his blade into the heart of an enemy—the impulse was coming back. The Dark Energy was starved, and the ailment that had riddled his body was worsening. It always was. Some days were just better than others.

Tomorrow—or perhaps it was already the early hours of the morning—he would find what Caster had on Geral. He wanted to learn more about the city he had once called home and about the lineage that now burned through him. Drexis had mentioned his family had a history with energy harvesting, so maybe he had information on that somewhere. He would also need to meet with Edwin and speak on the current status of Caster's army to begin preparations for seizing Ferguson. It would take some persuasion, but it would happen. Morei did not wish to waste time. If he was going to take Sorréle, he intended to do it as quickly as possible.

His other order of business was to learn of Syra's whereabouts. He knew she was from this city, but long gone. If she was within his grasp, he considered ordering a hunt for her. Then again, he also wanted to stay as far away from her as possible, especially if Sekar was involved. Information would not hurt, though. The more he knew, the better he could act.

Morei scratched his jaw. There was too much happening at once. He could not juggle this all forever without something slipping. A king was raised to know what he could and could not handle, and for how long. This was one of those situations that screamed danger in his mind's eye. If he didn't find answers soon, he risked losing everything he had worked for.

Morei still had so much to gain, and nothing would stand in his way. No matter the cost, he would make Geral pay for what they did to him, for what they made him to be. And he would do that by conquering everything, including Syra, the dead, Sekar, the fucking Dragon Rider who had slipped through his grip when he had been a foolish king, and every city that stood in his way. The world had not seen a monster, not yet, but they would.

LIGHT BRINGER

Syra didn't need to see Dryl to know that the Infernol was in absolute shambles. Shouts rang through the halls. She had triple checked her lock—although it hadn't helped the first time—and kept her sword strapped on. With everyone's attention turned on Keryn, Arik, and now Dryl, she didn't think people would pay much mind to her. But one could never be too sure.

Over and over, she reminded herself that these people hadn't known she was involved in any of this, but it did little to calm her nerves. Up in the cave, she'd at least been able to separate herself from all the noise. Here, it was all around her, just outside her room. Had word of Vic even reached anyone? Had the council relented and granted Dryl rule? By the sounds of it, people were upset, and if the turmoil was here, she was certain the south and the East Markets were a disaster.

She thought about the Crown of Gods, the demon, Dryl's arrival, and Henry Junok. There was no guarantee that they'd found the agent. Keryn had made it seem so, but she wondered now if there was more. They'd know about Dryl and the shift in leadership. It was ignorant to believe the council was made up of authentic people. When she saw Dryl again, she'd tell him.

"Thinking?"

Syra whirled around to see Sekar standing there with a curious expression. He had changed his clothes, now wearing black. The last time she'd seen him, they were standing with Keryn's body. That was only yesterday.

"The Infernol is losing their mind," Syra commented. "Dryl spoke to the council today, and by the sounds of it, it's just madness out there."

"Nobody ever likes change," he replied. "This storm will pass."

"Will it?" she challenged. "If the Infernol can't unite on anything, they'll end up killing each other."

Sekar didn't reply to that.

"Nothing to say?" Syra held up her hand. "Actually, what am I saying? You'll have some sarcastic remark about it, so save it. I'm seriously worried about him. Zane too."

At that, he raised an eyebrow. "The soldier that accompanied you?"

"Yes. He's missing." She didn't want to assume he was dead. Wouldn't.

"Shame," Sekar replied. He sounded genuinely concerned. "I kind of liked him."

She did too, and now he might be dead because of her. Syra knew it was more complex than that, but at this rate, it felt routine, people dying around her.

He unraveled his crossed arms and approached her. She had to look up to see his dark eyes. "Syra," he whispered, resting a finger under her chin. "Are you really worried about Dryl?"

She nodded.

That made the God laugh. "You don't know much about his history, do you?" When she shook her head, he said, "There are a handful of times Dryl should have died. He's broken more Guardian laws than anyone else I know. Remember, I spent nearly four centuries with him, so I know a thing or two. This is not a man you need to worry about. Zarek, on the other hand . . ." Sekar cracked a smile. "He's too stubborn for his own good at times. I'd worry about him."

That should have made her feel better, but it didn't. She knew he was trying to help, and she appreciated that, but she needed to see the Guardian herself.

Sekar was here, though, and that was what she had been looking forward to.

Pulling herself free, she rubbed a hand over her face and brushed her hair back. "Today, something happened," she told him. "I was able to harvest Chaos—"

"This is incredible," Sekar interjected.

"—but I went to the Soul Realm," she finished. "You know the few times I realm hopped? It was like that, but I was elsewhere. It was deserted, and this beast immediately saw me. I hit my head trying to get away, but then I was back here." She shrugged, unable to keep the excitement out of her voice. "I felt it. Chaos. I realized you can't chase it—her. She came to me. I thought if I mastered this, think of what I could do . . ." She was going to mention her dreams with Morei, but she trailed off.

The God stared. It was the first time in a long time that he looked absolutely mad with glee. Actually, the only other time she'd seen that look was when he brought her to face judgment with the Eternal Flame.

"No—"

Sekar snatched her from where she stood. His large frame wrapped around her to still her. "Tonight, we test it," he told her. "Tonight, you will show what you're capable of."

"But it's so soon," she pleaded. "I barely know what I'm doing." She knew she couldn't get out from his grip, not when he was so much stronger, but she still struggled. "I hardly think this is necessary."

"And miss the fun of this?" Sekar countered. His definition of fun was entirely different than hers. "Don't move now," he breathed into her ear. "Wouldn't want to lose you."

She stilled in his grip, even as the world around her shifted and a blue haze rippled. If he let go of her in the middle of a transport like this, there was a chance she could end up somewhere completely different.

Her boots sank into the familiar crunch of dead branches and soil. The crisp air now smelled of rot, and as the blue haze shifted, she saw the dense, dead trees. There were noises all around them—distant screeches from demons in flight. Syra had never noticed them before, but if she stared long enough, she could see the large wings of beasts cross the sky. Perhaps the very same as what she'd seen earlier. From the trees, wooshes and crunches echoed, whether from demon or beast, she did not know, and didn't want to.

"Sekar," she whispered, afraid to speak too loud. "What are we doing here?"

"Looking," he replied, and stepped forward. His eyes scanned the area, intense.

That didn't help. "For what?" she pressed.

There wasn't much to see, besides the branches, trunks, and dead leaves that never seemed to disintegrate. Even the sky wasn't visible, which left them mostly in the dark, save for the slight illumination that came from everywhere. She'd never noticed it until now—the glow from this world that gave them light. It emanated from everything.

She saw something a bit brighter ahead, fleeting before disappearing and reappearing. She squinted, watching, and realized that the light wasn't fading, but rather going in and out of the trees.

"A spirit," Sekar told her, but she already knew that. "We found what we wanted."

He stepped forward, and she followed. As they approached the spirit, she saw that it was a young boy, maybe no more than ten, and the dark hair atop his head bounced as he raced about, chasing something that only he could see. He was filled with pure joy, eyes wide, dark skin gray under the glow of his lifeforce.

Syra could see his clothing was untouched, simple and tan. Perhaps he had been a farmhand, but the grin on his face suggested he still possessed an innocence that had yet to be stolen by this realm.

When the boy saw them, he froze, and the smile fell. Already, his legs were stepping backward, his eyes widening in terror. Sekar shoved her forward, and she stumbled. "Your test."

She shot him a glare. "What am I supposed to do?"

He shrugged. "Your guess is as good as mine, Light Bringer."

Syra bit her tongue and returned to the spirit. Test. All right.

She took a step forward. Time, the boy did not look like he would flee, so she took another, and his arms relaxed. He looked around, searching for that unseen thing.

"You don't look like the others," he mumbled.

Syra was close enough now that she trusted he'd come to her, so she knelt on one knee to get to eye level. Offering the smallest of smiles, she said, "I'm not from around here. What's your name?"

She stole a quick look behind her to see the God still standing there, eyes locked on her.

"Erun," the boy told her. "Who's he?"

"A friend," Syra answered, although she wasn't sure that was an accurate description of their relationship.

This close, Erun smelled of nothing. The grayness of his skin shimmered when he moved, like sand in the sun. Syra had seen the dead before but not like this. Usually they were without such an illumination, such a lifeforce, and she wondered if this meant he was new, if the others had aged here a long while. Syra saw in his eyes the spirit of a child who had yet to understand the gravity of his situation. Perhaps he was chasing the friends he still saw in his mind; maybe his heart still beat with the living's.

This close, she felt a hum growing in her ears that could not be ignored. Syra looked left and right, thinking perhaps it was coming from an oncoming threat, but not even Sekar moved from where he stood behind her. This was not a threat, but something occurring between her and Erun. As she inhaled deeply, she caught the smells of baked goods and butter. The boy's eyes lit up. He smelled it too.

She could see it all in an instant. Erun's grandfather leaning over him, guiding his hands as he learned to knead the dough. All around, stone shelves were filled with dough ready to be baked or freshly pulled from the fire oven that burned bright to her right. A woman called, asking about how her boy was doing—

Syra blinked and watched Erun's face scrunch up as he realized that was only a memory. The smells were gone, the vision vanished, and the boy's eyes glazed over with fear. "Where am I?" he whispered.

He turned to run. He'd just figured it out—that he was dead. Syra snatched his wrist and spoke his name in a desperate plea for him to listen.

The world shifted.

It was the fields she saw first, but only for a moment. Then the dark alleyway. She was running—no, Erun was—and he looked back to see his pursuers chasing. They were older boys, three summers his senior, and they were bullies. They'd never liked him, thought he had life handed to him too easy with his grandpa taking him in as an apprentice without following the appropriate steps.

Erun knew there was a small exit up ahead that he'd used plenty of times. An escape route that nobody else could fit through, but he was still young and slim. Once he got up there, he'd shove himself between the buildings and cross over into the next street. Then he would be free. It would take the boys some time to backtrack.

Pride swelled his chest—mother would be so proud. She knew he was bullied at times, but she was always so thrilled to hear how clever he was. Mother always said he was a smart boy, that he just sometimes said the wrong thing to the wrong person.

Without thinking, Erun turned to slip in between the stone, but his shoulder slammed into something hard. He stumbled back and blinked, stunned, beholding the large barrier that now kept him from escaping. Panic consumed him. No. This wasn't right. Only yesterday, he was using this. Erun scrambled forward and tried to grab the large wood palate that now imprisoned him, but his hands barely scraped the surface before a force slammed into him from the left, sending him sprawling.

"Grab him!" Teryk ordered. Erun tried to swing a punch but his small fist didn't make it halfway to the other boy's face. He was hauled up and didn't even have time to plead before Teryk punched him. The hit dazed him. Something warm trickled from his mouth as he spit a tooth—blood.

Teryk grinned madly, flashing crooked teeth that had probably been beaten into their permanent location. As he stood there, looking like a savage beast, teeth bared and all, he produced a knife from his belt. "Want to play a game, bastard?"

He lashed out, and the blade struck Erun's cheek first. Even though it was dull, it cut right through skin with how hard the older boy swung.

He jerked backward, but it was already too late. The blade struck again, this time deep into his chest. It was wild, really, that Erun could see the handle of the blade jutting out from his torso. He had always dreamed of being the one to deliver the blow in grand games of how he'd protect his mother.

It didn't stop there. Even as his strength waned and the other boys dropped him, Erun watched as Teryk continued to stab him over and over again—

Syra stood abruptly. Her boot caught a branch, and she stumbled backward. A hand grabbed her and she yelped in surprise, expecting to see Teryk there with a maddened grin, ready to finish what he'd started. But it was Sekar, staring at her and pointing. He was saying something, but she couldn't hear him over the ringing in her ears.

She turned to see the boy, Erun, lying there. His body was made of stone, eyes wide open. And as she watched, bewildered, the stone crumbled into dust so fine that an unseen breeze picked it up and swept him away. All that remained was the impression his body had made in the rotted ground. Not even his clothes stayed.

Tears burned her cheeks, hot like the pain in her chest, and she raised her hand to point. Then her eyes found another problem.

Her hand.

It was no longer the fair skin she'd been born with, but a dull pink, like a burn that was still healing. The color turned blotchy on her wrist and disappeared altogether on her forearm.

And it burned. Horribly.

"Sekar," she wheezed. She felt overcome with anxiety, exhausted, and like she could run for the next twelve leagues without stopping, all at once. Her heart was erratic, like it couldn't figure out if it wanted to stop or sprint off without her.

"Syra." The god grabbed her, and she didn't argue. Couldn't. He spun her around so that she faced him, but her eyes were still locked on her hand. "You resurrected him. He's *alive*."

"But—"

"The body of this realm cannot exist if the physical one in the living is alive," Sekar cut in. "His body of this realm is of no use to him anymore. That's why he turned to stone."

As he said this, he embraced her in a tight hug that she could hardly reciprocate. Not because she didn't want it—the touch was comforting, real, and reliable—but her body wouldn't move. Sekar pressed against her as the world of rot faded from her view. The mist was colder than she remembered, especially in comparison to the heat of the God who now held her.

Syra's mind was frayed, her strength gone, but she could not shake the excitement that bubbled under the surface. The Chaos that shifted inside her knew this was it. The certainty in her soul could not be denied.

She'd found her gift.

THE SANDS OF TIME

The sun hovered just above the horizon, casting long shadows across the beach. The sky was a majestic array of oranges and pinks. Not a cloud touched the world above him, and Cyrus wondered if he would take flight. He longed for the taste of freedom, the wind rushing through his clothes and hair. There was nothing more liberating than being up there, where nothing could touch him.

Yet his boots carried him onward, toward the lapping waves of a sea he had never actually set foot in, only traveled over. When he was on the coast of Sorréle, staring ahead, he had known where he was going, known his purpose, but standing here now, he felt lost.

As he inhaled the warm and humid air of the waters, tasted the salt on his tongue, he only knew one thing: he wanted to be a Dragon Rider.

It was so much more than being bonded to Sozar, and he understood that now. It was more than swinging a sword and flying around wherever he damn pleased. There was so much to being a Dragon Rider that he had never considered before. Cyrus felt the hot hands of ignorance squeeze his throat. How many people had he let down because he had been so focused on himself that he'd failed to consider the implications of *what* he was?

The conversation with Hyle had played over and over. He'd never gotten to sleep, even well after the alcohol had worn off and Alaric had disappeared. When all the noise and laughter had settled, Cyrus had been left with the one person he'd been avoiding all night: himself.

Sozar had arrived shortly after, but he had requested some privacy. The dragon had obliged once he knew his Rider was okay. There he'd sat until sunrise, in the dining chamber. The wine had long since grown stale to his tongue, and his appetite had not returned. When the maids had shown up again, he'd allowed them to remove everything, telling them that he was just going to sit there.

Cyrus recalled his memories in vivid details—not from the perspective of the young man who had been running, but from the vantage point of a Dragon Rider. Where had he gone wrong? He'd let so many down. They had seen a Dragon Rider and expected the world from him, but he had never been able to see that until now. The people looked up to him, idolized him, and Hyle was right, he would be feared. There was simply no way to ignore that—he could not please the world.

If he continued to run and ignore the responsibilities that came with being what he was, he was failing not only himself, but also Sozar. The dragon was so much more than just a creature to be protected—he was the result of something extraordinary. This fate was not up to Cyrus alone to decide. If the dragon wanted to fight claw and teeth against their enemy, was Cyrus holding him back?

I fly where you wish to go, the dragon rumbled in his head. *Do not think I resent where our path has led us.*

Cyrus smiled, his thoughts uncensored to the dragon. Sozar's words were powerful, and they brought an immense peace that transcended any potential verbal reply. A bond like they shared went beyond words. He knew Sozar awaited him.

The dragon rested on the alcove, watching and enjoying the morning sun. When Cyrus was ready, the dragon would be too.

The heat of the rays caressed his skin, and he took a moment to enjoy the warmth. Carefully, he sat down on the beach and without thinking removed his boots and socks. He set them aside and ran his fingers through the sand. It was still cold underneath as he dug in, the heat of the day not yet having soaked deep.

Thousands of tiny grains cascaded from his hands and back to the ground. He watched, enchanted by the simplicity of it all. As the waves lapped against the shore, that sound that he now found himself fond of, he let his thoughts wander to places he didn't argue with.

There were times when he was ashamed of himself. Like when he'd punched another boy in the face because he was angry at him for stealing his food. Or when he'd snuck into the orphanage's galley one night and packed his pockets full of food so that he could eat more than the rest. He still remembered Miss Hans asking why the inventory was lower than usual. She was so angry about it that she forced everyone to strip naked and stand out in a snowstorm. Still, Cyrus had not confessed because he knew the punishment for thievery would have been far more severe than being uncomfortably cold.

When he was seventeen, he had pocketed gems and sold them to a buyer on the streets, so that he could have enough money to buy new clothes. Miners who were caught stealing from the findings were executed before the queen. He had been terrified to be caught, but he was also wearing fabric that was falling apart and wasn't being paid enough to even afford clothes—the city still taxed the miners who served the queen. They promised housing and a meal, but they didn't specify that the food was scraps, the housing was dingy, and the pay was not enough to live on.

Cyrus hadn't ever wished to confess to those memories. He had constantly told himself that he had been good, followed the rules, done everything expected of him, and to some degree, it was true. At the time, he had laid his head down on that dusty, flat pillow at night and told himself he was doing everything right.

To some, he had been. To others, he was a thief.

Recognizing that now, Cyrus saw his life differently. He had grown up fighting tooth and nail for a place in the world that wanted to devour him whole. Maybe that made him a fighter, or maybe that made him foolish. Either way, he was here now, on the beach of Delion in Creitón, watching the sea.

If he could talk to his younger self, he would tell him to keep his chin up. Above all, he would tell him to keep dreaming. Never could he have anticipated being the first Dragon Rider in centuries to roam these skies. Sure, Dameon and Ashtir were there now as well, but they were not the first. And that was something, wasn't it?

Cyrus took a deep breath and let his mind feel the world around him. He could feel the energy of the waves—a force stronger than anything he had ever encountered—and the energy that surrounded him now. The sand was made up of a force that he had come to recognize as nature's force. Light Energy. It was everywhere, and the easiest energy to manipulate.

Cyrus gave his mind over to that force. It was the first time he had felt so welcomed by the energy, like an old friend greeting him with overwhelming joy. He smiled, relishing the comfort and familiarity. For never having properly harvested and having no proper training, there was a great ease.

The force was not intelligent but reactive. Light Energy could not be communicated with and required only nudges to get what one wanted. It was primal, yet basic. That did not make it any less a force to be reckoned with. Light Energy had one basic need: to create. This came from the force's original reason for existence, the result of a cataclysmic event involving Chaos. The living world was an accident, a result of a series of random events, and the energy that now existed all around him was the tampered consequence of such an event.

That knowledge came with Cyrus's sudden connection to the world around him. The thousands of heartbeats from the tiny insects and sea life followed, their needs clear to him at once: to thrive. He felt all their life forces, like little orange auras scattered about in his mind's eye. They were so clear to him he could reach out and pluck one if he so chose.

A chill raced through him as the heat on his face grew stronger. Cyrus had never felt so alive. All around, the world teemed with immense life, down to the single grains of sand. Everything was made up of energy; everything reacted to his presence.

All it took was a little nudge to get the reaction he wanted.

As he sat there, lost in the intoxicating and enthralling pull of the world around him, Cyrus became aware of another, much stronger presence. The energy that emanated off this approaching person was bizarre, otherworldly, and intelligent. It spoke in a language he could not understand, and moved like an unsettled ocean through the person. The presence reached out to him and brushed over his mind, humming a tune he could not place.

You have found your purpose.

The voice was familiar, yet foreign. He heard it speak to him, felt it move through him, carried with it a weight of a hundred men—the power was overwhelming.

Open your eyes, Rider.

He did, without question. All around him, hundreds, if not thousands, of tiny sand particles hovered in the air. He was surrounded by a wall of it, moving in a slow circular motion. Cyrus reached out with his hand and brushed his fingers through the floating sand, and the grains reacted to his touch, breaking the wall. They moved without sound, sparkling like countless gems under the prideful gleam of the rising sun.

"You did it." The voice came from behind, and Cyrus turned in his seat to see Hyle standing there with a big grin on his face. That scar even stretched from his smile. The sudden change in concentration broke the spell, and the sand fell back to the ground. From behind the God, he saw Sozar watching from his place on the alcove. Affection flooded their link, and he swore he saw a shimmer radiate off the dragon that not even the sun could have produced.

"You never needed anyone but yourself," Hyle added. "It's incredible what the power of belief can do."

Cyrus stood slowly, his toes sinking into the sand. "I thought I was cursed."

"You were," Hyle confirmed. "But no curse can control a Dragon Rider forever, especially one with your strength in energy harvesting."

Cyrus shook his head as Sozar stood and began to approach. They were removed from the majority of the city's bustle, and Cyrus was relieved for that. He didn't want the stares of curious citizens with him now.

"I don't understand," he mumbled. "You knew?"

"I knew you doubted yourself," Hyle clarified, and stepped up to him. They were nearly the same height, with Hyle perhaps a hair's breadth taller. "Our mind is like the waters before you"—he motioned to the sea—"it is never-ending, constant, and it moves. We spend a lifetime trying to figure everything out, but many of us fail—many mortals. There is simply not enough time to explore an ocean this vast. But when we are bonded to a dragon . . ." Hyle smiled, his eyes growing distant. "We are exposed to some of the most extraordinary things."

Cyrus opened his mouth to ask more, but the God continued.

"Very few curses can be used against a Dragon Rider, and of those, even less is known about how to execute them. The rituals were banned during the Rider Federation's reign, and the council did everything in their power to eliminate all knowledge and texts regarding such dark practices. The curse that was given to you at such a young age was not meant to withstand the immense power of a dragon's bond. As Sozar has matured, so too has your bond. This has evolved your lifeforce, and it was only a matter of time before you were able to grasp your abilities."

The God turned his eyes to the lapping waves and fell silent. Cyrus did the same, sensing the heavy shift in the air between them. There was a lot on Hyle's mind. It was not his place to ask a God to speak, but to wait for when he was ready.

Sozar stood behind him now, his presence loud and clear.

"Her name was Kelise, and she was my world," Hyle mumbled. "Not a day goes by that I don't think of her."

His dragon. Cyrus did not have to ask to know that, he just knew.

The God turned his silver eyes on him once more. "Whatever you do, whatever decision you make, make it for Sozar. Life is not worth living if you must do it alone."

The heartache was palpable, the sorrow stank, and Cyrus swallowed the wave of emotions that struck him. Hyle had watched his dragon die, felt that bond be severed in what had to be unimaginable pain, and then instead of Death taking him away, he was destined to roam this world for centuries. Alone. If that was not the cruelest act of fate, he did not know what was. Gods were chosen at random, their souls judged upon their mortal death, and if they were deemed strong enough, they were made to serve the realm for an eternity. That was how it had always been told to Cyrus—Gods were once mortals. But while Kelise had been killed, so too had the man before him, only to be rebirthed into what he was now.

Hyle turned his back to the waters, and Cyrus followed. There Sozar stood, wings tucked up and head tilted in intrigue, one tooth poking out between his lips. An amused smile danced across the God's lips. "Aythen always had the same expression. Vikter used to call it her stink face. May I?"

Cyrus stared for a long moment, grasping the question. A God was asking for *permission* to approach Sozar. He could not believe what he was hearing, and couldn't believe a former Dragon Rider would feel the need to ask. Perhaps it was a social code from his time.

He nodded. "Of course."

Hyle faced the dragon and approached, his steps deliberately slow, as if doubting his own request. To see a dragon once more after centuries of not seeing one, living in a time when they were everywhere and then to see the world evolve without such majestic beasts . . . Cyrus imagined Hyle had to be feeling all sorts of emotions.

Pausing before the dragon, Hyle got down on one knee and crossed his right arm over his chest, dipping his head. Sozar huffed, and in an act that Cyrus had never seen, the dragon placed one leg in front of him, flushed his wings out across the ground, and crossed his head over his leg. It was a bow.

Hyle stood as Sozar straightened, and the God lifted his hand toward the dragon. Cyrus watched his shoulders tense as his skin met the soft scales of Sozar's snout. He was almost certain he heard an audible breath from the man, but he did not move. This was no longer Cyrus's moment, but Hyle's.

Sozar broached his thoughts, reflecting images of a beautiful white dragon with blue eyes. She was stunning in every way possible, and even her gaze held a mischievous gleam that he could see in Hyle's own. Kelise was massive, at least three times the size of Sozar now, and much older. They had shared the sky for centuries before she had been killed.

The images abruptly stopped then, and Sozar's chest rose and fell with a grating noise that Cyrus knew to be his way of showing sorrow. *He still blames himself for her death.*

Without a word, Hyle took his hand and ran it along the scales of Sozar's neck. He was cherishing this, Cyrus realized. This moment was significant for the God, even if he didn't share all the details. The world grew quiet. Not even time would dare interrupt such an event.

And then, without a word or warning, the God disappeared, leaving behind only a thin, wispy smoke that quickly faded as well.

A MEETING OF MINDS

Sleep had not come after Morei cleaned up the glass. Instead, he had paced the room, snuck looks under the bed and on the terrace, certain he was not alone. Morei was not a fool—a new king was as good as dead. Now was the time when assassination attempts were most likely. He had requested no soldiers outside his chamber for that reason—he just didn't trust them. If that meant lying awake and listening, then so be it. It wasn't like he was sleeping anyway.

It had taken quite a bit of ice-cold water on his face to rid Morei of the slumber that clung to his senses. He had awoken with a gift of new clothes next to his door, bound and wrapped in a basket. The seamstresses had worked overnight to get him clothing that fit and matched his royal title. He had quickly undone the parchment wrapping to find silk material, dyed in blue and silver, with the howling wolf along each sleeve. Silver threading accented the entire shirt, which had been paired with a pair of black pants with a similar thread accent. Satisfied, he slipped the new clothing on and was pleased to find that it all fit as promised.

Morei ran his fingers through his midnight-colored hair. It was too long now, and he messed with it in the mirror, annoyed. Finally, he dunked his hands into the water basin and dragged them through the locks. Then he threw his head back and saw that everything was in place. Perhaps in the next few days, he would get the cut he needed. He was not fond of its shagginess, although many, like Ezra, had preferred the look. There he was, thinking of the man again—it irritated him that he missed their friendship so much.

The man in the mirror was not the same who had left Geral. Those icy blue eyes were colder than Morei remembered, and lines forged by betrayal now decorated the skin of his face. Faint—some would say that age had gifted him beauty lines young—but to Morei, they were scars. Each one had been earned by the relentless fight against Destiny, Geral, and even himself. Some wore these with disgrace, even shame, but he would wear them with honor. There was not a day he had lived that he regretted. And if he had to do any of it again, he would.

He leaned forward and tugged at the collar of his shirt. The black veins had expanded some during his travels. He'd lived in a cloak for the majority of the time, but now, with nowhere to hide, it was quite clear how much this ailment had worsened. Lines decorated his torso and back with no clear direction, like an artist had thrown paint without looking. His arms, hands, and neck were covered—it was hideous. If there was one thing Morei was constantly reminded of, it was that if Dark Energy did not consume him first, this curse would. Time was precious, and he was no longer sure how much he had left before he would lose himself to the clutches of something sinister.

It was already changing him, that he knew. The Morei of two moon cycles ago would have felt some guilt for the harshness of his actions, perhaps even regretted them.

A knock echoed, and he straightened. Rhys was here to fetch him and bring him to Commander Edwin. With a final inhale, he turned and left the bathroom, heading to the door.

"Greetings," he said upon opening it.

The chancellor was momentarily speechless. Not because of the royal attire, Morei assumed, but because of the ailment that was visible along his neck where the collar of his shirt no longer reached. It was the first time Rhys had seen it, and it would be that way for everyone who faced him today and from now on.

If the chancellor had any questions, he did not ask them. "Good morning," he replied with a quick nod. "Ready?"

"Let us be off." Morei closed the door behind him, and they started down the hall. It was bright, and fresh-baked goods wafted through the air from the galley. He could almost make out the pungent smell of roast between the sweet scent of pastries. His thoughts wandered then to the methodical sound of their boots. This was familiar to him and brought him peace, regardless of how it was obtained.

"I have reviewed everything," the chancellor acknowledged after a fair bit of silence. "Are you sure about this?"

"If I wasn't, would I have asked for it?" Yesterday, late afternoon, Isla Caster had officially been reinstated as princess. Eventually, he did want to make her a queen, but only if he could trust her. It would be solely platonic. He did not wish for any more trouble, save to ensure the Geral bloodline would remain.

"No, I guess not." The chancellor was quiet for a moment as they turned the corner. "You have made a massive decision in less than a day that you've been here . . ."

His tone caused the hairs on Morei's neck to rise. "Would you prefer me to hide in my room while you made decisions behind my back?"

Rhys faltered in his step, and Morei didn't hesitate. In one quick motion, he grabbed the chancellor's throat and shoved him against the wall. Rhys gasped in surprise, but Morei squeezed harder, forcing him to still.

The king grew closer. "Don't you dare think I'm foolish enough to not see right through you." The skin on Rhys's face was growing red as he tried to get air. "Contracts signed, secret arrangements . . . you've had the council wrapped around your finger for how long now? It's impressive you didn't kill Drexis yourself, or maybe that makes you a coward. Which is it?"

The chancellor wheezed, unable to speak. The sound sent a thrill through Morei. All it would take was a quick snap of the neck to end him right here. Suddenly, the tough and daring chancellor didn't look so imposing anymore. He'd had his theory that Rhys was soaking up Drexis's spiraling health and enjoying authority, but he hadn't been certain until this moment.

Hopefully this would be the scare needed to keep Rhys obedient. This dynamic between them was a delicate dance between hunger and distrust. Both were starved for power and bred to be wary of newcomers. It was a surprise neither had killed the other yet in a mad frenzy to prove their worth.

Morei let go and adjusted the sleeves of his shirt as Rhys rubbed his neck and coughed. "Are we clear?"

The chancellor blinked and stared. A storm of emotions swept across his face. He could have lunged or laughed without surprising Morei. Then he raised his hand and ran it across the top of his head, as if to stay any loose strands that had gone rogue in the heat of the moment, before raising his chin at the king. "I think we've come to an agreement, Your Majesty."

"Good." Morei motioned to the hall. "Let's go, or we will be late."

There was no need to discuss further the reality of what now lay before them. Rhys didn't respect royalty, he respected power, and he was desperate to have it for himself. And now the chancellor knew that he could not continue as he had been. Morei wouldn't stand for it. If the king caught the chancellor acting without his permission, the man was dead. The big question was whether or not they could come to respect each other in the long run.

As they approached the commander's study, Rhys finally broke the silence that Morei had become comfortable with.

"Do you really believe Caster is capable of dominating an entire country?"

"I do." And he did, with his entire being. Caster would do more than just crush Geral, it would become the heart of an empire.

"Hm." The chancellor turned the wolf-head door handle. "Then like wolves, let's feast."

Inside, Edwin stood over a table with a large map rolled out. Books were stacked on the ground to the right, some covered in dust, with a handful of scrolls laid atop. The study was small, especially for a commander, but perhaps that was by choice.

As they piled in, Morei noted the sheath strapped to Edwin's left forearm, hidden under a dark tunic. The commander was armed—whether because he had ill intentions or because that was his backup weapon—so Morei made sure to take his place on the right side, so that he could see if the commander made any movement against him. The intentional placement did not seem to disrupt Edwin, as he reached for a mug of ale and took a long drink.

"Long time, no see," Morei greeted. The commander had seen him face-to-face with an ancient beast, betrothed to madness. Edwin was wary, but he was also stern in his values.

The commander set the mug down and turned his hardened eyes onto the king. "If you think I have any respect for you—"

"I didn't ask for it," the king interjected, and gestured at the map. "I'm here to achieve something no one has before. If you don't want to be a part of that, I am more than happy to find someone else who does."

Rhys's loud sigh did not go unheard. The chancellor was annoyed.

Edwin's jaw worked back and forth several times. Morei let him chew on his thoughts. If he was to strike, now would be the time.

But he didn't. Edwin swallowed, the lump rising and falling in his throat, and then those eyes shifted away as the door opened again. Isla stepped inside, dressed in simple pants and a pale blue tunic that looked more made for a man than a woman. Her hair was braided to the right, and her boots looked like she'd worn them for ten summers or more.

"What—" The chancellor's mouth fell open, and he looked at Morei.

"Isla," the king announced, and motioned at her. "Come in. We're just getting started." He watched the princess nervously close the door and take several steps toward him and away from the chancellor, who stood at the other end of the table. Rhys was still staring, those amber eyes twisted in disbelief, perhaps borderline rage. He was not happy with this decision. Or maybe he was not happy at being caught off guard for once.

That made Morei smile.

Edwin cleared his throat. "And . . . why is this woman here?"

"Documentation shows the Caster family has been keeping secrets for quite some time," Morei replied, keeping his voice steady. "You are looking at Isla Caster, Commander, the princess and only daughter of the late king." Edwin did a double take, likely recognizing her from the staff, and before anyone could say more, Morei added, "She will be working with me from here on out. Isla will observe and advise when necessary, but she has much to learn." He pointed at the map now. "Proceed, Commander. I did not bring her in so that she may be gawked at like livestock. Let's begin."

There was a long silence before Edwin reached over and grabbed his mug again. "All right. Let me tell you what is common knowledge. Caster possesses approximately 5,300 men prepared to fight at any given point. An additional two hundred cycle out as guards at the palace and are equally trained." The commander dragged a finger over to the port as he continued. "For ships, we have ten in use at all times—mostly for exports, but two are large enough to pack supplies and men aboard for travel. One of those is the king's ship, which has not been used in nearly a decade. In total, we have about a hundred seamen who work through almost every season, and twelve captains."

"Are these men trained to fight?" Morei asked.

"No. They have been raised by the waters, not with a sword to their throat. They are good and strong, though. I suspect they could hold their own in a scuffle without a problem."

"Understood." Morei crossed his arms. "So there's about five thousand men we could pull from for an army. The remainder would stay behind and uphold order in the city. Another hundred if we were confident in the remaining soldiers." Those numbers were disappointing, but he did not let it show. Geral was a city built on weaponry—it was only expected that their army be larger than any of the other cities. At its strongest, he'd had over seven thousand men ready and more in training. "How long is training for these soldiers?"

"Four summers, every season. Training includes strategy work, swordsmanship, handling extreme weather elements, and taking on a younger soldier to help with leadership development." Edwin shrugged. "We like all our men to be comfortable giving orders, even if they never have to."

Morei nodded. "I think it's a great idea. Helps with stress management too." Geral hadn't done the mentorship, so he was glad to see something different. "Do all your men have experience with the sea?"

"Some, but not all. In early training, soldiers are categorized by a series of tests. Then specialized training in those. Some soldiers have been training to fight on the waters—cannons, bows and arrows, that kind of stuff—while others take on different roles, like managing the defenses around the city and training in fire work."

That got his attention. "Fire work?"

"Aye." A grin spread wide on Edwin's face. "Caster has a defense that no other city knows about—fire. Those trained in it learn how to manage weaponry and bombs, along with our Ly'rün, which is a potent mixture that, when it combusts into flames, releases a deadly toxin in the air that makes the lungs swell up. The victim essentially suffocates to death—if they aren't burned alive first."

"The toxin works up to half a league," Rhys piped in. "I trained with it for two summers before I was pulled into my current position."

Ah. Morei nodded, intrigued. The chancellor was a complex character—he knew more than what he was letting on. "Tell me about your strategy in an attack."

Edwin spoke in great detail about the chain of command and how the soldiers know exactly where to go and what to do when the bell chimed danger. The commander talked about how the port could be fortified, how there were cannons hidden in specific wood panels that nobody else knew of, and how Caster could defend itself from any angle. The city was built for defense no matter which way the enemy came from. Resources were tucked away in secret where no citizen could find them, and passageways underneath the city provided instant access to anywhere they needed to go. Furthermore, and far more interesting, there was an entire canal underneath that led from the shore to the center of the city.

"It was originally used to torture prisoners," Edwin explained, "but now it's become a housing center for storing all the additional weaponry, Ly'rün, and anything else the king may desire."

Morei opened his mouth to comment, but another voice cut in. "How would they be tortured?"

It was Isla.

The commander tipped his head side to side and snatched up the mug, which was now half-empty. "Prisoners would be brought down there and tied. There are cracks all over and water drips incessantly. I'm sure you know where I'm going with this." Edwin took a swig. "Water torture. It was vicious, even by my standards, and I've done a lot over the summers. If you ask some of the soldiers, they make all sorts of claims about hearing screams still." At that, he rolled his eyes. "Stories."

"But why did it stop?" the king pressed.

"It was stopped before my time," the commander answered. "It's understood that this method ceased because it was too much for even our own men. Documents report that soldiers started refusing to go down there, especially when they knew a prisoner was going mad—said that when that happened, they could hear his screams for days after. Too much pushback, and the old king finally relented and ceased the practice."

It had been a long time since Morei had read about water torture. As far as he understood, Geral hadn't touched it in three centuries.

"I'd like to see the canal," Morei told the group. "I want to see where everything is kept, along with where the prisoners used to be taken. It doesn't have to be today, although I would prefer it before the end of the moon cycle. Will that be a problem?"

The chancellor blinked. "As you wish, Your Majesty. Although I must warn you that we will need to be accompanied by soldiers. Occasionally, there are stragglers who find their way down there and try to use it as their home when they don't want to pay taxes. In previous encounters, there have been attacks."

"That won't—"

"And if you don't let the soldiers do what they were trained to do, you will have bigger problems," Rhys finished, raising his brow. "Everyone here knows what you're capable of. You don't need to prove anything to anyone."

Morei held his breath, swallowing his sudden urge to punch the chancellor. He glared, and when his lungs began to scream for air, he obliged to the demand. "Thank you for that information, Chancellor. Please be aware that when I go down there, you will also accompany me."

"Very well." Rhys was clearly uncomfortable at the idea of going beneath the city.

"Commander," said Morei, "let's continue this discussion."

Topics flowed easily thereafter. It became quite clear that the more Morei showed curiosity and engagement with the army of Caster, the more Edwin brightened. Had Drexis paid so little attention to the soldiers that Edwin had grown used to the idea of doing this all alone? Now, he wouldn't stop talking. He poured another drink and even got some for Morei, who took it gratefully. After the stress of the last day, he needed it.

Rhys engaged as the conversation steered to seizing Ferguson. It would not happen tomorrow or even the next day, but the men worked out a plan. Ferguson had an estimated three thousand armed men—it was one of the smallest territories in the country, but Caster was the second smallest. With Ferguson being so private, there was no telling what weapons the city had. If they had anything like Caster's Ly'rün, then they would be in trouble—no amount of soldiers would help against a weapon like that.

That broached the subject of leaving Caster with only a handful of soldiers to protect the city. The army that would take Ferguson would be gone for at least two moon cycles—too long.

"Then we send half of that," Rhys offered, and gestured down at the map. "The Silk Family doesn't want war, never has. They may bend the knee before we even make it to their gates."

"Presumptuous," Morei observed. "Who's to say they aren't comfortable with such low numbers because they have an Energy Harvester among them? A well-trained one could wipe out an entire army."

"Couldn't be," Edwin replied, and took another drink—this was his third mug, but he was holding his alcohol well. "We have zero reports of such activity."

"Would you divulge such information?" Morei countered. "I wouldn't."

"Ferguson has always had a healthy relationship with Caster," the commander pointed out. "Prior to this, there's never been any reason to hide."

"You said that Ferguson has secluded themselves." The king grabbed his own drink and took a swig. The ale was mild in comparison to the stronger liquors. "They obviously have something to hide."

"Or they want nothing to do with any of this." Rhys motioned at the Dark Forest. "What if they've found something?"

The change in topic made everyone freeze. Morei kicked himself for not having thought of it before. "You think they've discovered something in that forest?"

The chancellor scratched his chin. "It's possible. I mean, I don't know what Geral was told, but we've always been told that the Dark Forest is cursed, home to the beasts."

"A gate to the Soul Realm," Isla whispered. Her honeyed voice brought everyone's eyes back to her. The princess stepped forward. "The maids heard a lot of things in the dungeons. Someone once claimed that the Dark Forest was home to wild dragons and ancient beasts." She leaned over and pressed a finger to the corner of the map. Her confidence grew when no one interrupted her. "They say there's a lake up here that smells of rot but no one can get close to. Not because of the smell but because there's a strange energy that exists there. It's unlike anything anyone has ever seen. A world between worlds."

Morei's first reaction was that he wanted to go there. Not to prove anything, but to explore. If there were secrets, he wanted to know about them. Ferguson had to be hiding information— it would explain their reclusive stance.

Full of resolve, he turned to Edwin. "Commander, I want you to identify your top two thousand soldiers. Ensure you have a second and third in command for the campaign as well. When you've done so, make sure these men are all aware that they will be traveling north—I want them to know exactly what we're doing and why. Tell them everything, if you must, but I need these soldiers on our side. If they don't know anything, then they have nothing to fight for. Chancellor"—he turned to face Rhys, who still stood on the other side of the table—"are there any Energy Harvesters in the city?"

A deathly silence filled the room.

"What?" Morei pressed, annoyed.

Rhys blinked and looked visibly bothered. "Three summers ago, Drexis ordered all publicly reported Energy Harvesters to be executed. He feared that any of them could betray the city."

Morei opened and closed his fists and flared his nostrils. A sudden surge of fury turned his vision red and made his hands shake. The. Fucking. Arrogance. How this city was still standing was beyond his understanding. It was only by luck and a violent reputation, it seemed. The politics were in shambles, chancellors were making decisions without their king, kings were executing their greatest weapon because they were afraid. It all made sense why Syra had fled now. He would have done the same in her shoes.

"There have to be Energy Harvesters who have not reported themselves," Morei replied as calmly as he could. "I want soldiers stationed in commoner clothing everywhere in the city. I want them observing. Anything that seems out of the ordinary, I want to know about it. I also want a list of all families that were impacted by the executions. If there's one Energy Harvester in a family, there might be another hiding. No reason not to investigate that." Junok was an example. The family's rich energy harvesting history had lasted through many generations. And, as Drexis had been so keen to inform, Geral possessed its fair share of Harvesting history.

In unison, the chancellor and commander said, "Yes, Your Majesty."

"Good. I also have one more request."

They eyed him, and he could see a flash of annoyance in Rhys's expression. "I need someone to go to Gamer's Village and fetch my steed, Sunny. His fake name is Jasper, and I provided the name Garrison for myself to the barn hand. There was gear left there for him as well." He chuckled to himself, caught up in a memory. "Send someone who is comfortable with a Shire. He's big and doesn't require whips. If I hear or see any sign that he was physically forced to do anything he doesn't want"—the laugh died on his lips—"I will kill you all with my bare hands. Send someone immediately."

"Yes, Your Majesty," Edwin replied without hesitation. Isla rubbed her hands over her arms, scanning the room.

"Chancellor," Morei said, "does the name Syra Castello ring a bell?"

His nostrils flared, and his chest rose and fell. Rhys tilted his head, regarding the king. "Thief of the Demon Killer. Who doesn't know her?"

"Does she have any family left in Caster?"

"No. Her father died in a housefire."

"Set by you," Morei added coolly. The chancellor raised his eyebrow, but he continued. "No family, and she flees across the world to escape you. Just out of reach. Shame, right?" He echoed the same words back to him and watched the color drain from Rhys's face. "Find her, Chancellor. Find her. Do whatever you have to do, but I want to know everything. Where she is, what she is doing." He leaned over the table, the vision of her and Sekar sealing his next words. "If she's within reach, I want her captured and brought here. If not, we'll find someone who can." He would not share the dream or his belief of what she meant to this world and to his reign. Not yet. It would scare these people if they knew who they were dealing with.

Numbly, the chancellor nodded.

"And the Rider, Cyrus from Diemon—" The words felt foreign on his tongue after so much time unspoken, but he relished the taste of them. "Track him down. I want eyes and ears everywhere. I want to know if the forest up north stirs from the sea winds that come from the Ashen Sea. I want to know when the Sorréleian River speeds up or slows down." Morei raised a finger, stricken by the ailment. "I want to know if anyone sees anything unnatural. You are to bring all text predating a thousand summers to me immediately following this meeting. Am I understood?"

The king would learn everything there was about ancient beasts, energy, and the old Vore World. The more he knew, the stronger he was.

They nodded.

"Then we're done here. Begin immediately. I want a report this evening on the status of the Energy Harvesters and potentials. Edwin, you've got three days to identify your next-in-commands and get the two thousand soldiers rallied. I don't care how you do it, just do it. Get them training and make sure their weapons and armor are the highest quality. The day after the new moon, they set off for Ferguson."

It was aggressive, but Morei did not want to waste any more time. He did not see any other path forward. The sooner he acted, the sooner he could stake his claim as the rightful king and raise an empire unlike anything the world had seen.

CURSED WITH CHAOS

ekar's words echoed in her mind, even as he paced back and forth before her with visible excitement. The Soul Realm clung to her senses, and she could see Erun's eyes staring at her from her place on the chair. Her hand remained an ugly pink, but the pain had faded to a dull throb.

His body had crumbled into dust, and Sekar had told her he was alive. Syra had resurrected a spirit. While she was thrilled that this was her gift as a Vore God, she could not shake the agony of that boy's final moments. She could feel the blade go right into her chest, over and over, could see that ugly grin watching her.

She had no idea what time it was, but she suspected that it was early morning based on how her muscles and eyes felt. They ached with an extreme exhaustion that demanded she lay her head down and close her eyes. Whether it was from being up all night, the collision of events in the last couple of days, or her use of Chaos, she couldn't tell, but she guessed it was a combination of all three. Energy harvesting took strength, so Chaos had to be the same for a God. In time, it would become easier.

"We don't know the consequences," Sekar said, halting his movement.

"Huh?" Syra tore her eyes free from the mark on her hand and looked up at him. She felt like she was seeing the chamber for the first time since they'd arrived back from the Soul Realm. It made her think of the Guardians and Zane. She hoped they were okay. There was no shouting outside the room, but that could change. Already, she was determined to find Dryl later today and sit down with him. She still had no idea where he'd been, and it felt like he had changed.

"I've never seen power like that," Sekar told her. "There has never been a God with the ability you showed. There has been healing, even a God who could literally make anyone the richest person alive, but not like this." He shook his head. "Syra, you must understand something. Every action a God does with the help of Chaos, there are reactions we cannot control. The ideology of Ghrynál is that every action creates a reaction, yes?" She nodded, having heard of it once before. "In the broad terms of the realms, that term applies too. As a God, you are responsible for ensuring balance and protection of Chaos, which is achievable by simply existing. However, when you harvest Chaos, this creates a reaction. But instead of an isolated reaction, you create a ripple effect. This ripple could be leagues wide—or even entire countries. Do you understand?"

Again, Syra nodded.

"Imagine me," he continued, and motioned at himself. "I can create illusions. I can change people's minds, tamper with their dreams, and show them anything they want, even if it's a memory they haven't thought of in decades. But these actions create a ripple effect. A simple dream could change someone's mind, which impacts their life and those around them. Or I can build an illusion that turns men on one another and creates a war. A reaction like that could devastate an entire country."

"And?" she pressed, wanting to hear more.

"Take a God like Eazon, who is known to be the giver of luck. He could grant anyone unlimited luck, or take it all away. Imagine if someone like Eazon with his gift gave Henry that—the ripple effect would devastate the entire world. Do you see where I'm going with this?"

She did, but that didn't mean she liked it. "Yeah."

His tone turned grave as he took a step toward her. "Nobody knows what the ripple effect is for bringing back the dead. We don't even know if this boy you brought back is himself. We don't know where his physical body lay, or even if he made it back. My concern is what will this do to not just the family, but the city, and then the country. That kind of power could change everything. It could establish an entire religion, which could cause an even greater ripple across the world."

Syra glanced at her hand and then back at him. "Then why am I given something that could cause more harm than good? Sure, I bring back one boy, but what if what I've just done causes the entire village or wherever he lives to turn on him and the family? More could end up dead because of what I did." She did not want that burden. "And can I even bring back just anyone? What could happen if I brought back a spirit that has roamed that realm for a decade? They'd have nothing to return to."

Sekar was already nodding his agreement before she finished. "You need to be careful, Syra. I knew you were ready, and I know I took you there, but I did not think you could bring back the dead."

Syra wasn't sold on that, and his words caused her to pause. "You think I believe that?"

"Believe what?" he countered.

"That you didn't know or at least think I could bring back the dead? You brought me there, Sekar. Why wouldn't you be honest with me? Does it make a difference if you did or didn't? The result is the same."

He eyed her but didn't reply. Syra had started to pick up on his patterns by now. He was never entirely honest. Maybe it was the result of living as long as he had, although she wasn't sure his true age, or maybe he just didn't know how. The world was cruel, and she didn't know his life as much as she wanted to. Either way, she was growing bolder, and she wasn't afraid to call him out anymore.

As he remained silent, she threw up her hands. "You're impossible to like, you know that?" She wasn't looking for an argument, just stating the facts. "The moment I think we've made progress, you do something that makes me question your intentions. You play the hero, tell me your regrets, but then when I try to give you the benefit of the doubt, you manage to screw it up. I don't know you," she confessed. She'd wanted to say that for a while now, and getting this all off her chest felt good, damn whatever the world was becoming.

"I've never known the real Sekar, no matter what you say. And that's fine. If you want to be a hero and squash whatever guilt you have for the past decisions you've made, that's great. But I can't keep doing this. You're messing with my head, and I can't tell anymore if that's what you want to do or you don't realize it—"

"Syra?"

The sound made her freeze. She looked at the door. That was Zarek, but why he was here at this hour was beyond her.

Sekar raised a brow at her, his usual cold expression back. "Got a date?"

She wanted to punch him but forced a deep breath in instead. Before she could say anything, Zarek spoke again.

"I heard you talking in there. Can you open up? I've got some news about Zane."

She reeled at that, and she slammed her leg into the table trying to make her way to the door. Sekar eyed her as she cursed vehemently at the furniture, and he crossed the room before she could make it.

"Do you really want to do that?" she warned. The last time the God had seen Zarek was at Raveer. The two had not seen each other since, and she was fairly certain the Guardian would stab Sekar.

He shrugged at her. "Couldn't be much worse than your attitude," he remarked, and opened the door. When the two beheld each other, he asked, "You didn't bring anything to drink?"

They stood there for what felt like an eternity. Syra waited, watching as Zarek's eyes traveled from Sekar to her and then back again. He knew that the God was training her, and she'd hoped that the Guardian had come to peace with everything, but his look suggested otherwise.

"I really don't like you," he said.

"I like your brother better anyways," Sekar replied.

"Don't bring Dryl into this."

"I didn't realize you were suddenly so prote—"

"Zane?" Syra interjected, and quickly approached the door. When the Guardian looked at her, she added, "You came here with news?"

There was a look in Zarek's eyes that she didn't like, and as they grazed over her, she saw them land on her hand. A muscle in his jaw ticked. "Your hand. What is that?"

"She found her gift," Sekar declared, as if it were his own to celebrate. With the way the Guardian stared, she wanted to shrink. "That is her mark."

"Mark?" Zarek halfway choked on the word. "It's not going away?"

"No," he answered.

Syra stared. She'd thought it was just an injury, a result of the Chaos. "It won't?" she asked. "But . . ." She couldn't wear gloves or long sleeves for the rest of her life. That felt entirely impractical. Her emotions were all over the place—she was glad to have discovered her gift, but she was angry that he hadn't warned her.

Sekar took a deep breath. "Every God earns their scar, Syra. This just happens to be yours."

"And where's yours?" Zarek challenged. "I don't see anything on you."

He raised his hand and pointed at his head. In a deathly low whisper, he said, "*Here.*" Then he lowered his hand and added, "I'd much rather have a little mark on my hand, wouldn't you?" It was said in spite, and she grimaced at his tone. She'd never considered the implications of using Chaos on the Harvester. And she'd never known Gods had these marks—scars, as Sekar said. Suddenly, her hand didn't feel so overwhelming. At least she could use it. If it was discolored, oh well, but she couldn't imagine what it had done to the God's mind.

For just a moment, Syra saw Sekar in a different light. Someone who was not entirely in control of his actions, and who acted the way he did because he was not entirely rational. Touched by Chaos in a way that would undoubtedly shift the way he saw the world.

She kept the conversation going. "Come in," she told Zarek, and pushed Sekar over. "I don't want us standing here."

Zarek's eyes bounced between them.

"He's not good with people," she commented, but it was more for herself. When enough space was left for the Guardian to enter, she motioned for him to.

"Zane's body wasn't found," Zarek said as he turned to face her. "But he's also not accounted for."

"What?" The air left Syra immediately.

The Guardian nodded. "He's missing," he clarified. "Nobody can find him, his chamber untouched, and he hasn't been seen. Missing."

"But how?" she asked. "I spoke to him yesterday. He came here, we chatted, and he left. Said he was going to help you. Didn't you see him?"

"I did, but that was before the fight broke out. We got separated in the mess of it all. When it was over and we didn't find him, I suspected he may have gotten knocked out or taken a blade. But he's not there. Bane's had men searching, thinking he dragged himself in one of the crevices in this place, but there's no sign of him."

Syra stared, the words not registering right away. Zane hadn't just gone missing. He wasn't like that. He was proud and if he was needed anywhere, he would show. If he was injured, they'd have found him. If he was dead, they'd have identified him. Gone made no sense.

"I liked him," Sekar said from behind. "Good sense of humor."

She didn't even address his comment. "And Eva?"

"No sign either," Zarek told her. "There are still scouters out, but we don't think their disappearance is related in any way."

"Well, how do you know?" Syra pressed. "She could have taken him as part of some bribe?"

"Someone like Eva doesn't need to bribe her way through anything," the Guardian responded. He scratched his jaw then, and she saw scratches on his knuckles. "At this rate, everything is still up in the air with why and how they disappeared. But we do think Eva's is correlated to Arik's death. Seems obvious."

"Yeah, and it seems obvious that Zane would be taken by Eva," she shot back. She couldn't fathom the idea that he had just vanished without significant cause.

Zarek dropped his hand and regarded her, then Sekar. "Dryl told me what you did."

"You're welcome," the God replied.

"I wasn't thanking you. I was going to tell you that you're sloppy."

He snorted. "They say practice makes perfect. I could try it on you next time."

Syra turned and shot Sekar a glare. Now was not the time. He smiled at her but seemed to take the hint for the time being. "What's happened with Dryl and the council?" she asked Zarek.

"It's still a disaster." He sighed. She wondered now if he'd been up all night. "There's no doubt it'll take the people a few days to get their arguments and fights out of their system. The council did hear what he had to say, but the vote didn't happen."

"What? Why?"

"They couldn't agree on anything. He's going to see them again today. Dryl's persistent, but he's having to prove to these people that the Infernol must shift focus. Keryn has kept them brainwashed for a long time, by the sounds of it."

Syra didn't like hearing this. She'd hoped for good news of any kind, but the Guardian hadn't offered anything positive. This was all a giant mess. "What if they don't approve of him? What if the reason they're not is because some of them are Lirallians?"

Zarek's nostrils flared. "We've already considered that, and we're still working through that to ensure that if there are any in this place, we'll identify them. Bane seems to believe he's narrowed the list down to a few dozen possibilities. The council is not on that, as of yet."

"Yet?" Syra echoed.

"More investigation is needed." His words were final, and she could see he was visibly irritated, no doubt by Sekar. "I need to get back," he announced, and started back to the door, but then he stopped next to her. "Don't forget what I said," he whispered.

He continued out, his steps not even faltering as he passed Sekar. She turned to see him go, feeling torn. She'd wanted to tell Zarek everything that had happened, that she'd found her gift, that she was growing stronger, and that the God he was so distrusting of had positive qualities. But none of that came out as he closed the door behind them without looking back.

She knew what he meant by those words. Everything he'd said about Sekar originally still held true to him. Even though Sekar had been consistent with training, Zarek didn't care.

"A pleasant Guardian," Sekar observed. "What did he tell you?"

There was no point in hiding that information. "He doesn't like you."

"The feeling is mutual."

Syra held her marked hand up. "Could you just leave? It's been a long few days, and I'm exhausted." She was devastated about Zane and angry that Zarek had been so cold. Nothing good had come out of the last day. The gift hardly felt worth celebrating anymore, and her mood had turned sour. Now that she knew it wasn't going anywhere—that she'd have this mark on her hand for the rest of her life—she felt like a giant pile of dung. She might as well have hung up a sign that said she was a God for the world to see. People would have questions, and she didn't have the strength to deal with them. Any of them—including the man before her.

"We don't want a tired princess," Sekar commented dryly.

Syra glared at him, even as she saw the mist take shape and he began to dissolve. "You have no idea how to be nice," she blurted out as he disappeared.

Now she was completely alone. She'd wanted this, but it made her feel vulnerable. Syra glanced down at her hand. She'd need a story, something to tell people so that they wouldn't ask questions. Why did it bother her so much?

Because it was yet another problem, and she hardly had the strength to deal with the ones already in front of her.

She wanted to sleep, but she didn't want to risk anyone breaking in. Then there was the fact that seeing Morei had become a rather unpredictable thing, and Sekar's warning still hung over her. If the king was as dangerous as the God warned, then she wanted nothing to do with him.

She could return to her cave. That thought teased her, but she decided against it.

No, she wanted to find Dryl. She wanted answers. If he said now was not a good time to talk, too bad. Syra didn't want to stay here, and she suspected that if there were going to be problems with fights, she wanted to get out now before it escalated with a new day. Sword on her hip, she wasted no time and left her room.

SAVAGES OF THE COUNCIL

Courage. It meant being bold in the face of terror; it meant doing something nobody else would do. The God of Courage was not the giver of such strength, just a symbol. He was a walking icon of what courage looked like, and Cyrus knew that now. While Hyle had not told him everything—far from it—he knew that when Hyle had been a Dragon Rider, he had seen and had to do things that no mortal ever would. He was a God made to teach people that there was a world beyond grief, yet he was also meant to inspire.

Cyrus had come to that conclusion as he traversed the halls of the palace with two soldiers. They were heading to the council chamber in response to an urgent summons. He had been warned ahead of time that this might happen, although he had been hopeful it wouldn't be today. After this morning and the long night before, he was exhausted, and a headache pounded with a dull but relentless thud.

The soldiers hadn't said much to him, except to intercept him and tell him he was requested at the council meeting. Nodding, he had fallen into step with them, finishing up the piece of bread he had been snacking on while he explored. It was freshly baked and one of the maids had ran up and handed it to him before scampering off. He knew it was an act of flirtatious kindness, a way to get his attention, which he appreciated. It was fun. The bread had been stuffed with berries and been sweet—delicious.

Now, as he approached the chamber, he wished he had some sort of drink to wash down the bitter taste of politics looming on his tongue. He loathed this game, but he'd anticipated it once Alaric had taken the throne. The king had slaughtered the soldiers who'd taken part in his beatings and torture, which Cyrus had never even gotten a say in, before he had ordered that Cyrus be treated like a royal guest.

That was sure to piss a councilmember off or two.

The soldier to his left cleared his throat and gave him a sideways glance. "Can I ask a question, sir?"

Cyrus raised an eyebrow. "Sure." Sir. A term he wasn't sure he liked.

The soldier licked his lips. "Could I pet your dragon?"

He almost laughed. Pet? If he thought Sozar was some mindless beast, the poor man had another thing coming! He forced a smile. "Of course, although you'll have to ask him first."

That made the soldier's brown eyes go wide. "Ask?"

He could hear Sozar snort through their link. The dragon was amused from his place in the courtyard. "Sure. You just walk up and ask if you can pet him. I'm sure he'll answer you."

The soldier paled. "He can . . . talk?"

"Well, how else do you suppose we work together?" Cyrus asked. He could not believe the ignorance, although he couldn't say he was surprised. He himself had had to learn on the fly—literally.

"We're here," the other soldier said, sounding not so thrilled. They were at a massive double-door entrance, which was already cracked. Cyrus could hear chatter from within. This would be good.

He turned to the curious soldier. "What's your name?"

"Luke, sir."

"Luke, come by after your shift tomorrow, and I'll introduce you to Sozar. He loves the attention."

Don't patronize me.

Cyrus ignored the jest and thanked the men before slipping inside, where he closed the door behind him. The talking ceased as everyone's eyes turned to him.

Alaric was at the head of the table, wearing a white and blue shirt that looked like it might be laced with actual gold. It was clearly a king's shirt—even the cuffs were decorated with sapphire gems that he was pretty sure were the buttons. It was a loud shirt, but Alaric looked quite pleased in it. On his hand was the same red ring from the night before.

"Cyrus," the king greeted warmly. "Please, sit."

He did so, sliding into the chair nearest to him. He was next to an older gentleman who could have passed for his father—if he knew who his father was. The man had a braided silver beard, and his skin was sun-kissed. There was a tattoo on the right side of his neck, which looked like it had probably been part of some crew sigil based on the gaping jaws of the skull.

"Cyrus, that's Lord Rendal. He served Delion's fleet for nearly thirty summers before being elected to join the city's council."

At the king's explanation, Cyrus nodded. This man looked like he belonged on the waters still and was stuffed into a royal attire that he would rather trade for a tunic and sea breeze. "A pleasure."

Lord Rendal grumbled and nodded before looking away. He did not look entertained.

Alaric didn't seem fazed. "Following him, it's Lady Treza, Lady Yan, obviously me, Lord Jexton, and my chancellor, Asher."

Cyrus nodded again. It was a small council. He knew Diemon to have at least eight members at all times, or so he'd heard from the queen herself when he'd eavesdropped. Perhaps it was easier to run a city with less opinions, less people fighting for a space to be heard.

The chancellor eyed him from across the table. He appeared to have gone gray at an early age. Asher looked no older than thirty, yet his braided hair was nearly all silver. With his deep brown eyes and honey-stained skin, he looked like he should be running a city, not advising one.

Alaric cleared his throat, and everyone turned to look at him. Cyrus was grateful for the break—there were too many eyes staring at once, like he was a piece of entertainment to celebrate or reject. Based on these judgmental gazes, he couldn't tell how any of them felt. From Sozar's thoughts, he could tell the dragon was intrigued by it all. It was clear Sozar had a curiosity for politics, which certainly didn't come from Cyrus, since he couldn't stand it.

He looked around, realizing nobody had anything in front of them, not even a drink. By the Gods, he was thirsty, but he would have to wait until after this was settled.

Alaric's dark eyes wavered over Cyrus as he started to speak. "Obviously, we are here on slightly unique terms. I did not request a recorder to document this meeting because I don't think it's necessary. I am also trusting we are all here for the right reasons."

He let that settle among them.

"Some of you have approached me about Cyrus, more so after the accident with my father." That was the first time Cyrus was hearing the word "accident" tossed into King Raj's death. "You want to know where his loyalties lie and so forth. Some of you—you know who you are—have even asked that he leave because the citizens are in an uproar over a Dragon Rider. Others"—his eyes landed directly on Asher—"have warned me about other political issues that this could cause."

Cyrus bit the inside of his cheek. His mother had abandoned him to the late king, and he was trying to accept that.

Knowing that there were people in this room who still wanted nothing to do with him was like pouring salt into the wound. Cyrus had gone his whole life trying to be a good person. If the council didn't want him, he was left alone. Again.

The king laid his hands on the table. It was interesting watching Alaric run this meeting. It fit him well, and authority came natural to him, likely thanks to many, many summers under the guide of his father. He was a son, a prince, and now a king who had spent his entire life exposed to this world of politics—it was all he knew.

"I have requested Cyrus be here, so that he may tell you directly his intentions. Perhaps this may bring some of you peace. If there are questions, hold until the end, and make sure they are respectful. This is a Rider, not just some sea scum who washed up ashore. Let's treat him with some respect."

The choice of words was interesting, but Cyrus didn't have time to consider that more before the council turned to him. Everyone's eyes blinked almost simultaneously as they awaited his response. It wouldn't be much, but it would hopefully put them at ease.

Cyrus raised his left hand slightly in a meek wave. He wasn't sure why, but it felt appropriate. "I don't come here with any intention but for peace." A loaded word choice, but oh well. The Demon King might live by the same mission statement, for all he knew. "I originally came here for answers about my heritage, which did not go as I had hoped, though I hold no resentment toward the city. Your king has shown me kindness and given me free choice."

Asher raised an eyebrow and glanced toward Alaric but did not say anything. Cyrus recognized it to be a look of disbelief—he didn't support the king's decision. And the others didn't seem to either. They had all anticipated something different.

Lord Randall spoke first. "We shelter you, and you do not give us fealty?"

"I never asked for shelter," Cyrus countered. "In fact, I didn't want any of you to know I existed. My intentions were to come here, get the answers I needed, and then leave. The fact that any of you know I exist was by accident." Or betrayal, but they didn't need to know the emotional details. These people had a city to run.

Lady Yan leaned forward. She was young, with straight black hair, but her eyes were cold and much older, drilling into him. "What are your intentions?"

The dreaded question. He had been weighing this one for a while, now knowing that Henry Junok was the one who had tricked him, taken the eggs, and given a false name. There was risk in both choices, but he had to consider which one may result in an uglier outcome. No choice was right, but one would hopefully be the lesser of two evils.

"I intend to recuperate here," he answered. The truth was, he intended to learn as much as he could about the world before flying off with some half-assed goal again. He'd learned his lesson. He needed a place to stay, to learn, and Alaric had promised him a sanctuary here. At least until he was ready to do whatever it was he chose to do next.

Lord Jexton nodded—he seemed like the only one who saw this as reasonable. "May I suggest something to the council?"

Mumbles of agreement. Alaric motioned for the middle-aged man to continue. He had rich ebony skin that contrasted well with the gold rings that lined his fingers and the green fabric of his garb. "I am only thinking of a possibility to appease both sides. Cyrus here wishes to stay, but the council—my guess—considers him a burden and political risk. Why don't we, if Cyrus would accept, utilize his skills and dragon for exploratory flights in the nearby islands? He could aid us with our hunts, keep an eye out for any incoming ships, and he may be able to offer information we don't know of." He shrugged. "Or we could bicker."

The offer seemed rather reasonable. "Services for housing," he voiced out loud, "with no pledge. Am I correct?"

The king nodded. "Aye."

He had no idea the consequences of not returning to Henry Junok, but he could not risk what could happen if he did. The false god might force him into violent servitude or even harm Sozar. If he didn't go, he knew that Sozar was safe, which was his priority. Henry had the two female eggs, which ate him up inside, but he was unwilling to risk the safety of his dragon for them. At the end of the day, he had to make a choice. All he could hope was that if the eggs did hatch, they were not destined to be mindless beasts.

"All right—"

The door slammed opened from behind and a man stumbled in, out of breath. He brought the thick scents of the pungent sea. "I'm sorry—" He was gasping for air, and soldiers encircled him. Cyrus watched the seaman raise a hand. His clothes were dirty, grime coated his sunburned skin, and his dark hair fell all around his features. When he raised his head, his chest still rising and falling, he spoke again. "A ship, Your Majesty . . . It has returned."

Alaric cocked his head. "We were not due for an import or arrival. This is not ours."

The man shook his head. "They insist they are supposed to be here. Your Majesty, they brought back something . . . something *strange*."

The king stood at once and motioned for the soldiers to give the seaman some space. "Continue," he ordered, and approached.

The man glanced to the soldiers, and then his eyes landed on Cyrus. After a quick double take, he licked his lips and started to talk. "There's a creature aboard. They say she's a shapeshifter of the sea, captured when they ventured too far into the Grave of the Sea—"

"A Tsu'ran?" Alaric whispered in disbelief. Cyrus saw the entire council go stiff. "Impossible."

"I promise—" He coughed. "I saw her myself. Your Majesty, they're just like the stories."

"Take me there."

"No," Lord Rendall said abruptly, and stood. Cyrus followed, feeling uncomfortable sitting any longer. "You mustn't go. You know what they say about them!"

The king had a wicked gleam in his eye, something Cyrus had only ever seen in Morei Geral. It was thrill—and a need to be there. "You do not need to be concerned, Rendall. I have my soldiers."

Cyrus glanced between everyone, not sure what the problem was. It was clear this Tsu'ran was dangerous, but he'd never heard of such a thing.

"Don't be a fool," Rendall snapped. "You know better—"

"Do not question me. Do so again and I will have your tongue." The king turned back to the seaman. "Apologies. Grand stories scare my council more than the sea does." He shot a glare at Rendall before continuing. "Is there anything else?"

The seaman looked so small next to the king, standing an entire head shorter. Cyrus was suddenly aware that if the man wanted, he could lash out. It seemed the soldiers thought so too, but Alaric did not let any concern show.

"There is one more thing," the newcomer said. The room had grown deathly quiet. "The captain has declared that he is the prince of Junok."

A BALLET OF SWORDS

There were few things that brought Morei more joy than the swing of a sword. The weapon was an extension of one's self—how he stepped, perceived, defended were all direct reflections of who he was as a person. Time slowed as he twisted, turned, and danced with the sword that had been his for many a summer now. The serrated edge was sharpened, the metal polished, and the leather on the hilt freshly oiled and treated.

His thoughts wandered in the training space that was now his alone. He had instructed soldiers to leave him be, to let him work alone for the time, and if he got the wild desire to exchange blows with someone, he would summon them back. For now though, he was satisfied with himself and the blade.

The training ring was wide and reserved for only the palace soldiers. This particular area was much smaller than the primary training ring just south of here, past the palace and toward the city center. Fighting was a trademark here, and when people had differences to settle, they brought it to the training ring, sometimes with an audience, sometimes without.

Weapons hung on the far wall, a usual spot for soldiers to pick and choose the metal of their choice. Grieves, braces, and various armory hung next to the weapons, but Morei reserved such attire for the field. The soil beneath his boots was fine, like sand, and the color of sunset.

The art of wielding a weapon happened in the mind, nowhere else. Morei focused on how his muscles reflexed and tightened with each step. He focused on the air that came and went at his request, the sound of his heart at its steady beat, and how the weight of his weapon was distributed along his hand. It was a dance with himself, one that he had grown to adore.

Morei took another step, then another, following the blade's song—and then he saw someone standing on the edge of the ring.

He halted and lowered his weapon. It was Isla, dressed the same as earlier. The princess looked startled at his sudden awareness of her, and she took a step back.

"What are you doing here?" he asked. His voice rolled off the stone and across the sand.

"I was just— Well, to be honest, I was watching." She laced her fingers as she spoke. "I didn't mean to intrude."

He raised an eyebrow. "Considering I've sent everyone away and you still managed to walk right in when I asked for privacy, I would say you did mean to intrude."

Isla didn't reply right away. The comment had caught her off guard, and Morei let her flounder a bit. "I can go."

"And then what?" the king pressed, stopping her in her steps. He eyed her form. Yes, she was fit, but that didn't mean she knew how to swing a sword. "Do you know how to fight?"

"N-no." The answer didn't surprise him. Isla had spent her summers carrying buckets of feces and water through dungeon halls, not in the training ring and mastering a weapon.

Morei gestured for her to approach the weapons rack. "Come then. Let's fit you with a sword to work with."

"I didn't mean to impede—"

"Yes, you did," Morei cut her off and stopped in front of the swords, chains, and scythes—yes, scythes. "Admit it and let's move on. Do you know if you are left- or right-hand dominant?"

As she stepped up next to him, he caught the distinct scent of apples and cinnamon, which he was more than happy to breathe. Isla shrugged and flashed the faintest smile, but he could see a thrilled glimmer in her blue eyes. This was exactly what she'd wanted, and he was more than happy to placate that deep desire to learn.

"From what I've tried before, I think I use my right hand," Isla answered.

"All right, then let's check weight distribution. Take this one." Morei reached up and snatched a short sword from the rack and handed it to her. It was lightweight—this one forged without the intent of crushing bone—and it might work for her frame. It was too light for him, but he was also a harder fighter than most. The weapons he used needed to be forged with a denser steel to balance his swing.

He watched the princess work clumsily with handling the sword, but it was clear from her grip that this was not the first time she'd tried. Her fingers were splayed evenly, save for the pointer, which was too far apart from the rest. "How does it feel?" he asked.

Isla rose and dropped the sword a couple of times. "A bit heavy."

"Heavy is good," he explained. "Too light and you risk throwing your sword in the middle of a swing. It'll make you off balance." The king saw another sword, slightly shorter, and grabbed it. "Compare with this one. If this is too light, we'll stick with the first one for now."

She leaned the sword up against the wall and repeated the same thing with the second weapon. The way her body moved with it, it was clear that this one was much better for her.

"I like this one," Isla told him.

He nodded. "It looks good on you too. Now"—he reached forward with his free hand and tapped her fingers—"close that gap. It will feel awkward at first, but with time, you'll learn to rely on it. If your fingers are splayed like so"—Morei copied her—"the distribution of strength is off. In a defensive fight, you'll lose. Come."

They approached the center of the ring. With his back to her, he could not help but be acutely aware that she could try to kill him. Her breathing and steps did not falter or change pattern. Isla was far more concentrated on his words than any motive of her own. Fascinating.

When they faced each other once more, Morei pointed his sword at her. "Bend the knee slightly, keep your feet shoulder-length apart, and place your dominant foot slightly ahead." Isla did so. "This is both an offensive and defensive stance. If the enemy comes at you like so—" Morei stepped forward and raised his blade. Isla flinched but kept her stance. "Don't be fearful. The enemy will know." He slowed the fall of the sword and let it gently tap the edge of hers.

"In the moments leading up to this," Morei said, "you can roll, jump aside, anything you want." They were only two paces apart now, and he lowered his sword from hers. "In the same stance, you can lunge for your enemy."

Now, he took five steps back and kept his sword lowered. "Hit me."

Isla's mouth fell open. "What?"

"Hit me," he repeated. "I have no defensive stance; I am not prepared. If you can catch me by surprise—well, you tell me what you want, and if I can do it, I'll do it." The king smiled. "Is that a deal?"

The princess looked between him and the sword in her hand. "I don't . . . I don't even know what I'm doing. What if I hurt you?"

"You won't." When she didn't act right away, he tilted his head. "Do you think I'd be doing this with you if I didn't see potential?"

She sighed and took her stance. It wasn't as clean as he'd have liked to see, but that was a concern for another day. The intent of this test was to see how she acted under pressure. Isla didn't know what he had planned, and he hoped to catch her by surprise. How she reacted would determine the kind of fighter she was.

Even as she started to run, he noticed her stride was too slow, uncertain—she was scared. Isla was clumsy as she raised her weapon just high enough to block her view, and he took that opportunity to sidestep and snatch her by the collar of her shirt.

Morei yanked her close and drew his own weapon up to her throat, all before she could cry out. Dropping his voice against her ear, he said, "*Always* be on the defense, or you're as good as dead." Then he shoved her off. "Again."

Her cheeks were flushed, and her breath rose and fell sporadically. Morei could tell she was startled, but he wanted her uncomfortable. It would reveal more about her than anything else. As she retook her stance, he said, "Don't ever block your view again, or I will personally ensure you never raise a sword. Go."

Isla charged, this time with a little more certainty, but he saw her hesitate just before reaching him. Her weapon rose before faltering, and Morei swung at the sword with his own. He struck it hard, and Isla let go of it as if she'd been stabbed herself. As the weapon fell, he wrapped a hand around her throat and brought the tip of his sword to her cheek.

"That was pathetic." Morei pushed her away and took a step back. This time, he saw how flustered she was. With two simple exercises, Isla looked like she might cry. As she picked up her sword, he snapped, "For someone who has spent their life cleaning dungeons, I expected you to be tougher."

Isla glared at him with glassy eyes. "You don't know anything about me." But the words came out in a whimper.

"I know you fight like a princess," he retorted. "Should I get some tea for you, *Your Majesty?*" The heat was building in his chest. Morei was not in the mood to be nice or placate the emotions of some girl who thought she was owed the world.

"How can I fight when I don't know how?" Isla yelled. Her tone was furious, her eyes dark. Good. He wanted her angry.

He spread his arms wide, sword and all, and asked, "Do you think I have any sympathy for you?" When she wiped at her eyes, he added with disdain, "Tears will not solve your problems, Princess. If you want to cry about this, then leave."

Morei turned around then. Slowly, he started to walk out of the center of the training ring, listening. The grip on his sword remained tight, his ears strained for the movement he knew would come.

Isla ran toward him, steps growing louder and louder until she was on him. Morei ducked and sidestepped, bringing his sword around to protect himself. Metal clanged deafeningly loud, and he saw the enraged expression on Isla's features transform her into something cold and dangerous. She grunted as the swords met, but she quickly withdrew and swung again, using both hands this time, as she delivered what would be a fatal blow. Isla wasn't fighting to train, she was fighting to kill. And he liked it.

Morei deflected her next blow, noting the strength. There was certainty in her movements that came with trusting the weapon. Isla was no longer second-guessing herself or the sword, she was pouring everything into each movement. It was heavy-handed and irrational, but it was still there, and if not for his countless summers of training, a disastrous mistake could occur.

Isla changed tactics and swung sideways at his head. Thrill bubbled under the surface, and he raised his blade to stop the swing. As the metal connected, the princess was already with-drawing her weapon and trying to stab him right in the torso.

Morei sidestepped. Her actions were sporadic, not thought through, which made her swings dangerous. He was watching her steps, her eyes, and how she shifted weight between her left and right arm. There was no offense by him, only defense, and slowly, they worked their way around the training ring.

Sweat poured off Isla's brow, and she gasped. Her strength was waning with each swing. The princess had used up every-thing in her frenzy, and with one quick adjustment, he nudged her blade out of the way and slid his own sword down to the handguard. Morei stepped up to her, forcing her eyes upward as he snaked his fingers through her hair and pulled back.

Isla didn't fight. Her sword dropped as she gulped in air like a starved animal.

"Well done," Morei whispered. Her eyes searched his—a deep sea-blue that he hadn't noticed until now—and he could feel her body shake from the exertion. A part of him wondered how long she would have gone before she had dropped from exhaustion. "We're done for today."

Her knees buckled slightly, and she wiped the droplets of perspiration from her brow. As they stood there, Morei knew this was the right time. He had been thinking it over, watching her in just the short time that she had been brought to him. There were many tasks ahead, including the Festival of Seasons. She was his risk.

"Isla," he said, and sheathed his weapon. "I am sure you are aware of the festival that is due to take place in three moon cycles."

She nodded between breaths, chest still rising and falling heavily. There had been no attempt to pick up her weapon yet.

"The king is to have a dance partner," he told her. "I want that to be you."

Her chest stopped moving, her mouth clamped shut, and she stared. It occurred to him then that she might not know how to dance, let alone have ever been the center of attention. The first dance would be on display for everyone to see.

"I—" Isla stopped short and snatched the sword up from the sand. "I am not sure that's such a good idea."

"Why?" Morei watched her eyes go to the steel in her hands. She looked like she wanted to crawl into a hole and disappear, but he didn't care. "You are a Caster, Isla. Why wouldn't I choose you?"

She looked at him pointedly. "I am not a queen."

"Yet," he insisted. When her shoulders fell, he added, "If you thought my plan was to bring you into the palace so that you could play princess all day, you're wrong. You are Caster blood, which means that no matter what you do, you will always have an influence on this city and what becomes of it. You can become anything you want. I see in you an opportunity, potential."

Isla glanced between the sword and him, her hand fidgeting on the handguard as if she suddenly didn't know how to hold it. When she spoke, her words were full of resolve. "You want me by your side to boost your support amongst the people."

He would not deny that—it had become his goal since learning of her. A Caster family member by his side would, as he had come to believe, change everything. He had anticipated going about this entirely alone—proving to these people that he had their best interests in mind—and he had been okay with it. After all, he was quite used to acting alone. But he could not deny the immense opportunity of using Isla as part of a way to win the citizens over. Rhys had been right about one thing—he intended to use Isla's tragic story as motive.

If she thought this went one way, though, she was wrong. "And you want to fulfill your purpose and bloodline," he pointed out. "So, it seems we both have motive."

He had given Isla the opportunity to reject her bloodline and leave, but she had accepted the offer. That told him everything—she might appear defenseless and even meek at times, but she was more than willing to become a confident ruler. She was born for it, and he knew that as well as he knew the desert sunrises.

Isla lifted her chin to him, the flush color of her cheeks having faded. "And here I thought you might have had a heart."

He scoffed and ignored those words. She was hurt—no, gullible. In time, she would learn that everyone had a motive. Kindness was never selfless. Morei was glad to give her this opportunity to embrace her heritage, but nothing was ever free. Surely she must know that after spending all those summers as a servant.

"I ask again," he said, "will you be my dance partner for the festival?"

They waited. Morei got the impression she was intentionally not replying right away, and that was fine. If she wanted to hold this over him, then so be it. He would wait, because he knew she would agree. Posing this as a question was just his way of making her feel like she had any say in the matter. She was too eager to learn to deny the opportunity.

With a single nod, she answered, "All right. I think we're on the same page."

He raised his brow. "So is that a yes?" Morei wanted her to say it.

"Yes," she told him, and crossed her arms. That same fierce expression from when she fought earlier appeared again now.

"Good." Morei could now inform the council that he had identified a dance partner. It felt like such a petty task compared to everything else going on, but it was important to make the people happy. If they wanted their festival, despite the impending war, then he would be more than willing to give it, especially since it would further cement his commitment to them. "Then we're done for today. You may retire and do whatever you like. If you have any questions, come to me directly. I'll be in my study."

As he turned to leave, he noticed she was still standing there. "Yes?" he pressed.

"That's it?" she asked. "No appointments or anything?"

That made him smile. She was searching for something to do, hoping to keep busy. That would make her a great queen. "No. Tomorrow though, I will summon you for discussions on policies and contracts and other such things. It'll be good to expose yourself to all the paperwork involved with ruling. If you wish to go do something productive, then go read. Educate yourself on Vore history."

He was willing to bet she had no official experience with education, no summers of studies under her belt. She had been raised a staff member, hardly respected in the dungeons, and she likely knew very little about the Vore World. When she nodded, he knew his instinct had been right.

"Okay," Isla said.

Morei left. His boots sank into the sand, and his steps were steady, but his heart beat with pure joy. He was glad to see progress already in Isla, and the more he saw of her, the more confident he was in his decisions.

His next stop—food. He was starving. Then the study.

THERE WILL BE PEACE

Syra found Dryl sitting alone in the meeting chamber where they'd been last night. He had nothing in front of him to show he was busy, and when he saw her, he looked visibly startled. Syra caught a glimpse of something she hadn't seen on the Guardian before—sorrow. It drew his face down, and his crisp red eyes looked dull, but just as quickly as she saw that emotion, it was gone.

"Hello," she greeted, but there was no response. Dryl turned his eyes downward to stare at the Vore map. There was no question about how the walk over here had been, to which she was ready to tell him there were people passed out in the halls, some with bruised faces and others drunk. There were no inquiries about how she was doing, nothing.

That worried her. Maybe he'd thought this would all be easy or that there would be little pushback. There was even the possibility that he'd thought he'd be welcomed back with open arms, especially with his extensive history with this place. But as Syra stood there, watching, she realized it couldn't be any of that. This was not Dryl's first day. He was not ignorant. He'd known what he'd be walking into, so this was something else entirely.

Zarek's attitude had been tense, cold. Had something happened with the two of them? A fight, fallout . . . something could have happened that caused the two brothers to be at odds again, and Syra grimaced. After all this time, maybe their relationship was irreparable.

She walked up and sat in the chair across from him. He did not turn his eyes toward her. Syra had never been on this end before. Guardians were tough, and in her travels, she'd never seen him like this. Here was a man who was agonizing over something only he could see. The words on her tongue died; the harsh words she'd been ready to say in irritation about how he'd spoken about her yesterday crumbled. All she did was stare. She wasn't used to this. Syra hadn't ever been the one to comfort a Guardian. She didn't know what to say.

Everything felt leagues from her grasp. The Soul Realm, Chaos, Sekar. She kept her hands intertwined in her lap, watching him. The map lay between them, and right now, it really did feel like they were countries apart.

Dryl shifted in his seat then, and she tensed.

"I never told you about Annabel," he said. His voice was low, and if not for the silence in this room, she was certain she'd be unable to hear him. "She was enslaved by her father and raised to be a weapon. She was one of the most powerful Energy Harvesters I'd ever met, but she was a shell of a person." Dryl looked at her now, grief-stricken. "Her father wanted to use her to dominate Creitón—he was the king of Barnǎl— and she wanted to run. I gave her that freedom, but it costed her everything."

Syra swallowed, and the muscles in her shoulders and upper back locked up. She didn't know why she was so nervous. The man across her wasn't a stranger, but she had no idea where he was going with any of this.

"I've spent my whole life trying to do the right thing for people. What I did for Annabel nearly took my life as a Guardian." He shook his head and sighed, defeated. "You are my Annabel, Syra. The world wants to weaponize you, but I want to set you free. But I can't. Not this time."

She dug her nails into the palm of her hand, trying to remain still, even though her head was spinning and she felt the anxiety rock her body.

"You are the key to keeping this"—he motioned around them—"alive. You are the only thing this world has that truly has its best interest at heart. If I could do this all without you, I would. If I could stand up against Liral and trust that it could be done without a problem, I'd do it. But I can't."

Dryl shook his head. "Your potential, what you are and will become, will change the realms," he continued. "If I don't use that to our advantage, then I might as well as dig everyone's grave. Your bloodline grants you opportunities in the Soul Realm that no Guardian can touch. Your love for this living realm will give you a perspective that is unmatched by me or anyone else." He looked like he was pleading with her. "I know you're confused, angry even, and I don't blame you. I walked in here and started saying things without saying hello. But I trust that you do or will one day understand that time is not on our side for pleasantries, even if I tell that to people like Bane. And I hope that one day, you'll forgive me for seeing you as nothing more than a means to an end."

Syra blinked. A rogue tear fell and dropped into her lap. She had known there were things she could not ignore. The realm fracture, the dying Soul Realm, these were things she had actively accepted and been prepared for. When Dryl had hinted that he wanted to use her, she'd been upset and betrayed. She'd been ready to share her opinion with him and how he'd treated her, but now she didn't have an argument to make.

That was why he was upset. What was happening here was because he was agonizing over telling her this, along with real-izing that he couldn't protect her anymore. Not like he used to. Maybe he and Zarek shared these words prior to the Guardian finding her. Putting it all together like that, Syra knew it was her time to step up. Dryl needed her. The Soul Realm did, she knew that, but it was more than that. The realms needed her. The future was dependent on her. It clicked in that instant.

"I understand," she told him. His eyes met hers at those words, and she felt more confident as she added, "I want to be what I need to be. I'm ready for that. A lot has changed since we last traveled together. I've had to change, Dryl, because things have happened that I've been forced to deal with." She raised her marked hand and showed him. "Last night, I found my gift. Last night, I realized that I'm so much more than I think." She lowered her hand, but it was like he hadn't even seen it. "I know now that I'm it."

He nodded, slowly. Syra waited for him to say something to that, to make a remark—anything—to show that he'd heard what she'd just said. But nothing happened. Instead, Dryl got up and walked over to the small decanter that was sitting on a table and poured himself a drink. He looked her way and then grabbed another glass. Once that one was topped off, he made his way back over and set them down, settling back into the chair.

Syra eyed the glass and its slightly purple hue. She was not in the mood to drink this early in the morning.

"It's tea," Dryl told her, sensing her hesitation. "Blackberry, at that."

Carefully, Syra wrapped a hand around the short glass and raised it to her lips. The liquid was warm, but it was subtle and fruity. She took a large drink before setting the glass down again.

"We have several major problems to consider moving forward," Dryl told her. His tone shifted; it was like she was staring at a new person. She couldn't tell if she was relieved or disappointed at how fast the subject had changed. "The realm fracture will take priority for obvious reasons, although we need to understand the source of where this fracture originated from before we can even begin to address it. I am hoping to put Zarek on that. He's got extensive knowledge on the Soul Realm, given his relations with Shevana. Once we know more, we can act on that. But in the living, we've got Henry Junok and Morei Geral." At the last name, Syra's brow went up, and Dryl noticed. "You are aware?"

"I've had several encounters," she confessed. "My dreams . . . they've become real at times."

Syra told him about those, along with Sekar's theory about the realm fracture. It felt good after holding on to this information. She'd hoped to tell Zarek, but their timing hadn't granted that luxury. The Guardian appeared satisfied with it all, and she quickly added the confrontation between Morei and Sekar and the use of Dark Energy. At that, Dryl's face dropped.

"Morei is one of only few ever in history to master an element of Dark Energy," Dryl said. "Between that and his political drive for power, he will cause irreparable damage to the world. His prophecy has always been of concern to the Guardians."

Syra wrapped her fingers around the glass. "You know about Morei?"

"Guardians do more than walk around with spirits all day," Dryl replied. "We're in charge of ensuring certain laws are never broken in the living realm, so we're constantly watching people."

This was news to her. "Well, how do you know you've broken one of these laws?" She didn't know of any rule she had to adhere to, beyond the standard city laws.

He smiled. It was the first time she'd seen it since her arrival. "You'd know." With a wave of his hand, he continued. "Henry Junok is a concern for obvious reasons we've discussed. Junok is already under his control, which means he now controls the largest port in this country." Raising the glass, he took a drink and set it down again on the Vore map. "These are things I will remain focused on uniting the Infernol under. We don't want another Lirallian Empire, but Morei's rise to power creates another potential empire—or worse, he aligns himself with Henry."

Her stomach twisted. "You think he'd do that?"

Dryl sighed. "If I could predict the future, I'd feel a lot more confident right now, but I can't. My goal is simply to keep the living realm from crumbling or being devoured by the demons escaping the Soul Realm." At that, he laughed, clearly caught up in his own joke.

Syra studied him as the gap of silence grew wider and wider. He would use her to help the Infernol protect themselves against Henry's forces. She would be the key to salvaging the Soul Realm, and her growing abilities would make her a dangerous person. Syra didn't have time anymore to be a victim, to self-doubt, or to question her potential and purpose. This was it. Dryl wanted her a part of these conversations to keep her engaged, and also because even if he didn't outright say it, he valued her opinion. She trusted him with everything she had.

"One step at a time." She gave his own words back to him. "We'll focus on uniting the Infernol. When we can confidently say we've got everyone's trust and the council supports you, then we'll turn our attention to gathering information on Henry and Morei. When Zarek has information on the fracture, we'll discuss those steps then." She nodded, but it was more to herself. This was their plan.

"Today, I'll be back at the council." Dryl leaned back. "I hope to have a productive discussion with them. Perhaps some more information on Zane and Eva too."

She nodded in acknowledgement and took another drink. When she set it down, she asked, "Can I ask you something?"

He raised one eyebrow, which she took as her opportunity to continue. "You didn't say where you've been all this time . . ."

She trailed off, unsure of how to end that statement. Did she want to know?

Dryl averted his gaze. "There will come a time when I will be ready to tell you. But please know that I used my travels to learn what I could, like with Volkeri Island."

Dryl had poured his heart out at her arrival, and now he was shutting her out. She'd expected, and wanted, more. An explanation. Something she could hold on to, so that she could justify having been abandoned.

She downed the rest of the tea in hopes of not saying something rude. Now was not the time.

"Keep training," Dryl said, moving on. "Make use of Sekar's expertise while he's around."

She swallowed, not liking the sound of any of this. "While he's around?" She had figured the God couldn't always be around, but Dryl made it sound so final.

The Guardian bared his hands and narrowed his gaze on her. "There will come a day, and it'll be soon, that Sekar will have to be your enemy. His commitment to Henry will force his hand. You must recognize that, Syra. There are things in motion so much bigger than us, and we must be prepared for anything."

She and the God had a complex relationship, and they'd made a deal. This journey had started with Sekar when he'd pretended to be a Guardian, and she couldn't fathom it ever turning sinister between the two of them, no matter how much he angered her at times. She rubbed her thumb over the scar of the Zyulë Bond.

Maybe Sekar had done that for more than one reason.

"I should go," she mumbled, and stood. Syra wanted to get out of the Guardian's way before the morning got any older—she knew he had a long day ahead. She also hoped to make it to her secluded spot before the rest of the Infernol woke up.

She wanted to think about last night, about what had happened, and if she had the strength, practice projecting herself.

"Syra," Dryl said. She turned around and saw him standing. His eyes softened. "You know I'll always be here for you."

She did, but hearing it in that moment felt like the biggest relief. "I know," she whispered back.

At that, she left and made her way back to her chamber. As she passed those who had been passed out previously, she saw some had already moved and others had disappeared. A few remained slumped over. Only a single staff member saw her, and the woman was carrying stew. When she saw Syra, she smiled big, which was a huge relief, and then continued on her way. It was nice to see a little bit of kindness after everything.

A SONG FOR THE SEA

Cyrus wasn't sure how he got involved with Alaric heading to Delion's port, but here he was, trekking alongside the king to the ship. A dozen soldiers followed behind, some already with their swords drawn, while Lord Rendall and Asher took up the rear. Sozar flew overhead, circling about and waiting for the right time to land. Cyrus had advised him to stay up there, away from all the prying eyes and excitement. For all he knew, this Tsu'ran was some stranded woman at sea and the city was just looking for a reason to be violent.

Extreme, he knew, but one could never be too cautious.

Citizens flitted about, and many stopped and stared at the progression as they went by. Some asked what was happening, while others were smart enough not to ask questions the king was surely not going to answer. All anyone knew was that this was the Dragon Rider—Cyrus couldn't hide his silver eyes.

The path to the port was well-loved—a sandy one accented by stone on either side. People stepped off the main path when they saw them coming and only got back on once they were long past. When Cyrus looked around, he anticipated seeing his mother but didn't. Good. He was in no position to look at her in the face and tell her anything, because he didn't trust his tongue on the matter, and he knew Sozar would be furious. He'd gone decades without seeing her; he could go decades more.

Alaric suddenly spoke. "I've always wanted to see a Tsu'ran."

Cyrus took this opportunity to confess. "I have no idea what we're talking about."

The nearby soldiers glanced his way, surprised, but didn't say anything, even as Alaric's mouth fell open. "What?"

He shrugged. "Diemon was super strict about what was shared."

The king shook his head in disbelief. "Fair enough. It's a sea legend too, so not like your people could do much with that next to the mountains." He flashed a smile, then continued. "The Tsu'ran is a creature of the deep seas. They take on the form of what we desire most. For many of the men stuck out at sea, that's a woman. You see where I'm going with this?"

He nodded.

"They are devourers of souls," the king explained. "They were born with one job—to steal our lives, because it gives them the strength to live theirs. Sounds like a harsh way to live, don't you think?"

One could say the same about the dead who still wander these lands, Sozar commented. Cyrus saw his point but chose not to mention it to Alaric.

"What will you do with this Tsu'ran?"

The king motioned to the sky and soldiers. "I shall get what I need, and if the creature so happens to desire a return to the sea, I shall grant that."

Cyrus did not like that answer. "Will you?"

A sly grin slid across the king's face. "You're picking up fast, Rider. Have you ever thought about joining politics? You'd do well."

He chose not to answer.

"A creature like that does not come to shore and ever see the sea again. They go mad when they stay too long out of water, and it's believed that even if you do return the Tsu'ran, it will be so driven by revenge for being taken in the first place, that it will haunt your port and sink your ships." Alaric's eyes were no longer wicked but sad. "Thus is the way of the sea, my friend."

"Doesn't sound like she came back willingly then."

Alaric bared a hand as they closed in on the port. "We don't know the story, so best we ask the Tsu'ran, hm?"

They were ignoring a major part of this revelation. Cyrus swallowed and asked, "What about what the man said? The prince of Junok?"

The Tsu'ran mention had stolen everyone's attention, Cyrus presumed. Alaric had shared a bit, but he sensed it was a legend that was in the blood of these people. A prince was simply that—a legend come to life was far more superior to these people. "He'll be treated with respect, given he is here for genuine reasons."

Cyrus didn't like that answer, spoken so loosely. "You think he could be here with ill intentions?"

Shouts and calls came from ahead, signaling the king's arrival. Seamen and women bustled about, getting out of the way yanking children with them too. The markets were alive, filled with all sorts of goods from both the waters and bakeries. Fabrics and weapons hung in some, while another seller strung fish. The smell was strong, and Cyrus's eyes watered in response. He had never been around fermenting fish, and after this, he was sure he never wanted to be again. The soldiers and Alaric and Asher paid no mind. This was normal for them— fish left out in the sun or freshly pulled from the blue waters ahead.

The boards creaked, and Cyrus was acutely aware that the waters lapped beneath them. This whole port was built over the shore. Despite having flown over the sea, his legs still felt wobbly from the idea that the only thing separating him from the deep waters was a piece of wood nailed together probably centuries ago.

A yell from ahead. "The king is here! Why is he here?"

Alaric did not wait for anyone to answer for him. "To see it for myself," he called back. Soldiers eyed him but did not say more. In a lower voice, he told Asher, "Let's get his name for later."

"Understood."

Cyrus raised his brow but kept his mouth shut. Now was not the time to show sympathy for a soldier who would be reprimanded for questioning the king's arrival. In the heat of everything happening, he was impressed with Alaric's ability to compartmentalize. All his attention was on the idea that the Junok prince and sea creature were here, and then there was Alaric, worried about the training of his soldiers.

But just as his thoughts were spiraling, they were yanked above water. He saw men pulling ropes and chains off a ship. His eyes landed on the dark shimmer of blue and green—hair that looked to be the color of the sea, unmistakable. Large, slit-like eyes of a stunning, vibrant green blinked as they scanned the area. The woman's skin was decorated with strange black markings, sigils that he could not decipher, and she wore a simple, short dress—prisoner attire. The shackles on her wrists were made for beasts, wide and sturdy, not for the delicate woman they chained.

His mouth fell open, even as Alaric began to order his men to surround them. Cyrus wanted privacy, yet this was all being put on display. It felt like they were exploiting this creature.

The thick stench of the sea washed over Cyrus, but he couldn't determine if it was from the woman or the seamen who held her. The ropes that were wrapped and knotted around her waist revealed a beautiful figure underneath, but he remembered Alaric's words and forced his eyes back to her own. They were on him, otherworldly, and he swallowed. It was like staring into the pit of a dark hole. There was something disturbingly powerful beneath that gaze, and he could feel it tug at his soul.

Sozar's presence forced its way into the forefront of his mind. *It's got the lifeforce of a dragon.* His words tumbled out quick. *This is a shifter of great power.*

Then why the chains? Had the metal been forged with an unbreakable force? It would be the only logic behind this scene before him.

"Welcome to land," Alaric announced. "Is there something we can call you by?"

The Tsu'ran cocked her head to the side and smiled, revealing dagger-like teeth that still managed to look beautiful on her. Cyrus blinked. "They call me Kan Sëri."

"Sea Master," Asher quietly translated. The coloring on his cheeks looked to be a shade lighter.

"She came aboard willingly," a voice announced from the ship behind, standing atop the gangway that connected the vessel to the port. "But one can never be too cautious with such power—she's under a spell, so your men may rest easy." The man had black hair that hung past his shoulders. His rich green eyes could have passed for gems, and his frame befit a warrior. A tattoo raked up the side of his neck, an illustration of bones and a vine. He had an air of authority that preceded Alaric's question.

"You must be Nerius," he greeted. There was a shift from the surrounding men, but no one took the prince's words seriously. They were wary—rightfully so. Alaric kept the conversation going with ease. "It is a pleasure to have your bloodline this far south."

The prince of Junok stepped down to meet them eye-to-eye. He stood about Cyrus's height and made his stare quite obvious. "A Dragon Rider. This is quite the meeting, isn't it?"

"Aye," Alaric replied, and reached a hand out to shake with the prince, who took it. "You captained this ship?"

Nerius nodded. "A storm came, and Captain Jones was in the wrong place at the wrong time. Got flung overboard and lost to the raging waters. I was nominated to sail her from then on."

"Ah." Alaric motioned at the Tsu'ran like an object on display. "And this?"

"Came aboard willingly," Nerius repeated, his eyes hovering over the woman's a moment longer than expected. "She saved us from the Grave too. I owe her my life."

The king nodded. "Yet you bound her and cast her under a spell. Who is your Energy Harvester? People of that nature generally don't sail the seas."

"Me."

Cyrus studied the captain. He knew Junok blood to be rich with energy harvesting skills, but this man was rubbing him all the wrong way. He eyed Alaric once more, noting that his chancellor looked like he'd rather be anywhere but here.

"Wrangling and chaining a Tsu'ran is no easy feat," Alaric replied. "Why would she"—he looked at Kan Sëri—"come aboard willingly, unless there was a reason?" His question was not said in offense, but Cyrus had spent enough time now with the king to note the undertone. Alaric didn't trust Nerius, not yet, and he wasn't happy with the answers he was getting.

The captain raised his brow. "She is nomadic. She abandoned her kind."

Cyrus didn't like that answer either. He was preparing to say something on the matter when Asher cut in.

"Your purpose then, Captain?"

Nerius nodded, as if realizing why they were all there. "Storm's coming, just north of here, past the Hil Islands. She's a nasty one—been ravaging those waters for days and growing stronger—and we wanted to shore up before we got caught in any of that. With your permission, we'd appreciate housing— with payment, of course—if you will accept us."

Alaric stared at the prince for a long moment before he gestured with his chin to the Tsu'ran. "Then why is this here?"

This. They were past formalities. His tone suggested he had heard something he didn't like. The hairs on the back of Cyrus's neck stood on end.

"She told me to come here," he answered. "Said she wanted to give the Delion king a message."

It all happened too quick for Cyrus to react, but the woman's form shifted from solid to liquid. The chains and rope could not contain such a thing, and she—it?—slipped between the cracks of wood of the boards. Men started to shout, swords were drawn, Sozar roared, and Nerius stood there with a big grin on his face.

A groaning sound came from all around, like the port itself was protesting against a massive weight. People bolted as the waves grew violent. The dragon's wings were coming up from behind—Cyrus could hear the woosh of air as Sozar slowed his decent. Already, he was moving backward, and still trying to find Alaric. Where had the king gone?

Then he saw him, surrounded by soldiers and screaming. He slashed his sword over and over. The Tsu'ran was trying—

The entire ground gave out with a deafening crack. Weightlessness came first, and then the cold and bitter slap of the waters engulfed him whole. He held his breath and felt the burn of the salt scrape at his eyes as he desperately searched all around for some direction. Up. He needed to go up.

A hand grabbed his leg and dragged him below.

His back was on fire, his hands slashing out at anything he could grab onto, yet nothing came. He kicked, and his lungs screamed for air. Sozar's presence was thrashing against something massive. He needed to act now or drown.

Summoning the energy from all around, he directed it at the grip on his leg. A pulse of white light flashed through the water, and his heart seized when he saw it wasn't a hand . . . it was a tentacle.

They were everywhere.

A frenzy of voices rushed his mind at once. Cyrus's connection with Sozar was severed in an instant as he was encompassed by a force so starved, he could hardly focus. Dark Energy. He inhaled, taking water with him, as he started pulling himself upward. The panic kept him going, the literal need to survive making his limbs burn with adrenaline, even as his lungs were on fire.

Air. He needed air.

Cyrus broke the surface of the water, arms flinging upward. He spit water out, coughing violently, as his body demanded air immediately. Head swimming, he blinked and looked around. "Sozar?" he called.

When he didn't get a response, he screamed across their mental link. *Sozar!*

Bodies lay everywhere. Cyrus pushed one aside as someone above him called out that there was a survivor. The voices that had ambushed them had ceased, but he could not shake the exploited feeling in his soul, as if he had just been put on display to be judged by something he didn't understand. He hardly had time to consider those implications as he heard gasps and cries. He swung around in the water and saw, just in time, Sozar's head surge out of the water.

Wings wide, the dragon struggled to get out. Cyrus tried to call for him again, but more shouts tore his gaze away. There was Alaric, thrashing in the water.

He looked back at Sozar. The dragon was taking flight right out of the water, and clutched in his massive claws was the Tsu'ran in its sea form. Reddish-brown tentacles failed to lift as black blood dripped from the gouges that covered the body. Sozar was flying with heavy flaps away from the port, keeping low.

The dragon was fine. He would have to be fine. Cyrus continued to tell himself this as he spun in the water and swam over to Alaric, who seemed to be fighting an unseen force.

"Alaric," Cyrus insisted, finding it harder to talk than he anticipated. "Alaric," he repeated, louder.

The king gasped and spun around. His eyes were wide, black pits, and he blinked. As quickly as Cyrus saw the look, it was gone. He wrapped an arm around Alaric's and started to swim ashore. Already, people were helping the survivors up. They hauled Cyrus and Alaric out with incredible ease, countless hands grabbing their soaked clothes.

As his hands met the solidness of the wood, Cyrus gasped for air properly. He stared at the wet wood grain, mind racing. All of that had happened far too quickly. Someone draped a large cloak over him, and he took it gratefully. Turning about, he saw Asher checking on his king, whose mouth was set already in a thin line, eyes distant. He had seen something. The Tsu'ran had done something to him in those waters. Cyrus did not have to ask to know that—it was written all over his face.

The dragon's presence flooded his mind and Cyrus turned to the sea. He could not see him. *Where are you?*

Sozar flashed images of the sea and the creature hanging from his grip.

He didn't like that answer. *Drop it and leave it.*

No.

Cyrus was going to answer when Sozar continued over him. *It seeks to destroy. If it remains too close to the city, it will return. I must fly outward.*

The words didn't satisfy him. Even now, he felt the stretch of their bond as the dragon flew as fast as he could. He could sense Sozar's urgency, knew the dragon was afraid the Tsu'ran might awaken with more strength than before. Cyrus did not have to tell him what to do if that happened, although he could not fathom the idea of not being there.

"Rider," a soldier said suddenly. "Let us get you warmed up."

He shook his head. "No."

The man looked surprised, so Cyrus added, "I will wait for my dragon. Go. I shall return when he returns." He left the crowd and approached the edge of the port, where the wood had been shattered and devoured whole by the waters below. Some boards still floated, others had been crushed, and bodies still remained, faces devoid of life. They had likely suffocated to death.

And Nerius . . .

Cyrus looked back to the ship. Nobody was paying attention, the chaos of the scene too great, but Cyrus saw him standing there, aboard. A woman with great horns stood next to him, and before his eyes, massive wings sprouted from her back. Her gold eyes stared into Cyrus's soul as she wrapped Nerius into the folds of her great wings.

And then they were gone.

Cyrus stared, dumbfounded, for a long while. It wouldn't be until someone put mead in his hands that he would return to stare at the sea in wait for Sozar.

The world was a strange place, and it was only growing stranger.

TWISTED AFFAIR

he water was warm, blessedly so, and Syra took her time in the tub. She scrubbed her skin with a sponge and lathered herself in lemon and mint, taking care to let the mixture settle in her hair until she was satisfied to rinse. With care, she worked her fingers through the red locks, running them through the water until everything was out. When that was done, she rested for a while, clipping her hair up in the process, so that it would not continue to get wet. The hour was late, but there was no one waiting for her.

She closed her eyes and let her thoughts wander on their own. Her heart beat steadily, her movement was sluggish, and she found herself devastatingly close to slumber on occasion, but never quite close enough to be summoned. It created a rhythmic cycle for her, where she was just relaxed enough to not worry or fret, but not quite tired enough to fall asleep.

The day had dragged on more than she wanted to admit, but she was grateful that there had been no shouting outside in her hall. Perhaps the fights were already winding down, or they could have moved to another place. The Infernol was huge, and there were plenty of places for people to cause an uproar.

The conversation with Dryl hung over her, even now. She was in a far better mindset than she had been that morning, but it still didn't settle the nerves that shook her every now and then. Dryl wanted to weaponize her. Continue to train, strengthen her abilities, that was her task, so that he could leverage her when the time was right. If it had been anyone else asking, even Zarek, she may have fought back more. But with Dryl, she knew he was genuine. She didn't love thinking that one day, she might be the only thing the Infernol had against an enemy, but there was a certain level of peace knowing that Dryl and Zarek weren't going anywhere.

Tomorrow, she hoped to see Zarek. They'd left off on the wrong foot. Not that the timing of any of that had been fantastic. It would make her feel better to see the Guardian and chat, even if it was about the weather. With Zane missing, she was now aware more than ever that anyone could disappear from her life in an instant. Death was a very real thing, but there was a strange, haunting presence knowing that someone could vanish without a trace. There was no closure.

One step at a time. She told herself this even as her thoughts raced about. Sekar was on her mind now. It had only been a handful of days for her since he'd arrived back in her life, and she felt like she had progressed so much already. She'd harvested Chaos and found her gift, but so much had happened, too. The God's presence had uprooted her life.

She wondered if she'd dream of Morei again, or of someone else. If she trained more on the skill, maybe she could control who she saw. Though maybe her dreams were correlated to her ability to project, like she had with the Soul Realm. If she mastered it, she could be anywhere and see anything.

The water was getting cold, which was disappointing. The changing temperature was ruining her relaxation. It meant she would have to get out of here and move to the bed. It wasn't a lot of work, but it sure seemed like it. After the last few days, Syra felt like she could disappear for the next twelve days without regret.

She didn't want to think more, so she slowly rose from the tub, water running off her body in loud waves. Reaching for the robe, she wrapped it around herself and tied the knot. It was a soft and silky green—probably one of her favorite things since arriving here. There was nothing quite like taking a bath after a long day and dressing in a warm robe and curling up under the sheets.

Clip pulled from her hair, Syra took a moment to braid it. The locks had dampened quite a bit since putting it up, but it was still wet, and the braid would help with the knotting overnight and give it extra wave tomorrow morning when she took it out. Small things like that made her still feel like a woman and not some grungy, worn-out, *fierce* warrior, as Zane liked to say.

One final look in the mirror behind the basin, and Syra was ready for bed. Making her way out of the bathroom, she was relishing the idea of burying her head into the pillows. The world felt so quiet tonight, a first in a long time. She snatched up the history book she'd been reading and sat down. The cushion felt extra soft tonight.

She could see the door from there, and for a moment, she stared, trying to confirm that the lock was in place. It was. Death's Sword lay at her side, and she reached over to the table she'd pulled over to double check the latch was unhooked, so that she could unsheathe it at a moment's notice. As great as the idea was of sleeping without a care in the world, she couldn't. Not here. There were too many risks to turn a blind eye to, and Syra was still a bit shaken up from Garett and the others, no matter how tough she wanted to act.

When she was certain no one was coming and there was nothing else she could do, she leaned back. And found herself next to Sekar.

"No." The word came out instantly, and Syra bit back a groan of frustration. She just wanted one evening to herself.

Things were finally slowing down just enough for her to take a breath, and now he was here. "I'm not training tonight. I need sleep."

He had his legs crossed over one another and his arms behind his head. Sekar hardly looked her way as he said, "I didn't come here for that."

"Okay?" She studied his expression, trying to gauge some direction from him. At times, he was incredibly difficult to read. Their earlier exchange of words slipped through her head, and she wondered if he was back to discuss more about her abilities, or maybe have more to say about her dreams and interaction with Morei.

He didn't say anything, and she waited, a bit annoyed. Syra leaned over and set the book down next to the sword. She couldn't help but think of Dryl's words or Zarek's hatred for the God. Lying here now, she wondered if they'd been right all along.

"There was once a God who thought he could control the world," Sekar said. She stopped what she was doing and looked over at him. "He'd seen it all and thought he knew exactly what Destiny wanted. He was so confident in that, that he believed he could predict any future. When he met a young man ostracized by his own family, they became friends. At the time, neither realized what the other was."

Sekar's eyes stared up at the ceiling. Syra watched him, afraid he might disappear if she blinked.

"Then, one day, this God's friend did some extraordinary things. So incredible, in fact, that this God believed this was exactly what Destiny wanted. They forged an alliance then and there, not just with words, but with souls. Each possessed a piece of the other's soul because they believed that together, they could change the world. But you see, the God was foolish, Syra, because he took for granted the ability to choose.

Now, centuries later, he is bound to a man who has taken his choices away."

Syra stared, speechless. This was his own story. The alliance with Henry Junok was beyond words or blood bonds. She had absolutely no idea how that was even possible, but she suspected it was the work of Chaos.

Slowly, Sekar turned his eyes to meet her own. "I lied to you, Syra. I told you that I regretted having felt anything for you, but the truth is, I regret the man I was. Every time I look at you, I'm reminded of my mistake."

In the heat of his confession, all she could focus on was the relief she felt at hearing those words. She hadn't realized until now how much they'd clung to her. "Can't you end it?" she asked. It was a futile question, but she needed to hear it from him.

He smiled. "If I could, I'd have done so a long time ago. Ending such a bond could cause devastating consequences to not just those involved but the world, because Chaos is involved. The death of a God is not anything ordinary." He turned his eyes back up to the plain ceiling. "Even Gods are afraid to die," he mumbled.

Syra thought of Dryl's warning. She'd asked if she was safe with him, and he'd said yes, but now she wasn't so sure. "You will have to choose a side one day," she told him. She had said this once before, and he'd dismissed it.

He smiled. "One day," he echoed, "but that is not today." The God turned his attention back to her. Those eyes had seen so much, lived through centuries, and now she beheld them. "Remember our deal?"

She nodded. He'd train her, but in return he wanted her time. How could she forget?

"Good. Let's play a game," Sekar told her. "Let's imagine a world where we are not separated by war, or motive, or even Gods. We're just people who have come back from a night out, two strangers who know nothing of each other. Will you do that with me, Syra?"

That was easy—too easy. "Okay."

Sekar offered his hand, and she placed hers in his. His fingers wrapped around her, engulfing them whole. "There was a festival. Dancers, drinks, and all sorts of people out. It was a miracle we didn't get lost in the crowd or separated."

Her heart seized. This could not be a coincidence. "The Blood Festival?"

Sekar's eyes glimmered. "That's what it was. Glad you could remember. When I saw you tonight, drink in hand, I couldn't resist approaching."

"I was watching you too," she admitted, and felt his hand squeeze her own. This was fun—innocent, perhaps, was a better word to describe what they were doing. "You made it obvious that you were looking at me. Did you know that?"

"Maybe," Sekar replied. "I wanted to see if you were interested in me or not. Didn't want to waste my time otherwise."

"What about all the dancers?" she asked. "Did you like the show they put on?"

"Of course. It's not often you get to experience a festival like that. Don't forget the men and women with their giant hats and throwing fake blood around too . . ." But even as he said it, his voice trailed off. He was no longer looking at her, and a palpable tension settled between them.

He obviously had something on his mind.

Syra waited for him to continue, but when he didn't, she said, "What's on your mind?"

"The festival," he told her.

She wanted to continue to play along, but she was uncertain of the direction this was going. More specifically, she was uncertain about how she would react if Sekar made any gesture toward her. Despite everything, she could not ignore the way he made her feel. It was the way he undressed her with his eyes, the warmth of his skin, and that smile that could be seen from leagues away. He was cunning, confident, and a bit mad, and that terrified her.

Syra took the chance to pull her hand free, but his fingers tightened, refusing to let go. The God's eyes were on hers once more, starved. "I didn't tell you the whole story," he said, and propped himself up on an elbow.

Under that gaze, she felt small. His grip was like iron, and she knew she wasn't going anywhere. "What is it?"

His thumb rubbed against the palm of her hand, slow and deliberate. "I told you the memories were real. Do you remember that?"

She nodded.

"What I didn't tell you was that the feelings were just as real," he stated.

Almost immediately, she opened her mouth to protest and tell him he was being outrageous, but Sekar yanked her forward and pressed his lips against hers before she could react. The heat, tension, and desire molded quickly into a kiss that Syra couldn't remember starting. Her thoughts froze in place, her hands grabbed any part of him she could find, her body burned with need. In less than a heartbeat, she felt entirely . . . like a woman. Wanted. Needed.

He let go of her hand and placed it against her chest, pushing her backward. Sekar climbed on top of her and shoved his fingers through her hair, just as another hand slipped right between the robe's folds. His lips were on hers, their tongues dancing, as she adjusted her legs to accommodate his body over hers.

She moaned into the kiss as his hand fondled her breast. She laced a hand through his hair and shoved him deeper into the kiss, wanting his body against hers more. It had been a long time since she'd felt this way, and she wanted to ensure he understood just how bad she wanted him.

He pulled her head back suddenly, breaking the kiss but hovering just over her lips. He squeezed her breast and moved down to her neck, where his hot breaths sent shivers down her back.

"You smell wonderful," he complimented, and started to kiss her more softly. As he made his way up to her ear and nibbled, she reeled underneath him. She could feel him smile against her ear—

Syra sat upright, jolted awake. Grabbing her clothes, she felt the robe and quickly looked around to find herself completely alone. The lantern had nearly burned out, offering just the faintest of glows. Her body still felt under his spell as she asked, "Sekar?"

Nobody answered.

Bewildered, she pulled the sheets higher, unsure of when she'd passed out. Her hair was wet, so she'd obviously finished her bath and braided her hair, but the space between that and now was unclear. A dream, she thought, another vivid one.

But it *was* real. Syra was not a fool. She scanned the room, certain she might see the God somewhere. Looking over, she saw Death's Sword with the book on the small table. Syra was annoyed at herself because she'd so willingly accepted his affection, even with everything she knew. But in the heat of the moment, she'd believed him, believed the world they'd created—two mortals who had gotten caught up in the festivities of the Blood Festival.

Syra stared at the ceiling. The God had turned his gift on her. He'd gotten into her head, exactly what he wanted. She could almost see his smug expression. Yet, she wasn't mad—this was him. He was the God of Dreams, and this was how he had fun. He was also extremely dangerous. Henry Junok or not, this was not someone she ever wanted as an enemy.

Syra cringed, realizing her affection for him had never waned. They had come a long way together, and she wasn't ready to believe that he had ill intentions, not after everything he'd done. Sekar could and would be an asset to her. She would prove it. She simply could not accept any other outcome.

Syra let her shoulders rise and fall, realizing what the future held. It would not be easy, and there would be hundreds of obstacles in her path, but she let her imagination run wild. One day, she would be the queen of the Soul Realm. The place would be restored to its original greatness, the realm fracture would be resolved, and there would be peace. There would be work, but nothing great ever came easy. And she was not alone—she had incredible allies and friends. One day, she wouldn't have to worry about looking over her shoulder or whether someone might stab her. She'd be safe, free, and in control of her own path. There was a life out there that she yearned for, and she intended to have it.

It would take war, but for the first time in Syra's life, she was ready for it. The world had changed—and so had she.

LUCK OF THE RAVEN

Two days he had been king of Caster, and Morei felt like he was already losing a grip on his control.

For one, it took everything in his power to not kill Rhys. The chancellor's devious demeanor felt like an invitation for him to just thrust his blade right through the man's heart. The impulse had been so great when he'd wrapped his hands around his throat that he'd momentarily forgotten that he was king.

When Morei looked at people in passing, he didn't see them as they were, he saw what he could do to them. The images were violent, always. And when he'd had that control over Isla, he couldn't shake the terrible desire to snap her neck just to hear the sound.

Yet he knew he was where he belonged. So much was at stake. Morei was driven by the overwhelming need to make Geral pay, and he was also determined to show the world what he was capable of. An empire was that answer.

Isla was proving a quick learner. She had been so fascinated by everything so far that it had made Morei excited to teach her. She always asked questions, was attentive, and with the Caster library now at her fingertips, he hadn't seen her without a book tucked under her arm. Her excitement was contagious, and on more than one occasion, he had looked forward to seeing her to teach her the ways of rule. That didn't mean he entirely trusted her, but he did think in different circumstances, they could be genuine friends and not two people determined to use one another.

The council still had a lot of adjusting to do. Morei wasn't thrilled with the current schedule or how he had come to learn only yesterday that they did not openly share their trades. In Geral, it was common practice to discuss trades that each lord or lady participated in during such meetings. He would not have secrets here.

He eyed the scroll he'd been writing in earlier that evening. Morei had taken to jotting notes and phrases down about his journey. He'd even gone so far as to name the thing: *Vorelian Scrolls*. The title was basic, but his intention for it was to tell his side of the story. He had no idea where it might lead him, but perhaps one day it would be a book for future kings and queens. It surely helped him get his thoughts down about things, like the politics and his current predicament, predictions and his view on the world.

Tomorrow, he should hear from Edwin regarding his task on identifying his two thousand soldiers and those who would command the army. He was eager for that. Next to him, lying on the desk, was the list of families who had had an Energy Harvester executed as part of Drexis's mad plan. The list was not as long as he'd hoped, but he was also well aware that there had to be distant family members not listed, although they likely didn't live here still if they weren't.

Doing this made him reminiscent of Ezra and the life he'd once had. It felt like a lifetime ago that he had summoned the four Energy Harvesters to the courtyard in Geral, determined to train them. Deep down, he wished he could continue to work with Ezra. The man had an exceptional gift and had already learned the basics—one day, he would be a force to be reckoned with. Here, he was having to start over.

He scanned the list. Three families had already been crossed off once investigation had discovered that the only remaining members were either dead or so old they were near death. That left twelve other names, four of which he'd had records pulled for and now looked at. Scrolls starting decades ago identified each family member and their heirs, updated with every new birth or death. He eyed the one closest to him, which had torn from age. He would need someone to transfer all this data to fresh scrolls—these were well past their use, and he sensed the sea's harsh conditions were to blame. At that, he peeked over the parchment. The terrace doors were open, granting him access to the night sky and distant waters that he could not see.

Morei looked at the record. *The Danshins.* Four family members still lived—a mother and three sons. Based on these dates, it appeared that all three sons were between nineteen and twenty-four summers. Wait—Morei squinted to pick up the faded ink. The oldest was dead. Victim of the execution. He glanced at the other two and saw their occupations listed. Eli, nineteen, worked the port, and his brother, Grant, who was twenty-two, was a seaman. That didn't surprise Morei, not when the port was the largest income for the city.

He did, however, find interest in them, especially with a brother having been an Energy Harvester. Morei put them aside for later. Tomorrow, he would have Rhys send some men in common clothes and watch Eli from afar, see what they observed—and if Grant was in the city, then him too.

Morei took a sip of his Kendell's Milk. Always a strong go-to when he had to review things like this. Paperwork was grueling, but he enjoyed it, these quiet moments where he could gather his thoughts and prepare for the next day. Satisfied, he picked up the next one.

The Marlens. Morei studied the family, but the only thing he saw was a fresh entry for a daughter who appeared to have been born only last summer. The son, executed, had been only ten. Morei raised an eyebrow in silent acknowledgement and then rolled this one back up. They were not what he was looking for. He wanted strong and ready blood.

The next three families were the same disappointment. Children too young, or there was simply no family left to call upon. He went to take another drink but found the glass empty. Morei sighed. The decanter was on the other table. Originally, he had poured the drink with the intent to sit and ponder, but he had found himself at this desk.

In the dim light, he got up and grabbed his glass. Based on how stiff his muscles were, he'd been sitting there for a bit longer than he realized, but he was not tired. He'd top the drink off and continue on his way. Actually, he would just take the decanter over to the desk. No point in fooling himself—he was sure another drink would be poured before the end of the night.

A whooshing sound caught his attention, and he stopped.

Morei waited, listening. When it didn't happen again, he grabbed the decanter and topped off his drink to the rim. He wasn't used to the sounds yet, and he suspected it had to do with the breeze that quickly rushed through the room, smelling of potential rain. Morei had never experienced a real storm from the sea, but he'd heard they could be monstrous in size and ferocity.

As he set the decanter back down, he turned and froze.

There was a man in the study. No, it was Reyd, the man who had harassed him at Gamer's Village. Reyd was eyeing the scrolls on his desk, his ringed fingers scanning the writing. That dark hair was tied up in a bun, but a few wavy strands framed the man's face as he peered down. He was dressed like he was prepared to join the pirates—a V-cut white tunic that revealed an array of ink Morei had not seen before, a leather belt that possessed a sheathed sword, and loose-fitted pants. Between the jewelry, stubble, and attire, the only thing Reyd needed was a captain's hat.

And to get the fuck out of there.

"You've been busy," Reyd said, and looked up at him with those otherworldly eyes. Eyes that looked like they'd seen everything the world could ever offer and more. Morei was angry at himself for not seeing it before. It was so obvious now that this was not just anyone. This was a God.

"I'm in no mood for this." The last time he had dealt with a deity, the queen of Junok wound up dead and his title had been stripped. "I advise you to leave. I am not here to play games with your kind."

Reyd didn't look perturbed. "Careful what you say, *Your Majesty*. I'm not here to kill anyone."

Morei swallowed. He knew what had happened.

Reyd also knew he had the upper hand based on that grin. "I know what Sekar did, what he took from you. He's one of the ancients, and he certainly thinks he can do anything, doesn't he?" Reyd waved a hand around the study, which now felt small. "If Sekar wanted, he could take this and turn it to dust. What gives a God like him the right to just destroy lives simply for a good time?"

Morei swallowed, finding his tongue. "The same reason you're here without an invite. To fuck with me."

Reyd came around the desk and approached the table where the decanter was, where the king stood. Quickly, Morei stepped aside, not wanting to be so close, but the God didn't seem to mind. He poured himself a drink. "I'm a huge fan of Kendell's Milk, you know. Glad to see you've got such good taste."

Morei was ready to stab this God for intruding on his life. In fact, he was tired of all of them. Not a single good thing had come out of these deities. There was once a time when he would have cowered before such power, but now he was just angry. This was out of his control.

He was prepared to open his mouth, to give this God a piece of his mind, but Reyd spoke first.

"Something abnormal happened to you, Morei Geral. That curse you have, it's marked your lifeforce. From leagues away, I could smell it off you. The Inere did too. That beast you faced?" Reyd said it casually, even though the mention drove a blade through Morei's chest. "Like moths to a flame. As the curse grows stronger, so too does this *scent*." He shrugged. "Just thought you should know."

Morei couldn't believe what he was hearing. This was so beyond his understanding. He still had no idea why the beast—the Inere—had spared him, and he certainly didn't have the army needed to defeat something like that if it came to the city.

"The Gods are at odds," Reyd said, and took a drink. "Some want you dead, some want to see what you're capable of. I like to think I'm here for the show."

Morei was certain he was going to be sick. He had been so determined to keep his head down and focused on the current situation with Caster. It felt like he'd just been punched in the face. He had to set the glass down to keep from dropping it.

"Don't look so upset. I'm not a bad guy, and if you keep Kendell's Milk around, I'm more than happy to tell a story or two." Reyd downed the rest of his drink and laughed at some unheard joke. "Some say I'm exceptional with luck, so you might want to keep me around."

That gave Morei pause. He eyed the God harder, no longer sure how he should handle any of this. He had a lot of questions, and he wasn't sure where to begin, so he started with the basics. "Who are you, really?"

A cocky smile stared back at him. "You're not thinking straight, Morei. I already gave you that hint."

A knocking caught his attention, and Morei turned his gaze to the doors. "Your Majesty?" Rose peeked her head in. Morei felt his heart drop. She would not know who this man was, but he did, and that made the entire situation worse. He would have to tell her that Reyd was a guest—an unwelcome one, but he'd refrain from sharing that part.

"Oh—" She stopped short and frowned. "You have a raven?"

He was taken aback and looked behind him. Reyd no longer stood there. In his place was a raven with a white tail feather. The bird cawed and fluttered his wings, as if getting comfortable, then turned one large black eye to the king.

Morei gaped. It was the same raven he'd fed in Gamer's Village. Reyd was the raven. Reyd was a God. The hint he'd given suddenly broached his mind with a serrated edge.

This was Eazon, the God of Luck.

A SANCTUARY FOR THE RESTLESS

Six Days Later

Cyrus's life had changed. A lot. The man who had left Sorréle had been terrified of his own shadow. The man he was today had survived a near-fatal whipping, spoken to a God, and faced a Tsu'ran, and was now making his own decisions.

Sozar had changed a lot too. The dragon was fierce, merciless, and would only grow bigger and bolder the older he got.

Delion's port was still being repaired. Watchers had been stationed day and night to be on the lookout for any possible return of the ship. Cyrus lay awake most nights, thinking about how quickly things had changed and how his first reaction had been to protect rather than to run.

Word of the Tsu'ran attack had no doubt reached the ears of Barnằl and Saveen, and those who called the sea home would carry the story far and wide.

And they would carry with it the word that a Dragon Rider had been present, and that it had been Sozar who had carried the beast back into the depths of the sea. Cyrus wasn't sure how he felt about that notoriety yet. He'd spent so long trying to avoid all the publicity. Yet he had accepted that if he was to be a Dragon Rider, he was going to be known. Some would come to love him; others would despise him. Hyle's words had not left him.

When they were no longer in immediate danger, Cyrus had learned that there were only a handful of other documented Tsu'ran attacks on cities. These sea shifters remained far from land and tended to stay in the Grave of the Sea, an impossible passageway for ships.

Cyrus had adjusted to royal living for the last handful of days. When Sozar had arrived back from ridding the port of the Tsu'ran, Cyrus had returned to the palace to find Alaric requesting that he, Rider of the Sea, be granted the pledge of the city to him, not the other way around. Cyrus had refused, even as Asher had stood there with a document in his hand that would provide Delion with official documentation of their pledge to Cyrus.

After several back-and-forth discussions, Alaric had relented and said that he wouldn't make Cyrus sign anything, but that he would be signing something himself. A pledge that while he was king of Delion, the city would always prioritize the safety and security of Cyrus before anyone else. If any new ruler happened to take over—whether by death or choice of the current king—that new ruler would have to talk to Cyrus and the council about the current promise.

Cyrus didn't like it. It still felt like Alaric was pledging everything this city was to a cause Cyrus didn't even know about, but he had little say in the matter.

Alaric treated him to great feasts, and the council eyed him with less discontent and more acceptance too. They had spoken little on the situation with the Tsu'ran, although when Cyrus had told Alaric what he'd seen with the horned woman and

Nerius, the king had nodded once and requested that Asher gather information.

His back had healed significantly, although it was starting to scar. He could tell by the tug of skin and the way it puckered that it would not heal all the way, but that didn't bother him. He had plenty of emotional scars, and a physical scar was just like a decoration. More importantly, he was alive, and Sozar was okay. If he could still fly with ease and swing a blade, that was what mattered.

A God had graced his life. Troubled, but still a God. Hyle had granted him a gift of healing and had also given him a perspective that he had not considered fully until it had been laid out before him: he was a Dragon Rider, and that meant he was capable of incredible things. The only person holding him back was himself. The strength and resolve it took to make decisions came with time, but Cyrus felt like he was getting better and starting to understand what Hyle saw in him.

Today would mark the first day of sword training. He was okay swinging a blade, but that was only because he'd grown up swinging a pickaxe. He was used to the weight, just not the method. When he had approached Alaric about learning more hands-on work, the king had jumped at the idea and said he'd bring in his most trusted trainer for it. Even he, who had been trained by the same man, would attend when he could. The trainer, Magnus, knew Cyrus was healing from an injury, and they would go easy to test how far he could go.

Sozar would watch. The dragon had insisted on being present for training, which no one had objected to. Cyrus knew it was because Sozar wanted to protect him if anything went amiss, but it was better to remain optimistic with Alaric than to tell him that he didn't trust his men. The king was going above and beyond to prove that Delion was a sanctuary to the Rider.

Upon further investigation, they had come to learn Cyrus's mother had fled with the coin she'd earned from turning him over to the late King Raj. She'd left everything at her house, only taking bare essentials. She'd slipped away one night without anyone's knowledge. Cyrus suspected she'd found refuge with one of the pirates she'd done business with.

Against his wishes, Alaric had placed a bounty on her head, declaring that she was an enemy to the city. While the king was certainly trying to prove his friendship to the Rider, he had ways of doing it that made Cyrus uncomfortable. Cyrus had to tell him that if she were found, he didn't want to know, for his own peace of mind. At that, Alaric had gotten a wicked gleam in his eye and said that would be no problem.

Yet, beyond all those political and royal traits, Cyrus had found a friend. He was certain of it. He knew the king of Delion saw him as more than just a man, and he had to be okay with that. Cyrus had to embrace who he was. After everything he'd been through, there had been only one person who had ever looked at him as nothing more than a man. Zorya.

That was, if the princess of Razan forgave him for abandoning the city to Dameon's schemes. He wanted to believe she would, but he wasn't sure. It wasn't like he had left on the best of terms with her, but he still held on to the memories and hoped she was well.

Under different circumstances, he'd have flown across the world for her. He'd have gone back to her and declared where he'd been wrong and that he did care for her, but that he needed her to be safe. She couldn't be safe with him—not now, and possibly not ever. He was a Dragon Rider, forged by betrayal and destined to find trouble. His path needed to be walked alone.

The sound of the hall changed, his boots echoing with a faraway sound that made him slow. Cyrus blinked and looked around. It was darker, warmer.

"You are a fool if you didn't think I'd stop by and say hello," the voice said from behind. "But you Riders have always had an incredible gift at ignorance."

Cyrus stopped, and he turned to see Henry Junok standing there. His red robe complemented the mass of sigils etched into his skin, and in one hand was the *Book of Liral.* Along with it, a blade drenched in midnight and rubies. Behind him stood another man—tall, with dark eyes and short hair, and a look that said he would rather be anywhere but here.

"How . . ."

Henry gestured to the man behind him. "Gods are incredible, aren't they?" Then his eyes turned downward to the book that Cyrus had practically carried across the Vore World. "So kind of you to hold on to this for me. I've been looking for it for quite a long time."

He nodded, still unsure but not willing to ask anymore. He didn't trust his tongue. When he tried to reach out to Sozar, he found he couldn't. The world around him didn't exist, which meant he was at the mercy of whatever this God wanted.

"I'm not here to take you back," Henry told him. "I am only here to remind you that every choice has a consequence, no matter how honorable you think they might be."

Again, he didn't speak.

Henry stepped forward, and Cyrus stepped back. That seemed to amuse the man. "Scared?"

Cyrus opened his mouth but then shut it again. Nothing he said now would matter.

"You've done what I expected you to do. You lack conviction, and everything you've ever done proves that."

The insult hurt, but he didn't let it show. "Go," he whispered.

"Ah, so proud." Henry's eyes shifted, now menacing and cold. The next words terrified him. "Dameon and Ashtir send their regards."

And then they were gone.

Cyrus stared into the open space of the hall. The lighting was normal, the air rich with the sea. Sozar brushed up against his mind, concerned. The dragon knew something wasn't right but had no idea what had just transpired, so Cyrus relayed everything by images. When he was done, Sozar was unsettled.

They wanted to scare you.

It had worked. No matter how tough he was trying to be, there was nothing right about what had just happened. He had so many questions, but he knew none of them could be asked without going straight to the source. And that source happened to be a God and Henry Junok. The *Book of Liral* was now in the hands of the most-feared man of history, and while Cyrus had never been able to read it, he felt a surreal sense of dread wash over him.

Still, as he stared into that empty hall with its stunning pearl-white flooring, he became more and more determined. He would not be afraid. Fear was a method of control that he refused to fall victim to.

No, he would be ready. He had no choice but to become the strongest, most powerful Dragon Rider the world would ever see.

VORE TERMINOLOGY

Ashýon *(Ash-ee-on)* – Outer region of the Soul Realm. It has become the home to the majority of the demons and is the most dangerous region of the realm. No Guardian will travel to this territory. Beyond demons, great beasts roam the area that are not seen anywhere else.

Assane *(Ah-sane)* – Northeastern city of Diyră. One of the only major cities to still allow for smaller territories to be ruled by tribes, the tribal territories make up the vast landscape of Assane. The primary income varies between tribes, but eccentric and unique gods are well known to come from this region.

Barnăl *(Bar-nahl)* – Eastern city of Creitón. A brutal past with strong armed forces. Historically remembered as the city that enslaved its princess. Supplies cities with ships, gathering supplies through a deal with the ancient Venkar City.

- Tyrik Village – Small and quaint, but best known as the village massacred during the White Horn pirate raid approximately 434 summers ago.

Caster – Eastern city of Sorréle. Known for its high crime rates and violent culture, the city's economic income weighs heavily on the production of wines and trading. All goods, exported or imported, must pass through Caster's Port, giving the city a significant advantage over all others.

Cer'han *(Ser-hahn)* – A flying creature that comes from the Soul Realm. Many have referred to it as a 'demon dragon' because it embodies similar characteristics, such as wings, snout, powerful jaws, and talons. They live for decades and can be as small as a hand or as large as a home. Aggressive, territorial, and hard to kill.

Chaos – Often referred to as 'the mother of energy' or 'Mother.' Without Chaos, there would be no Vore World. Dark Energy and Light Energy are both sub-energies to Chaos. All things, including the realms, are linked to the mother of all energies.

Creitón *(Cre-ton)* – Nicknamed 'pirate country.' There is no clear record of whether Creitón or Eiyrӑl came first, and the answers will vary by individual. This country is well-known for its ports, ships, and the cultural significance of the sea. It is true that most of the pirates Vorelians meet consider Creitón their home, but it is certainly a well-established country with strong values. Main cities: Barnӑl, Saveen, and Delion. Lesser cities: Venkar City, Ruby Village, and Tyrik Village.

Crystónity *(Cris-ton-ity)* – Branch of Drügalism. This monotheistic religion only celebrates Sekar and does not consider the other deities significant. Crystóns are secluded worldwide, but the City of Liral is the only location to practice openly.

Cu'cel *(Su-sel)* – Sinister illness responsible for the deaths in Geral. Old Tongue translates to 'evil' or 'ungodly.' Refer to Grënyl for a description.

Dark Energy – A more prominent form of energy, sometimes referred to as 'the sister of Chaos' or 'the dead's power.' This energy is raw, untampered, and pure, derived from the souls of the damned locked in the living realm and unable to pass into the Afterlife. Dark Energy is nearly impossible to master by an Energy Harvester, given the incredible power of the force. This power is often known to consume and kill the harvester and is considered a bad omen by most Vorelians. Dark Energy is embodied in the purest elements: water, wind, metal, and fire. Historically, only two have mastered the energy: Selena Delcate (wind) and Henry Junok (metal). Morei Geral (fire) is now the third Vorelian to master it.

Delion *(Dee-le-on)* – Northern city of Creitón. A quiet city that keeps to itself. It is commonly referred to as the heart of Creitón because of its central location, although the city remains compact and smaller in stature, unlike Saveen and Barnăl. Do not be fooled by the city's quiet demeanor, as the toughest citizens live here, with many working the sea as their source of income.

Diemon *(Di-mon)* – Northwest city of Sorréle. The city of gems, or as some refer as 'the gem city.' Stationed up against the Releuthian Mountains, its primary income is from mining and jewelry.

Diyră *(Di-rah)* – Founded over 1,500 summers ago and well-known for its gruesome history. At the height of the Lirallian Empire over four centuries ago, Henry Junok led a bloody domination that slaughtered millions, now known as the Diyrăllian Massacre. Main cities: Assane, Raveer, and Junok. Lesser cities: Nighthunter Federation, Jasper Village, and Whale Village.

Diyrăllian Massacre *(Di-ral-lian)* – The largest massacre in Vorelian history that occurred over four centuries ago. The Lirallian Empire carried it out under the guidance of Henry Junok. Millions of lives were lost across Diyră, and the summer has become known as the 'Blood Summer.'

Don'sul *(Dawn-suul)* – A ritual that restricts Energy Harvesters from harvesting. This ritual is considered dark and is prohibited across all four countries. Most successful when performed on a child less than five, but it is still used on adults, although results vary.

- This was performed on Cyrus by Henry Junok.

Drügalism *(Druug-al-ism)* – The primary religion of Vorelians, embodying all five Gods: Helyna, Greve, Hyle, Eazon, and Sekar.

Eazon *(E-zon)* – God of Luck. Ritual of Contact: a bundle of Krye placed on a cloth and surrounded by candles.

Edanzín Blade *(E-dan-sin)* – The blade used in the Commitment Ceremony of the Guardians. While the vast amount of information surrounding the process of the Commitment Ceremony remains a secret, this blade has been confirmed. The user of the blade is specially trained and must undergo a mental evaluation after each use to confirm that the power of the blade has not negatively impacted the person (in this case, Guardian). The master of this blade is called a Herän (Her-ahn).

- Only one Herän can exist at any point in time. The blade is bonded to the chosen individual until they relinquish that. In any case, relinquishment can be through death or by choice. In unique cases, by force.

Eiyrǎl *(Eye-ral)* – An ancient country with conflicting settlement records, although many agree it was well over 2,000 summers, with some estimations as high as 3,000. With no clear indication, it is well-known as the Dragon Riders' home. The ancient country holds traditional Vorelian values that are entirely lost to many outsiders. More interestingly, Eiyrǎl is withdrawn from many political movements and is independent of a lot of activity with other countries. Main cities: Kalic, East Razan, West Razan, and Rider Federation (destroyed in the Great Fall).

Ferguson – Northeast city of Sorréle, more commonly referred to as 'the silk family.' Ferguson's economic income is primarily from clothing, specializing in silks. An eccentric group of people that remain withdrawn.

Firóle *(Fur-ole)* – Giant serpents that once ruled the lands of Diyră and traveled openly. One of the ancient beasts. The Firóle were hunted for their scales and fangs during the height of the Dragon Riders, driving them to extinction. Very few remain and stay in hiding. They are ancient beasts and possess many characteristics like a dragon, such as telepathic communication and intelligence.

Fräurune *(Fraah-rune)* – Translates to 'Lady of the Dead.'

Geíon (Ge-ee-on) – A highly evolved and intelligent species of demon. They are violent, bloodthirsty, and constantly seek control. They are active users of Ön'grusah with theories stating they have evolved because of their use of this force. They loathe the Honuyál.

- Ka-Geíon (Kah-Ge-ee-on) – A higher and more powerful Geíon. Have the capability to conjure their own bodies, so they can look like anything. Many of these Ka-Geíons take the body of people because it allows them to walk among the living.

- Gor-Geíon (Gore-Ge-ee-on) – A lower and less powerful Geíon. They cannot conjure bodies like their brethren, so they possess the living. Any possession or soul bondage with a person is not permanent. This is because their own lifeforce slowly devours the lifeforce of their victim.

  · Morei Geral, prophesized Demon King, is soul bonded to one.

Geral *(Geh-ral)* – Western city of Sorréle and nicknamed 'the black-smith's city.' Geral's economic income weighs heavily on the trade of metals, including armor and weapons. A city that takes pride in its strength and independence.

Ghrynál *(Ghrin-all)* – A philosophical belief quite literally translating to 'the path forward.' Everything has a cause and effect; every action dictates a different path. The mother of energy,

Chaos, knows all paths forward. It was once revered in traditional Vorelian culture but has since become less known, specifically in Sorréle and many parts of Diyră. Guardians of Death adhere to this philosophical approach.

Gonsín *(Gone-seen)* – Translated from Old Tongue to 'leader.' A high form of respect when this term is used.

Gray Realm – The space between the living and Soul Realm. Often believed to be the realm closest to Chaos. Given its vast and uncontrollable environment, no one goes here, and it is acknowledged by Energy Harvesters or Vore students. Very few cultures address the Gray Realm. Sekar is believed to be the only God who freely travels to and from the Gray Realm, using its volatile and secretive nature to his advantage. With so little knowledge of this realm, no one truly understands what or if anything lives there.

Grënyl *(Greh-nal)* – Ailment associated with Sekar. Old literature discusses Grënyl to be the mark of the Dark Lord and how he identifies his next victims. Symptoms include black rotting pieces of flesh, fever, and mental deterioration. Sekar utilizes this tactic to weaken the life force and bring them to the Gray Realm, a space between the living and dead realms. Ancient texts theorized Grënyl only came to those with fractured loyalty to the Gods, such as Greve, Hyle, Eazon, and Helyna.

Greve *(Greeve)* – God of Strength. Ritual of Contact: wooden posts with letters nailed to them, followed by a hand gesture over the heart.

Guardian of Death – Warriors that belong to the Soul Realm. They are responsible for the guidance of souls from the living to the Afterlife. Guardians are also responsible for the protection of the Soul Realm against all forms of threats. They are mortal boys taken before ten after a tragedy and raised in the realm of the dead. Countless summers of training and mastery of their skills and emotions make them savage competition in a swordfight. Upon training completion, they undergo the Commitment Ceremony, which involves the bondage of a lesser demon to their soul. The ultimate test is surviving this ritual, and those who do are honorably gifted Death's Sword and become a Guardian of Death. Details of the Commitment Ceremony are not shared; Guardians do not speak highly of the seven-day ceremony and a few that have emphasized that it is unbearable. The iconic characteristics—pale blue skin, red eyes, black hair, and Marking—all result from the ceremony. In cultures where they are less accepted and perceived as bad omens, they are called 'Death Seekers.'

- Shevana ceased all further training of Guardians, and the numbers are now the lowest they've ever been.

Helyna *(Hel-e-na)* – Goddess of Love. Ritual of Contact: a glass of wine with use of the phrases 'Love is endless' and 'Helyna bless you.'

Honuyál *(Hon-u-al)* – A grotesque and ruthless species of beasts. They are power-hungry and feed off souls. They follow traditional values and place a high emphasis on female rulers. Noted traits include leathery skin, large and strong bodies, dagger-like teeth, slit noses, and tusks. They have amassed numbers in the Soul Realm.

Hyle *(Hile)* – God of Courage. Ritual of Contact: silver beads with a small wooden sun, widely named 'Hyle's Beads.'

Indül *(In-duul)* – A flower harvested on the outskirts of Venkar City. The flower produces a toxin that can be fatal in high doses. Ingestion of the toxin will create hallucinations and other symptoms. Only a master herbalist should work with a flower this dangerous.

Inere *(E-near)* – One of the ancient beasts of the Vore World. This giant beast is covered in shell-like armor. Large pincers, a dozen beady eyes, and ten legs. The Inere burrows underground and comes above ground only when threatened or curious. Can live up to 400 summers.

Junok *(June-oke)* – Northwest city of Diyră. The largest territory of all Vore cities and best known for its gory history and rich Energy Harvesting bloodline. The Junok family is most notably known for Henry Junok, despite the family's expulsion of the prince and his title from the family lineage. Junok's Port is the major port of all trades for Diyră, making up a significant amount of city income.

Kalic *(Kal-ick)* – Eastern city of Eiyrăl. One of the smallest cities in the world. Well known as one of the only cities to enslave people still. Its brutal punishment system and predefined roles make the city ancient in its practices. Primary income is weapon and armor production.

Kan Sëri *(Kahn-Sar-e)* – Translates from Old Tongue to 'Master of the Sea' or 'Sea Master.'

Krakí *(Kra-kee)* – One of the ancient beasts of the Vore World. Eight tentacles, larger than any ship, and territorial. In some cultures, like Creitón, these beasts are revered. They live deep underwater and occasionally come up out of curiosity. Highly intelligent and hold grudges. Can live up to 1,000 summers.

Krisár *(Kris-har)* – One of the dark rituals of old Vorelian practices. Involves the consumption of the participant's blood and the recital of an ancient text spoken in Old Tongue. A blade of power must be used in the ritual for it to be successful. It is forbidden in most cities across the Vore World, given its highly dark association with the dead and curses. The ritual was outlawed after the fall of the Lirallian Empire and all books associated with Krisár and equally dangerous rituals were said to be burned.

Ku'sar *(Kuh-sar)* – Old Tongue for 'Death Dancer.'

Leangé *(Lee-an-gee)* – One of the most important books of the Soul Realm. This book possesses all sorts of information regarding the history and creation of the Soul Realm, along with natural laws. This book is one of the few that was saved when Shevana, the current and longest standing ruler, set fire to all material in an attempt to withhold information and increase her political power.

Lifeforce – More commonly known as soul. This is the energy that makes up every living thing or object. Depending on what region of the Vore World visited, one will hear either soul or lifeforce.

Light Energy – The weakest but most malleable form of energy, as it is impure and tampered with. All life is made of Light Energy. All Energy Harvesters lean heavily on this form, as its ease and stability make it reliable. Commoners often refer to this form as 'magic,' which indicates a lack of education in energy.

Ly'rün *(Lie-rune)* – A potent mixture of chemicals that combusts into a deadly fire when used. A fatal gas is released during this, which can spread for half a league in all directions. Anyone who inhales this will experience swelling of the lungs, hallucinations, and bloody tears. No records exist of any survivors.

Móermism *(More-mism)* – Spiritual religion. Followers place their value and respect in energies and are considered extremely spiritual, often praising Mother, or Chaos, as the ultimate deity. This old practice is seen rarely but is scattered throughout the world, and followers are known best as Móers.

Mo'lüre *(Mo-lah-ure)* – The commoners call it a unicorn. The creature is created with pure Dark Energy and has been nicknamed the 'Walker of Realms' because of its ability to dissipate and reappear wherever it wants. Nobody can touch the creature without permission. Doing so will cause the Mo'lüre to consume the lifeforce of the person. Ancient stories say that to see one is a good omen for this creature does not show itself to anyone without intention. There are only a handful of sightings throughout Vore history.

Nighthunter – The best assassin in the world. Trained for up to eight or more summers under the guidance of skilled assassins and must earn their sword in training. They hold tremendous value in the Old Laws and will hunt anyone.

- Upon the formation of the Nighthunters, a deal was made with Junok. In return for land, the Nighthunters would never take a bid against the Junok family.

Nighthunter Federation – A southwest city located on the panhandle of Diyrǎ. The city is well known for its zero-crime tolerance and is the only city in the world to offer asylum to all refugees. However, the Nighthunters are more than just soldiers, but the best assassins in the world. An underground market allows travelers from around the world to come and bid for a Nighthunter. The federation is a hotspot for illegal trade.

Old Laws – Old text written over 200 summers ago. These laws were the original promises of the Nighthunters and define the guild. To break one of the Old Laws is to break the oath of a Nighthunter.

Ön'grusah *(Ohn-gru-sah)* – Translated to 'evil energy.' This is a form of energy that has been abused, contorted, and twisted into an all-consuming force. While many of the Soul Realm believe the Ka-Geíon are responsible for this, it is still unconfirmed which species of demon is to blame. However, it has been confirmed that Ön'grusah is responsible for the current state of the Soul Realm.

- Studies on Ön'grusah are few. Those that have spent time researching this malicious power have theorized that it is alive and moves with the intelligence of Chaos. This could be the result of evolution—the force growing stronger and smarter when faced with any form of threat. Although one theory is that Ön'grusah was created with the use of a God's heart, which would explain the theory that there is a direct link to Chaos. There are no confirmed reports. To study Ön'grusah, one would have to venture deep into Ashýon, where it is believed the heart of this evil energy lies. This is extremely dangerous.

Oth'al *(Ahth-al)* – The book dedicated to the Guardians and their laws. All information regarding the Commitment Ceremony, their order, and training is covered in this book. As of current, the book is lost.

Rauna *(Raw-na)* – In old stories, she is the ancient queen who fell in love with the God, Zyne. She was killed by her own citizens.

Raveer *(Rah-veer)* – Eastern city known for its brutality and ancient values in Diyră. The city has become revered for its armed forces; they are trained for twice the number of summers than the standard soldier observed in other Vorelian cities. The primary city income is metalwork.

Rider Federation – North city of Eiyrăl, or the remains. The city was destroyed over 800 summers ago during The Great Fall. The city's remnants offer sanctuary to strange beasts, volatile energy, and secrets. Often, citizens of Kalic and Razan come to offer gifts and say prayers.

- When it stood, the Rider Federation was glorious and home to some of the most influential people in the world. The federation kept peace among the cities worldwide and led massive explorations.

Rül'Cril *(Rah-Cril)* – Translates to 'Crown of Gods.' This relic was one of the three forged by Henry Junok in his reign. It earned the name because it has the power to make any beast a mindless slave to the user of the crown. Sekar remains the only God with the knowledge on how it was forged. Henry Junok never got the chance to use it.

Saveen *(Sa-veen)* – Western city of Creitón. Saveen drives global trades of jewels and unique goods. The city is known for its exquisite architecture and attitudes, but they are masters of the seas and should not be misunderstood.

- The prince of Saveen, Dameon, is the second Dragon Rider to soar the skies in over 800 summers.

Sekar *(Seh-kar)* – In traditional culture, known as the Dream Walker or God of Dreams. More recently, heavily regarded as the Dark Lord, God of Darkness, and unacknowledged by some cultures altogether for the belief that such action brings bad luck.

- Ritual of contact as Dark Lord: blood sacrifice and recital of cursed text. Punishable by death if caught performing this ritual in most cities.

- Ritual of contact as Dream Walker: Prayer before bed. The method of contact is through dreams, so many would pray to Sekar for him to visit and guide them while they dream.

Sorréle *(Sor-rel)* – The youngest country of the Vore World, founded over eight centuries ago. The establishment of this country originates in a political dispute between families in Diyră. Main cities: Geral, Ferguson, Diemon, and Caster. Lesser cities: Gamer's Village.

Soul Realm – The realm of the dead. Commoners refer to this location as the 'underworld,' but this is inappropriate, as the Soul Realm lives parallel with the living—not above or below. Souls pass into the Soul Realm and exist until they are ready to be guided to the Afterlife. It is ruled by a select family who the Gods chose to uphold the responsibility of caring for the dead. The Soul Realm is critical to the living—it brings order and balance to the energy system. If the Soul Realm fails, the living will follow, and vice versa.

- The Soul Realm was notably once beautiful, with flowing rivers and vivid colors. It has since become the embodiment of ghastly and horrible imagery. The malevolent forces entered with permission under the guise of promised power and slowly devoured the land.

Soul Speaker – People who have a connection to the dead. They see, hear, and speak for the deceased. Some cultures regard Soul Speakers as bad omens, while others revere their gift.

The Great Fall – The fall of the Rider Federation. Upon the death of her Rider, Vikter, Aythen went mad with rage and destroyed the city. It is said only a handful escaped the carnage, but what happened to the survivors remains unknown.

- Prior to The Great Fall, two Dragon Riders fled in the middle of the night with their weapons and gear. What became of them remains undetermined—no further dragon sightings were reported, and no one by the iconic silver eyes was documented following the destructive events. Cyrus is believed to possess one of the Rider's Swords that was saved before The Great Fall.

Tsu'Ran *(Su-ran)* – Shapeshifters of the sea. They live in hordes and call the Grave their home. They transform into anything their victim most desires. Souls are what they consume. Powerful creatures that in their natural form look closer to a small Krakí.

Ve'hem *(Veh-hem)* – Old Tongue for 'the burdened one.'

Vor'gal *(Vore–gal)* – Old Tongue for 'the pit' or 'underworld.'

West and East Razan *(Rah-zan)* – Western city of Eiyrǎl and second largest in the Vore World. Rich in ancient culture and values and is considered one of the oldest cities. One of the only cities in the world where people will walk without a weapon in the streets. Energy Harvesters are welcomed and highly regarded. The Razan family occasionally opens their gates and allows citizens to explore the vast palace. An extensive underground tunnel system accommodates the palace. Income varies, given the city's adaptability to economic changes.

- West Razan was once known as Suniyr *(Sun-ear)*, a city of occult followers. Approximately 1,100 summers ago, Suniyr was dissolved by Razan after a political war. The Suniyr family was executed publicly.

Zimbórism *(Zim-bor-ism)* – Branch of Drügalism. This religion identifies Greve as the primary God and is heavily recognized in Diyră, although there are a small number of Zimbór followers across the Vore World.

Zyne *(Zine)* – A Vore God who many believed was the moon in ancient Vore beliefs. He fell in love with a mortal, Rauna.

Zyulë Bond *(Zule)* – A type of energy bond that doesn't identify a master. The equal relationship that results is often referred to as a God's Bond. Both individuals must remain alive; the death of one will result in the partner's death. This peculiar characteristic makes it both dangerous and extremely useful. Both participants must adhere to the rules of Krisár. Individuals of Zyulë Bonds possess a silver raised scar on their wrist and are extremely valuable in some traditional cultures.

ACKNOWLEDGEMENT

I think it's safe to say that after the third book, you might start to guess where this is going. All the acknowledgements of who made this possible, and why I couldn't do it without you. You know who you are. For this time, though, I am going to do things a little bit differently.

I'm going to tell you a story.

When I was about nine, I wrote my first story. When I was twelve, I wrote what would one day become a story I couldn't stop thinking about. And when I was thirteen, I wrote a story that my teacher told me was too long. The requirement was six pages, but I wrote fourteen. The truth is, though, I didn't think I was a storyteller. I never once imagined myself going down this road, telling grand epics, and sharing it with the world. I simply wrote because it was as big a part of me as my left toe. Did I make you laugh? Good.

So when I shared a story with, at the time, my best friend from middle school, she straight up told me it was boring. Actually, she fell asleep and *then* told me it was boring. All fifteen handwritten pages. I guess unicorns and dragons weren't her jam. That's okay. Years later and many, many jokes about "it's kinda boring" and I've come to realize that she didn't say that to be cruel, she said that because she was and has never been a reader. But it's safe to say that statement stayed with me.

Even today. Miah, I hope you're doing good and enjoying life to the fullest. Life was not kind to you in the beginning, and I hope you found your purpose.

A few years and fifteen random drafts of retellings later, I ran into what would undoubtedly become a prominent figure in my journey. His name was Jay and for legal purposes, I won't tell you his last name. But he's an author and I met him one night while I was bartending at my local restaurant. I was actually supposed to call in sick that night, but I decided against it because the place was already short-staffed. While I poured margaritas and beers, Jay told me his big dreams and I immediately was entranced. Who wouldn't? At the time, I was beginning to realize that my writing was more a part of me than I originally believed. And this Jay was my one-way ticket to making this dream come true. I agreed and gave him my number (and yes, stalked him on Google), and we agreed to meet up somewhere public to discuss the future of my writing.

Sounds kind of cool, right?

Jay read one of the roughest drafts I have ever written and told me I needed a lot of help. That's okay, I was ready. I knew it. And I wanted to play in the big league. I actively agreed to take his help because I saw no other option—I was still in college, worked up to fifty hours a week, and was actively caring for senior dogs with my family that needed around-the-clock care. But world be damned, I was going to make this work.

So when he told me to read a 500-page book about some military excursion and tell him the "beats" of the story and essentially a play-by-play of each chapter, I hesitated. What about the military genre aligned with my yearning to write fantasy? Even at that age, I knew this was odd. What about reading a book could teach me anything new? Frankly, at that age, I'd probably read nearly 300 books in just a couple of years but had slowed down dramatically because of, well, life. Stephen King and other works of horror and fantasy were my go-to.

It's safe to say I fell behind *fast*. I couldn't read fast enough and frankly, a little bug in the back of my head told me this wasn't learning. This was placating someone who thought they could mold me into the exact storyteller they thought was successful. And Jay, well, Jay wrote apocalyptic military works and declared himself above the King. Red flag.

When life took the wheel and I couldn't keep up with my little reading assignment (which was anticipated to be done in two weeks), I was upfront with him. And instead of respecting the senior dogs and my education, he berated me over email. Told me I was full of excuses, that "I would never become anything if all I did was make an excuse," and "that I would never publish anything."

Yeah. I cried.

Because you see, I tend to try and take on a lot. It's how I thrive, and when I had to be honest and say I couldn't read fast enough, it destroyed my sense of confidence. Dramatic, right? Blame the Virgo in me. I was young still and naïve. But I wasn't full of excuses. I just had priorities and at the time, reading some dry military book was not one of them.

Despite all that, I kept writing. In secret. Holed up in my room on late nights, I scribbled madly away in my notebook, retelling the same damn story over and over because I swore it would be bigger and better with each new draft. And it was, but the story was and will never be for publishing. That story was for me to find my voice. And after fifteen years of writing, the big C word hit. Ugh, I know. Sorry I have to bring it up.

At that point, my life had slowed down a lot. I was working in the restaurant industry and finishing up an EMT program (a story for another time). When I got the call that my local restaurant would be closed until further notice, I was stunned. I think we all were.

So in the first week, I found myself watching *The Lion King*. Live action. Some of you know this story, some don't, but I am going to tell it in full this time. In the first half hour, I watched Simba struggle for an identity, despite having everything handed to him. He was the heir, the chosen one, the one the people (or in this case, animals) would eventually turn to for guidance. And when his father was killed and Scar turned him into the villain, it hit me. The feeling was so deep in my soul that it took my breath away. I can still recall that moment as clearly as my cup of coffee I had this morning.

I saw a son born into royalty. The sole heir. I saw a boy raised to be the king his father was, someone the people could rely on and turn to for guidance. Everything was handed to him. Yet, he was born with a ticking time bomb. He was born into a prophecy he had no control over, or so Destiny states. The name Morei was easy to come by, and that's because the countless drafts I had written over the years had a character named that. It was a name that fit like a glove, just don't tell OJ Simpson that.

But what I haven't shared is that I have a deep fascination for the human mind. The way people tick, the abnormal psychology, the biological makeup of what makes us who we are. All of it. If it wasn't some freaky "is she really watching this" show, it was something on psychology and killers. Particularly serial killers.

Yeah, yeah. I'm one of those. But not in a "fan girl" kind of way. Specifically in a "what biological, genetic, and environmental factors makes someone do that" kind of way.

It became integral that I tell the characters' stories that reflect this. I was and am a firm believer that older fantasy works always did it right with the character development. If it takes a book for a character to come to terms with their purpose, then so be it. But it shouldn't take a chapter or less for a character to realize their purpose or to suddenly have a change of heart. It's a dozen, sometimes more, sometimes less moments that add up over time, and I was determined to respect that philosophy.

We all know what happens here. The birth of an Empire. Yeah, that's right. You know I had to say it.

But the truth is, the *journey* to get here was the birth of an Empire. It wasn't the first few lines or the moment I watched *The Lion King*. It was the fifteen years I spent writing in secret, being told my story was "kinda boring" and that "I was full of excuses" and "I'll never publish." Those distinct moments forged the foundation of this Empire.

Determination is the storyteller's pen. Desire makes up the ink. We're all a little mad, I think, when we stare at a document or notebook and put words down for sometimes hours on end. Despite what the world does to us, we return to the vast worlds we have created in our heads and feel an overpowering need to transfer these visions into something physical. It isn't a hobby, it's an identity. And we need to embrace that.

So that's my story to you all. I've never shared my journey in such detail before but when I look back and see the then and now, I am in awe of what we are capable of. Keep writing. Whoever you are. One day, it'll be worth it.

Keep your swords sharp, Vorelians.